Six Postcards
Home

W/D

Also by Michelle Jackson

One Kiss in Havana

Two Days in Biarritz

Three Nights in New York

4am in Las Vegas

5 Peppermint Grove

Published by Poolbeg

Six Postcards Home

Michelle Jackson

POOLBEG

F/5316212

Published 2013
by Poolbeg Press Ltd
123 Grange Hill, Baldoyle
Dublin 13, Ireland
E-mail: poolbeg@poolbeg.com
www.poolbeg.com

1

A catalogue record for this book is available from the British Library.

ISBN 978-1-84223-560-7

Typeset by Poolbeg Press Ltd in Sabon 11.5/16
Printed and bound by CPI Group (UK) Ltd, Croydon, CR0 4YY

www.poolbeg.com

About the author

Michelle Jackson is the bestselling Irish author of five previous novels, all published by Poolbeg Press. All five – *One Kiss in Havana, Two Days in Biarritz, Three Nights in New York, 4am in Las Vegas*, and *5 Peppermint Grove* – have been translated into foreign languages including Dutch, German, Portuguese and Norwegian.

In October 2010 her first non-fiction title *What Women Know*, which she co-wrote with Dr Juliet Bressan, was published.

Extracts of her work and articles have been chosen for publication by the Journal.ie, the *Irish Daily Mail*, the *Irish Independent*, the *Irish Times*, the *Sunday World* and various Irish women's magazines. She also contributes to newspapers on a variety of topics, including travel and education, and is travel editor of *Suburbia Weddings Magazine*.

She is a native of Howth, County Dublin, where she lives with her husband and two children.

For further details, her website is www.michellejackson.ie.

Acknowledgements

I would like to start by thanking you, the reader, for purchasing this book – it is your support that makes it possible for authors to write in this increasingly difficult climate. I would also sincerely like to thank Poolbeg Press and all the terrific staff who have published my first five novels and now my sixth.

Special thanks to Gaye Shortland my editor, whose eagle eye and nurturing care over the last five years have been more educational than a Master's in English Literature.

Thanks to Kieran Devlin, Paula Campbell, David Prendergast and Sarah Ormston who have been wonderful, and especially to Ailbhe Hennigan who has given me the inspiration to become a travel writer.

Thanks too to Ros Edwards and Helenka Fugelwicz, and all at their literary agency in London, who tirelessly seek new homes for my novels in different languages.

This book was started many years ago but I realise now that I needed to write my previous novels before I could finish it. I also needed a gentle nudge from two inspiring writers who, after a weekend of Prosecco and chocolate, gave me the confidence to write this love story. Thank you Maria Duffy and Denise Deegan.

Thank you to my special readers who have been a constant support as always: Clodagh Hoey, Tryphavana Cross, Carla Cerasi, Angela Forte and Wendy Buckley.

Writing is a lonely process but we are blessed to be working in an age where social networking has connected so many of us and I would like to thank all the writers, readers, friends and acquaintances that I have made on Twitter and Facebook.

I would also like to thank all my 3D friends who help me to get my books to this stage by being there in different supportive ways, whether it's in my job at Malahide Community School or with my children who attend the Burrow National School, or just meeting me for a cup of coffee to get some rest between the writing of chapters.

Thanks to Emma Walsh of the *Bord Gáis Energy Book Club* for the endorsement and quote.

Finally all would be impossible and worthless without the love and help I get from my wonderful family. There are not the words to thank my parents, Jim and Pauline Walsh, who I love and adore. I am so blessed.

My sweetest love to my husband Brian and children Mark and Nicole, with thanks for being the most wonderful and beautiful family a woman could have.

For my mother, Pauline.

Prologue

Barcelona

Karen stood trembling in the foyer of the bleak three-star hotel. It was late afternoon, and the shadows from the huge palms outside danced against the yellow-ochre buildings. The fountain, in the middle of the Plaça Reial, erupted as she stared out through the hotel door. It had taken a long time to get to this point in her life and now that she was here the occasion felt surreal.

Greg walked over to where Karen stood, a large key dangling from his hand. He reached up and tenderly brushed his other hand against the side of her face.

"Don't want to change your mind?" he asked.

She shook her head. Words were no longer necessary. The words they had spoken in the little café on Las Ramblas were a prelude to now.

She hankered for her youth and wished she hadn't had to go through so much to get to this moment in time. They were a shadow of their former selves who had languidly strolled through St Anne's Park and dipped their toes into the icy waters of the Burrow Beach.

The walk to the lift seemed to take forever and their breathing quickened as they arrived on the second floor. There was

1

electricity in the air as they located the room and he fumbled with the lock. They stepped into a small room flooded with light. The shutters were flung open and the cacophony from the square echoed up and into the room.

Karen switched on the light beside the bed as Greg walked over to shut out the noise from the revellers down below. He closed the shutters and drew the curtains then turned to look at her.

The moment was perfect – the moment was now.

He slowly walked over to where she stood. He leaned forward and his lips gently met hers – suspended in perfection before opening and thirstily drinking her in. With eyes closed he navigated her shape with ease and removed her shirt to reveal her black lace underwear.

She hungered for more, tugging at his T-shirt. They were no longer in a square in Barcelona – they were back in 1982. The yearning of years of love would soon be fulfilled.

Part 1

Hi Karen

The lads are having fun on Inis Mór. Stephen has got off with a young one that looks like Peig and Frank has fallen in love with a sheep.

As for me, I really miss you, Karen . . .

See you Wednesday
   Love, Greg xxx

21-06-1982

Karen Forde

21 Clontarf Close

Clontarf

Dublin 3

Chapter 1

Karen

Clontarf, Dublin, June 1982

I held the card to my chest and closed my eyes. He missed me – that was all I needed to know. And now I had his words in writing. It was the first time that Greg had written to me. He said that he wasn't much of a writer and I hadn't pushed it. But I cherished the card and would keep it by my pillow at night beside my photograph of the two of us together, taken at the photo booth in Boyers on North Earl Street the second time we had been to the city centre together. We had come into the city by bus and had just been browsing through albums at the Golden Discs store on the corner. I bought a Billy Joel album that day for ninety-nine pence even though I didn't like him very much. But there were two songs that reminded me of fun I'd had with my best friend Linda and that was enough reason to buy it.

I loved being on the bus with Greg. We timed our trips perfectly even though the bus timetable and the arrival of the actual bus seldom matched. He would get on the Number 31 at Sutton Cross and sit at the front beside the driver. He knew lots of the conductors and would only pay his fare as far as Sybil Hill in case I was late and he'd have to get off the bus. Then when I'd see him he'd press his face up against the window to make me laugh and I would hop on. I always blushed with pride when we

5

sat at the back of the upper deck, he with his arm around my shoulders. One day our neighbour Mrs Peters tut-tutted at our kissing in front of everyone. It made me chuckle to remember the look on the old busybody's face.

I ran upstairs and placed the postcard beside my bed. Then I reached under my pillow and pulled out the black-and-white image of myself and Greg. It was in a plastic wallet where I also kept my Grove card. The Grove was a disco for teenagers held at St Paul's school every Saturday night; it also ran on Sundays, but I was never allowed to go during term-time because of having school the next day.

I hated my Grove photo – it was taken shortly after I'd had my hair permed. I was so glad that the curls were growing out now. They were still quite tight when I'd met Greg and I often wondered how on earth a hunk like him had asked me to dance when I resembled a poodle. I'd had a sneaking suspicion that night, three months before, that Greg O'Sullivan had only asked me to dance because his friend Stephen fancied Linda. But, after three weeks of snogging and phone calls and playing happy foursomes, Linda had gone and got off with BOB and broken Stephen's heart. BOB was so cool – he used to let his cigarette hang between his lips for several seconds before lighting it. He wore a tight denim jacket that was real seventies but it wouldn't matter if he wore a paper bag – all the girls swooned when he entered the Grove. His name wasn't really BOB either – it was Barry O'Byrne but he was too cool to be called that. Rumour had it that even a couple of his teachers called him BOB. Linda thought she would be the one to win his heart and actually get going with him. He took her up to the stage – snog central zone – behind where Cecil the DJ worked his magic on the decks and asked her to meet him the next night. But Linda wasn't allowed to go to the Grove that Sunday night because her cousins were calling over. I felt that I should have had sympathy for her but I was so cross with her for breaking it off with Stephen that I couldn't bear to listen to her sobbing.

At first I was concerned that Greg might break it off with me after what Linda had done to Stephen, but I needn't have worried. The following day he and I took our walk to St Anne's Park, which had become our recent Sunday afternoon routine. Instead of discussing our friends or anything else, we found a quiet spot beside the orchard on the branch of an old tree that resembled a seat and happily drank the sweet taste of each other's lips for hours. I had kissed three other boys before I met Greg but they were very different. One was a holiday romance, one was a disaster during my first time at the Grove and the other was at a night of spin-the-bottle in Linda's house with her older brother's friends.

Kissing Greg was different from anything I had ever expected love to feel. And this was definitely love. Madness sang about it – *"It must be love, love, love!"* – and I wanted to scream from the rooftops that I knew exactly what they meant. It was so wonderful and thrilling and I felt as if I could take on the world. Before Greg all that mattered was silly stuff like getting 100% in my exams or winning a hockey match for my school. Hockey practice was one of the first casualties of our relationship. I told my mother that if I was going to get into Trinity then I would have to spend more time studying. It wasn't a good ploy in hindsight because the first thing to be affected after meeting Greg was my grades. It was more serious for Greg as he was sitting his Leaving Certificate but instead of concentrating on his books he was cycling down to Clontarf any chance he could get to see me.

My mother was willing to let it pass as I was only in fifth year and the real pressure wouldn't start until next year. Besides, my mum adored Greg – there wasn't a mother on the north side of the city that wouldn't love him. He was tall and polite and Mum believed that he would look after me. Even Dad liked him and he never commented much on anything that wasn't linked in some way to Manchester United.

I popped the postcard into the book beside my bed and put

my Grove card and the photo with it. I would have to find an album or box to keep my precious mementos in. For now I would go to my job in the supermarket on Vernon Avenue and hope that time passed quickly until Wednesday and the boys' return.

Chapter 2

Linda tipped her friend on the shoulder, causing her to drop the tin of beans that she was stacking on the lower shelf.

"Linda!" Karen groaned. "You frightened the life out of me – I thought it was that mad old Mrs O'Dea stalking me again."

"Ha ha – is she still trying to get you to be her slave? Putting her stuff in her basket for her?"

Karen got to her feet and wiped her brow. "She's batty – thinks she's back in the sixties – someone should tell her that it's 1982 and everyone serves themselves nowadays!"

"My gran is the same. She says they'll be expecting us to fill up our own cars with petrol next!"

"I can't see that happening – not in Clontarf anyway," Karen said adamantly.

"So what time are you finishing here?" Linda asked.

"Six. Do you want to do something later?"

"Yeah, defo, 'cos when loverboy comes home on Wednesday I won't be seeing much of you before I go to Irish college."

Karen gave her friend a playful thump on the shoulder. "I'm not that bad – we still see each other lots."

"You probably haven't noticed but you are always in Greg's house these days – if he's not in yours of course."

Karen had noticed. He was the first thought in her head every day when she woke up. She felt guilty about how little time she was spending with Linda, but her friend would be gone soon for three whole weeks to the Gaeltacht and she had to understand that things were changing – they were growing older and she was in a proper relationship with a boy.

"I got a postcard this morning from the Aran Islands!" Karen said. "I wish my parents had a house down the country like Greg's."

"It would be cool, wouldn't it?" Linda agreed. "Actually I got a card too – from Stephen. I was surprised."

Karen's heart leapt. "Oh, he must still have a thing for you, Linda – do you think you might get back with him?"

Linda shook her head. "It was really nice of him but I think he's more interested in getting the foursome thing back – that way he'll see more of Greg. You must understand the effect you two are having on the rest of us – it's not the same any more. It's taking a bit of getting used to. Stephen and I never clicked the way you and Greg do. At least I'll be away for most of July."

Karen felt guilty as she listened to the newly deflated Linda but in another way she didn't care if she was being selfish. All she wanted was to see Greg's gorgeous smile and bright blue eyes – and those lips – the lips that she could sit and kiss for hours on end. And, if Linda going to Irish college meant that she could see Greg every day without guilt, then she didn't care.

"I'm sorry!" Karen squeaked.

"It's okay." Linda shrugged. "I'll be back here when you finish work at six."

"Hey, will you ring my mum and tell her that I'm meeting you after work? We can go to the Capri for chips and eat them down at the statue."

"Okay – will do."

The supervisor scowled at Karen from where she sat over at the till – she was only a couple of years older than her but was a full-time member of staff and had been working there since she was fourteen so she felt very superior.

10

Karen returned to the task at hand but in her head she was in the park walking along by the river and Greg had his arm around her shoulder, the way that she loved to be held.

* * *

"So how does it feel being separated from Greg – like now?" Linda asked.

Karen swelled with pride. Linda was always the one who was more attractive to boys, with her auburn curls and big green eyes. She had kissed at least a dozen fellas but Karen hadn't minded being her sidekick – it had helped her to meet Greg in the first place.

Karen kicked out her legs and stretched them across the rocks as she took a fat chip from the paper bag.

"It's been okay but as the week has gone on I'm finding it harder to picture his face so I have to look at his photo more and then I remember."

The stink of vinegar wafted from the bag of chips, making Karen turn her head out to the sea. They were under the shadow of the statue of the Virgin Mary; this was always their spot, where they had come over the years to sit and discuss first the cutest boys at youth club and more recently those in the Grove. The sea was a dead calm, painted soft pastel hues of powder-blue, lilac and grey. A tanker chugged into the bay and disappeared behind the tall stripy ESB towers in the distance, which billowed smoke into the clear sky.

"Mum says I can go to the Cricket Club when I come back from Irish college."

Karen swung her head around. "No way – they serve drink there – how will you get in?"

"I'll have to go with Tommy and he's not too happy about that – but he's promised Mum that he will watch me."

Karen didn't know what to say – she wished *she* had an older brother like Tommy. "I don't think I'll be allowed go – it's easy for you being the youngest."

"I have to spread my wings – you and Greg will be an item

forever – well, a long time anyway – and if I don't get out more I'll never meet anyone."

"We might not make it to the end of the summer!"

Linda tut-tutted as she liked to do. "No, you two are in it for the long run – I can sense these things. My granny reads tea leaves – it's in our family – the gift!"

Karen felt elated by her friend's predictions. She wanted to be with Greg forever – she couldn't imagine herself kissing anyone else for the rest of her days.

* * *

Karen woke and looked at the alarm clock beside her bed. It was nine o'clock. Only eleven more hours and she would see him. It was a Wednesday and in the summertime the Grove was on three nights a week. They had planned their reunion just before he left. They would meet at the bus stop on Mount Prospect Avenue and walk to the Grove together – maybe sneak in a couple of bottles of Stag 'down the Anne's' beforehand, but she knew that the thrill of seeing him would leave her heady in a way that alcohol could never make her feel.

This day at the supermarket would just drag, she told herself – but the sun shone through her bedroom window – a good omen for the day.

Suddenly she heard the phone ring out downstairs.

Her mother called out, "Karen, it's for you!"

Karen pulled on her dressing gown and ran down the stairs. She reached out to grab the phone from her mother who wore a big grin as she passed the handset over.

"It's Greg!" she said – as if Karen hadn't guessed.

Karen put the phone up to her ear. "Hi there!"

"Hello, you! Hey, someone must have fixed this phone because I've been trying it every day since we got down here and it wasn't working – it's one of the older phones and you have to press the A to be connected. You know the type."

"I do. It must be lovely down there."

"Yeah, it's all donkeys and aul' fellas with wellies and caps. They only get RTÉ 1 in the local pub – the picture on RTÉ 2 is all fuzzy."

"So you missed *Top of the Pops* – Captain Sensible is still number one. Oh and 'Freebird' has re-entered the charts at number three."

"I love that song!" he sighed.

"Umm, me too!" It was the first song that they had danced to. She knew then that Greg liked her because he hadn't broken away when the fast instrumental bit came in. "Tell Frank I think he's right about 'Fame' though – it's definitely going to be number one."

"Are you and Linda still drooling over that wimp Bruno from the film?"

"Linda is – but I kinda prefer this big goofy Irish guy I know – don't ask me why!" Karen pursed her lips to stop any giggles from slipping out.

"And would this big goofy guy happen to be in the middle of an island in the Atlantic Ocean and desperate to get the train back to Dublin?" he asked eagerly.

"Oh well, I'm not sure, but I'm hoping that he will be at the Grove tonight." Karen could feel her legs tingling as the conversation developed. She wanted to see him so badly.

"Right. So he'd better drag his companions out of their dusty beds and make sure he doesn't miss the boat!"

"I think that would be a tragedy," Karen agreed.

A pause first and then the phone bleeped, demanding another ten-pence coin.

"I miss you – can't wait to see you."

"Me too –" but Karen wasn't able to finish as the line cut off.

She held the phone to her chest for a moment and closed her eyes. The familiar sound of his voice would be enough to get her through the rest of the day in the supermarket. She could imagine his face on each tin that she stacked.

Chapter 3

Karen opened her wardrobe door and ran her eyes over her clothes. She still had some Mod-style dresses, which seemed old-fashioned now. Greg liked her in her hippy dress but that didn't seem fashionable either, now that they were in summer. She decided on a simple geometric canvas dress that tied at the waist with a white cord. It would be nice with her new navy sandals and denim jacket. She drew her turquoise sparkly eyeliner along the rim of her lower eyelids and blinked. The addition of some black mascara and pink lip gloss and she was ready.

"Make sure Greg walks you home!" her mother called as Karen ran down the stairs.

"I will!" Karen answered, slamming the hall door behind her.

She was free and all the excitement of Saturday night on a Wednesday was thrilling. She walked on air along Mount Prospect Avenue. Her heart pounded – it had been one of the longest weeks of her life. She heard the squeaky brakes of a bicycle from behind her and turned around. It was him.

Greg hurriedly climbed off his bike, his eyes wide with the same joy as Karen's.

"Hi!" he said.

Karen didn't know what to say. She was filled with so much love she could burst.

"Hi!"

Neither knew who should make the first move.

Karen hovered on the edge of the footpath – her heart thumping out of her chest. She loved his sandy hair and his fringe which was always falling into his eyes. She reached up and possessively flicked it to the side, away from his face.

Greg gripped the handlebars firmly with his left hand and moved closer to the edge of the path. She was almost at his level as he stood on the road and she on the grass verge.

The waiting was over and the pent-up longing disappeared for them both as their lips met. Karen was so overcome she thought that she would cry. She had never missed anyone this much – ever.

They slunk into their natural rhythm of warm French kisses and lost track of time. He rested his right arm around her waist and she put her palms on his shoulder blades. The tension between them was perfect and passersby could not but smile at young love in action.

"I'm glad you're back," she said as they pulled away briefly.

"So am I! I wanted to see you before the lads arrive. They said they would meet us in the Anne's – Stephen's got some booze."

"Oh." Karen was disappointed – she wanted Greg all to herself. But, still, she would have all the slow sets with him later. "Is Linda coming?"

Karen shook her head. "She can't. I think she's getting ready for Irish college."

"Aah, Stephen will be disappointed."

"So he still has the hots for her?"

"Yep – afraid so. He was kissing anyone with a pulse in Aran and then sobbing into his pints over her!"

"I think Linda has her sights on other things – she wants to go to the Cricket Club in September."

"Is she allowed?"

"Yes. I think she's bored with the Grove."

"That's a pity."

"Are any of the other lads coming tonight?"

"Yeah, Frank is, so he can keep Stephen company. Some of the lads will meet us in there. Do you want to get on the crossbar?"

Karen nodded and hopped up on the bicycle. She held onto Greg tightly as they wobbled along the road to St Anne's Park.

Frank and Stephen were already at the sixth tree along the avenue on the left-hand side. That was their spot and other groups of park revellers knew that it was their territory.

Stephen had opened a can of Harp and was gulping it back. Frank preferred spirits and sipped on his naggin of Powers Whiskey.

They grinned at their friend – he was on such a different tack to them.

"He was a right pain on holiday, Karen – he's no fun any more – thank God he has you back!" Stephen said grudgingly.

Karen giggled. She longed to tell Greg that she had been in a state of high anxiety all week without him.

"Frank, did you get any Stag for Karen?" Greg asked.

"Yeah – just one can though – I'm broke after the holidays," Frank said, taking the tin out of a plastic bag.

"Thanks, Frank – how much do I owe you?" she asked.

"Don't mind him! I gave him money to get it." Greg scowled at Frank.

"I don't feel like drinking much so this is fine – thanks." Karen didn't want to cause friction. Already she was changing the dynamics of the group and Greg had made it clear that she was his priority over his friends.

"Scooby and Yogi are in the Grove already so we'll just knock these back quickly, okay?" Frank informed them.

"That's fine," Karen said, looking up at Greg for approval. She would be happier in the Grove where they could blend into the background and find a spot where they could be alone.

When the last can was drained they started the short hike to the large school hall just outside the park.

"Who's got Polo mints?" Frank asked.

"I have," Karen said, passing them around.

They had to disguise the smell of alcohol before entering the Grove. Frank lit up a cigarette and suggested she took a drag to get rid of the smell of the Stag. Greg looked on protectively as she put her lips around the tip of the cigarette and drew her breath. Greg never smoked and neither did Stephen. It was one of the little holds Frank had over the girls – he always provided them with cigarettes, to the annoyance of the others.

Karen loved to smoke but her mother was very much against it – even though she smoked herself. The fact that Greg didn't smoke had helped her to stay away from cigarettes but Frank knew it was her Achilles' heel and enjoyed the reaction he got from Greg when he shared his cigarette.

"Thanks," she said, pulling away and slipping a Polo mint into her mouth.

They fell into line outside the school hall where the teenagers waited to have their ID cards checked and their breaths smelt. The Polo mints were a dead giveaway that alcohol had been consumed by the crowd but the bouncers seemed happy enough to let them slip in if they seemed coherent.

Greg was quick to grab Karen's hand and drag her into the corner of the hall where their gang usually hung out. It was early in the evening and there were plenty of chairs free – only a couple had coats draped over them to mark the territory. Greg slipped his arm around her as they reached the plastic chairs that he had occupied as a student during term time.

"Do you want to dance or sit?" he asked.

She sat on the nearest seat and he snuggled up beside her.

They surveyed the pimply faces of those around – the greasy-haired girls who hid behind their glasses and gangly boys who had not yet grown into their tall frames.

Karen and Greg were king and queen of their domain and in

a position of power that most of those lurking and skulking around the hall wished they were in too. Everyone wanted to be in love. Music from Genesis belted out from the speakers – a prog rock classic that everyone at the Grove knew well.

He turned to look into her grey-blue eyes. "I missed you."

That stillness passed over them that happened whenever they were together. There may have been two hundred or more teenagers in the room but at moments like this they were the only people in the world.

"I missed you too," she whispered.

He kissed her again and this time it was more delicious than when she had met him on the road. She was full of him. The smell of him and the taste of his lips were fresh to her again and she wanted their mouths to stay joined forever. This was much more than she ever imagined she could feel for anyone – even her first crush Donny Osmond could never have made her feel the way that she felt at this moment. She could die for this boy and if they were put on a desert island forever then she would be happy.

The music changed to the strums of Led Zeppelin and 'Stairway to Heaven', but instead of dancing or talking she rested her head on his shoulder and let him soothe her by gently stroking her arm with the protective palm of his hand.

"This is heaven," she said.

"Mmm, I want to stay here forever." He sighed deeply and when he spoke again the tone of his voice had changed. "Hey, I'm in deep shit – the lads broke a window last night – I put a board up and hammered it to the frame but my dad will kill me when he finds out!"

Karen lifted her head. "How did they do that?"

"We were playing football inside the house."

Karen rolled her eyes. "Why didn't you fix it before coming home?"

"We'd have been delayed – I was dying to get back to see you and there are no glaziers on the island."

19

"When are your parents going down?"

"Maybe on Saturday – or sooner. I'm going to have to tell them."

Karen's heart thumped. She had only just got him back – she didn't need an upset that would ground him or take him away from her again.

"Hey, let's dance to 'Stairway'," Greg said. "I know you love it."

They stood up and wrapped their arms tightly around each other as if their lives depended on their closeness. The last week had been hell – she didn't want to lose him again.

Chapter 4

Karen opened her eyes and the first thought that came into her head was the mammoth kissing session she had shared with Greg. She ached when she thought about him and wished that he was in the bed beside her now. That would be an incredible experience. Something she could only try to imagine. He had walked her home from the Grove and cycled back to Sutton afterwards. She wanted to let him into her house but it was too late.

She cupped her breast the way that Greg had done as they stood at the garden gate. She wondered how her softness had felt for him. His moans had assured her of his pleasure. The night was bright and calm and watching him hop on his bicycle and disappear down the road left her feeling sad. But this morning she felt much better. She would work until one o'clock and then he was coming to meet her and if the weather was good enough they would go to the beach.

"Karen, do you have to be in work today?" Monica Forde called up the stairs.

Karen looked at her watch – it was a quarter past eight and time to dress. "I'm up!"

She dragged herself out of bed, wishing that she could lie

there and think of Greg until she saw him later. She pulled on her jeans and tied back her hair with a bobbin. She wished her hair was straight again – she often felt like a poodle with her hair tied back but Mrs Corcoran in the supermarket insisted she wore it that way. To make matters worse, she had to wear a work-coat too, which always seemed to be grubby.

She went into the kitchen where her mother was ironing some shirts for her father and taking a drag from the end of her cigarette.

"Did you have a nice time last night? I didn't hear you come in – I slept so much better knowing that you were with Greg."

"It was great, thanks." Karen hated the hundred-question scenario that seemed to thrill her mother. She went over to the press and poured herself a bowl of cornflakes.

"In my day you had to be on the last train home from the dance at ten o'clock. And you wouldn't be going out in the middle of the week either."

Karen switched on the radio to drown out her mother's reminiscing. Radio Nova was her favourite and she loved to hear the latest sounds. 'I've Never Been to Me' played out and Karen felt a shiver of embarrassment at some of the lyrics. She just hoped her mother wouldn't get all preachy like she had the last time that she heard this song.

"And who sings that one now?" Monica asked as she carefully folded the sleeve on her husband's shirt to get the edges just right.

"Charlene – she's American."

Monica inspected her work proudly and hung the shirt on a hanger. "Ah, in my day you had to wait weeks before an American singer was on the radio – and it was only the BBC radio that played songs for young people. You have so much these days."

Karen couldn't listen to any more. She gulped back the last few cornflakes and lifted the bowl to her lips, draining the last of the milk.

"Don't do that in front of your father – he will have a fit. You weren't brought up in a barn!"

Karen grinned. Her father couldn't give a toss how she did or didn't eat her cornflakes, but her mother liked to use him to inflict her own standards on the family.

"I'm off, Mum," she said, giving her mother a peck on the cheek.

It was dry outside but cloudy and not a beach day. Still, she would be with Greg and that was all that mattered.

The four hours spent stacking shelves and sweeping felt longer than at any time the previous week. When it was coming up to one o'clock her heart started to pound with excitement. How could she still be feeling this way after three months? Somehow the week apart had made her sure of her strong feelings for Greg. A tiny part of her had worried that he would go off her while away with the lads but from last night's experience she was confident that the trip away had had the opposite effect. And of course she had the postcard as written proof that he had missed her.

"Can I help you with that?"

Karen looked up from where she was kneeling, stacking tins. He seemed to have grown in the week that he was away.

Greg held out his hand and she took it as he helped her up.

"I must have stacked a thousand tins today! I thought the day would never end," she said. "Didn't we say we'd meet outside?"

"I'm making sure that your cruel boss lets you go on time."

"Oh, I'm going, don't worry. Just let me go into the storeroom and I'll take this coat off."

Greg admired her figure as she disappeared into the back of the shop. He was anxious and excited. His parents had packed up the car, piled his little brother and sister into the back and set off for Aran – and his older sister Tara wouldn't be home from the bank until seven o'clock at least. He hoped that Karen would be keen on his suggestion.

When Karen returned she had brushed her hair and draped a

sweatshirt over her shoulders covering a baggy T-shirt. She had shoved her bikini into a beach bag with a towel just in case.

"Ready!" she said, swinging the bag in the air. "I guess we won't need our swimming stuff though."

Greg shrugged. "The sun is trying to push through – we might be lucky . . . but . . . I have another suggestion . . ."

Karen was all ears as they walked out onto the street. She could tell by his body language that he was anxious in case she wouldn't approve.

* * *

There was a free row of seats downstairs at the back of the Number 31 bus and Karen sat on one of them.

Greg cycled along behind, keeping perfect pace so that she could see him at all times along the way.

They were almost at Sutton Cross and Karen felt her insides would burst with excitement. It was the first time that he'd had a free house and they would be in it alone together. He hadn't said what they would do when they got there. He didn't need to. It was obvious that their relationship had been taken to another level although there was no event to mark it – until now. Only a minute more and she'd be getting off the bus. She pressed the button on the metal pole to signal the driver to stop.

Greg was dismounting from his bicycle as Karen descended the steps. His face was red from the physical exertion but Karen hoped that there was another reason for his flushed expression.

The sun had decided to come out and play now and the clouds were only tiny fluffs of cotton wool in the sky.

They passed through the laneway from the Howth Road and took a short-cut to Offington Park. It was the most American layout of any housing estate in Dublin with fashionable bungalows on large plots. They didn't have walls around them like the houses on Karen's road but nobody ever seemed to walk on the open lawns – even the dogs didn't wander past the invisible boundaries. Linda said that only posh people lived in Offington, but Karen thought that Greg's family were not a bit snobby. His father had a big job as a surgeon in the Mater Hospital and that was why they could afford luxuries like houses down the country. Karen's mum had heard of him and said that he was always being quoted in the newspapers. He drove a classic sports car and it was parked in the driveway now as they had taken the mother's family estate on the long drive to the west of Ireland.

Greg fumbled with the key as he opened the front door. He parked his bike in the porch and led the way for Karen into the hall.

There was a distinct smell to Greg's house that was different to that of any other she had been in before. It smelt of him, even though none of the other members of his family carried the same smell.

They walked into the kitchen and Greg fussed around like the novice host he was.

"You must be starving – what would you like for lunch?"

"I don't mind." Karen shrugged.

"I make a mean toasted ham sandwich."

She nodded her head enthusiastically and watched him set to work.

The way that he fumbled around the worktop made her smile. He was eager to impress and she was flattered. Karen had to agree with Linda's assessment of the residents of Offington as she looked round Greg's kitchen – it was very posh with a breakfast bar and high stools, which were very American. The kitchen had French doors that led out onto a patio with plant pots and plush sun loungers.

"I thought we could sunbathe if you like – it's got really nice now."

The back garden wasn't overlooked like at Karen's house, which meant that they would be in total privacy. It sounded like a very decadent thing to do and she did have her swimsuit after all.

"Okay, I suppose we should make the most of the sun while it shines. We've had so much rain." Karen felt that this was a move in the direction she suspected they were going. She had seen him in his swim trunks before on the couple of warm days in June after he sat his Leaving Cert exam but there were others around. This would be just the two of them and it felt very grown up.

Greg was all fingers and thumbs as he served up two toasted sandwiches and two glasses of orange juice. Every now and then he'd brush his hand over hers or give her a peck on the cheek.

Karen was feeling braver by the time they finished eating and she climbed down from the high stool.

"Where should I change into my bikini?"

"Eh, you can use Ella's room if you like – she won't notice."

Karen went down the corridor to where Greg had pointed out his little sister's room and quickly changed. She could hear Greg in the room next door, opening and shutting drawers. Her bikini was made from pink-and-white striped fabric and tied in a halter-neck. It made her feel so much more mature than her sixteen years. She wasn't sure what to do with her towel and decided to tie it around her waist as a kind of wrap-over skirt.

When she returned to the kitchen Greg was already there and wearing his swim shorts. He had poured more juice into their glasses and the French doors were open wide. Two straw mats were placed side by side on the grass and covered with beach towels, looking far more appealing than the loungers where they would be lying apart.

"Will I put the radio on?" he asked.

"Oh, I'll do that," she said, taking the beat-box over to the back door. "Will I put it on Nova?"

"It's already tuned in to it."

Toto blasted from the speakers: *Meet you all the way, Ros-a-ana yeah . . .*

Karen walked out onto the patio. Greg followed, observing her silhouette and hoping she would make a beeline for the mats.

He needn't have worried. She wanted to be as close to him as possible and sat down squarely in the middle of one of the beach towels.

"It's certainly heated up," she said, taking a glass of juice from Greg. "Thanks."

"It's great to have the house to myself. Tara might stay out later tonight so you can stay for dinner – plenty of food in the freezer. I can do crispy pancakes too and green peas."

"Sounds very tempting – I'll have to call my mother at some stage though."

Greg nodded. They had all day to spend in this way.

"Do you have any baby oil? I don't want my skin to peel."

"Tara will definitely have some in her room – I'll get it." Greg jumped up and returned seconds later with a bottle. "Would you like me to help you put it on?"

Karen lay face down on the towels. "Okay!"

It was with military precision that Greg carefully applied the layer of oil on her back and shoulders.

"Would you like me to do your legs?"

"Yes, please," she smiled and held her breath as he ran his palms along the insides of her thighs.

"Would you put some on me?"

"Of course." Karen sat up and poured some oil into her hand then ran it along his chest. She put more on his abdomen and felt the strong muscles that had developed from playing rugby. He was thin but by no means skinny, his torso defined already into a V-shape.

"What about your legs?"

His smile and raised eyebrows said it all.

Her hands grazed cross the fine hairs on his legs – skimming quickly over the area around his upper thighs.

"Come down here and lie beside me."

She did as she was told and let him put his arm around her.

It was one of those silent moments that didn't need words. Every now and then he would turn his head and kiss the side of her face. How was it possible to feel this relaxed, content and happy next to another human being?

Karen didn't want to break the spell but she was concerned that his parents could appear at any moment – what if they had forgotten something and came back?

"Did you tell your dad about the window?"

"No – I'd say he'll reach the house by about six or seven this evening and then he'll call here – provided that phone box on the island is still working." He laughed.

"Oh, and what will happen when he gets home?"

"I'll get grounded or something but he won't be able to check that I stay home and you know my old lady – she won't even remember the next day!"

Greg's mother wasn't like most mothers. She was vacant to say the least. Karen worried that she didn't like her but Greg assured her that she treated everyone with the same reserved disdain and what she had shown Karen was the best welcome to anyone he had brought into the house. Karen was grateful for his kind words but still not convinced.

"Does Tara know about the window?"

"Tara can only think of one thing – and he drives a Toyota Celica and works in the same bank as she does."

It was true. Even Karen knew how much in love Tara was with her latest flame. And the neighbours' net curtains did rustle at the roar of his super engine as he belted up Offington Avenue.

"So forget about everyone else – this is time for us," he said, stalling to find the perfect moment to kiss her. Then he asked tentatively, "Do you want to continue this inside?"

Karen's heart beat loudly in her chest. Was the undressing a prelude to something else? She had sworn that she would keep her virginity until she was eighteen at least. Really she wanted to keep it for her husband. Would she be strong enough to stop Greg if it went too far? She knew that this was late in her cycle. Linda and she had listened carefully in biology and they could work their days out perfectly. But still it was risky and her mother's friend had just announced at forty-three that she was having baby number five after using the rhythm method. She decided there and then that she wouldn't do it. They hadn't had the talk about it but she couldn't go all the way – so far they had only been to third base. She and Linda had both been there and letting a fella touch your bare breast seemed enough for them. But, going into the house almost naked, she realised that she wanted more. She had to say something but didn't know how.

Greg sensed her apprehension and took her hand. "I won't go all the way if you don't want to."

Relief washed over her. She said a silent prayer to the Virgin Mary, thanking her for helping Greg to read her mind.

"I think it would be better to wait – I've never . . ."

He seemed as relieved as she was and stopped and held her closely to him, kissing the top of her head. "I haven't 'done it' either. We don't need to."

They were so much more relaxed now and walked straight down the hall towards his bedroom. It was messy but that was no surprise – she had been there before. But not like this. They playfully flung their nubile bodies onto the bed and wrapped their limbs around each other. Soon they were lost in the sensations of licking, stroking and caressing each other's bare skin.

Greg slid the triangle of fabric that covered her breast to the side and put his lips to her nipple. He tickled it gently with his tongue and made her shiver.

Karen wondered how he knew to do that – she had never thought that a fella would want to do such a thing. But it was pleasurable for her to hear his groans of delight.

His fingers traced the outline of her shape with featherlight strokes as if she was made of a fragile porcelain or precious metal.

And that was how he made her feel – precious and fragile and wonderfully womanly.

His fingers hadn't far to travel to skim along her bikini

bottoms. He caressed her fleshy buttocks, skirting along the gusset every few strokes for a brief second or two.

Karen was torn between begging the Virgin Mary for strength and the desire to separate her legs. It was a huge step to let him touch her down there – she wanted him to do it but was scared that all sorts of things would happen if she did. His parents could turn back and walk in the door and find them there – Tara could have a headache and come home early from work – her mother could take the bus out and knock on the door, wondering where her daughter was – all highly unlikely but, still, these were the distractions that she had to deal with while longing for him to slip his fingers under her bikini. In the end her desires took over and as their tongues melted into each other she parted her thighs and gave him the signal to explore. His fingers were long and strong but moved slowly and carefully inside her. She was dripping with adolescent juices and the strong smell of sex.

They had no idea how long they spent like this before they stopped and realised what had passed between them. It was an intimacy that had moved them both deeply.

"I never imagined that it would be like this," he said, his cheek touching the side of her face, their legs entwined.

"I feel so much closer to you now."

"Me too. I wonder what the others would think if they knew how we'd spent the afternoon!"

"I think Linda would kill me – she'd send me off to say a novena to Saint Jude, the patron of hopeless cases! What about Stephen?"

"I don't think it would dawn on him that we would do something like this."

Karen giggled. There was something lovely and innocent about Stephen – he wore his heart on his sleeve always. There was something innocent about them all but what they had done couldn't be called that.

Whatever it was, it felt right.

"I'm going to take a shower," Greg announced. "Do you fancy joining me?"

Karen nearly fell off the bed. "Maybe, but with my bikini bottoms on – and you must keep your shorts on, okay?"

He nodded reluctantly and they raced each other to the shower. A bottle of Brut aftershave rested on the shelf.

"Is that what you use?" she asked.

"Yeah, I splash it on all over!" he said, mimicking the boxer on the TV advert.

They let the water flood over their bodies, their bare chests brushing closely and intimately.

She brushed his wet fringe to the side and held her hand on his cheek for a moment, the water rushing down his face and travelling along her arm, holding them together like two parts of the one person. Neither wanted to leave the comfort of the shower but they were disturbed by a ringing on the front door.

"Oh God – who's that?" she gasped.

"Don't move – I'll look out the bedroom window." Greg took a towel and went out to see from his sister's bedroom. He tiptoed back into the bathroom. "It's Stephen. If we don't answer he'll go away."

Karen shivered and he put a fresh towel around her shoulders.

The doorbell rang out again.

"Shit. I bet he's spotted my racer in the porch and knows I'm here."

"What do we do?"

"Just wait." He listened. "I think he's riding down the driveway now – yes, he is. Phew! Maybe we should get dressed."

Karen nodded. "I think we should."

They met in the kitchen and didn't have to wait long before the doorbell rang again.

This time they answered.

"Took you long enough," Stephen complained bullishly as he padded into the hall. "Oh, you're here," he said to Karen.

"Nice to see you too, Stephen."

"Sorry – I didn't mean it like that. Where were you – out the back?"

Karen and Greg looked at each other urgently.

"Yes!" they both said. "Out the back."

Stephen sat up at the breakfast bar and rested his arm on the counter. "Well, I hope that you're ready for the call from your dad – he's going to kill you."

"That's good coming from the one who kicked the ball through the window."

"I told you we should have fixed it before coming home – so what if we'd missed the Grove?"

Greg gave Karen a knowing look that said a multitude – Stephen simply didn't understand.

"So what are you two doing for dinner?"

"I'm going to make crispy pancakes."

"Sounds good. I told my mum I was coming here to keep you company, Greg."

Karen and Greg looked at each other.

"Are you two going to the Parish Fundraiser in the youth club tomorrow night? Tickets are two quid and Frank is selling them."

"Count us in," Greg said. "Will it be okay with your mum, Karen, if you come out this way to Sutton?"

"Oh, you've reminded me – I have to ring my mum," Karen said. "But, no, she won't mind at all – yeah, let's go to that tomorrow."

Karen went into the hall and lifted the receiver.

Monica answered almost immediately. "Karen, where have you been? I've been worried sick!"

"Hi, Mum – I'm in Greg's. I told you that I was meeting him after work."

"But you said that you would meet Linda here at four – don't you remember?"

Karen groaned. She had completely forgotten about her best

friend. And it was Linda's last night in Dublin before she set off for Galway.

"Is she still there?"

"No, she's gone home and she's waiting for a call from you. When will you be home?"

Karen looked at the clock on the wall. It was five o'clock already – how had time gone so quickly?

"I'll go straight to Linda's house now then."

"You need to let me know where you are, Karen – you might think you're grown up but you're only in school."

She didn't need reminding. She wished that she was waiting for her Leaving Cert results like Greg. If only her mother knew what she had been doing for the afternoon. She was a young woman and she wished her mother would treat her like one.

"I'd better not stay on the phone – this is costing Mr O'Sullivan a fortune."

"All right but let me know when you arrive in Linda's house."

"Okay, Mum, stop worrying."

She dreaded the call to her best friend. She had neglected her completely and this was her last chance to see her for three weeks. She dialled Linda's number – she knew it off by heart like all of her friends' numbers.

"Hello."

"Hi, Linda, I'm so sorry! Can you forgive me?"

Linda huffed at the other end of the line. "So are you coming to say goodbye?"

"I'm on my way there now – I'll be as quick as I can."

"Mum says you can stay for tea."

"Great – see you soon."

"Okay then," Linda said and put down the phone.

Karen went into the kitchen. Greg was unwrapping the pancakes.

"I have to go," she announced. "I forgot I was to meet Linda earlier and she's leaving for Galway tomorrow."

Greg's face fell and Stephen threw her a look that said that he had won this battle and had Greg all to himself for the evening.

Greg followed her out to the front door. They stood in awkward silence, neither wanting to leave the other.

"I'll call you later?" Karen said.

Greg nodded and leant down to plant the softest kiss on her lips.

It stayed there all the while she walked to the Howth Road. As she jumped on the Number 31, which arrived a few minutes later, her mind was in a haze of milk and honey and nothing could bring her back to the mundane or humdrum.

The bus ride felt like seconds and she was let into Linda's house by her mother.

"Hello, Mrs Maloney – thanks for inviting me for tea."

"Oh, sure, Karen, we will miss you while Linda is away. Go on up to her – she's in the bedroom."

Linda was folding some T-shirts as Karen came into the room. She turned and smiled at her friend. She couldn't stay mad at her for long.

"So what had you losing track of time today then?"

As if she had to ask.

"Greg's folks went down to Aran early so he had a free house . . ."

"Ahh, playing mums and dads, were you?"

How did she know? Karen's mouth hung open.

"You have to spill – come on!" Linda said, flopping down on to the bed.

Karen plonked down beside her. They always told each other everything but this was different – she'd hate it if Greg spoke about what they had done.

"We were sunbathing."

Linda raised her eyebrows in disbelief.

"Well, for a while anyway . . . why can't I keep my news to myself? It's not fair!"

"So did you go past three?"

Karen wanted to scream 'What, are you a bloody mind

reader?' There was no point in hiding it even if she could – anyway, Linda would be gone tomorrow to Galway. "We went to six."

Suddenly Linda got really animated and jumped up from the bed. "Oh wow – what was it like?"

Karen blushed. "Eh, nice – I mean amazing. Nothing like you see on TV. It was really intense."

"Were you not scared he'd go all the way?"

Karen shook her head. "No, we discussed it before going to the bedroom."

Linda stood up and stomped up and down the small box-room shaking her head. "You actually talked about it – I can't imagine that, Karen – you two are so far ahead of the rest of us."

Karen did feel more mature after her afternoon experience. It was thrilling and scary and wonderfully romantic. Nothing seemed the same after it – even sitting on the bed talking to Linda felt different to the way she had been the week before while Greg was away.

"Don't do it while I'm in Irish college – please?" Linda begged.

"I won't." Karen shook her head. "I told you there's no way I'm going to do it until I'm married."

"You won't last the way you're going." Linda shook her head. "I think I'm just jealous."

Karen didn't know what to say. But then Mrs Maloney called from downstairs and the two walked down to eat the sausages and mash smothered in gravy that was her signature dish. If they were lucky there would be ice-cream wafers or fig rolls and custard for dessert.

Chapter 5

Work went quickly for Karen the next day. She had been sad saying goodbye to Linda the night before but three weeks would fly by.

There wasn't enough hot water in the tank for her to have a bath when she got home and the showerhead attached to the taps dripped pathetically with barely enough water to cover her body without shivering. Her father would allow the immersion to be left on for only an hour during the summer. She wished she lived in a posh house like Greg's. The water had flowed powerfully as they had stood in the cubicle the day before.

It was such a shock when she thought about what she had done, but satisfying too. She wondered if they could slip back there tonight – the house was close to the community centre where the fundraiser would be held. But on second thoughts it might be better to wait.

Greg was going to meet her at the bus stop at Sutton Cross at seven-thirty. His voice was dreamy when he had called the night before to make arrangements. Stephen had stayed until ten o'clock – long enough to make sure that it was too late for him to cycle to Clontarf.

"Your father will be there to collect you at twelve," Monica

Forde called to Karen as she raced down the stairs.

"Can he make it one – please?"

Monica came out to the hall where Karen was standing. She took a hard drag on her cigarette. "I'll try and convince him to wait until twelve-thirty but that's the very latest."

Karen brushed her lips against her mother's cheek before she ran out the door. "Thanks, Mum!"

It was so bright and mild that it felt like the middle of the day. Everything seemed so much better now that Greg was home.

The bus was only five minutes late – good going, she thought, as she paid the conductor. She bobbed up and down on the front seat in excitement. Butterflies flitted about in her stomach at the thought of seeing him. All the thrilling emotions that she'd had at the start of their relationship were back. In the distance she saw a figure standing at the bus stop. It didn't look like Greg. When the bus came to a halt Karen could see that it wasn't Greg – instead it was Stephen and skulking against the wall sucking the last bit of nicotine from a cigarette was Frank.

Karen craned her neck looking for Greg but she couldn't see him.

As she descended the steps of the bus Greg's two friends stood waiting to escort her.

Confused and disoriented, she asked, "Where's Greg?"

"The shit's hit the fan, Karen," Stephen explained.

"Big time," Frank piped up.

"Greg's dad rang late last night and told Greg he had to go down immediately to Aran. He has to get the glass and help fix the window."

Karen hoped they were joking and looked around for Greg to jump out from behind the post box or a wall. "Seriously – where is he?"

"On a train to Limerick – he missed the one this morning and is going to be in even more trouble. His dad had a lift arranged to bring him to Doolin to catch the boat. I wouldn't like to be him." Stephen looked at Frank as if they both knew something that Karen didn't.

"So what will I do?"

"We've been told to be your chaperons and look after you," Frank said, offering her a cigarette from his red box of Carroll's.

Karen took one without speaking and let him light it with his new silver Zippo.

Frank flipped it shut so that it made a loud click. "You're in safe hands. You're allowed dance with us but no one else – okay?"

"I feel sorry for you, to be honest," Karen said. "What if you fancy a girl and want to ask her to dance?"

"That's why there are two of us. Jackie Quinn isn't going so Frank doesn't mind . . . isn't that right, Frank?"

Frank scowled. Karen didn't know who Jackie Quinn was but she presumed that she was the girl that Frank had been snogging at the Grove last time at the end of the evening.

"You are really kind," Karen said but a part of her dreaded the evening. She still hoped that they would arrive at the community centre and Greg would be there.

* * *

There was a poor turnout at the disco and at ten-thirty Karen wished that she had asked her dad to collect her at twelve. She'd much rather be at home staring at the photo of Greg than sitting in a hall full of strangers from Sutton and Howth. Stephen was chatting to a girl over by the DJ and Frank was sitting at her side chain-smoking all evening.

Then the night seemed to look up as a couple that Frank knew came over and joined them.

"Karen, this is Orla and Pete – Pete was in school with us." Frank turned to the others and explained: "I'm minding Karen for Greg."

Orla waved in a truly friendly way that put Karen at ease. She sat down beside her and started to chat while Pete and Frank lit up cigarettes.

"Hi, I've seen you at the Grove with Greg. He's so nice. How long have you two been going out now?"

"Three months."

Orla smiled and nodded her head.

"How long are you going with Pete?"

Orla flicked back her long blonde hair and batted her blue eyes. "Two years," she said proudly.

Karen felt so far out of her depth she wanted the floor to open and swallow her. But they weren't a showy couple – they just seemed so mature.

Michael Jackson's 'Don't Stop 'til You Get Enough' suddenly blasted from the speakers. Pete sprang into spontaneous dancing and Orla leapt up. As they moved in unison and perfect harmony Karen thought of herself and Greg the day before. Could this be a prelude to how they would be in two years' time? She hoped so.

Suddenly Frank's attentions were turned to the door as a stunning girl with cropped black hair entered the hall.

"Oh God – Jackie Quinn is here!" he gasped.

The stunning girl scanned the room and her eyes passed over Frank and then quickly turned back when she saw a girl at his side.

"What will I do?" Frank asked. "She said she didn't want to go steady with anyone at the moment."

"Put your arm around me quick!" Karen said. "If she thinks you have another girl already she'll be interested in you."

Frank frowned. "What?"

Karen took his arm and pulled it across her shoulders. "There, do nothing for a few moments until we see what she does." She could feel Frank's heart pounding. "Relax. She's been looking at you since you put your arm around me!"

"B-b-but she hasn't looked my way at all."

"Girls look out of the corner of their eyes – don't you know anything?" she said, clicking the roof of her mouth with her tongue.

"But what if she thinks we're together?"

"That's what we want her to think. Tell you what, now would be a good time to go to the loo. I'll wait here and I bet she'll follow you outside and bump into you. Look, Stephen is on his way over now – I'll be fine."

Frank wasn't convinced but he did as she suggested nonetheless.

"Hey, what's with the arm business? That's taking our job a step too far!" Stephen said.

"It's okay – it's for a good cause," Karen explained. "Sit down and I'll tell you what we're up to."

Frank went out through the entrance doors and, sure enough, thirty seconds later Jackie followed.

"Come on, let's dance with Orla and Pete," Stephen suggested.

And that was what they did until half past twelve and it was time for Karen to be collected.

* * *

Four days later and Greg still wasn't home so Karen consoled herself by writing to her best friend.

Dear Linda

You'll never guess what happened. Greg's dad went mad when he found out about the broken window and made him go back to Aran – it's Tuesday now and he's still not home. Stephen has been good and checking up on me every day – but it's because Greg told him to. I went to the Parish Fundraiser in Sutton on Friday and Frank scored with a girl called Jackie Quinn – she's too cool and wouldn't like us at all. But he's totally smitten. I guess I'll have to buy my own cigarettes from now on – or even give them up.

I hope that you get Top of the Pops down there – or are you not allowed to watch English TV? Well, "Fame" is at number one at last – no surprise! I met your mum in the supermarket and she said that you are in a very nice house that's not strict at all. I bet that's easy for her to say. I wish that you could ring. I'm feeling so confused. I also met this couple called Orla and Pete – you'd probably know them to see – they've been going together for two years – can you believe it? He's really cool and they are both great dancers. I feel like I know them already – it's really strange. When I spoke with them it felt like we had talked before. Anyway the good news is that Greg is let come home tomorrow – his dad got him to do some painting while he was down there for punishment. Thank God the phone box is working and he calls me twice a day.

I'll finish this letter off and write again when I have some more news.

Do chara

Karen

PS You aren't missing much.

* * *

Karen readied herself for his arrival. He was calling to take her for a walk in St Anne's Park. They didn't want to go to the Grove – they needed time on their own.

Her dad answered the door and started to chat about any changes that might be made before the football season started back.

Karen's heart filled with pride as she heard her father and boyfriend speak man-to-man downstairs. She dragged a brush through her hair and put on some lip gloss before joining them.

He had got taller in the few days he had been away – or maybe it was broader. Greg looked up and smiled as he saw her descend the stairs.

"Hiya!"

Declan Forde took the cue to exit. He left the young couple

and went in to where his wife was sitting in the kitchen.

"Great that you made the early train back," Karen said. "Do you want to leave your bike here?"

"I've already put it around the side."

They walked out into the sunshine, passing some local kids playing on the footpath. Karen lived near a gap in the hedge of the park and the kids entered it that way.

Once in the park Greg put his arm around her shoulder and they stopped by a tree for a snog.

"I didn't think I'd last," Karen said, pulling away.

They continued walking randomly in the direction of the rose garden.

"I didn't think I'd last either. My dad was furious – I knew that he would be but this was like I'd never seen before. You don't know my dad!"

"I haven't seen him much – only that time he was working on his car in your driveway."

"Yeah – he thought you were gorgeous and it's not like him to comment on anyone that comes into the house. He's very odd – I suppose being a surgeon makes you that way. But he's hard on us – especially me. He's at the top of his game and he's frustrated at me because I'm not as clever as him. I don't know who I'm like – sometimes I feel like they picked up the wrong baby in the hospital."

Karen had never heard him speak about his family intimately before. Nor had she seen such pain in Greg's face as he spoke. "I hadn't realised. What did he do?"

Greg took a sharp breath. "He has this way of putting me down – making me feel completely useless – it's like his way of pushing me to do better. I wish he'd realise that it has the opposite effect."

Karen was feeling terribly guilty – wondering if she had hindered her boyfriend's progress. Maybe they should have seen less of each other back in May and June.

"Are you worried about your Leaving results? Maybe if you

hadn't met me you would have studied better?"

Greg shook his head. "I don't care what I get in the Leaving – I'm not like him – I don't want to be a doctor and there's no way that I'm going to get the grades anyway."

"But what will happen if you don't do well?"

"My dad said that I'll have to repeat and make something of myself. He puts me down about everything that I've done over the last two years – the broken window was the final straw for him. He said that he'd trusted me by letting us use the house and I'd let him down – again."

Karen's father was distant at times, with his head in his paper or watching TV – the way most adults behave – but she always felt that he was proud of her and he only ever encouraged her. When she had got her last report her mother made her show it to him and he thought that four C's and three D's was a very good result – it was a long way down to Z was his way of seeing it. Declan was a fireman who had left school at twelve. He worked in a factory until he was called up to be a fireman and had no great desire to do anything more in his life. However, he was a changed man this last while since the Stardust tragedy. He had worked tirelessly that night in February 1981, and although he had pulled some revellers to their safety he, like so many of his colleagues, was left with terrible mental scars as so many young people lost their lives that night. He thought his wife had "notions" at times and after experiencing such horror thought she needed to let up and stop putting pressure on Karen. As long as she was healthy and safe, that was all that mattered to him. Karen loved her dad fiercely and couldn't imagine how it must feel to have an awkward relationship. She felt bad for Greg and listened as he talked on about his inadequacies and lack of self-confidence.

"I'd never have known that you felt this way – I'm glad that you told me."

Greg nodded. "It's great to have you to talk to. Stephen wouldn't understand and Frank's dad is dead."

Karen's mouth dropped. "Oh, I didn't know – that's awful!"

"Yeah, he died two years ago – lung cancer. His mum is worried sick about his smoking but there's nothing she can do. It's mad but he wasn't a smoker until his dad died and then it's like he took over where his dad left off."

Karen wished that she hadn't encouraged him and made a vow there and then never to smoke again – not with Frank anyway.

Greg stopped and wrapped his long arms tightly around Karen. "I'm sorry – this was meant to be a happy walk – I was dreaming about it while I was painting the walls of the cottage."

"I feel honoured that you're telling me these things. It's the only way we'll get to know each other better."

They kissed some more before walking the circumference of the old and new ponds and deciding they would go back to her house and listen to some Santana. Her mum had agreed that he could stay for tea.

Chapter 6

It was almost time for Linda's return and Karen was concerned because she had thought so seldom about her best friend over the last three weeks. She and Greg had met up with Orla and Pete twice at the Grove and enjoyed time dancing with them. Frank was having an on-off fling with Jackie Quinn and Stephen was feeling very left out in the cold.

Summer was racing away on Karen and soon she would be back in school and studying for her Leaving Cert. Greg's results would be out in a matter of days and if he did badly she would feel terrible. Greg had picked up a job in the Marine Hotel but so far had managed to arrange his hours around the time that she spent in the supermarket.

It was definitely her best summer yet and they had money to buy records and clothes. Karen had bought a pair of blue Sasperilla skinny jeans in O'Connor's with her previous week's wages and worn them to the Grove. She felt so gorgeous in them and they made her bum look great. Greg kept caressing her in them and she loved it. He even managed to get his hand down the back of them one day when they were all around in Frank's house. Nobody would have known what he was doing – they were having their own private petting session on the couch while

Santana played on the record player and the others discussed *Fame*.

It was often that way now – she and Greg in their own little world even when they were with the others. She hoped that wouldn't change now that Linda was home. If only she would go back with Stephen then they could all be happy couples again.

* * *

"I'm off out to get a few messages – will you be here when I get back?" Monica called up the stairs.

"No, Mum – I'm going around to Linda's at one and then we're going into town."

"All right but be back for tea at six."

"I will." Karen put her lip gloss into the pocket of her denim jacket. She was wearing the Sasperillas. She hadn't told Linda about her new jeans in a letter – she wanted to see her reaction.

It was a ten-minute walk to Linda's house. All the way there she thought about her birthday which wasn't far away now. Greg wanted to go somewhere special – grown-up – now that he was earning money working in the hotel. They had some crazy conversations over the last couple of weeks and had even come up with the notion of running away together. Karen wished that she was a rebel and brave enough to do something wild but it had been drilled into her head by her mother to aspire to greater things – Monica warned her that she didn't want to be reliant on her husband for money and decision-making.

Linda was already in the garden when Karen reached her house. The friends hugged awkwardly and went inside.

"So what was it like?"

"I don't think you'd have stuck it, Karen. The food was awful and we had five hours of classes a day."

Karen shuddered. "I most definitely wouldn't have – oh, it's great to have you back! We've been going to the Grove twice a week and we had a barbeque down on Dollymount one night."

"I thought you said I wasn't missing much?"

Karen smiled. "Well, you weren't – I mean there's no sca – apart from Frank and Jackie Quinn."

"Why do you always use her surname?"

"I just do – she's not like us – she's *sooo* sophisticated – I don't know what she sees in Frank. She doesn't wear clothes like us. But wait until you meet Orla – you'll love her – she's just like us."

"It sounds like it's all been cosy couples since I left – I'm not going to be lumped with Stephen, am I?"

Karen grimaced. "Well, that's it – Stephen is going out with someone too."

Linda rolled her eyes. "So I'm going to be on my tod then if I go to the Grove? Well, the Cricket Club is starting up in the middle of August and I'll be going there instead. Anyway, it doesn't matter – come on, I'm dying to go into town and look at the shops – I'm just glad to be back in the land of the living!"

* * *

The two friends sat on the top of the bus after buying some eyeliner in Roches Stores and eating an ice-cream sundae in the Ilac Centre.

Karen's head was full of thoughts of Greg. Things had changed in such a short time and she hoped that her friend would understand.

"Have you thought about what you want to do for your birthday?" Linda asked.

Karen winced. Her friend was a mind reader – she didn't want her seventeenth birthday to be a cause of friction between them but she knew how possessive they were of each other on important days of the year. Linda's parents had invited her to go down to a caravan in Wexford, which would mean being away for her birthday. Before Linda had gone to Irish college Karen had said that she would go – but now she wanted to spend the day with Greg.

"Would you mind if I don't go to Wexford? Greg will be getting his Leaving Cert results and I want to be here for him."

Linda had expected as much. She had wanted to get it out of the way – know where she stood.

"I never thought a fella would come between us, Karen."

Karen hadn't either. The guilt was huge – she couldn't expect Linda's parents to change their holiday arrangements and they would be disappointed that Linda wouldn't have a friend on the holiday.

"You could stay with me in Dublin?" she said.

Linda sighed. "I don't think so – you'll be with Greg. I can't say I blame you. If I had hit it off with Stephen I'd probably be the same." She turned to her friend and observed the worried look in her eyes. "So is this it – have you met 'the one' at sixteen years of age?"

Karen didn't know how to answer. The thought of spending the rest of her life with the same man was terrifying – but the thought of being apart from Greg was even more so.

"Tell you what, I'll come to the Grove with you this weekend and play gooseberry to keep you from feeling guilty," Linda said. "And it doesn't matter about Wexford – Mum said I don't have to stay all the time – I can come up early and stay with Tommy so I will see you for your birthday."

Karen felt much better. They almost missed their stop and ran giggling and laughing like they used to down Sybil Hill Road.

Chapter 7

August 14th 1982

If she'd had a fairy godmother and had been granted a wish to have anything she wanted for her seventeenth birthday she wouldn't have changed a thing. Greg was meeting her on the bus and they were going into town to have lunch in Solomon Grundy's. She had walked by the restaurant on Suffolk Street several times and longed to eat in there. It looked so American and trendy – a step above Captain America's, although thrillingly she had seen the Boomtown Rats eating burgers there the last time she went with Linda. That day they had ordered chocolate sundaes and Coke because they had given over most of their money to a fortune teller in the Dandelion market. That was one of the first times that she had been allowed into town but still it couldn't beat the excitement of today.

She waited at the Howth Road for the Number 31 to arrive, her heart beating as it pulled to a halt.

Greg stood up and came to the door to greet her. They ran upstairs but the front seats were already taken so they went down the back of the bus.

Greg carried a bag with the Golden Discs logo all over it. She knew that it was her birthday present and she hoped beyond hope that it was the album that she wanted – ABC's *The Lexicon of Love.* The bus journey always flew when she was with Greg and they were walking across O'Connell Bridge in minutes. The brown murky waters of the River Liffey below stank and Greg gave her the woolly hat that he had in his pocket all year round to put over her nose.

The hat reeked too but Karen didn't mind – it smelt of Greg and if he had let her she would have happily slept with it under her pillow at night.

Along Westmoreland Street they strolled, laughing and joking at the sights of the city and the roar of the buses. A horse and cart trotted by laden with vegetables and slowing the traffic. The blackened stone walls of Trinity College came into view next, reminding Karen of the mammoth year she would have ahead of her if she hoped to study there. Greg would have his results next week but they wouldn't talk about that today.

They passed the tobacco store with fancy pipes in the window and the ludicrously expensive fur store with the doorbell that you had to ring if you wanted to enter.

And then they were on Suffolk Street.

There was a queue at the door of Solomon Grundy's but that was to be expected and they had to wait ten minutes before being seated. Karen hoped desperately that they would get the table where the lifesize pig sat. Greg whispered something in the waitress's ear as they were brought to the table beside the pig which was a good compromise.

The menu was printed on big cards and described exotic Italian food. Karen had heard about the pizzas and was dying to try one.

They ordered two Cokes.

Then Greg reached out and held her hand.

"Do you like it?"

"I love it – this is brilliant."

"I'd love to spend the whole day with you – not go to the Grove tonight. If only my parents were away and we had the house to ourselves like before!"

Karen blushed. She had thought about that day often since. In some ways she was happy finding a space amongst the dunes in Dollymount Strand or along the cliff behind the gorse bushes in Howth. But when winter came they wouldn't be able to do their courting outside. They would cross that bridge when they came to it. But she was pleased that it prevented them from broaching the subject of having sex – she had lost control of herself the last couple of times and it was Greg who had held back. Now she understood how easy it was to be swept away and how girls got pregnant. Laura Murphy in sixth year had a baby hours after finishing her Leaving Cert – she almost wasn't allowed to sit the exam at all only the nuns were afraid of her father. Some said that he had been in the IRA but Karen didn't believe that anybody in Clontarf could be in the IRA. Laura Murphy had used a johnny too but the story went that it had burst. Karen wondered where they had got it. She knew her father had them – she'd seen them once in the drawer beside his bed. But she couldn't take one because he would definitely count them and wonder where it had gone. His friend Matt was a policeman and able to get stuff like that – and bangers and sparklers at Halloween that he confiscated from the women on Moore Street. It still didn't stop them selling them though.

"What are you thinking about?"

Karen shook her head. "Sorry, mind drifted off there – sparklers and bangers."

"Sparklers and bangers? You're crazy!" Greg laughed and leaned forward and kissed her. "That's why I love you, Karen Forde!"

They both flinched at the remark. It had just dribbled out of his mouth.

Karen blinked at him wide-eyed and felt the blood rush around her body. She reached out and touched his forehead, gently moving his fringe away from his eyes.

"I think I love you too."

Greg smiled wider than she had ever seen and leaned forward to kiss her again. "I've wanted to say that for ages."

Karen nodded. "Me too. There never seemed to be the right time."

The waitress came over and put two massive plates down in front of them with huge pizzas smothered with mozzarella and tomatoes.

"Eat up," he grinned cheekily but something had changed between them.

* * *

The next morning Karen was walking on air. She rushed downstairs and put on the album that Greg had bought her. She wiped it with a static cloth before placing it carefully on the deck. *The Lexicon of Love* was sprawled across the cover of the LP. She didn't know what a lexicon was and she didn't care. Greg didn't like this music but he knew that she did so he had bought it for her. He'd joked about it damaging her taste in music and it must have killed him to walk up to the shop assistant and pay for it. But that's love – and since he had declared his feelings in Solomon Grundy's she had felt invincible.

"Are you not going to tidy your room, Karen? It's in an awful mess up there." Monica was vacuuming just inside the door as she spoke.

"I want to listen to this, please, Mum – can you turn the Hoover off?"

Monica huffed and took her cigarettes out of her pocket. "I'll make myself a cup of tea but don't play that too loudly."

Karen watched the needle lift and move over the edge of the vinyl. There was anticipation before the start of every record – if the needle slipped and didn't make the edge it would destroy that fine point and need to be replaced and she didn't have a spare. But it landed properly and the strains of ABC's 'The Look of Love' filled the air.

Karen danced around the room, hugging herself with her eyes closed. She was seventeen – no longer sweet sixteen – and had been kissed and her boyfriend had told her that he loved her and she loved him and everything was perfect and wonderful in the world.

Chapter 8

School changed everything. Karen realised that the wonderful warm cocoon of summer would soon be gone. Or maybe things changed the day that Greg got his Leaving Cert results. He had got one honour, in economics, and he'd failed Irish. His other subjects didn't rise above a D. Greg's dad had threatened that either Greg went into the Institute of Education and got a good Leaving or he could work as a porter in the Marine Hotel for the rest of his life.

Karen felt so guilty but Greg assured her that he would have got the same results whether or not he had been going out with her.

"My dad doesn't understand – I'm not like him. I don't want to be a surgeon. I don't want to be a doctor or anything to do with medicine."

They lay on the heather at the top of Howth Head with the Baily lighthouse in the distance. She imagined herself and Greg 'doing it' on this very spot one day. But not yet.

Greg had given her his jacket to lie on and they both stared up at the blue sky above their heads.

"Do you ever wonder what we are doing here?" she asked.

"Hiding from Linda and Stephen?"

Karen laughed. "No, silly!"

"Well, I'm hoping we came here to make out!"

"You're mad, Greg O'Sullivan. You know what I mean – why are we on this planet – why are we alive?"

"Because the alternative isn't very appealing."

"Do you ever doubt that there is a God?"

"I don't really think about God as being a person or a great leader – I'm not sure that he exists at all – not the way we've been taught in school anyway. He's more than likely an alien."

"I believe in aliens too," she said excitedly. "I didn't know you did."

"Well, considering we haven't a clue what's in our own galaxy – let alone what's outside – how can we write aliens off?"

"I'm glad we agree on that – but I do think God is watching over everything – but he's probably not the way he's described in the Bible. You know, when I was a little kid I'd lie awake at night for hours and hours worrying about the possibility of nothing."

"I don't get it?"

"What if there was nothing – if God had never existed and he hadn't made the world and planets and galaxies and aliens? Imagine if there was just nothing."

"Well, we wouldn't be here to worry about it."

"Exactly – so why is there something now?"

"This is why I love going out with you, Karen – I never know what's coming out of your mouth next." He planted a kiss on her cheek. "You know, there are times when I feel things and I can't explain it but it's like I know they are about to happen or will happen in the future."

Karen was getting keyed up by the conversation. "I get those feelings of knowing things all the time. Like the first time we met . . . it was like I had met you before or something."

"Maybe in a previous life? There are people around the world who believe in reincarnation."

Karen believed in it too – now. She had definitely shared time with Greg before – there was a bond between them that was different to other relationships – even with members of her own extended family. She couldn't explain these feelings inside her but there were times when she knew him better than she knew herself.

"So what do you want to be in this life?" she asked.

He slipped his arm under her neck to support her lovingly and turned his head so that he could look right into her face. "I'd like to be your lover." He smiled.

She poked his ribs playfully. "No, seriously!"

That was when he swiftly turned and propped himself up on his elbow so that he was almost on top of her. "I am being serious."

Karen quivered beneath his intense stare. God, she loved him so much – she could melt into him right at this moment. Their lips met and they lost track of time as they usually did when together this way.

"Do you think we should go home?" Karen asked after they had languidly petted as much as they could in such a public setting.

"Probably." Greg said, helping her up to her feet. "Hey, let me take a photo before we go – I want to remember this moment."

He took a tiny camera out of his jacket pocket and put his arm around her.

"Come closer – I want to get the lighthouse in the background."

"How do you know you'll get both of our heads in?"

"I know what I'm doing. I want to be a photographer someday," he grinned.

"You never said you liked photography before."

"Could you imagine my father's reaction if I told him? It's our secret – you're the only person I can tell."

Karen felt a surge of pride that he had confided in her. She felt sorry for him that he couldn't be his real self with his father but she understood that photography would not be an accepted profession in his house.

She got into position by his side and he put his arm around her. His reach was long and the tiny lens seemed to be pointing in the right direction. "I want to remember this day forever," he said.

He clicked and they kissed and walked arm in arm towards the summit where the 88 bus was waiting to take them down the hill to Offington.

* * *

Greg's mother had asked Karen to tea which was a rare invitation and she felt that she couldn't say no. His dad would be there too and his little sister and brother.

Karen thought they were checking her out in some way and felt awkward as she walked through the front door.

Greg was often invited to eat in the Fordes' house and he always got the red-carpet treatment. But things were stern in Greg's house. His mother had made an effort and cooked a chicken – but she had waited until Greg came home to tackle the chip pan which she was terrified of in case the hot oil caught fire. His little brother Simon was expertly opening a can of beans and Ella was putting frozen peas into a saucepan.

"It's a co-operative here, Karen dear," Jean O'Sullivan said with a thin smile.

Shortly after the plates were put on the table, the front door opened and Mr O'Sullivan came in. He ignored his entire family and smiled at Karen.

"Hello, Greg's friend!"

"It's Karen, dear – you know Karen," Mrs O'Sullivan prompted.

"Of course I do!" Mr O'Sullivan frowned. "It's nice to see you properly at last. I'll just wash my hands and then join you all."

Greg whispered in Karen's ear while his father was at the sink. "He's always washing his hands – all the time."

Mr O'Sullivan was tall and handsome with a receding hairline. He had a severe expression on his face even when he tried to smile and be jovial – like he was doing now.

"So, Karen, did you do your Leaving Cert also this summer?"

Karen hadn't expected him to go in for the kill this early – she hadn't put a chip in her mouth yet.

"No – eh, I'm sitting my Leaving Cert next year."

"Ah, so you'll be studying this year – are you hoping to go to college?"

"I'd like to go to Trinity and –"

"Good choice!" Mr O'Sullivan interrupted. "I went there myself – so did Jean. In fact we met there."

Karen looked at Mrs O'Sullivan – she couldn't imagine her studying anything. She seemed so distant from the conversation.

"What did you say, dear?" Mrs O'Sullivan asked vaguely.

"Trinity, Jean – it's where we met. And where did your father go, Karen?"

"My dad didn't go to college . . ."

"He's a fireman," Greg interrupted this time.

"Oh – was he involved in the Stardust last year?"

Karen nodded. They didn't speak about the tragedy in the house – her dad wasn't able to.

"So many young people lost their lives that night," said Mr O'Sullivan. "I've had to do skin grafts on many over the past few months – terrible."

And suddenly the talk of college and careers made no sense or mattered at all.

Chapter 9

What are you getting Greg for Christmas?

The scrawled note was passed along in religion. It was a hardship to sit through double religion on a Friday afternoon but they were seniors now so their exam subjects were all carefully timetabled to be in the mornings – with priority given to English, Irish and maths of course.

Linda had crumpled the note up so small that Karen wasn't sure what it was when Deirdre, who sat beside her, passed it over. It had come from the other side of the room.

Karen had been dreaming about Greg all through the day – the weekends couldn't come quickly enough. September had been a nightmare and she was exhausted getting up in the mornings. Sometimes she only spoke to Greg for half an hour every day – there were even days when they couldn't speak for that long, when their parents put them off the phone. It was okay for Greg – they had three phones in their house so he could find somewhere private but Karen had to sit in the cold hallway while her family walked around or over her.

Her mother kept telling her that she had to focus on her career – that it was the most important thing in the world. Monica regretted her lack of education every day. It was true

61

that she was a sharp woman who hadn't used her talents. She was only forty but acted older at times as if she had given up. She had married Declan Forde for love – her sister had married a professional man for the size of his wallet and now drove around Sandycove in south County Dublin in a brand new Audi 80. It wasn't that Monica was materialistic but she realised that a profession was the only way to improve yourself and with the current recession getting steadily worse her daughter would need to be well equipped to face the hard slog involved in finding a job. There was always a risk that she would go off and emigrate like so many of the graduates who took the boat and train to London and further afield. But without education she had nothing.

Karen sighed and found a scrap of paper to answer Linda's note. This was only the end of October and she hadn't thought as far ahead as Christmas. Linda had, however. She had met a guy called Dave at the Cricket Club two weeks ago and swore that she had found 'the one'. Karen had a feeling that he was only 'the one for now' but didn't want to burst her friend's bubble.

She scribbled on the piece of paper: *Not sure yet. Probably a record. I'm broke since I gave up working in the supermarket. Want to come back to my house after school?*

Karen sent the scrap of paper across the room. A few minutes later she looked over at Linda who nodded. They hadn't long to wait now. Only a few more months and they would be free from this place and she could meet Greg whenever she wanted.

* * *

"What do you mean you don't know if you will be with Greg at Christmas?"

Linda's intensity annoyed Karen at times. Everything had to be decided here and now.

"It's not the same now that we are in winter," she said. "The nights are dark and cold and we're only getting to see each other twice a week at most – sometimes I feel as though he is changing and sometimes I feel like it's me."

"B-b-but you two can't change – I'll lose all hope in love forever if you split up."

The words cut Karen to the quick – she couldn't imagine splitting up nor did she want to.

"I need to concentrate on my studies," she said. "I'm keen to make something of myself, Linda."

"Oh, and you think I amn't? I'm hoping to do law in college."

"Yes, and that's great and everything, but you are much more clever than me – and you don't have the same pressure as I do – you know what my mum is like."

"Yeah, but your dad doesn't give a toss."

"I worry about things – I need to be able to support myself. Things are changing in the world and it's not like our parents' time – I think all women will have to work in the future."

"Well, I'm not going to be all doom and gloom – there's plenty of time for that when we are older. What's brought this on anyway?"

Karen sighed. "It's just Greg – he's going into town every day now and he's got so much older in his behaviour – he meets up with Orla and Pete sometimes – they're both in college now. Orla is doing drama and Pete ESc. He thinks they are great and wants us to go into town to meet them on Saturday night."

"And will your mum let you?"

Karen sighed. "What do you think?"

Linda felt for Karen – it was tough to be the eldest. "Will you not try? Tell her you're coming to my house and we can meet up in the Neptune bar – I think Dave wants to go there and Tommy and his mates will be in there. We'll be safe – just hop on the bus and come back this way after. I might even drag Dave to the Grove."

Karen was pleased at the prospect – she still loved the Grove – that was her comfort zone.

Everyone was growing up too quickly all around her – she

wanted it all to slow down. She wished it was the summer again and things the way they were, but in her heart she knew that they had changed forever.

* * *

It was a damp miserable night in Dublin. Karen had bought a new duffle coat and sprinkled musk oil on it. She wanted to look older but didn't know how to. At least she was tall. She didn't like having to lie to her mother and prayed to God that she wouldn't find out. All it would take was a nosey neighbour to spot her on the bus and she would be snared. She longed for a cigarette but had been trying really hard not to smoke since she heard about Frank's dad.

"Bye, Mum," she called out, making her way to the door.

"Hold on a second there!" her mother roared. She had a serious look on her face. "I was talking to Mary Maloney the other day when I was getting the messages and she said that Linda is now going to the Cricket Club – I don't want you going there – they serve drink, I believe."

"It's not on tonight, Mum – we're meeting at Linda's house and then we're all going to the Grove."

"And will Greg be there?"

Karen nodded. "Of course he will."

"Just make sure that he walks you home safely, mind."

Karen kissed her mum on the cheek and left. If only she could go to the Anne's the way they used to in the summer. That would be brill. But the Anne's was scary in the winter and a girl had been raped jogging in broad daylight the week before. At least there would be a crowd in the Neptune.

Linda and Dave were standing at the bus stop when Karen got there. She hoped that Dave and Greg would get on okay. It was always a risk when fellas met from two different schools. Although Greg wasn't really in school any more – now that he was going into the Institute he might just as well be at college.

Dave went to Joey's, a school in Fairview, and was a really happy chap – just the sort Greg and Stephen and Frank loved to take the piss out of at the Grove.

"Hiya – you got out okay?" Linda asked.

Karen nodded. "But I think my mum suspects something – she asked me about you and the Cricket."

"Don't worry," Linda said. "I said I was going to Dave's tonight."

"No way – we'll definitely get snared – I told my mum we were all going to your house before the Grove."

The Number 31 pulled up and Greg was sitting in the front. He smiled cheerfully as the others clambered on.

"The top is full," he said.

Karen sat beside him and every thought and care vanished once she was by his side.

"Hiya," he grinned and kissed her on the lips.

She was home.

* * *

The Neptune bar was set in the basement of a pub called The Flowing Tide, opposite the Abbey Theatre. There was a diverse mix of people upstairs – local men with worn-out faces and hardened expressions that mellowed after their pints of plain. Women who wore headscarves and those who permed their hair with rollers sat along the wall but there were also artisans and actors who would later be moving across the road. Downstairs, however, was for the young. The Neptune had a cross-section of youths who had ridden into the city on motorbikes. There were others wearing embroidered denim jackets, copying their favourite album covers from groups like Boston, AC/DC and Thin Lizzy. The girls who wore peasant dresses and New Romantics fashion wouldn't be found here. However, there were some in hippy dresses and others like Karen wearing their painted-on Sasperilla jeans. Karen wore her red T-shirt and rainbow braces under her denim jacket and duffle coat and felt that she looked like a college student at the very least.

The air was thick with smoke and pints of Harp and Guinness lined the bar. Every Saturday night was like Christmas in Dublin City. And the fears that Karen had before in her own house disappeared. Orla and Pete were already there and Greg was relieved to see them – he had been civil to Dave on the bus but there was no way that they were going to be friends – and anyway there was a very good chance that Linda would be bored with him soon.

"Come on, let's go over to Pete and Orla," Greg urged.

Pete was putting back a pint of Harp while Orla sat in terrible form with her arms folded.

There were so many bodies pressed against each other at the bar that Karen readily agreed to go over to the corner.

"Hi, Karen – haven't seen you in ages," Pete grinned.

"That's because you've been going to the Pav." Greg turned to Karen. "If you do get into Trinity that's where all the heads go."

Karen was daunted yet excited by the prospect.

Pete stood up. "Do you want to sit in there, Karen? There's not much room."

Karen didn't want to leave Greg's side but she didn't want to seem rude either so she slid in beside Orla. As she did, she could hear Greg whispering into Pete's ear, asking him what was the matter with Orla. Embarrassed, she glanced at Orla who didn't seem to have heard or, at least, didn't react in any way.

"Ahh, she's in her flowers," Pete muttered, seemingly not too bothered that Orla could probably hear him. "She's not happy with just studying drama so she has to turn every bloody situation into one. I'm getting another pint – do you want one?"

"A Smithwick's, please – here's a fiver – and can you get a pint of Stag for Karen?"

"Put it away – my grant came in this week so I'm in the money." Pete disappeared behind the mangle of bodies.

Orla's expression changed the instant that Greg sat down beside her on a free stool.

"Hiya, Greg – I'm glad that you came in."

Greg didn't notice that Orla was flirting with him – but Karen did.

* * *

Later at the Grove the night wasn't panning out to be the fun they had all anticipated.

Dave and Linda had gone back to her house before the last slow set and Orla and Pete had a flaming row by the stage.

Eric Clapton's 'Wonderful Tonight' started up and without speaking Greg pulled Karen onto the dance floor.

"I wonder what's up with Orla and Pete?" he said.

Insecure feelings had been bubbling inside Karen all night after they had left the Neptune. Orla had plonked down on the back seat at the top of the bus – making sure that she sat beside Greg.

"He's probably feeling the same as me."

"What do you mean?"

"Well, it's obvious – Orla was all over you earlier – I think she has a crush."

Greg threw his head back and laughed. "Don't be silly!"

"I'm not – Pete noticed and so did I. Even Linda said it to me and she wasn't here half the night."

Greg shook his head. "Well, he has nothing to worry about – you are my girl!" He kissed her gently on the forehead.

She held him so tightly for that dance that she couldn't breathe. She loved him more than she had ever loved anyone in her life and wanted to always feel this way.

Chapter 10

Karen

Clontarf, Dublin, November 1982

Greg and I were in my bedroom and I was sick inside after what had happened earlier.

I'd been trying to forget the scene in the front room when Pete had called around.

All the while I was so obsessed that Orla fancied Greg that I had no idea that Pete had feelings for me. But he had called around after tea and asked if we could have a chat. It was strange but I liked Pete and I thought he wanted some girly advice about Orla. I didn't smell the alcohol on his breath at first – not until he moved closer to me and said that he had been thinking about me all the time and had to kiss me.

I couldn't believe it – we were in the good room where my parents bring guests and I hadn't expected him to lunge forward and kiss me the way that he did. The fact that my brother Niall walked right in and found us in what looked like a deep snogging session made it worse. I had pushed Pete away but from my little brother's point of view I was having a good snog.

I was firm with Pete and explained that I was going out with Greg. He seemed distracted and started to rant that Greg and Orla would soon be an item and I was terrified by the thought. When I eventually shoved him out the door I was shaking and wondered when would be a good time to tell Greg.

But why did Pete think Greg and Orla would get together? What didn't I know? I was suspicious of Greg in a way that I had never been before.

Mum called up the stairs to see if we wanted a cup of tea and I was relieved when Greg went out to the landing to chat with her for a while. I was tetchy and not sure how best to bring up the subject. I lay down on the bed and when Greg came back into the room I had a frown on my forehead.

"What's wrong – you've been quiet since I came here this evening."

And then Niall chose to burst into my bedroom and start pointing at me and giggling. "Karen was kissing a boy in the good room earlier!"

I couldn't believe it – Niall was annoyed with me because I took the last bag of Tayto from the cupboard earlier but this was not fair. I grinned at Greg nervously but his face turned puce.

"Get out, Niall – I wasn't kissing anybody!"

"Yes, you were – I saw you! And Mum said she's getting me Taytos tomorrow and not you!" Then he stormed out of the room and banged the door.

I could hear my father berate him from downstairs.

Greg had a look of utter disbelief on his face and I sat up on the bed nervously.

"He's messing – I was going to tell you." My tongue was twisted.

"You were going to tell me what? Who called around earlier?"

"Pete, Pete called and was talking rubbish."

"Talking rubbish or kissing you – which was it, Karen?" His lip quivered with anger and I thought I was going to throw up.

"Pete said that he had feelings for me and tried to kiss me."

"Tried or *did* kiss you?"

I could never lie to Greg – I didn't need to – surely he believed me?

"He did but I pushed him away – honestly."

"I can't believe it, Karen – you've been going on all the time about Orla and me and it's you and Pete that have been messing around."

I was mad and stood up so that I could face him. Why didn't he take my side? I was the injured party after all. I took a deep breath and tried to keep control of my feelings. Greg was furious and hurt, so I needed to tell him exactly what had happened. But when I tried to explain the situation it came out worse. I was the innocent party but that wasn't the way Greg saw it – he figured that my harping on about Orla fancying him was a cover-up for the fact that I fancied Pete. He didn't believe that I was more shocked than anyone by Pete's behaviour.

Something snapped inside me and I let rip. "If you don't believe me then I think it might be a good idea if we take a break."

The words had rolled off my tongue before I realised that they had shot out. They created a deathly silence between us.

His face changed expression instantly.

I was more concerned about being wrongly blamed – I hadn't kissed Pete on purpose. A break didn't seem like a drastic thing to suggest – it was really common. Jackie and Frank had them all the time – we used to joke that they were on a break more often than off it. But they always got back and we would too – wouldn't we? Anyway I needed to make a stand. I hadn't been unfaithful.

But as I looked at the astonishment on his face I wondered if perhaps I had misread the situation – maybe a break between us wasn't something that could be fixed the way Jackie and Frank did it.

He flapped his arms in anger and despair and it was then that I realised how huge his presence was beside me and how much I really loved him. Then he stopped and just looked at me. He didn't kiss me but he put his arms around me and whispered in my ear. I'll never forget his words.

"I never thought you would do something like that to me, Karen."

I trembled inside – I was the injured party and he was making me feel guilty. Still I needed a lifeline so I said, "I'll call you before Christmas and we can meet and see how we both feel then."

He nodded but it was like he didn't believe that I would.

When he was gone I felt as if I had severed my right arm. It was like I was all alone in the world in a way that I had never been before I had known him. I fell down onto the bed and sobbed my heart out into my pillow.

When my mother came upstairs an hour later I was still crying.

"Is everything all right, love?"

"I broke it off with Greg."

She sat down on the bed beside me and stroked my hair gently.

"He was a nice lad – there won't be many along like him."

Something flipped in my head when she said that. How could she possibly tell what type of a fella Greg was? I had been blamed for getting off with Pete when Pete had got off with me.

"We're just on a break."

"Greg's not the sort of lad you take a risk like that with – I saw the poor fella go out the door and I guessed what had happened and my heart broke for him."

She made me feel so cruel and heartless I hated myself but I hated her more. There was no way that she could have figured out our destinies before they happened. Anyway, it wasn't my fault – Pete had kissed me and Greg didn't believe me. I would never cheat on anyone on purpose.

Chapter 11

I didn't want to go to the Grove again after New Year's Eve. I couldn't bear to think of the Grove and our corner where we had sat snogging for hours that sweet summer long. The sound of New Year's Eve was definitely 'Come On, Eileen' by Dexys Midnight Runners. The solid wood floor practically erupted from the pounding of hundreds of feet dancing on the one spot. Every fella in the room had someone on his shoulders in a massive rocking and rolling.

But the moment imprinted on my brain forever is when I went up to the stage where all the serious snogging happened behind Cecil the DJ. A nice guy had just asked me to dance and he seemed cute – but I was too distracted thinking about whether I would bump into Greg or not so I wasn't really giving him much of a chance. He gave me a little peck on the cheek and asked was there a song that I'd really like and he would ask Cecil to play it for me. It was thoughtful of him so I went along with him. Of course, he could have been trying to get me up on the stage and if I agreed he'd think it was code for a good snogging session. There was no sign of Greg so I had nothing to lose. Jim or Tim was his name – or something like that. Poor bloke didn't stand a chance once we ascended those steps.

I came out from behind the curtain where Cecil played the decks and that's when I saw Greg and Orla. They were lying down on the floor with all the other snogging couples, their arms wrapped tightly around each other's waists while they licked the faces off each other. He didn't look like that when he was kissing me – at least I hoped not. I was holding a young fella's hand and intending to do the same thing but I couldn't bear to kiss anyone for the rest of the evening after that. I told Jim or Tim I had to go and ran off to find Linda.

She was the best friend anyone ever had: she'd just got off with BOB again and he wanted to take her 'outside', but she ditched him and we got our coats and went home while I roared crying the whole way. I had to apologise next day for interrupting her session with BOB but she said I did her a favour and she felt empowered by being the one to ditch him this time. Mind you, I was pretty hysterical. It shouldn't have come as such a shock – I'd predicted it a couple of months before. Pete was nowhere to be seen and neither was Stephen or the rest of Greg's crowd. So Orla and Greg must have gone to the Grove together.

I can't explain that numbness – that raw sharp ache in the pit of my stomach as I watched them together. I realised that I had made the biggest mistake of my life and I didn't know how I could possibly get him back.

Linda had told me to call him the day after we broke up – to talk to him at the very least.

"What did you think you were at, kissing Pete?" she scolded me.

"I told you! He took me completely by surprise. It was weird the way he called around out of the blue like that. I had no idea what he wanted."

"You can be really feckin' stupid sometimes, Karen." Linda rolled her eyes and I felt like crap.

"Greg should have believed me when I said I didn't want to kiss Pete."

"Jayney, Karen – you didn't have to admit it to him!"

"He should have felt for me – getting pounced on by Pete."

"He's a bloke – they don't see things that way – as far as he's concerned, you kissed someone else."

"But I didn't mean to – I didn't want to."

"You should say sorry to him."

But I was hurt and too proud.

Then Linda managed to convince my mum that I was mature enough to go to the Cricket Club – so that's what we did two weeks into the new year – and Greg and Orla were there. I didn't know where to look. And then on the way to the toilets . . .

"Hi, Karen, I thought you'd be studying."

It was Greg. He had walked right up beside me. I died inside. I wanted to thump him on the chest and demand an explanation and throw my arms around him and hug him deeply, all at the same time.

"Well, I do need to get out at weekends," I said defensively. "Just the one night."

"Who are you with?"

"Linda."

He seemed relieved when I said that – did he think that I had met someone else?

"And what about you – who are you with?" As if I didn't know.

"I came with Orla – she's hoping Pete will be here – she wants to get back with him."

I wasn't sure if I believed him – I desperately wanted to but it hadn't looked like that at the Grove on New Year's Eve.

"What happened to them – why did they split up?"

"I don't have much time for Pete – I'm sure you understand why." He looked at me severely and I winced. "Apparently he's having problems with money and his family. I promised Orla I'd help her look for him – she has no friends – she gave up everyone while she was going with Pete."

And I wondered what he was doing now by acting as chaperon to Orla – was he going to exclude everyone else too?

I didn't know what to say – it hadn't occurred to me to delve deeper into Pete's life. My home life was so simple, I took it for granted. That's another way that we were different – Greg had such a complicated way of looking at his family.

"You've become very pally with Orla then?"

"We are good friends." He nodded. "She's on my bus every morning going into town."

I bet she is! I thought to myself. She could get tons of buses from where she lives yet she conveniently hops on the 31 coming from Howth. I hated myself when I thought this way – you see, I liked Orla – genuinely. When she was dating Pete I loved her – wanted to be with her all the time. But just because I had taken a break from Greg didn't mean that she should step in and be my replacement.

"And you were at the Grove on New Year's Eve, weren't you?" I shouldn't have said it so accusingly but I couldn't help it.

Greg seemed really taken aback. "You were there? I didn't see you that night."

I wanted to say 'That's because your tongue was in Orla's mouth'. "I was there with Linda," I replied and was proud of myself for being so calm.

"Oh, I was hoping to see you there. I know it sounds silly but I went with Orla because she was hoping to meet Pete."

Oh yeah? Was he lying to me? It was too much for me to take in.

"Well, I saw you with Orla so I guess we're quits – difference is I didn't want to kiss Pete and you didn't believe me."

Greg stood back defensively. "Orla said that you always fancied Pete when we were together – she noticed things that I didn't."

"Feck off, Greg! Maybe Pete did fancy me but Orla is the one that fancied you. We should never have hung around with them."

Just then Linda appeared with a glass of vodka and orange

from the bar. I took it from her gratefully and knocked it back in one gulp. When Linda blended back into the haze of bodies in the room Greg pulled me over to the wall and put his arm protectively above my shoulder.

"So have you decided how you feel now about us?" he asked.

I was riveted to the spot. How I felt? I wanted to scream. I wasn't the one that had got off with Orla on New Year's Eve – okay, I'd almost snogged some bloke called Jim or Tim who was gifted at embroidery and had crafted Thin Lizzy's Black Rose on the back of his denim jacket but he wasn't someone who was going to mean anything to me. It wasn't as if I was snogging Pete – Pete had snogged me and if it hadn't been for my little brother blurting it out maybe Greg would never have known. I felt like the injured party here and Greg was putting the blame right back on me.

"I thought we were meant to meet up the week before Christmas to talk," I said.

"Yes, but you didn't call."

"I did. I left a message with your sister Ella. She promised me that she would tell you."

Greg threw his eyes to heaven angrily. "For God's sake, that child couldn't remember her name sometimes! Why didn't you try again?"

"She's twelve years of age – she's old enough to give a message. Besides I did ring again and got your mother next time. She said she would tell you too."

"This is exactly what I've been saying to you about my family." He looked sad – not angry any more.

"You could have rung me!"

Greg just stared at me. I could tell that he wasn't prepared to answer that.

And I felt cruel.

Suddenly Orla appeared and she grabbed Greg's arm. She didn't smile at me. She had set her sights on him months ago and I had played right into her hands. I felt such a fool.

Part 2

Greetings from London!

I bumped into Linda on the Tube and she said that you are coming over. I'm living in Hammersmith. Linda gave me your number. Maybe we can meet up? She said that you would be here by 3rd June.

Miss you
Greg

27-05-1986

Karen Forde

21 Clontarf Close

Clontarf

Dublin 3

Chapter 12

Karen

Clontarf, Dublin, May 1986

It arrived out of the blue. He was the last person that I expected to hear from. I wondered what had prompted him to write to me now – maybe he had seen sense and broken it off with Orla? I read the card again but there was nothing to suggest that – he was very casual. I had read into things before with boyfriends and been completely wrong. But with Greg it was different – that strange energy that passed between us whenever we were in the same room – or the same building.

I wondered why Linda hadn't told me that she'd met him – maybe she hadn't wanted to upset me. It was only two weeks since the house party in Harold's Cross held by a science faculty student when I got all maudlin about Greg. The same disastrous evening that I ended up snogging a vet! There were times when I think I just snogged someone because I didn't want to be alone – or maybe I was searching for the one to make me feel the way I did whenever I kissed Greg. If I kissed enough fellas surely one would top him.

I'd been dating Eamonn for a year. It was a good match on paper. He was Pre-Med. He wasn't my first Med student either. I should have learnt my lesson after Rory. They have this superiority thing – thinking that they are above all other

81

faculties in the college. You see them in the Buttery with their scarves dangling like badges of honour – they skip the queue too without batting an eyelid. Sometimes I think I'm the only one that notices things like that – I've become very angry lately and I can't understand why. Maybe it's because I'm studying Philosophy and English – Arts degrees are at the bottom of the pile.

Linda says I need to meet a good lover! She's been milling through the guys and having a great time by all accounts. I've only slept with two fellas, Rory and Eamonn, and although I enjoyed it – sometimes – Rory was too clinical. I guess I should be happy that I didn't get pregnant. Eamonn's father is a surgeon too – like Greg's dad – they are in the same hospital. I never asked if he knew Mr O'Sullivan though. I was afraid to go there.

But back to the vet – that was a really low point. The end-of-year Science bash – which I gate-crashed, it has to be said – was Linda's attempt to introduce me to a different circle. Linda is great at getting invited to parties – she has the knack. I notice the law students are always in the know with everything happening in the college. I can't tell you why I keep going with Med students. I don't pick them – it just happens. I'd be sitting in the Pav bar down beside the Science faculty – it would be smoke-filled and heaving with rugger types etc and then out of the blue someone sits down beside me and I'd think – he's nice – hey presto, a few minutes later he's telling me he's Pre-Med and my heart sinks because I think of Greg's dad and then Greg and it spirals from there.

Linda says I'm obsessive and wouldn't give a damn about him if he weren't going with Orla for the last three years. But she couldn't understand – that awful feeling that, if only I had gone to the Grove that night in April 1983 when he got going with Orla, he could have been with me instead. But I only had myself to blame and it went back to that night in October that I wished I could erase forever . . .

* * *

I had thrown myself into the preparations for my mock exams after that night in the Cricket Club. I didn't want to go out and anyway my mum said that I needed to focus on my studies for just a couple more months and when I got into Trinity I could go out as much as I wanted.

Linda was frustrated because she was brighter than me and didn't need to do the same amount of study. She would easily get her grades for Law and it was difficult for her to understand that I had to slog to get into Arts. Besides, she was doing easier subjects – I should have taken home economics instead of physics. I thought that I would be learning about the planets and why we are here and what life's all about – but Linda said I should save my curiosity and take Philosophy when I get into college. Sometimes I think she knows me better than I know myself – she's kind of psychic. She swears that I will end up with Greg. I like to believe that she is right. Maybe that's why I've been trying to spend this time focusing on other things.

I was in the middle of some revision when I heard my mother downstairs on the phone and I knew before she said a word that it was him.

"Karen, it's Greg on the phone!"

I jumped up and ran downstairs. Mum smiled at me as she handed over the handset but covered the mouthpiece. "You should have stayed with him," she whispered. "Lovely fella."

Her words fell like salt on a wound – didn't she know I thought that too?

I was shaking as I took the phone.

"Hello."

"I'm sorry that I've taken so long to ring. I want to explain about that night in the Cricket."

I did wonder why he and Orla disappeared straight after my exchange with Greg.

83

"Yeah?" I was ready to listen.

"Orla got very upset after Pete arrived. He had drunk too much and ignored her."

I didn't remember Pete being drunk – he'd had a few all right but wasn't falling all over the place. "So where did you go?"

"I took her home."

"You could have come back."

"I did."

I nearly died when he said that – you see, I was so upset I ended up getting off with a rugby bloke who kissed like a washing machine. Greg must have seen me.

"So why didn't you ring sooner?" I huffed to distract him from that disaster.

"I don't know what you want, Karen."

How could he? I didn't know myself. I was seventeen for God's sake!

"I'm sorry – I don't know what to say."

"Do you want to meet for a walk?"

I did.

We arranged to meet an hour later at the Sybil Hill end of the Anne's – he didn't want to see my parents and I understood. I told my mum I was going out to get fresh air. She didn't mind me walking in the park on a Sunday on my own because there would be plenty of people around.

He was standing at the entrance wearing his duffle coat and denims. He looked good.

There was an awkwardness between us though and I wished so much that we could return to those days when we would stroll along the avenue arm in arm.

"I want to clear the air," he said.

"Yes, me too."

"I need to tell you that I was really upset when you broke up with me."

"But I explained to you that Pete pounced on me and you didn't believe me."

"It didn't mean that we needed to take a break – 'a break' means breaking up," he said firmly.

"I'd hoped that you would come around to seeing it from my point of view. Look, Orla and Pete messed us both up and I don't trust either of them."

"I certainly don't trust Pete but Orla is different – she's vulnerable."

I didn't agree – I thought she was a manipulative little cow but that wasn't the issue and we were getting side-tracked.

"Look, Greg, you didn't try call me and I threw myself into my studies."

"Just like that?"

"Yes! My studies are important to me. You see, I'm not like you, Greg. I live in an ordinary house and my dad has an ordinary job and it's a big deal for my mum that I make something of myself – I'm the eldest in the family and it's her dream."

"What about your dream?"

"It's my dream too – I want to go to a posh college and live in a nice big house in Sutton like you do – my family doesn't have a second house down the country – my parents don't go on foreign holidays."

"Don't tell me this comes down to money?" He seemed cross with my explanation.

"Of course not – it's about making the most of my life. I live in a terraced house. Bet you don't have fig rolls and custard for dessert!"

"We don't have dessert – my mum doesn't like to cook. My parents are away at the moment – yours take care of you."

We stopped walking and looked at each other. I desperately wanted to go to his house again. I wished I could wind back the clock to nine months before and be in his bedroom.

And then he said it. "Do you want to come back to my house for the rest of the afternoon?"

My heart pounded. He didn't need to ask twice. We were sitting silently on the top of the 31 twenty minutes later.

* * *

I loved that familiar smell I got when entering Greg's house – it smelt of him. Greg cleared away the breakfast dishes and the newspaper that had wrapped his chipper dinner the night before from the kitchen table. He seemed anxious, now that I was here.

"Do you want a drink of something?"

"Have you 7Up?"

He opened the fridge door. "No – some red lemonade left over from Ella's party?"

I nodded.

We went into the living room and he put *Rumours* by Fleetwood Mac on the stereo.

"How's Stephen?"

"I haven't seen that much of him since he started college. Frank is working now in a newspaper – the *Irish Press*."

"Wow, good for him – how did he do that?"

"His uncle knows an editor in the Golf Club and he's giving him some sort of apprenticeship. He's still going with Jackie Quinn."

"Ha – I didn't think that would last."

Greg handed me the glass of lemonade. I could read his mind. He hadn't thought they would either but everyone thought that we would. And it was all my fault.

He didn't sit beside me on the couch like he would have if we were still going out – instead he took the big reclining chair in the corner where he had a perfect view of me. He was inspecting me with his gaze. I longed to know what was going through his head. And then he started.

"I miss the time we spent together – you helped me make sense of myself. That's why I was so cut up when we broke up."

He was pouring his heart out and I longed to go over to the chair and hug him.

"I've been talking to Orla about it and she was feeling the

same about Pete. He changed when he went to college – it happens, I guess."

"I think it's like that for me – you may as well be in college – things changed in September."

He shook his head. "Things changed when Pete called around to your house. But I'm sorry that I never got your messages – I would have rung back. Christmas wasn't easy when I didn't hear from you."

"It wasn't exactly great for me either. I dragged Linda to the Grove a couple of times but you weren't there."

"No, I didn't go. You see, when Pete broke it off with Orla she needed someone to talk to – she was in a bad way. You have to understand they were a long time together. And there is other stuff too – that she told me in confidence and I wouldn't be a friend if I told you."

Still no admission that he had got off with Orla. Well, I'd better not bring it up now that we were working towards fixing things up.

"I don't mind if you can't tell me Orla's private stuff," I said, "but I don't think you can judge a relationship by the length of time people spend together."

Greg nodded. "I know. We had something special and I want you to know that I'm grateful for the way that you made me feel. That's really all that I want to say."

He might as well have punched me in the stomach. Was that what this was all about? I'd hoped that it was something more. Were we ever going to get back together?

Seeing me at the Cricket Club with that rugby guy must have been the last straw for him. I realised I had better say something about it.

"I'm sorry about that night at the Cricket – I hadn't meant to get off with someone." Damn, that seemed to be what I did when I couldn't cope with my own feelings. "I know what it looks like but I was single – and I was cross with you for not believing that I hadn't kissed Pete – he kissed me."

"You only had to wait half an hour. I left immediately after I saw you with that rugger head."

"He was nobody – he meant nothing."

"Then why did you do it?"

I had no answer for that. I shook my head. After Pete kissed me that time it's like I didn't care who I kissed, but all I had to show for my time away from Greg was a couple of snogs and none of any great pleasure.

He stood up and moved over beside me on the couch.

"I agree that we are both young and we have a lot of living to do. But I miss you in my life, Karen – can we at least be friends? I loved our crazy chats about life and the universe and everything. If we could at least get that back I'd be happy."

"But you've got to trust me – I really didn't cheat on you, Greg, and I was hurt that you thought I did."

"I couldn't stand to think of you with someone else – especially Pete who was our friend. But we know he can't be trusted." He paused. "I have to admit something, Karen – yes, I did kiss Orla on New Year's Eve at the Grove. I don't know why I did it. We really were there because she was looking for Pete. I guess it happened because we were both miserable and lonely. She's still mad about Pete and that's why I've been spending time with her – no other reason – and all the time I've been missing you. So can we be friends again?"

I wanted his friendship and maybe more.

"Yes, it would be great to be friends again – I'd like that too."

He let out a loud sigh of relief. "Brill! So do you want to stay and eat here? We could go to the Grove later – I told Orla I was meeting her there."

It stabbed me to the core to hear that.

"Okay – I'll ask my mum. Can I use the phone?"

He jumped up and enthusiastically made his way into the kitchen to prepare our tea. I looked at my watch. It was almost six o'clock already – time had a habit of racing when I was with Greg.

I didn't think too much about what I was going to say to my mum. I was pleased to be getting back on track with Greg and although there were still old wounds on both parts we could do friends to start with and see how it went. My clothes were scruffy and I hadn't even my lip gloss with me but it didn't matter. I had five pounds and miraculously found my Grove card in the pocket of my duffle coat before coming out so had that too.

Mum answered.

"Hi, Mum, I'm in Greg's and he's asked me to stay for tea and we are thinking of going to the Grove later. I won't stay till the end 'cos I know it's a school night."

"You most certainly will not stay until the end because you, young lady, are not going to the Grove! I have just come out of your room and it is filthy. There are sweet wrappers on the floor – crumpled sheets of paper and even dirty socks. I can't see your dressing table you've got so much junk on it! You are going to get on the next 31 and come home straight away. I've dinner here for you – and did you go to Mass? You said that you would go to half past five in Raheny."

I'd lost track of time – everything had melted away while I'd been with Greg but I hadn't expected a response like this. Why wasn't she ecstatic that I was spending time with Greg again? Wasn't that what she wanted?

"But I need to go – you have to understand – I'm friends with Greg again."

"That's all very well but you can see him next week and go to the Grove on Saturday. It will always be there."

I panicked. This was a turning point in my life – how could she not understand? I had to go to the Grove. If I didn't it would spell rejection to Greg. If I didn't go he would get going with Orla. I just knew it – don't ask me how I knew it but I just did.

"You are to get on that bus right now!" Mum commanded. "And that's the last I'll hear of it."

Greg walked me to the bus stop and hugged me before I got on it. I felt I knew something that he didn't – maybe I was psychic like Linda. But I cried the whole way home to Clontarf and the next week I heard the news from Frank.

Chapter 13

London, 1986

There were many reasons why I was so excited packing my bags for my stay in London. It would be great living with Linda and the engineering students she shared with – in fact we would be the only girls in the house. It was just as well – neither of us was tidy. I always blamed my messy habits for not going to the Grove that night Greg got going with Orla. Linda said I shouldn't beat myself up over it – my mother would have found another reason not to let me go to the Grove. Either way Mum wielded the hand of fate that night and I hadn't spent time with Greg on my own since. It upset me that we couldn't renew our friendship after all. I was able to remain friends with other boyfriends but maybe that was because they didn't mean as much as Greg. I still met Eamonn for the odd drink in the Buttery and we were able to laugh about our break-up. He'd sent me a Christmas card too – he even said that he'd write to me in London.

I folded my black leather jacket carefully and put it last in the suitcase. Mum had said that London was warmer than Dublin and I wouldn't need it but I loved the shape of it. Sade had a jacket just like it – she wore it on *The Tube* the previous week when she sang from her new album. I loved *The Tube* – it was so much cooler than *Top of the Pops*. You only ever saw videos of groups on *Top of the Pops* – even the number one. Mind you, I wasn't as obsessed with music since I'd started college. I'd moved on. That's why I couldn't wait to go to London. They had so many more shops, department stores and markets. Almost everyone from college was going to be there. It was like the whole of Dublin's student population had moved en masse.

Linda said she'd like to move there permanently. I got scared sometimes when I heard my friends talk about finishing their degrees – they all wanted to go and live abroad. Most wanted to go to America. Even Eddie from next door was over in New York illegally, working as a carpenter.

I knew that I would stay – I loved dirty Dublin. But I looked forward to my adventure in London.

* * *

Euston Station was the biggest train station I had ever been in. Linda was there to meet me and I was glad because I wouldn't have had a clue how to get to Kensington from there.

"Welcome to London!" She hugged me and took one of my bags. "Did you bring the Tayto?"

I nodded.

"Thank God! I'd kill for a packet. How was your journey?"

"Not bad, but I got off the train at Crew to buy a sandwich because there was no buffet carriage and it nearly went off without me."

Linda huffed. "That damn train is like a cattle wagon – it's always so crowded. Last time I had to stand most of the way – the floor was manky so I couldn't even sit on that. Next time I'm flying."

"But is it not too dear? I know Ryanair have slashed the prices but we're here to make money."

"I'm making a fortune in tips in this restaurant called Biggles – I might be able to get you some hours there too. Most of the lads in the house are cleaning up working on the roads and buildings."

"Oh cool – that's what I need to hear. And have you any word on other jobs for me?"

"They are doing interviews in Harrods tomorrow for the summer sale if you fancy that? It's five pounds an hour and might be good to start with?"

Linda dragged me over to the kiosk where there was a huge queue but it was moving swiftly.

"You need to get your railcard – you can use it on the trains and buses. Did you bring the passport photos that I told you to?"

I had, so we did our business and took the Tube from Euston to Earls Court. We had to change from the Victoria line to the Piccadilly at Green Park which wasn't easy with my case and so many people thronging the tunnels. Linda pushed me over to the right-hand side on the escalator – she said that was the slow lane. I couldn't understand why everyone was in such a hurry. They reminded me of ants in a massive colony under the ground.

"So what's the house like?" I asked as we started our short walk to Lexham Gardens.

"It's really good. There are about eight flats and three are let out to Irish students. A gang from Bolton Street were kicked out last week so I don't know what's going to happen to that flat – they have to do a big clean-up job, I think."

"How much damage can you do in three weeks?"

Linda laughed at me. "Wait until you see the parties – the house rocks all night most nights. The beds are taken in rota because there aren't enough."

I wished Linda had told me details like this before I'd agreed to going along with her plans.

"Where will I sleep?"

"I've a blow-up Lilo for you. I got one for myself too. It works great – and some of the lads will definitely fail their exams so they'll be going home by the end of July to study for repeats in autumn."

"Is there anyone nice in the house?"

"For you?"

"For either of us?"

"One of them is cute – you wouldn't even snog the others. But there are some gorgeous architects in flat six."

"Ah, we'll have to go to their parties then." Suddenly I was prompted to ask about Greg. I couldn't believe it had taken me so long to ask her. "I had a card from Greg. He said he met you?"

Linda nodded frantically and started to jump up and down. "Yes, yes, I forgot to tell you – I met him on the Tube. I knew there was something I had to tell you."

"Well?"

"He's after cutting his hair really short – looks like he's in the army. He's working on the buildings – making a fortune, I'm sure."

"And is Orla with him?"

"Yes. I have no doubt she has her spies out now that she knows you're in the city."

"Maybe he didn't tell her I was coming over?"

"Not if he has any sense. Which he mustn't have – to be going with her. Oh, look right – we are about to pass the best kebab shop off the Cromwell Road."

It was a grubby-looking takeaway with the slab of lamb attached to a rotating skewer in the window.

"I don't think I'd eat anything out of there," I said.

"Ha! Wait until you're famished after a night out and you will give your right arm for one of those – they're gorgeous."

"I'll have to take your word for it." There was a lot that I would have to learn if I was to survive my three months in London. And if I met Greg I would have to be careful because nobody could mess with my head the way he did.

* * *

I settled in well and after two weeks adjusted to my spot in the

94

corner of the living room beside the tape player. I brought over some mixes I'd made from Radio Nova but there were loads of cool radio stations in London that played even better music than the Irish pirate stations. Capital was my favourite. One of the guys in the flat was a big Leonard Cohen fan and he introduced me to his music. Liam was his name and he was really sweet – sometimes he played the 'Sisters of Mercy' on his way out to work in the morning to wake me up. I wouldn't get off with him or anything – he was more a brotherly friend. Linda said he fancied me but I didn't want to create any awkwardness in the flat.

It was nice and airy – we were on the third floor. The house must have been enormous before it was divided up. It's in a really posh part of London – all of Kensington was like that. Linda was so clever to get us a slot there. Some of our other friends were way out in the suburbs and had huge commutes every day. We could have walked into the centre of London if we were stuck and anyway the night bus from Trafalgar Square went right by the Cromwell Road. So far we had been to the pictures in Leicester Square and had plans to go to a massive night club called the Hammersmith Palais – there's always a big crowd of Irish there apparently. And Linda wanted us to go to this really cool nightclub on Shaftsbury Avenue called Limelight some night – I couldn't wait.

I got the job in Harrods and it was grand. I was the only Irish person working in the food halls from what I could see. There was a lovely girl called Rhonda from Newcastle working on the fruit and veg in the hall next to me. She looked about twenty-five but was thirty-four. She had to wear a silly white hat and overalls – thank God I could wear what I liked as long as it was smart and not trousers. Rhonda had served Billy Connolly. She'd met so many famous people over the years. She'd even met Lady Diana who came in when the shop was shut to the public at Christmas to do her shopping. Rhonda said that she was really lovely and stunningly beautiful. I wondered if I would meet anyone famous? London had such a buzz – it's so different to Dublin – I could see why people stayed here. Everyone had loads of money too. It reminded me of Greg and the words I'd said to him when we were kids about making something of my life. Maybe I was too harsh and unsympathetic to his views on financial and social status. It was easy for him not to care about things like that because money was never an issue for his family, like it was at times for mine. I was not influenced by money but I did like nice things and there's nothing wrong with that. Why did my thoughts always start and end with Greg? Why did I bring his postcard with me to London? Because his hand had touched it and his tongue had licked the stamp? I worried for my sanity at times. And why hadn't he rung the flat yet? Linda warned the guys to pass on any messages and so far there had been three calls from my mother and I'd got them all. Maybe he'd changed his mind about ringing. Orla might have been giving him grief for talking to me at the Trinity Ball. If she was still with him, that is . . .

* * *

It was Linda who'd arranged for me to go to the ball with Alan McConville, a guy in her class and what I would call a typical law student. She fancied his friend Eugene and I wasn't bothered about going at all – the ticket was really expensive and I hated queuing for it. I'd bumped into Orla in the queue the year before and we had blanked each other.

Anyway Alan was nice and by the time it came around to the ball I was looking forward to it. It's not like we were going to be dating after it or anything. Besides, Eugene had rooms in the college which was really cool. We felt like VIPs. After our meal in Zachary Stingers in Abbey Street we went straight to the rooms for a few scoops before joining the mayhem and madness down in the quadrangle. There were mind-blowing green lasers bouncing off the buildings. Everyone had to walk under a canopy as they came through the entrance and produced their tickets. All the girls tottered across the cobbled stones that did not suit stiletto heels. It was a really good year because the Pogues were playing and Something Happens.

I wore a black maxi dress with a print of a tropical bird on the front and had used a new set of heated rollers to get my hair really wavy. Linda wore a shocking-pink strapless dress with a balloon skirt and looked amazing. It's always easier for the guys who couldn't go wrong with a black tux.

We got to see all the headline bands and were getting hungry so we went into one of the halls. I was on my own at that stage because Alan had gone to queue for some beer.

I got a fright when someone tapped me on the shoulder. I had guessed he would probably be there as it was Orla's last year in Trinity – unless she did a Master's. But I hadn't expected to see him on his own or for me to be on my own. All the times that I had bumped into him in the Buttery, or walking around the campus, she had been glued to him like a limpet.

"Hi, Karen."

"Hi, Greg – it's nice to see you – having a good time?"

He seemed anxious and flustered. "I was hoping I'd bump into you. It's been a while."

"Well, I guess it has since we've been in a position to talk." I couldn't resist the little dig.

"How are you keeping?" he asked.

"Grand – really grand – I'm having a great time in college. What about you?" I noticed my speech was a bit slurred and so was his. It must have been about half twelve at this stage.

"Oh, it's all right, I suppose – I'm glad this year is over."

He gazed right at me and that was enough – I didn't feel the need to speak – it would only ruin the moment.

Suddenly someone screamed from behind me and pushed me out of the way. I toppled and fell on my bottom.

Orla was standing next to Greg, holding on to his arm tightly. It was at that moment Alan appeared holding two beers in plastic pint glasses. He put them on a window ledge and helped me back onto my feet.

Orla was hysterically babbling and sobbing.

"Why don't you take your howler away?" Alan snapped at Greg.

I was shaking – surprised at my reaction or lack of it.

Greg looked back as he and Orla left and Alan handed me a pint of beer.

"You okay? I saw all that from a distance."

I nodded. "Yes, thanks – just as well you were there."

"What's your woman's problem?"

"I don't think she likes me."

"Well, you can say that again." He raised an eyebrow.

"Um, I was going out with her boyfriend for a while, when we were kids."

"Oh, I see. Fancy a walk outside?"

Alan was really rather sound and I hadn't realised it until then. He didn't try to snog me and I was glad about that. We went over to the theatre in the Arts block and watched Freddie White. He sang the Tom Waites song 'Martha', which was one of my favourites. It reminded of Greg for no particular reason except the first line of the chorus where he refers to the past as 'the days of roses'.

Chapter 14

London, 12th June 1986

There was a knock on the door from one of the Indian women living in Number 2 flat. It happened to be me that answered it.

"There's somebody on the phone downstairs wanting to speak to Karen Forde," she said sternly.

"That's me – thanks for letting me know."

"Can you please be brief because I am waiting to hear from my interview for a job position?"

"I'll do my best," I said and belted downstairs.

I hoped that it was him – I had a feeling.

"Hello?"

"Karen, it's Greg."

My heart thumped. I didn't know what to say so I just said, "Hi."

"How are you getting on? Have you settled in?"

"Yes, fine – I'm working in Harrods. What about you?"

"I'm working on a building site but I'm mostly driving so it's not too bad. I thought I'd give you a couple of weeks to settle in."

"Where are you living?"

"I'm in Hammersmith – Linda said you're in Kensington – very nice!"

"It's a great location but we're living on top of each other – the flat is meant to hold four but there are ten of us now – we managed to pick up a couple of strays this week."

"That happens – we're sharing with four others but it's a really small house."

There it was – the 'we' word. So he must still be with Orla.

"Sounds like a palace," I said.

"I thought I'd chance my arm and see if you were in. Don't you work on Thursdays?"

"It's my day off – I get a different day off each week but I always work on Saturdays."

So he still had the gift of sensing where I was. It didn't surprise me – I had known that he would ring when I woke up that morning. Something inside told me that today was the day.

"Of course – I guess everyone works most days. I just took Orla to the train – she has to go home for her uncle's funeral."

My heart dropped. He had to wait until she was away to phone me.

"So has she got her break yet?" I'd have broken her leg for her happily. God, I hated myself for having such thoughts of her.

"She has been for a few auditions but is working in Laura Ashley three days a week."

"When are you going back to college?"

"I've dropped out – I didn't sit my exams this year."

I wanted to scream at him – how could he be so foolish? This was because of her. He was throwing his life away so that she could follow her dream.

"Will you not go back to college at all?"

"Commerce wasn't me – I want to be in business but on my own terms – I don't want to be stuck in a boardroom moving pieces of paper around and smoking cigars. You don't need a degree to be an entrepreneur."

"What will your dad say?"

"I haven't told him yet. He'll get the idea when I don't come home in September."

My heart sank to the ground. I didn't think that he would emigrate – but I was so off the mark with his ambitions that I wondered if I knew him any more.

The Indian woman appeared again and tapped me sharply on the shoulder. "Excuse me, please, can you leave the phone? I am expecting a call."

I frowned at her but empathised.

"I've got to go here, Greg – it was great talking to you . . ."

"Can we meet for a drink? Say the Punch and Judy in Covent Garden – tomorrow after work?"

"I won't get there until nearer seven but, yeah, why not?"

"Great – I'll see you then."

I hung up and skulked back up to the flat. The bedrooms were full with snoring bodies from the night-shifters so I made myself a quick sandwich and went out for a walk to clear my head.

I was a woman now and we were very different from the teenagers who had walked hand in hand through the park as kids. But I was feeling vulnerable.

I hadn't managed to find anyone to make me feel the way that I did when I was with him. I couldn't decide why. Maybe it was because he was my first love – or maybe because I had never slept with him. I knew that while he was going with Orla I was cruising for a bruising, as Linda would say. But still he held a part of me that I wanted back – I wanted to feel that way again and the prospect of being on my own with him was thrilling. I didn't have long to wait.

* * *

Fridays were usually busy with Sloan Rangers thronging the place looking for preserves and biscuits to take home to Mummy and Daddy. Then there were the wealthy wives of Knightsbridge who never ever carried cash and used their Barclay Cards to buy a pot of jam. I didn't think that people like that existed – I wasn't sure if they did in Dublin but there were thousands of them over in London. And as for the DINKYs – the Dual Income No Kids Yet – they thought they were something else and couldn't spend their money quickly enough.

This Friday I was agitated because time wouldn't go quickly enough. I was curious to know why Greg was still anxious to make contact – I wondered what was going through his mind.

I had my lunch in the staff canteen up on the top floor of the building, where there was a terrific view over Knightsbridge and Kensington. I wasn't really hungry but forced a plate of lasagne down my throat and drank some bottled water. I found it strange the way people bought bottled water in London. Linda said that you couldn't drink the tap water because it had been through twelve people's kidneys by the time you drank it – disgusting.

Back at work, Rhonda waved over at me every hour on the hour, doing a kind of countdown to six o'clock. Such a sweetheart. I'd told her about Greg and she thought I should lay my feelings on the line. I was not so sure.

* * *

Covent Garden was only five stops away from Knightsbridge so I was there by six-thirty. I popped into a chemist on the way to Covent Garden market and bought some eyeliner and mascara. I hoped I didn't stink because it had been a really warm day and I could smell the rubber pong from the Tube on my shirt. I'd taken off the brooch that I had worn at the top button of my shirt and opened the collar. My skirt was so long it went down to my ankles – it was one of Linda's. My black pumps were my own. There was no need for a jacket in London except late at night – my mum had been right – it was warm here.

A juggler was entertaining crowds of people in the square outside the market and I decided to watch for a while to collect my thoughts. I had to be clear about what I wanted here. I wanted Greg back but how could I think that six months with me would carry the same weight and importance as three years with Orla?

Then again the year I had spent with Eamonn was not on the same Richter scale as the six months I had with Greg. And, of course, he had done 'it' with her too. Though I sometimes wondered about that. I'd spoken to Pete at one of the free gigs in Trinity not long ago – he had a beautiful girlfriend who was very cool and showing all of her assets. Pete had a couple of drinks on him but he wasn't holding back when he spoke about Orla. "That psycho – she doesn't know how to enjoy herself! I wouldn't be surprised if she's still a virgin," he'd quipped.

Pete was someone who had changed completely since those Grove days. I suppose we have all changed since then. I did think he was a bit harsh calling her a psycho though – until I saw her in action at the Trinity Ball, that is. I didn't hate Pete or blame him for my split with Greg – Greg should have trusted me and we should have communicated more about the kiss, but I guess we were only seventeen and in hindsight I now know we weren't experienced enough in relationships.

The crowd applauded the juggler and I checked my watch. It was six forty-five as I made my way slowly to the Punch and Judy.

The outside drinking area was thronged with yuppies coming straight from work. I went inside to the dark cellar bar – the counter and furniture carved from dark mahogany and exposed red-brick walls aged by years of nicotine stains.

Greg was at the bar surrounded by dozens of men in sharp striped shirts with braces holding up their trousers.

He wore a T-shirt and Linda hadn't exaggerated when she said his hair was short, but he still had a bit of a fringe – it suited him.

"Hiya," he said.

"Hi," I said. I couldn't have felt more awkward. It was balmy outside but the smoke was thick inside the bar.

"What can I get you?"

He seemed tense but who was I fooling – so was I.

"A vodka and Britvic please."

Greg got himself a pint of lager and we took our drinks outside. There was a table free but there were no stools so we stood up like most of the customers.

"It's great to see you in London – away from everyone. Do you like it?"

"Yes, I do – there's great *craic* in our house. Our flat's beside Earls Court and all the Aussie bars – there's even one with 'Bruce' and 'Sheila' on the doors of the toilets."

"The Aussies certainly know how to enjoy themselves – they get on well with the Irish. They generally only stay the year though – it's their year out. Walkabout, they call it."

"I couldn't imagine going to Australia – maybe some day."

"It's a big world out there." He arched his brows and I felt I could melt.

"I think I'll stay in Dublin – I may not get a job after I finish my Arts degree but I can try."

"You can always become a teacher."

"I don't think I'd have the patience. I'd love to get a break like Frank – working in a newspaper is the only other alternative with an English degree."

"Frank is one of those lads that if he fell on his face he'd land on his feet."

"Do you hear much from the lads?"

Greg shook his head. "I heard Stephen is in America this summer – we haven't spoken for two years."

"That's a shame – you used to be such good friends." I'd heard Stephen's side of the story and it was harsh – he was a solid friend to Greg always and he hated seeing him play the part of Orla's lackey. Greg didn't need to hear that Stephen had written to me and was now my friend.

"He had issues with Orla – it's a long story. But, you see, Orla needs a lot of understanding – she's had a difficult time."

I didn't want to listen to these – excuses? Explanations? He could have broken it off with her if he didn't love her.

"So how are your mum and dad?" I needed to change the subject.

"The same – Ella is a right little brainbox and wants to do medicine so that is keeping Dad happy at least. Simon wants to be a formula one racing-car driver – but give him time."

I smiled. He was such a cute kid – much as I imagined Greg must have been.

"So what about you?" I asked. "Would you not be better off getting your degree?"

"Orla needs me – she doesn't have much money and there's only a small window in acting to make your mark. I was bored in college all last year. I could get into a good company and learn more in one year here than in ten years in UCD."

He was probably right but I still thought he was foolish to chuck it all in to facilitate Orla.

Why had he asked me here – what was this about?

I took the plunge. "Why did you ask to meet me, Greg?"

His face softened.

Just then a pair of stools became available next to us and he ushered me over to them. We were sitting close to each other now and the crowd melted into the background and the only voices we could hear were each other's.

"I asked you to meet me because I hate the way we ended – I wanted you in my life as a friend when we split up and I don't want to think that I can't see you or speak to you."

"You should have words with your girlfriend then – she's the one with the problem."

"And I wanted to talk to you after the scene at the ball. She was out of her mind that night – she's on medication, you see. She has very serious depression."

I couldn't believe what I was hearing – I felt sorry for her but the way she was holding Greg's career back was appalling. How could he let himself be trapped in this way? What had happened to the fun thoughtful fella that I had dated?

"You look shocked?" he prodded for a response and I didn't know what to say.

Now that he mentioned it, 'unstable' was how I would have described her at the Trinity Ball.

"So is Orla your future? I mean, obviously she is or you wouldn't have chucked in everything in Dublin."

"Look, I'm helping Orla – she needs me now – her parents were never supportive of her dream of becoming an actress and she's so talented."

She was a drama queen all right, I had to agree.

"But nobody should hold another's career back for the sake of their own," I said delicately.

"When she gets on her feet I think we will probably go our separate ways. I need her too – I was never happy in college. I wanted to get away from my parents and especially my dad."

"But you can do that without . . ." I had to stop myself. I couldn't believe my ears. Why had he brought me here to tell me this?

"I want to be friends with you, Karen."

"Even though your girlfriend can't stand me? I don't know what I'm meant to have done to her."

"I think she feels threatened by you – before we went out I told her how much I loved you and she knows that I have feelings for you."

We were getting somewhere now – what kind of feelings, Greg?

"But we haven't been in touch for three years!" I said. "This is the first drink we've had together since that night in your parents."

I hated thinking of that night – I wouldn't mind but, after my mother insisting that I come home because of the state of my room, she never even checked that I had tidied the room before going to bed. Not going to the Grove that night had changed the course of my life, I was sure of it, but I had scuttled home like the kid I was because my mum was cross with me.

"That was the night when Orla opened up and told me how she felt," he said. "That she no longer missed Pete and instead wanted to be with me."

So I was right all along. Her timing was perfect and my timing was crap. But sitting with him now, I felt like he was still mine.

"I don't want to talk about Orla really," I said.

"I just want to explain that it was the mixture of alcohol and medication that made her react that way at the ball. She feels very inferior around you."

That's a good one! After all, she's the supremely talented actress. I hated myself and I hated Orla for making me have these feelings. I had to do something about it as being around Greg was bringing out this nasty streak in me.

But nothing he said excused her behaviour at the ball.

"Karen, can we leave all that in the past and keep in touch, please? I miss you in my life."

There were those words again – he missed me – and I missed him.

"And how is Orla going to feel about this?"

"I'll try and explain to her – she'll be upset when she gets back from Dublin and her uncle's funeral so I won't drop it on her straight away."

"It will have to be above board – I'm not meeting you behind her back."

"And I wouldn't expect you to. Hey, do you want to go for something to eat?"

"I'm going out with Linda tonight – I promised her. I can see you on Sunday?"

He seemed happy with that. "Will I call over to you in Kensington?"

"Sure why don't I meet you at the Tube somewhere? What about going to Hyde Park? We could meet outside the Tube – at Hyde Park Corner?"

"That sounds great – what time?"

"Eleven? The noise is something else in our place at weekends

– but I think I'm getting a turn in the bed this Saturday night because one of the lads is going home for a wedding."

"That's it settled then . . . have you time for another quick one?"

"Okay, but it will have to be quick." I wished I hadn't said I would go out with Linda but I couldn't put myself on a plate for Greg either – things had changed and although 'friends' was good, that was all he was offering.

* * *

The smell of bacon and sausages wafted down the stairs as I climbed the last few steps to our flat.

Inside, Linda was smiling and had a frying pan in her hand.

"So come on, spill the beans," she urged while expertly flipping a fried egg. "What had he to say for himself? Do you want a rasher?"

"Okay, thanks, yeah – well, he wants to be 'friends'."

"So he's still going with Orla."

"It's weird – I don't think he knows what he's at himself – he's dropped out of college and seems to be supporting her because she's depressed and wants to be a famous actress. I think that's about the gist of it."

Linda shook her head and I could tell she didn't approve. "He's not the lad I thought he was. God help her if she does get depressed though."

"He says she's on medication and that's why she had the outburst at the ball."

Linda was busily putting on more food for me but was listening attentively.

"I think she should get off that quick then, whatever it was," she said.

"So what are we doing tonight?"

"I have a surprise for you – I think you'll like it – we're going to Limelight!"

"Oh, is that the fancy new nightclub you told me about?"

"The very one!" she beamed. "Liam and some of the lads want to come with us so I said they could, but told them not to cramp our style if we see any fellas we like."

That was why I loved living with Linda – she was my rock and always there for me – from the sound of it, Greg didn't have anyone like that.

Chapter 15

There was something about parks and Greg and me. I felt much more comfortable going to meet him in Hyde Park than at Covent Garden. Maybe it brought me back to those halcyon days we spent in St Anne's. I'm sure the weather wasn't always sunny but in my memory the sun shone whenever we were together.

He was already outside the station when the steps led me up into the light.

And it was like we were back to square one – nobody else in our way and the world was our oyster. With the Wellington Arch to our backs we strolled along the footpaths towards the Serpentine and the promise of water. It was a hot 26 degrees and the sun was high in the sky.

Greg was wearing jeans and I could tell that he was roasting.

"Do you want to sit down over there by the trees?" I asked.

"I'm parched – wouldn't mind."

"I've some Perrier in my bag if that's any good?"

"Great, thanks."

All the benches were taken so we found a spot underneath an oak tree to shelter from the baking sun. He offered me his rugby shirt to sit on and I felt nostalgic. This was far from the gorse bushes and heather on Howth Head but there was something so familiar and comfortable about the scenario.

"How did your night go on Friday?"

I nearly choked when he asked – had he been there in an alcove watching me make a holy show of myself? I'd blamed him for my drinking too much and getting off with Liam at Limelight. I shouldn't have – but, you see, I did things like that still. It was like I'd no control over my emotions and I became desperate and needy after seeing Greg. That was why it was a good thing I was with Alan at the Trinity ball – he was a really sound guy. However, I should not have kissed Liam – he was a brotherly friend. Maybe if I hadn't seen Greg I'd have had more sense or strength. But a part of me craved love and attention and, the way I saw it, Greg was with Orla and I was on my own.

"Eh, the Limelight was cool – we were afraid some of us wouldn't get in but we all did in the end. It's in an old church on Shaftsbury Avenue – do you know it?"

"I've passed it a couple of times."

"The gear was amazing – some of the guys were dressed really weird. Oh, and Boy George was sitting in an alcove sipping a cocktail."

"I'm glad you're having fun." He gave a little giggle and threw me that look that I hadn't seen since we had been going out with each other.

"And what about you – are you having fun?"

A look of melancholy swept over his face and that was the first time I recognised that expression for what it was. There had been times when he had looked that way when we were kids – how could I not have realised what it was before? It was like he carried the weight of the world on his shoulders. It was that sensitivity that made me love him so much back then and now long to feel his arms around me once more.

"I wouldn't call it fun – more of a challenge. I'm not being unkind and blaming Orla – I'm on this path with her at the moment and I've chosen it for myself. I need to make my own mark away from my parents and all that I grew up with."

"Why does it have to be so hard?"

"I'm not sure – it just does." His eyebrows arched and he took a deep breath before speaking again. "You see, the happiest time in my life was those few months that I spent with you. It is the only time I can remember when my dad didn't get to me – I didn't feel inadequate. You lifted the burden."

I was gobsmacked – how could I not have known what was going through his head all that time we were together? All this time I had thought he had given me a special confidence by going out with me when, in fact, it was mutual.

"I didn't do anything."

"That's just it – by being yourself you carried me off into a simple world of fun and I was a different person."

"So, are you trying to say that this person who likes to beat himself up and make life difficult is the *real* you?"

He didn't need to answer – his stare said it all and I knew that he was more himself with Orla than me. How could I not have realised it? I felt so dumb.

"I know who I want to be – I want to be that person who went out with you – but we were only kids then and I wonder if that person is gone forever?"

I wanted him to stop – didn't he realise what he was doing to me with those words? I wouldn't allow him to shatter my illusion. I had him firmly placed on a pedestal and that was where I wanted him to stay.

I lay down flat on my back, afraid that I was going to cry. I didn't want him to see me like this. He had confused me beyond anything I had expected to feel.

He joined me on his back and we looked up at the clear blue sky. We could have been anywhere in the world lying like this. It was the same view we had seen on Howth Head.

"Sometimes I think I'm living in the past," I announced when I had controlled my urge to cry, and I really believed it.

"It's not a bad place – I'd go back there."

"Well, we can't do that but who knows what the future holds?" I needed some little branch of hope from him to suggest that maybe in the distant future our timing would be right.

"Sometimes I think the future has already been written – don't you?"

He was scaring me now. I wanted to make my own future.

"I hope not," I said.

"But I know one thing."

"What?"

"There is no denying this special way that I feel whenever I'm with you."

He turned his head and we looked at each other. In that moment we could have kissed – it's what we would have done in the past – but we didn't. We froze in the moment and an invisible aura of love and peace surrounded us. It was all he could offer and, for now and where he was at in his life, it was enough.

"I still have that photo, you know," he said at last.

"Which one?"

"The one I took on Howth Head . . . that day . . ."

I had my copy of the two of us in the photo booth and would cherish it forever. "Which day on Howth Head? There were so many days – they all blend into one sometimes. Oh, the one you took with the lighthouse. You never showed that to me."

"I got a couple of copies – sentimental fool, huh! I meant to give it to you that day when you came back to my house but it never happened."

That day . . . that damned day that was the turning point in my life as I often thought. But we had a chance now to turn it around. We were doing something about it and this was a good start.

He sat up suddenly. "Come on – let's go somewhere for lunch – what do you think?"

I nodded. We'd had enough heavy conversation for the moment.

As we strolled through the park we chatted like we used to

and I was relieved. We came out at the Marble Arch entrance and walked along Oxford Street until we came to a Pizza Hut.

"This okay?"

I loved Pizza Hut – there was so much restaurant choice in London.

We sat at a table by the window and ordered a deep pan pepperoni to share and some Tab Cola.

"Think I prefer Solomon Grundy's," he said with a grin.

I was chuffed that he brought it up. I'd been thinking about it too since we stepped inside the door.

"Tara is getting married," he said suddenly.

"To who?"

"Charlie – some new bloke in the bank – he's a typical yuppie."

"Wow – when is that?"

"It's not until Christmas. Dad is going mad. He never wanted her to join the bank – he wanted her to go to college – but Mum thinks she's right to get married so emotions are running high."

"Well, look at it this way – she had to work in the bank to meet her future husband. It's ser-e-ser-endipty!"

"The word is 'serendipity'! And you're the English student!" he chuckled.

"I always have trouble pronouncing that word."

"Well, then, it was serendipity my bumping into Linda on the Tube and getting your number – or maybe it was fate?"

"But according to you our fates are sealed."

"Yes, but maybe our fates are what we want them to be."

"And maybe you should be studying philosophy instead of me."

"You were always a little philosopher, Karen."

Linda would have said the same. But now it seemed I had been philosophising through rose-tinted glasses.

"What about your brothers? What are they at?"

"Harry is doing his Inter Cert and Niall is doing his Leaving Cert so it's exams all the way in our house."

"Time flies when you leave school, doesn't it?"

"I hate to think how much quicker it will be by the time we are thirty."

But I didn't want to think of us at thirty – I didn't want to know the future – I was happy with here and now. We wandered down Regent Street and spent three hours sitting with the pigeons at Trafalgar Square. He bought me a hotdog from a street-seller and we ate it at the Embankment with the River Thames for our backdrop. It didn't matter whether we were in Howth or London, I felt as if we were the centre of the universe when we were on our own together and everything and everyone else only the chorus.

As the night drew in he walked me back to my flat in Lexham Gardens. The stars were invisible against the city's polluted sky but there was a magic in the air as we strolled by the beautiful mansions on the way. He wouldn't come in. We hugged before he left and I was hungry with anticipation for when we would meet again. He said that he would call after he had spoken to Orla.

It had been a perfect day.

Chapter 16

It was a little awkward with Liam but he was doing his best to be sweet and funny and cheerful. I felt so bad. What was wrong with me? Why did I always get off with someone when I felt devastated about Greg? Still hoping to kiss Prince Charming and get that thrill that I used to get with him . . . I wondered, if we had kissed in the park on Sunday would we have felt the way that we used to? I didn't need to answer that – I knew that we would have.

Liam, however, was a lovely kisser and so gentle and kind. He was from the country and different to the Dublin lads. His parents lived on a farm and he talked about the animals and the crops and all that he used to have to do before he moved up to Dublin. He was given scholarship rooms in Trinity – he was really bright by all accounts. And although I didn't think it at first he was kind of cute – though not Linda's type at all so I could see why she wrote him off from the start. I really liked him and wanted to stay friends – so I shouldn't have messed up by getting off with him at the Limelight. It would make things really awkward for the rest of the time in London.

Linda had a few words with him though and explained that I wasn't interested in going out with anyone, so he had been really good at giving me space and not crowding. I wished that I could fall in love with him but with Greg to the forefront of my mind at the moment I wouldn't be doing anyone any favours by dating them.

Linda got us all tickets for the proms the following week – I remembered my granny always loved to watch the last night of the proms on the BBC. We weren't going to the last night though – we were seeing a composer called Gluck. Linda liked to hang out with the music types sometimes and fancied herself as a connoisseur of music. She was a typical Law student – always on the mooch.

I really wished Greg would hurry up and ring me. He'd said that he would after he'd spoken to Orla and I hoped for more days like that lovely one that we'd spent in Hyde Park and Trafalgar Square.

* * *

The Albert Hall wasn't that far away from where we lived and it was a beautiful evening so we decided to walk en masse. There were eleven of us – some of the architects from the other flat and a few other students who were staying in Earls Court joined us. We had tickets for the stands but it wasn't that crowded so we stayed downstairs and sat on the floor. A couple of lads were exhausted from working on the buildings in the heat all day and lay down. The music wasn't exactly funky but some dancers came out in full dress as worn in Baroque times and we had to stuff hankies in our mouths to stop the laughing. Linda was snorting so loudly she had to go out to the loo. Just as well the tickets were only a fiver. It was good being a student – lots of little perks with ticket prices.

We decided that we'd had enough culture after that and went back home – the architects had nominated their pad for that night's party.

Much as I tried I couldn't get Greg out of my head. It had

been a whole week since our walk in Hyde Park and I wasn't sure what I was expecting from our friendship but I wanted something to happen.

Liam was moping around the flat like a lovesick puppy and was beginning to annoy me. I desperately wanted something to happen to liven up my love life.

What I wanted was Greg back.

* * *

Three weeks later I packed in my job in Harrods – it was all right to start with but I needed to earn more money. Besides, Linda had moved on and got a really good job working in the office at Marks and Spencer – she didn't tell them that she was only a student staying in London for the summer – they promoted her after a week. That's Linda for you. Anyway, she passed on her job in Biggles restaurant to me and to my surprise I loved it.

The décor was on an aviation theme – there were little pilot puppets hanging from the ceiling and the walls were covered from top to bottom with posters about flying shows and airlines.

The lunchtime punters were mostly businessmen in suits. They loved my Irish accent and I always played it up and exaggerated words like 'thurty' and 'grand'. I made as much in one week there as I had in three weeks in Harrods. I flirted with them all and my confidence grew. It had taken a pounding waiting for Greg's call . . . which never came. July was almost over and he knew that I was going back to Dublin early in September. I made the most of my time in the flat and avoided getting off with anyone else. Liam had forgiven me by then and we were friends again – just friends.

It's always when you think that things have settled down that something happens – and it did!

I was in Biggles clearing up after the two o'clock rush when three men in suits came in. I didn't recognise him at first as I was so busy – he knew me but was biding his time.

I went over to the table in the corner with my pencil and notebook in hand and there he was.

"Hello, Karen," he smiled at me.

It was Alan McConville.

* * *

Alan rang the next night. He said that he had tickets for *Cats* if I'd like to see it.

I loved that song 'Memories' from the musical. Elaine Paige sang it – Radio Nova used to play it back when I was going with Greg. But I had to knock him out of my head – I had to get over him. So much for 'friends' – he hadn't tried to contact me at all so I figured I'd a right to go out with Alan. He was not the most exciting guy in the world but he was kind of sophisticated beyond his years.

Anyway, I agreed to meet him at Leicester Square so I was frantically trying to get into the shower before the others got in from the building sites and messed it up big time. I made a huge effort and wore my Levi 501s and a pink T-shirt. They felt great on and were much cheaper in London than in O'Connor's in Dublin.

"Off on a hot date then?" Liam said as I grabbed my keys and a light floral jacket I'd picked up in Top Shop earlier.

I wondered how he knew. I just smiled at him and ran for the Tube. I got the Piccadilly line to Leicester Square and Alan was standing outside the station on the cinema side.

He'd had his hair cut and it didn't look as red as it had in Dublin – more blond. He had a nice colour on his skin too and his green eyes widened when he saw me.

"Hi, Karen."

"Hi, Alan! Thanks for inviting me out."

"Hey, we have to make the most of our time while in London."

"So you're not planning on moving over here once you finish like everyone else?"

"Naw, I like Dublin. Bit of an old stickler like that."

It was refreshing to hear someone with the same mindset as myself. I felt everyone was going with the herd, droning on about emigrating. Even the posters at Dublin Airport promoted it – there was a horrible one of a pile of graduates clad in capes and mortar boards with the slogan: 'Our Greatest Export!' Well, I was not and would never be a commodity.

"Are you hungry?" he asked.

I was absolutely starving – I was also sick of the Biggles menu and fancied a real change.

"Kind of – have we time before the show?"

"Plenty of time – we could try the Aberdeen Angus Steakhouse – there's one around the corner here."

I was impressed when we were shown into a snazzy booth with a view of the hustle and bustle of London life passing by the window. A pair of punks – one with a green Mohawk and the other with a pink one smiled in at us. Baby-pins hung from their noses and one wore a Union Jack jacket while the other's gear was completely plastered with studs – including his dog collar.

Alan and I turned to each other and laughed at the same time.

"People are crazy over here, aren't they?" he said.

I nodded and watched as he went through the menu and ordered for me – he suggested the fillet steak and said I had to eat it medium rare.

My mum only ever cooked meat one way – well done – so it was a lesson in cuisine that I was getting. He was right about the steak when it arrived and he was right about the wine too. I had only ever drunk Liebfraumilch in Dublin – there were two types to choose between: Blue Nun or Black Tower.

Alan gently introduced me to the flavours of St Émilion – a red French wine that tasted very bitter to start but after he explained about the fruity flavours and how to savour the taste it definitely grew on me. It was also the most expensive bottle on the menu and I was a little in awe of Alan's lavishness.

We finished the meal off with some sticky toffee pudding then set off down Long Acre towards the New London Theatre. It was only a ten-minute walk but it felt less as we chatted about the sights and smells of the city. I told him I loved the choice in shops like Top Shop and Debenhams and Next – I'd stocked up well and would take lots of clothes back with me to Dublin. I could afford them with all my tips.

The New London Theatre was built in the round and the stage was open and modern. The set was a wonderful mass of giant garbage tins and cardboard packaging enlarged so that the cats looked true to scale. The actors were painted in spectacular feline colours and crawled out from the sides of the stage and from behind the audience. I'd never been to a musical before and my eyes were spellbound during the entire performance.

It struck me later that I had managed to watch it and eat dinner without thinking of Greg once. Alan made me feel special – everything was about me and what I wanted. We went for drinks during the interval and he ordered me a snipe of champagne which must have cost a fortune.

Alan impressed me with more than my first taste of champagne. We took the Tube home from around the corner in Covent Garden and he walked me to Lexham Gardens.

As we came to the door of the flat I turned to him and asked him in.

"I had better get home," he said. "I'm staying with relatives in Holland Park – I've had a lovely evening, Karen – see you in Trinity, I'm sure."

I was gobsmacked when he turned on his heel and headed off down the road without as much as a peck on the cheek. I wondered had I been such bad company that he didn't want to see me again?

* * *

Linda was curled up on the couch listening to her Walkman and reading a book. Everyone else was out or asleep in bed.

"Hiya – how did you get on with Alan?"

I shook my head. "I haven't a clue! I thought we were having a lovely evening – he must have spent a fortune on the night – took me to the Aberdeen Angus –"

"Oh, what did you have?" she interrupted.

"Steak and red wine."

"Oouuh!"

"I know – he's very posh, isn't he?"

She nodded. "I thought you didn't fancy him though?"

"I don't – I didn't – I'm not really sure how I feel about him. I thought he liked me and then when we got to the flat and I asked him in he said he'll see me in Dublin – what's he at?"

Linda smiled, sage-like. "He's setting you up for college next year – I bet he has plans for you!"

"Don't be silly – what do you mean 'plans'?"

"He knows that you aren't that keen on him so he's teasing you – bet he wouldn't hear of you paying for anything!"

"No – he paid for everything."

"Watch this space – he's a bit older than us – I saw the way he looked at you at the ball – he played it very cool but he has the hots big time, I bet."

A part of me hoped that she was right – I didn't want to think that my company was that bad. But then I had to ask myself did I really like Alan and I couldn't honestly answer that – when I was with him he intrigued me though it was nothing like I had felt with Greg . . . but then nobody but Greg made me feel the way that he did.

Chapter 17

I kept myself busy for the rest of my time in London. My heart missed a beat every time the phone rang out downstairs but it was never Greg and a part of me knew that he was not going to call. He must have thrashed it out with Orla and she must have forbidden our friendship.

It was the day before I was due to leave London and I was really looking forward to seeing my mum and dad – I had even missed Niall and Harry. Living with so many lads in the house with all of their messing meant that having only two would be great peace. I'd had my own bed for the best part of August – Linda had been right about that and we had a room, just the two of us. The pong of stinking feet as we walked into the lounge in the mornings was awful.

It had become a tradition to put on a party for whoever was leaving the night before they left. I was going home on a Friday so everyone would have work next day but that made no difference.

I'd bought too many clothes and had to buy another suitcase – it was just as well I was flying home. The job in Biggles had set me up nicely for my return to college.

And then the unthinkable happened. The phone rang and I knew this time it was him.

My heart pounded so heavily in my chest I wasn't able to be angry the way that I had planned to be when I spoke with him again.

"I'm sorry that I've taken so long to call – I just remembered you saying that you would be going home in September – I'm glad you're still here."

"It's my last day." I didn't mean to sound short but I was hurt and yet desperate.

"Can I come and see you – are you working?"

"No, I've just finished packing."

"I can be there in twenty minutes."

"Okay."

I went into a state of high anxiety trying to decide what to wear and how to look. I changed four times and in the end decided on what I had been wearing originally – an oversized sweatshirt and leggings. I gathered up my hair into a scrunchy and layered on my beads and bangles.

He was outside our flat on time. We didn't say much initially but fell into the relaxed world that was ours only.

We took the Tube to Leicester Square and walked down Charing Cross Road.

"Where are you taking me?" I asked.

"It's a surprise – I'm not sure if you've been here – and you can't go home without seeing something that I think you will really like."

This was the old Greg back to me – not the melancholy Greg that I'd walked through Hyde Park with. I wondered had he mustered up the good mood because he knew we had so little time. I didn't care. I was so happy just to be in his company that I didn't harp on about Orla or berate him for not calling before. The few hours we were about to spend would be precious.

We chatted as we walked down St Martin's Place until we came to Trafalgar Square.

"You're taking me to see the pigeons again?"

"Not the pigeons," he grinned. "The paintings." He pointed

over to the classic dome of the National Gallery.

He took my hand and his was warm. My own felt so small inside it.

We made our way hand in hand to the gallery. Inside, he swept me up the stairs.

"You seem to know where you're going . . ."

"Shhh!" he grinned cheekily.

I'd been in the National Gallery in Dublin once with him – one lazy afternoon when we were kids – he loved art and especially photography. He had a real eye for seeing beauty in the most amazing places.

"Almost there."

The halls and rooms were thronged with tourists and a cacophony of foreign languages echoed through the building.

"There it is!" He stopped at a painting.

A beautiful montage of water lilies and reflections painted in pastel pinks, lilacs and sagey greens.

"Oh, it's like the old pond in the park!" I said suddenly.

He nodded vehemently like I had passed some sort of test.

"Yes – you see it too. I knew you would. It's by Monet."

"You're crazy – is that why you brought me here – to see if I saw the same as you?"

And then his eyebrows arched. "I knew you would. It scares me sometimes that I know what you're going to say every time you speak. Sometimes I think I know you better than I know myself."

Damn you, Greg.

His hair had grown again and I put my hand up to his fringe and flicked it to the side like I used to always do. This time he held my hand there like he never wanted me to stop.

"Well, what am I thinking then?" I said.

"The timing isn't right now," he said gently.

"Will it ever be?"

"I don't know but you must finish college and do what you set out to do."

"It's only an arts degree," I said.

"It's what you will do with it that matters and I know you want to do great things."

"And it's okay for you to flunk out of college?"

"It's what I need to do now – you do understand."

I didn't.

* * *

When I got back to the flat Linda was pacing the hall. I got in the door at a quarter to nine and by the look on her face I wished I'd stayed out longer.

"Where the hell have you been? I've been worried sick about you!"

I'd never seen her so manic.

"I was with Greg."

Linda rolled her eyes and crossed her arms. "The whole house has been waiting for you – Liam has even got finger-food organised and we're going to play Wham all night just for you!"

I loved it when Linda was like this – it showed me that she cared. She was like a soul sister and always there for me.

"So anyway – what did Romeo want? He left it to the last minute to call, didn't he?"

I shrugged. "He wanted to say goodbye."

"Well, at least you are here now."

I might have been there in body but my spirit was back in the National Gallery. I couldn't tell how long it would take me to get myself together either. When we left the gallery we held hands for the rest of the time we were together. Everybody raced around us like they were in an old movie and we were protected by an invisible bubble from reality.

We window-shopped our way up Regent Street and stopped at Liberties. That was where we picked out the fabric for the curtains in our house in Howth. We had it all sorted. I would be the bread winner and he the stay-at-home husband. He'd have my dinner ready for me every evening and rub the soles of my feet. He'd make sure the kids would be tucked up in bed and I would have time to read the newspaper. Only the best-quality fabrics and curtains would be allowed in our home, which would be the epitome of style.

Then he took me to a pub on Old Bond Street and we ate pork scratchings and drank beer and laughed at the thought of being old.

"Don't you ever wish you were already old?" he said to me.

I was surprised by his question. "Why would I wish that?"

"Because then we would know – we'd know whether we had made it or not."

The thought scared me and stayed with me all the way back to the flat on the Tube. The thought of being old and not being with him.

But I had to concentrate on getting back to Dublin and finishing my degree. It was what he wanted me to do.

Chapter 18

February 1988

Linda was right about Alan – like she is about most things. He did have plans for us but continued the charade of showering me with attention one moment and then withdrawing the minute I acted interested. I got tired of the cat-and-mouse game but just before I dismissed him completely he officially asked me to go out with him.

I said yes. I was lonely and missed Greg. I hadn't had a card or phone call since I'd seen him in London and as far as I was concerned he was going to marry Orla despite all his hints and implications that our time would come.

I got a 2-1 in my degree and, after encouragement from my tutor and Alan, decided to do a Master's – my parents were happy to support me with it too. I spent the summer of 1987 in Dublin – Alan's dad had amazing connections and he managed to get me an internship with a new Irish fashion magazine.

I did feel like I was missing out in one way – Linda spent that last summer of college in a candle factory in Hyannis with a big crowd. But she liked me dating Alan. She always knew where I was and we still had our girls' nights.

Over that summer I found myself becoming more reliant on Alan. He always paid for everything, which annoyed me. His family were loaded and lived in a mansion in Monkstown. His mother didn't approve of me but his father liked me. Alan had no brothers or sisters so he was the golden child of his family. They had massive expectations of him, as he had for himself. He wanted to be a barrister.

Linda on the other hand was working on getting into a company with lots of hot rich men so she could retire – she'd already decided that she was going to be a housewife. She was out of control.

I did still think of Greg – but Alan was good to me, even though he could be fiercely possessive at times. However, it was like he realised when he was behaving this way and knew when to stop.

So Valentine's Day came and Alan had organised a table for us at the Trocadero restaurant in Andrew's Street. It was a beautiful restaurant and he had brought me there once before. There were monochrome photos of famous actors in silver frames lining the walls. I wore a pink dress with a shiny brocade and crossover front and, of course, shoulder-pads. My hair had grown long and it flicked out well when I used my curling tongs.

Alan suggested we had a drink in O'Neill's across the road from the restaurant. It was on the corner of Suffolk Street and we had to walk by what used to be Solomon Grundy's – a new restaurant had set up in its place. I still had trouble being certain places that belonged to Greg and me – like the old pond in St Anne's Park. I never took Alan there, nor would he have wanted to go.

Alan opened the door of the pub and that was when our paths crossed.

It was Greg.

His fringe was long and floppy in his face. I wanted desperately to brush it away but he looked at me as if he'd seen a ghost.

"Karen."

"Hi, Greg," I said. I wanted to do something dramatic – I wanted Alan to disappear. I needed to know if Greg was still with Orla.

132

I turned to Alan and saw that he recognised Greg instantly from the Trinity Ball. I could sense his hackles rising as he put his arm around me.

"I thought you were in London," I said.

"No, I'm not . . . I'm here."

I had never seen him so flustered before.

"What do you want to drink, Karen?" Alan said.

"I'll have a Dubonnet and lemonade."

Alan tried to draw me away but I resisted. All the time Greg and I just stared at each other.

"I was going to call you – I'm only back two days – I was hoping we could meet," Greg said.

I was frantic – Alan obviously sensed the chemistry between Greg and me and was frowning.

"Are you staying in Dublin?" I asked.

"No, I'm going back to London but things have changed – I've got a new job and I'm not going out with Orla any more."

I was speechless – I wished Alan would just go but yet I felt bad because he was my boyfriend.

"Do you want a pint or what?" Alan asked Greg gruffly.

"No, thanks. I'm meeting friends and they said if they weren't here they'd be in O'Donoghue's."

"You'd better go to O'Donoghue's then, hadn't you?" Alan said.

"I haven't seen Karen for a year – there's no law against talking," Greg snapped.

I hated tension and didn't want a bust-up after all this time. I owed it to Alan to respect our relationship but this was Greg and I needed to speak to him.

Greg turned to me and smiled. "I'll be in touch – I know where you live." Then he pushed past Alan on his way out the door of the pub.

Alan went to the bar and bought the drinks but knocked back his pint quickly.

"Come on. We have to go to the restaurant – they won't hold our table – not on Valentine's Day."

I knew that he sensed my discord.

When we reached the restaurant I played with my food and tried to stomach some of the pork and swede. Alan had ordered the St Émilion for old times' sake but I couldn't think of Alan and me in London. I was off on my own tangent in Hyde Park and the National Gallery and I felt horribly guilty and unfair to Alan.

* * *

I waited for the call from Greg but it never came. I thought about him for a few months after that meeting and Linda managed to find out information for me – according to her sources Orla had broken it off with Greg and she was going out with someone else. Greg was apparently living abroad now but her source wasn't sure if it was France or Belgium. I put him to the back of my mind and carried on with my relationship with Alan – the months turned into years and eventually I found myself thinking of Greg only briefly: once or twice a day – more often on his birthday, of course.

Part 3

Hi Karen

It was really great seeing you. You looked yum! Still can't believe you're married. As I said, I'll be home again the first week of February.

Hope to see you then.

Take care
Greg ☺

Paris 8-12-1992

Karen Forde

2 Sandy Lane

Sandymount

Dublin 4

Chapter 19

Greg

December 1992

I had written the card a few times but wasn't sure if it was the right thing to do. I mean, she was a married woman after all. I still couldn't believe it. How the fuck had that happened? Life was passing me by and going home this time was different. Now, only Ella lived with Mum and Dad and so many of the lads had emigrated. I couldn't remember the last time that I had seen Stephen. When did I lose contact with everyone at home? Probably when I moved in with Orla. If truth be told I had lost a lot of myself living with her. The heaviness still sent a shiver up my spine when I thought of the pressure she put on me and our relationship. There was always that threat hanging over me. It was the strangest way to get out of a toxic relationship but fixing her up with my friend Kevin was the only way to break the ties. She had threatened to kill herself on so many occasions that I got to the brink of wishing that she would. I hated myself even more for feeling like that. The responsibility of another's life in your hands wrecks your head. Ironic how smoothly she found Kevin as her new surrogate – convenient that he had a cushy job in finance. Not that I was in the least bit bitter – well, maybe I was a bit when I realised that I'd wasted so many years shacked up with a psycho while the one woman I really loved was busily living her life to the full. I didn't feel jealous – that's the strange thing. I never felt jealous where Karen was concerned. You see, if you really love someone – truly love them – I believe that you just want what's best for them and their happiness is the most important thing. Even if it means that they will be happy without you.

But it was strange meeting her again in Dublin after all this time.

I tried to remember what track was playing in the Summit last Saturday night when we met. Some grunge or maybe it was that cowboy singer – the one that sings 'The Dance'. It freaked me out the first time I heard it – reminded me of her. Karen could tell you which track – she could give you the date of any song's release and was seldom wrong.

Tinsel covered the frames of the mirrors behind the bar – it's very Irish to have tinsel everywhere. You notice funny little differences like that when you've been living away as long as I have.

The Summit Inn is a great spot to meet mates or bump into 'new heads' that eventually become lifelong friends – the sort of pub where auld lads drink during the day and the 'beautiful people' come to in the evening. I didn't recognise her at first because I was just intent on getting a pint. I was meeting my sister Tara and she hadn't long because she was going for dinner with her 'outlaws'. I was keen to have a bit of a chat and leg it into town where some of the lads from the old class in college were having a session.

So it was pure fluke that Karen and I were both in the same place at the same time. But then again, when we met in London we came to the conclusion that there is no such thing as a fluke. Karen would always say things happened for a reason. I can't imagine the bloody reason she had to go and get married though.

She looked really classy – like someone who owned a horse or lived in Dalkey with Mummy and Daddy. She was wearing a red jacket and a pair of jeans that showed the shape of her ass beautifully – she always had a fantastic ass. The ponytail was what threw me – I'd never known her to wear her hair that way. It made her look young – mind you, she hadn't changed a bit. She was with a couple of girls from work and had just ordered three glasses of Heineken and lime and a packet of dry roasted nuts.

She didn't see me at first. There was an auld lad sitting on a stool beside her and when he got up to go to the 'can' I stepped in and filled the gap. I studied her profile as she spoke to the barman but she spotted my reflection in the mirror and turned her head.

"Greg!" she blurted and then looked at me with those blue-grey eyes that always floored me.

"What does a fellow have to do around here to get a drink?" I said, trying to be smooth, but I was shaking like a leaf.

"I'll get one for you." She called to the barman: "A pint of Smithwick's!" She turned to me. "Still drink it?"

I nodded. I was chuffed that she had remembered – of course I've drunk more wine recently living in France but when I'm home I like my usual pint.

"Well, this is good luck bumping into you," I said. "I'm going back tomorrow."

"Where are you living?"

"In France now, Paris."

"I can't believe that I haven't seen you in . . . it must be . . ."

"Almost five years!"

"So you're just home on a visit?"

"Yes, to see my parents. God, you look great. You are well and truly a sight for sore eyes."

"Ditto."

And she reminded me of Demi Moore in that film *Ghost* as she said it. I remember Isabella dragging me to see it in the cinema a couple of years before and I hadn't wanted to go but I got into it and was thinking of Karen for most of the movie.

I'd thought about her more than a few times since I'd moved to Paris – there were days when I'd be somewhere and the thought of her would just hit me and I'd wish she was there too.

"So what are you doing in France?"

"I'm involved in cheese and a bit of this and that." I could see that she was amused. "So what about you – what are you doing?"

"I'm working for a magazine now."

"So you're doing some writing? Like it?"

"It's fun – not exactly what I aspired to but we have a great team. How are your folks?"

"Oh, they're grand, thanks – well, the same." I paused – I had to know. "Any man at the moment? Or is that a silly question?"

I could tell by her expression and the way her smile disappeared that she had.

"Well, actually I'm married . . . two years."

I swear to God if someone had taken out a blade and ran it cross my chest it wouldn't have had the same impact as those words. I thought I was going to choke.

So I forced a grin. I had to ask more. "Right, very good – so do I know him?"

"He was with me the last time we met – in O'Neill's, remember?" Her pause suggested she was hiding something as her expression changed. "He's from Monkstown – we were in Trinity together. Maybe you can meet him next time you're over."

"Yeah, I'd love that." *Like a hole in the head!*

"And what about you? Married?"

I had to take a sharp breath. "Not married, no, but I'm living with a Frenchwoman for the past three years. She's pretty cool. I met her at a wine tasting – she has a vineyard."

"That should complement your cheese business nicely." Karen said it in a way that was trying to be nice but I could tell she was surprised too.

What did we expect – I was never going into the priesthood

and she would never make a nun – not with those tits. I had to try so hard to keep my eyes off them but her cleavage was showing and I yearned for the days when I used to have part-ownership of them.

"I can see you with some chic little Frenchwoman," she teased.

I had to change the subject – it reminded me that Isabella would freak if she saw me chatting to Karen this way. She could read me like a book.

"Are you still living in Clontarf?"

"No, we moved to Sandymount when we got married but I really want to get back there. It's difficult to drag a southsider to the northside."

"You know, I couldn't imagine you living anywhere but Dublin, Karen."

"Well, you know me – I am a homebird."

"Listen, give me your number and address. We should keep in touch. I come home to see my folks a couple of times a year."

"You won't call though – you promised you would that night in O'Neill's."

This was news to me. I had phoned four times – I'd even called out to her house and spoken to her mother.

"Eh – it was you who didn't return my calls if I remember correctly."

She tilted her head with that look of surprise that I really loved. "No, you didn't call. I waited to hear from you – gave up after eight months and then Linda found out that you were living in Belgium or somewhere like that."

"I was here for two months and I did call several times. When I eventually went to your house Monica explained to me that you didn't want to see me – that you were serious with Alan and were upset by my behaviour when we met in the pub."

I thought her eyes were going to pop out of her head.

"She said *what*?"

"Did she not tell you that I called around to your house and left my number to get you to call?" I knew my answer. She had turned as white as a sheet.

"Greg, my mother never said a word about you phoning or calling to my house."

I would have struck Monica if I'd seen her at that moment. First my mother had let us down when we were on a break by forgetting to tell me about Karen's call and now her mother hadn't told her about my visit.

Karen ripped the corner off a Heineken beer mat and scribbled her phone number on that. As she wrote she held the tip of her tongue between her teeth and lips. I always loved that funny little habit and used to tease her when I caught her doing it.

"There you go." She handed the piece of card to me. "Now you'd better call next time you are home. I don't have to rely on my mother to get messages. I've my own house now."

"I will, I will," I promised. "I'll be back in February and I'll call you then. I'll even send you a Christmas card. Put your address on there too."

But she knows I'm not much of a writer so a postcard would be as much as I could muster.

Besides, I wanted her husband to see it – that bastard Alan got lucky. I know it sounds crazy but when we met it didn't feel as if she was married to someone else or like I was living with Isabella – it was weird. What was it about us and that incredible feeling of being the same person? And what the hell happened to time? There were moments when I felt like I was still eighteen and this was just something I was doing for a couple of years – living in France – finding myself. It's in our make-up as Irish people to go off and spread the love around the world, isn't it? I didn't intend to stay away forever – I mean, there would probably come a time when I might well live in Sutton – or Howth – maybe a nice big house around the back of the hill like we talked about when we were in London. Close to where we used to disappear behind the gorse bushes and the heather. God, how I kept from riding her I'll never know. It was enough for me then just to lie beside her and look up at the sky. Two love-struck fools who had no idea that one day we would turn around and be grown up.

That's how I felt now. I was almost twenty-eight. I'd grown up and not realised it. I slipped the card into my back pocket. I'd pop it in the postbox on the way to work.

Monsieur Cheval had a suspicion that I was leaving and I was only treading water until we moved to Bordeaux where Isabella's father's vineyard was. He was about to hand over the care of it and it was a big responsibility to ensure that she made a success of it. She was on a mission to do so much with her life. Compared to me. I felt like I was drifting. I'd got into catering in London – never thought that would be my thing but I enjoyed it and had to jog regularly to make sure I didn't put on too many pounds. Food and drink are good industries to work in – people are always going to need and want them and I'd met so many interesting people along the way.

Chapter 20

February 1993

When the plane started to descend over Dublin Bay and Howth came into view on the left I got that sense of belonging that doesn't happen when I'm anywhere else in the world. Then the tiny isthmus of Sutton appeared and I could make out my folks' house in Offington. And Karen popped into my head first and foremost.

My mother was collecting me at the airport. I folded the *Irish Times* and put it into my bag under the seat. The headlines told of the sad news of the death of the tennis player Arthur Ashe from AIDS – nobody seemed to be exempt from it – so many stars had lost their battle with it over the last few years. And to think you couldn't get a condom in Ireland when the AIDS virus hit the news! It was such a parochial small-minded country in so many ways and it was only when you travelled abroad and saw what was on offer in the rest of the world that it became infuriating.

I couldn't talk to my father about certain things – he was adamant that abortion should never be allowed in Ireland. He was such a bloody hypocrite because there were plenty of girls from the posh suburbs of Dublin getting shipped over to London every day for their abortions. An Irish solution to an Irish problem.

They didn't even have divorce for Christ's sake. I wondered sometimes if most of my parents' generation would have stuck together if they had? Who knows? I'd managed to get over my fear of my father – I just saw him now as a pathetic relic of an age that had to move over and make room for a new liberal Ireland. I wondered would I have ever got to this stage in my life if I'd stayed. That was one of the good things about living abroad – you could move on.

The baggage hall was always crowded and Dublin airport had an air of panic about it that I didn't find in other airports. Or maybe it was just me that felt that way.

My mother was standing behind the barrier and looked pleased to see me. And I was glad to see her – I never looked forward to seeing my father. He had got more austere over the years – and pompous. He seemed to have a God issue, believing that he was superior to the staff that worked under him. The elitism of a small minority here made it infuriating for someone like me who realised that I had outgrown my country. It happened, I guess.

"Ah Greg, you made good time." She hugged me and pushed my fringe out of my eyes – the way that Karen used to do. It was the first time for my mother to do it though.

I wondered what she thought when she saw her little boy now – the emigrant returning for his constitutional visit.

"It's lovely to see you back so soon – your father and I are going down to Aran for a birthday party on Tuesday so I'm sorry that we won't be able to bring you back to the airport. What day do you go back?"

This was typical of my parents – I had got used to it over the years. I knew I wasn't special to them but they could have waited until I went back to Paris. I wasn't offended by her second comment either, asking when I would leave.

"I'm staying until Friday – Isabella wants me to go to a conference with her next Saturday. Will Ella be around?"

"Oh, she's got a boyfriend and your father doesn't approve –

I'm having a terrible time. He has a tattoo."

Things kept getting better every time I returned – the boundaries were pushed a little bit more – maybe one day we'd see divorce.

We got into my mother's car which she had changed again. A Nissan Micra and I practically had to hold my knees up to my chin. She turned on the radio and Whitney Houston sang out of it – a monotonous ballad – 'I Will Always Love You'. I doubted even Karen would have liked it.

One good thing about living in Sutton is that the airport isn't far away and I was soon unpacking in my old bedroom. I loved the familiarity of it – my mother had left it exactly the way it was when I went to London in the summer of 1986.

That photo I took of Karen and me was kept in an envelope in the bottom drawer of my chest of drawers. I could kick myself now when I think of how I let her slip away when we met in London. It was an ideal opportunity to rekindle our feelings and she was keen to get back – I could tell. But Orla had such a hold on me.

The phone rang and my mother answered. I could hear her shrill voice along the hall.

"Hello, Karen – lovely to hear from you – yes, he is – he's here."

I took the phone from my mother and wasn't sure what to say.

"Hi, Greg – I thought I'd chance my arm and see if you were over yet."

"Your timing is amazing – I'm straight in the door from the airport." How the hell did she know I was in the country? Was there some sort of homing device linking the two of us?

"I got a feeling that you had arrived."

Unbelievable – well, maybe not – it said a lot about the special connection we had.

"So when can we meet up?" I asked.

"I've a day off on Tuesday – how does that sound?"

I didn't want to wait until Tuesday to see her – how the hell could I get to see her now?

"Oh, I was hoping to see you today."

She paused before answering. "Well, I'm going to my parents tomorrow – I could meet you for a little while then."

"Great – what about Clontarf? Just say where . . . the Dollymount Inn?"

"That's always packed on a Sunday . . . Clontarf Castle at three . . . oh, I have to go here – see you then."

She hung up so abruptly it made me wonder if I'd said something wrong. She seemed tense and nervous – not the way she usually spoke.

"How nice to hear from Karen – did she know you were coming home?"

"I sent her a card at Christmas and said I'd be back in February."

"She was a nice girl," my mother said vacantly then waltzed over to the fridge and nonchalantly poured from an open bottle of Chardonnay.

It was three o'clock in the afternoon and I wondered if this was the norm. I would have to check with Ella.

"So how is Dad?"

My mother ran her finger around the rim of the wineglass. "Oh, you know your father . . . he's . . . the same." She shrugged and took a slug from her wine.

"Is it not a bit early for wine? Even in France we don't drink it on its own at this time of the day."

My mother rolled her eyes. "What else would I be doing, Greg?" she said and disappeared out the door.

She'd been hard hit when Simon moved out – Ella had warned me. It was one of the reasons why I came back so soon. And as for my father, well, I was unlikely to hear any information about his marriage from him.

I went back up to my room and lay on the bed and closed my eyes. The journey from Paris wasn't taxing. With so many flights and new airlines and routes from Dublin it was closer than it had been a couple of years ago.

I liked Paris. It had a flair and a style all of its own. My eyes were constantly opened to wonderful new visual feasts and sensations. Isabella encouraged me to get a camera when I told her that I wanted to be a photographer. It cost an arm and a leg but it has been a good hobby. Last year I took it to Versailles and created a montage of images that I was very proud of. Every day is a photo opportunity in Paris – even when sitting on the Champs-Élysées enjoying a glass of Stella or drinking coffee on the Left Bank.

I loved Isabella – she was so funny – like a modern-day Bridgette Bardot. Not as incredibly sexy as Bardot – more conservative – but she was blonde and petite and good for me. But I guessed I'd be happy with anyone after the five years I'd spent with Orla. We lived in the centre of Paris in a chic part of the 6th arrondissement. Actually all of the 6th was chic and we were close to Saint-Germain-des-Prés and the Île de la Cité too. I woke each day to the aroma of freshly baked croissants and baguettes from the boulangerie next door. Isabella had taught me so much about food and wine that I could almost call myself a connoisseur now.

I definitely wouldn't be experiencing those things if I had stayed in Dublin or even London. I went to Paris to get experience in food after working in a franchise in London. It was a bit mad the way I ended up in food after I left working for the construction company. It suited me much better. Orla didn't like me working with food because so much of what I had to do involved working after six and attending launches and tastings. London was definitely on the up with food – they had incredible restaurants and some chefs were becoming celebrities on the TV and stuff. But I wasn't involved in the making, only in the sourcing and organising, and it didn't really matter what your product was – once you've got the business acumen you could make anything into a viable company. I guess I realised that when I was in college and that's why I didn't regret leaving UCD for a minute. I had more experience after working in London for four years and Paris for three than if I had ten degrees. Speaking French was difficult and I was far from fluent. But I managed to choose the best ingredients and send them over to enough London businesses to keep me comfortable.

Of course Isabella wasn't short of a bob or two either. She was determined to make her wine the best in the Bordeaux region and she had plans involving me helping her with it. To be honest, at times I felt a bit like I was heading into another co-dependent relationship like with Orla – on a completely different and healthier basis of course, but it was still following Isabella's dream and not mine. But then I had to ask – what was my dream? What was I searching for?

Karen popped into my head again. I found it hard to believe that Monica had denied me the right to contact her. If she had done it on purpose, what was her reason? I always thought she liked me – but then maybe she liked Alan more and didn't want me rocking the boat with her daughter. She had sat me down with biscuits and tea and let me chat for hours waiting for Karen. She must have known all the time that she would never arrive. I was disappointed in her but there was no room for blame now. This was the way things had turned out and I had an opportunity to see if Karen would allow me to make it up to her.

Chapter 21

The castle hadn't changed much – there had been talk of building an extension but the neighbours had quashed that. It was a beautiful Gothic building with the style of a medieval palace. It was mad to think that the composer Handel lived here nearly two hundred and fifty years ago, before he premiered his famous *Messiah* in Dublin.

The bar area did meander and I had to check out a few tables before finding her sitting in an alcove reading a paper. She had 'grown up'. I knew it sounded stupid – we were adults now but it still was strange to see someone from your youth doing things that only older people did. She looked up and smiled – and I was thrown back to square one all over again.

"Hi, there!" She stood up and kissed me on the cheek. "I've just ordered a coffee – would you like one?"

"I can't drink the coffee in Dublin – it's like dishwater."

A frown appeared cross her forehead and I hated myself instantly. How pompous did I want to sound?

"What I mean is I've got used to drinking it strong. Anyway, I'd rather have a Coke."

I'd never known her to be defensive about anything as simple as a cup of coffee before – I hadn't expected her to change. I suppose I would have been happier buying a bag of chips from the Capri Café and going for a walk down the wooden bridge to the statue. But we weren't sixteen and *she* was married.

Karen asked the waitress to get a Coke and started to smile. "I've been married to Alan too long – sorry for that!"

I had no idea what she meant by 'that' but would try and find out.

"How long is it exactly now?" I asked.

"I got married in 1990 – too young, eh?"

"Is there ever a right time to get married?"

Karen picked up her cup of coffee and sipped. "I thought I was very mature at twenty-four. It just seemed so easy and the right thing to do at the time. I had no idea what had happened to you and I was thrown after seeing you in O'Neill's that Valentine's night – after my summer in London."

"God, yes, that night – I was in a right mess that night. I got such a shock when I saw you – my head was all over the place. You see, I'd only just finished with Orla – my first taste of freedom in Ireland again. Anyway I thought I'd get to see you again and that's why I called over to Monica's."

"I asked my mum about that and she said that you never called."

"I'm not asking you to believe me over your mother but I'm telling you the truth – I sat with her and chatted for hours, waiting. She hinted that you were very serious about Alan."

Karen took a deep breath. "Monica is very serious about Alan. She thinks he's the perfect son-in-law and only sees him through rose-tinted glasses."

I could tell then that she believed me.

"I wish I'd known that you called. I honestly thought that you didn't."

"Three times. I should have written you a postcard."

"She could have hidden that too. I know you're telling the truth." And her eyes were sad.

But it wasn't time for blame – maybe it was just our fate.

"Our timing has been awful, hasn't it?" I said.

She wasn't smiling this time. She nodded and took another sip from her cup.

I hated to see her like this – the worried expression – it didn't suit her.

"So, you married the guy from the Trinity Ball?"

She nodded – almost embarrassed – and took another sip from her cup.

The realisation that I had let her slip away from me with that pillock landed on my jaw like a punch for some reason. I was curious to know more details but then another part of me wanted to make believe that she wasn't married at all.

"Do you mind if we get out of here?" I said.

She seemed relieved by my suggestion and jumped to her feet. I paid the waitress on the way out and we ventured into the chilly spring air. The daffodils and crocuses were threatening an appearance around the verges of the car park and we decided to take my car and go for a drive.

"Where to?"

"Howth, please."

She spoke so meekly I hardly recognised her voice. There was a sadness around her that I had never known before. I always felt revitalised after spending time in her company but this time I felt like I had to cheer her up – our roles had changed. I was the one flippantly on an adventure but she was playing a character in a soap, or maybe it was real life.

* * *

I plumped for the Summit Inn car park and it was a good choice. The Baily Lighthouse was bright and clear as were the Dublin and Wicklow mountains in the distance.

"Do you want to walk down the path a bit?" I felt like I was pulling teeth. I'd never known her to be this quiet.

I followed her lead along the path – she walked as if she was in a trance.

"I miss the northside," she said. "The view is so much better from this side of the bay. There's a poor aspect of the hill and then nothing but flat land from the southside."

I hadn't thought about it before – but there was so much I hadn't thought about my own city. "I miss Dublin – but I might come back."

"You *won't!*" she said with vehemence.

"Why do you say that?"

"I just know – you know it too. I knew Linda would come back."

I felt defensive at first but then again maybe, as usual, she knew me better than I knew myself. There was little here for me now.

"Frank is living in New York – did you hear?" I said.

"Yes, actually – I bumped into him one day when he was home – he's living with Jackie Quinn."

"Why do we always call her by her full name?"

"Not sure – she's the sort of girl who commands that type of respect, I guess – she's working for Versace as a designer so I hear and he's working for the *New York Times* – looks like they are the golden couple after all."

"Funny that – you never know how people are going to turn out when you are kids."

"I wonder how I'm going to turn out now."

The way she spoke was ominous – I found it difficult to find traces of the old Karen – the positive light-hearted girl that saw the good in everything. It was like a damp cloth had been put over her and she was now just existing rather than living. She was too young to be this way. It had to be her husband's fault.

"Karen – I hope you don't mind me prying, but are you okay?" I had to know if it was me or something else. Maybe she felt like she was doing something wrong.

She turned to me and looked up into my eyes and that was when I knew that something was really wrong. "Please, will you hold me?"

We stayed there for what must have been ten minutes but felt like an hour. She was shivering but it wasn't from the cold. This was a different kind of discomfort – she was a little girl again and I wondered where the bright cheerful woman that I had loved as a teenager and pined for in London had gone.

* * *

She had agreed to meet again on Tuesday and promised that she would be in better form. I was baffled. Why did she want to see me and then not want to talk and then make more arrangements? I realised that guys were simple – I used to think that I was complicated and she was the one with her head clear but after the display on Howth Head I was scared. And whatever was going on for her I knew that I had a part to play in it. I didn't know yet but I hoped to find out over the course of the week that I was at home.

This time I met her in town and she looked beautiful – back to the old Karen. My Karen.

"It's cute to meet at one of our old haunts." She smiled as she said it and lit up the air around us.

We stood outside Switzers window where two months before throngs of children had been brought into the city to see the fantastical window display of polar bears and Christmas characters. It was one of the things that I missed about Dublin and I was glad that I got to see it this year. It proved that the child in me was still alive.

The Diceman came strolling down the street, wearing a picture frame and long black wig: a walking portrait of the Mona Lisa who winked and made funny faces if you put a coin into his pouch.

"Look, it's the Diceman!" I was delighted to see the famous street performer.

"Oh yes, but I believe he has AIDS," Karen whispered in my ear. "It's just awful."

"I'm sorry to hear that – I only read about someone in the paper on the flight over – another celebrity."

"I'm still not over Freddie Mercury's death."

I knew how much she loved Queen – another band that we disagreed about – but, still, there were more that we agreed on.

"Where do you want to go?" she asked.

"I like McDaids – is that okay for you?"

The air was sharp and cold and it was good to settle into a cosy pub with a welcoming smile from the barman. Full of character, it was a good choice.

I was wondering if she was happy working on a magazine or if she felt like she had sold out. I would have to be careful how I spoke to her about it – she was fragile and not reacting to anything the way that she would have in the past.

I put a glass of Heineken and lime down on the table in front of her beside my own pint of Smithwick's.

The pub was unusually quiet – as to be expected on a Tuesday afternoon in February.

"How is work going? Tell me about the magazine."

"It's not exactly the sort of stuff that I expected to be writing."

"It's a women's magazine?"

"Yep, and it's glossy and good quality but I think I'd like a newspaper better."

"Well, what's stopping you – what about the *Herald* or the *Press*?"

"Alan wouldn't like me commenting on politics or anything that he considers the male domain."

I was flabbergasted. Karen was letting a man dictate what she should or shouldn't write about.

"But what about your career? You worked so hard to do well."

"Alan says it doesn't matter what I do because once we have kids I'll have to give up work."

My blood was starting to boil. But I couldn't be too hard on her. It wasn't that long ago that I was in a relationship where I was made do things that I didn't want to – it had all turned out well but only after a hell of a lot of grief along the way. But maybe with my experience I could help her.

"So you're planning on having a baby soon?"

She became very uncomfortable with the question and lowered her head onto her palms, covering her eyes.

"Well, I'm not." She looked up but I could only see anger in her eyes now – not sorrow. "He thinks he's bought me; and I only have myself to blame, because I let him."

I couldn't stand listening to her speak like this – it went against the grain. This wasn't Karen.

"He sounds very opinionated – your Alan."

"He's just a bit old-fashioned, I guess. He is very protective and good to me. He has a lot of strong points."

"I hope so because you deserve the best, Karen."

She laughed and lifted her glass of beer and took a sip. "But I'm not the best for him – he could have got better. There are tons of women out there who would love to be with an up-and-coming young solicitor like him – he'll be a barrister soon."

Why was she speaking this way? I hated to hear her put herself down.

"Wow – good for him. But does he make you happy? Does he make you laugh?"

Karen gave me a puzzled look. "Laugh? Alan doesn't make anyone laugh. Laughing isn't his thing. He's got too much to do with his life to laugh. He's fiercely ambitious."

I never thought that Karen could end up with someone who sounded so cold and calculating – mind you, she had always had ambitions to have a nice house and nice things. Maybe she was right to marry someone who could provide for her lavishly. It wasn't on my agenda for things to achieve. I wanted to be wealthy and successful but all in my own time. I didn't want to settle into middle-class boredom in my twenties. I didn't want to end up living like my parents and couldn't stand the thought of Karen doing it.

"Sounds like you're well set up for when you do want to start a family." I was fishing and she knew it but I wasn't sure how much she would tell me.

"We'll see . . . So what are your plans in Paris? Tell me – I want to hear everything about your exotic lifestyle."

She perked up when she asked me the question so I wanted to entertain her. God knows she'd cheered me up enough times over the years.

"Well, I was exporting French food to Britain. It was going well but I'm winding it down now as I'm relocating to Bordeaux once I go back. Isabella has already moved there and when I get back to Paris I'll be returning the keys of our apartment and moving the last few bits and pieces with me."

"How is it, living in Paris?"

I couldn't lie to her. "It's amazing – you would love it so much. Waking on a cold winter morning as a mist rises off the Seine and over the bridges. The parks are stunning and I don't need to tell you about the museums."

I loved watching her eyes light up as I spoke. "No, please tell me – what about the Musée d'Orsay? Alan proposed to me in Paris. I wanted to go and see the Monets but we hadn't time in our schedule – Alan had our itinerary all worked out."

I bet he did, I thought to myself. I was angry with him for choosing Paris to propose to her – I'd have liked to have proposed to her there. Alan was a right slick fucker by all accounts.

"Ahh, he shouldn't have let you leave without visiting the D'Orsay." I know it was childish but I couldn't resist the little dig. I'm not surprised she changed the subject.

"Are you doing any photography?"

"Yes, I have a good collection made over the last couple of years. When Isabella visits Bordeaux it's a great excuse for me to snap at the markets and parks. Oh, but it's only a pipe dream – I'd never make a living from it – I'm happy to be making a crust in the food business – excuse the pun."

We laughed together and it felt great. It was the first time that I'd seen her relax. We strolled through the Green and Trinity and window-shopped along the way.

Then she looked at her watch and shrieked. "Oh my God! It's nearly four o'clock – I'd better get home and make the dinner."

"Do you cook every evening?" I asked.

She nodded like a scared child.

"What's the matter – can't he cook for himself for once?"

"He's a good cook but only does it for dinner parties – he likes me to be home."

It was bizarre – a strange gloss came over her eyes like she was hypnotised.

"Would Alan mind if he knew you were here with me?"

Karen bit her lip. Of course he would – she didn't need to answer. I hoped that my hunch was wrong but I felt that there was something she wasn't telling.

"Karen, can I see you again before I go back to France?"

"I don't know how – I'm back in work tomorrow."

"Some evening?"

She checked her watch again. "Alan sometimes goes to the club on Thursdays – I'll ring and let you know – I could say I'm meeting Linda."

"That would be perfect – you can come to my house in Sutton – my parents will be in Aran."

We looked at each other, remembering. "I'll go – thanks for a lovely day – I can't remember the last time I had one like it."

I could – Hyde Park was like it – only the roles were reversed.

Chapter 22

Thursday came and I was nervous. Karen's scared face had popped into my head quite a few times since Tuesday. My parents had left for the west of Ireland and Ella saw it as an opportunity to stay in the dingy flat in Harold's Cross with her tattooed boyfriend.

He must be bad if she didn't even want me to meet him.

I cleaned the place up and made sure that I would be the perfect host for my special visitor. I'd achieved little with my mother – she hadn't opened up or spoken to me the way I wished she would. But I was now convinced that the reason I was back in Dublin was to help Karen and not my mother. My mother had issues for sure but what was happening with Karen was more urgent – more urgent for me too. I was on the cusp of making big decisions with my life and I needed to be sure that there was closure between us. But while she had no children there was still a thread of hope for us, I felt.

The phone rang and I rushed to answer it.

"Hello?"

"Hi, Greg. Guess what? I've a free pass for tonight."

She sounded buoyant and giddy.

"What do you mean?"

"Alan just called. He has to go to Shannon to meet a client so won't be home. I guess that means that I can go straight out to Sutton after work if that's okay with you?"

"That's perfect by me. Wow, both of us with free houses!"

"You sound like you're seventeen," she laughed. "See you shortly after six."

After her call I wondered if this was possibly the world turning finally in our favour. Her husband and my parents were both out of the way for the night. You couldn't make it up. The stars were shining on us at last.

She arrived at ten past six and I had candles burning in the living room and a roaring fire in the grate. Isabella had shown me how to create ambience in our apartment.

"Oh, that's so lovely and cosy," Karen said. She took her hat and coat off and blew heat into her palms. "I'm impressed, Greg. Isabella is a lucky woman to come home to this treatment every evening."

Isabella would be mad if she saw this but I managed to put her to the back of my thoughts – I was here with Karen and there was a reason for it.

"Ha, we eat out a lot in Paris – I'm sure that will change when we settle into our new life in Bordeaux though."

"Can I give you a hand?" She followed me into the kitchen.

"Not at all – I have it under control. Do you want a cup of tea – or a glass of wine?"

"I'd love a cup of tea, thanks."

She sat up at the breakfast bar and I was thrown right back – more than ten years. She looked exactly the same. Her hair was loose and wild the way I liked to picture her in my mind's eye.

"I made lasagne – hope you like it."

"Yum – thanks."

"And I have a nice Châteauneuf-du-Pape that I brought over for my dad but he will never drink it and it's better that we drink it than my mum does."

"Why do you say that?"

"Oh, it's something I've noticed the last couple of times I've been home. She likes to take a tipple during the day."

"Is that why you are back so soon – are you worried about her?"

Karen had that look of concern on her face now and I wanted to hold her. It wasn't going to be easy . . . I'd have to control my urges this evening unless she gave me a clear signal that she wanted something more.

"Big time – I guess I feel guilty living away and now with only Ella living here I wonder if they notice how bad she's got? I think when you see someone occasionally you notice changes that those living at home just don't see."

"Something smells great."

"Oh, the lasagne!" I rushed over to the oven and the edges of the pasta had turned black. "I think I've burnt it!"

She joined me at the oven and we laughed as I made a mess of carrying it over to the draining board.

"I'm sure it's going to taste lovely," she said. "We can cut the corners off."

It was such a great situation to be in – the house to ourselves like this. But it did feel like we were playing at being grown-ups – like real life hadn't kicked in yet or something. And all the time I had a hard-on.

After dinner I remembered the photo that I had kept in my drawer upstairs. I wanted her to have a copy.

"Hey, I've just remembered – hang on a minute." I fetched the copy I had made and put it on the table in front of her.

She picked it up and her eyes widened with delight as she looked at it.

"You were right – you got the lighthouse in and the picture of the two of us right in the middle." She sighed and ran her finger over the image. "Do you ever wish you were back there?"

I wanted to say 'all the time' but I didn't.

"Come on, let's go into the living room."

I stoked the fire up with some logs and she sat on the sheepskin hearthrug.

"Come and join me down here," she beckoned.

"I'll get us some more wine."

"Not for me – I've got to drive home and I've already had two glasses."

I couldn't help what next came out of my mouth. "Of course you could always stay?"

Her eyes were wide with desire when she looked at me. She looked so vulnerable curled up on the rug.

"If only I could," she said.

"Alan's not coming home . . . I'm staying here on my own . . . why not?" Then I lost my nerve and backpedalled. "I mean . . . we could just keep each other company . . ."

"How would I explain if he found out?"

The air between us was thick now with a tension unlike any that had passed between us before.

I joined her on the rug. There was a nice blaze now and the flames reflected off the moist red of her lips. I wanted to bite them. I couldn't make the first move – she was a married woman. If anything was to happen it would have to come from her side.

"So – do you want to have a sleepover?" I said.

She sighed and smiled nervously. "I think you already know the answer to that – but it's complicated. You know how it was when you were with Orla in London – things were difficult for you then and I didn't put you in this situation. We aren't the type of people to cheat behind another's back."

Maybe I wasn't at one time but I'd have no problem doing it now. I didn't give a damn about Alan or Isabella – we'd missed out on too many chances and this was perfect. Why did she want to go and bring Orla up?

"Orla was a different scenario – she held me to ransom. I'm so angry when I think back now on all the years that I wasted with her. She threatened me with suicide if I left her."

Karen's face scrunched up. "She did what?"

"That time when we met in London – I tried to explain to her

164

that I wanted to be friends with you but she swore that if I contacted you she would commit suicide – she used it all the time to get her own way."

Karen frowned. "I can't believe that you let her control you that way. And what is she at now? She obviously hasn't committed suicide without you?"

"Nah – she's living with a friend of mine actually – a wealthy chap – they've settled in Richmond. Getting married next year."

Karen shook her head angrily. "I could strangle that wagon!"

"Believe me, I would if I could get there before you. But, to be fair to Orla, she fulfilled a need in me to break away from my dad and the pressures that he put on me. That's something you didn't really get about me, Karen – I'm over it now but there was a time when I was kept down by him. That's why I'm worried that my mother has taken over from where I left off. I feel bad for her."

"Well, it messed up any chance we had of getting together."

Now, that I did not want to hear!

"But you obviously love Alan – or you wouldn't have married him?"

I longed for her to say something terrible about him – that she didn't love him and would leave him for me.

"Alan is like a bloodhound – he knows what he wants and he gets it at any cost. He's successful and is only at the start of his career. He has big plans and I am part of them."

"I hope that these plans are what you want too."

"Well, I don't want a baby yet so that is a problem."

"So you're still . . ." this was delicate and I knew I was stepping over a line, "using contraception?"

She shook her head.

My heart sank. "Well, then, the chances are that you will get pregnant soon."

"You need to be having sex to get pregnant!"

I couldn't believe my ears – if I was married to Karen we'd be shagging every night.

"You mean you don't do it?"

"Sorry . . . I can't say any more."

She looked away and I thought she had shut down on me. While I searched for what to say next, she spoke again.

"Alan wants a son and heir more than anything. I haven't told a soul this – I don't know what is wrong with me – but I don't want to be a parent yet and I don't know if I ever will. I . . . I don't know if I should ever have married him when we don't see eye to eye on such a vital matter."

In a way I felt sorry for the bastard but still it gave me hope.

"You don't have to stay married – you could always leave him?"

Karen shook her head. "I can't leave him – there's no divorce in this country – don't you remember?"

"But you could go and live somewhere else – somewhere there is divorce."

"I'd like to get away from here for a while but I love Ireland – it's my home. Even you said that you might come back here some day."

"I did, but then when I'm here a while and I see the limits that are put on people and the regulations that hold progress back I think I am right to live abroad." I paused. "What you're saying is that you don't see any prospects of breaking up with Alan?"

She stared deep into my eyes and I wondered why she was holding back – why she couldn't talk to me from her heart. I had come clean and told her all about the mess that I'd been in with Orla – the constant threat of her suicide every time something didn't go her way, every time I said something that she didn't agree with. It seemed bizarre now when I looked back on that time and how I let her control me. I knew Karen well enough to realise that she wasn't being completely honest with me. What was she hiding?

Everything about tonight was perfect. Everything was in place for us to fulfil our love at last. There was nothing stopping us.

"Karen . . . we know we love each other . . . so what if I asked you to marry me? Would you leave Alan for me?"

I was so pent up with emotion and desire to jump her bones I would do or say anything.

She smiled at me sadly and flicked my fringe away from my eyes. She left her fingertips on my cheek for a few moments, driving me crazy inside.

"I'm married, Greg. Like it or not, I can't just do whatever I want now. There are too many other people involved. My parents, Greg's parents, we have extended family and our lives are cut out – I'm not a free spirit wandering around the continent like you are. I have commitments – a mortgage – a job. I would love to run away with you . . . but there's one reason why I can't right now and you have to trust me."

One reason? What did she mean? An angry ball of fire leapt in my stomach. I'd had enough talking – it was all this bloody talking that had kept us apart for so long. By the sound of things I was happier in my relationship with Isabella than she was with Alan, but I was willing to go all out to get her back into my life. What was stopping her? I reached out and grabbed her in my arms with a force that took us both by surprise.

"Please, Greg – it's not okay. I wouldn't want our first time to be like this – full of deceit. Would you?"

"Yes, I bloody would! I want to have you on the spot right now."

"The timing's not right – I respected you when it wasn't right for you in London."

"That's because I was a feckin' eejit back then – brainwashed by Orla. I thought we had loads of time – I didn't think you'd go and get bloody well married!"

She pulled away from my grip on her and I felt hurt.

"I'm fighting for you now, Karen, dammit!"

She jumped up on hearing the force in my voice and I wished I could take my words back.

"Please, Karen – don't pull away – I need you tonight."

"You have to trust me – I can't tonight – I will explain why another time – but I won't ever two-time anyone."

She was right – I was letting my emotions take over, dragging up the past. I needed to calm down. I didn't want her to slip away again and I had to make her see it.

She stood up and went over and got her coat from the settee. None of what she had said made any sense to me.

"I have to go – I will explain why I couldn't stay soon – I promise."

She kissed me on the cheek before heading out the door and I was left wondering what it was all about. I had no idea what she was talking about and why she didn't feel the same urgency as I did.

* * *

It was three months later that I got a letter in the post – sent via my mother. She hadn't opened it, fair play to her. I read and re-read it but all I felt was confusion and a terrible sense of loss.

Dear Greg,

I'm sorry that it has taken so long to get around to writing this.

I'm sure you were confused after I left you that night in Offington last February. I was confused too. Things have not been easy for me and I couldn't tell you the full story without betraying my marriage.

I do wish we had spent more time together and I can't stop thinking about what might have been. You are so much braver than me – I'm a simple girl really. You will be a fabulous entrepreneur or photographer and have an exciting life that you wouldn't have with me. I do wonder what would have happened if I had stayed that night. It's probably for the best not to dwell on it.

Things have changed here. Alan is always working. He stays in town some nights – Linda has got engaged to a doctor called Bill – unbelievable – they've been dating only a couple of months. He took her off to Monte Carlo to propose. The wedding will be next year or so.

Will you let me know if you are coming back to Dublin? I'd love to see you.
Take care
Karen

I was completely confused after getting the letter. She had explained nothing – just made tantalising references to 'the full story'. She expected me to trust her reasons and leave her with the ball in her court. I was angry and hurt and I didn't reply.

Chapter 23

March 1995

I decided to stay away from Ireland for a few months – it turned into two years. Besides, I was busy with the vineyard. Maybe I was hiding from the troubles between my parents – or maybe I was hiding from Karen. Whatever it was I became accustomed to French ways and my understanding of the language improved to the point where the locals were willing to speak to me without correcting every sentence.

I kept the letter from Karen in a secret compartment in my suitcase – beside the photograph that I took of the two of us at the Baily Lighthouse. I've looked at it on more than a few occasions. I still couldn't make sense of what had happened in Dublin. I really should've contacted her but it didn't seem like the right thing to do. She'd been adamant that she wanted to stay married to that gobshite Alan.

Then Frank called to say that Stephen's dad had died. He was anxious because he couldn't get back for the funeral. He said that Stephen had moved back to Dublin after spending eight years in New York and he felt that this was my chance to make amends. I needed to see my parents and I hadn't made it home for Christmas and things were quiet in the vineyard so I booked a cheap flight with Ryanair and found myself in Dublin airport.

The funeral was to be held in Raheny church. I hadn't been there since I'd been going out with Karen and the couple of times she'd dragged me to Youth Mass. I wondered if she would be there but put it out of my mind. I did feel bad about not replying to her letter but I really didn't know what to say. I'd laid my heart on the line that night in my parents' house and I couldn't do that again. It was probably the right thing to do in hindsight. I was fortunate to have Isabella – she was good for me.

* * *

Funerals are depressing at the best of times but there was something so much more difficult about going to them in the pelting rain. The church was crowded. Mr Owens was hugely involved in the GAA and generations of players filled the church. He had been a fireman too, like Karen's dad, and I wasn't surprised to see Mr Forde at the top of the church. I wished Frank was here – he'd understand about things like this – losing his own father at such young age. I wondered if that was why he was that bit more mature than the rest of us?

Frank had briefed me on Stephen's situation – he was working in computers in America and was now involved in the launch of a new product that was coming this summer to Dublin. I'd never put Stephen down as a nerdy type but this new product was sexy according to Frank and we'd all be using it soon. It was called Windows or something like that. The pace of life was so much slower in France and less inclined to change – I hadn't seen many mobile phones – not like London where they were becoming almost common.

I started to recognise a couple of faces as the congregation followed Stephen and his mother up the aisle. Scooby and Yogi from school and the old Grove days – jeez, Scooby had turned grey. We were all hitting thirty – what did I expect? Stephen was as pale as a ghost and his sisters were in floods of tears.

Mr Owens couldn't have been more than fifty-five – he

always looked so young and trim. But Frank had said that a lot of firemen who had worked the night of the Stardust tragedy were dying young. The asbestos fumes had poisoned them and given them cancer.

And then I saw her – she came in the side door and pushed into the pew next to her father. Her face was thinner than the last time I had seen her. She was pale too. I wanted to go straight over but had to wait until Mass was said and the coffin was brought outside and the church emptied.

She seemed surprised to see me and put her hand up to cover her mouth.

"Hi, Karen – I wasn't sure if you'd be here."

"Hi! Are you back living here?"

I shook my head. "Frank rang me so I flew in for the funeral – it's been a long time since I've seen Stephen and I wanted to be here."

"Are you staying long?"

"Only two days – it's literally a flying visit."

"Are you going to the Shieling after the burial?"

"Yes – I am, are you?"

She seemed flustered. "I don't know . . . but I'm going to the graveyard in Sutton – do you want a lift?"

"That would be grand, thanks."

I felt so awkward. She was still the same to me but my head was firmly ensconced in the vineyard and it had helped me to put Karen to the back of my mind. It was the first time that I felt old. When Frank's dad died it was different – we were all so young we couldn't relate to the idea of mortality. But this was different – this was the passing of our parents' generation – we were all heading into middle age whether we wanted to accept it or not. Frank and Jackie were married. Scooby has a kid, Frank said. He was working in a company called Eircell – there was a market for mobile phones in Ireland in that case. Yogi was living in a squat in London – it was good of him to make the journey. Life was changing so much and I was in an oasis on the vineyard with Isabella. It wasn't a bad place to be – but it scared me in another way.

Karen was driving a brand new Volkswagen Golf.

"Nice car."

"Thanks," she said. "I wanted one before I was thirty."

"But you are still only twenty-nine!" I joked.

"*You* don't have long though, do you?"

"Ha – you remember my birthday!"

"Of course I do. It's a major milestone. Alan was thirty in December and we had a party in his parents' house. It was bloody awful."

She turned on the radio and quickly pressed play on a cassette as we drove off.

"They sound good – who are they?"

"Oasis. Have they not reached France?"

"Music isn't Isabella's thing."

"What about you – are you not allowed to listen to music?"

I didn't know how to reply to that.

"This track is called 'Live Forever'," she said.

She focused on the road – her hands heavy on the steering wheel.

"You didn't reply to my letter," she said after a while.

"You didn't say much in it."

I was being defensive – I felt I'd a right to be after she rejected me without proper explanation.

"I said I wanted to see you again."

"I stayed away – this is my first time back since then."

"Because of me?"

I didn't need to answer. "Where's your dad?" I asked instead.

"He's getting a lift with one of his friends from the fire station."

"It's scary to see your friends' parents die. I never thought that I could feel this old. Maybe I need to go off and do something different with my life."

"Running a vineyard is pretty exciting – how's that going?"

She was businesslike in her tone and I hoped I hadn't offended her.

"It's good – we did well for our first year – but the real test will be over the next five. Bordeaux is the home of younger wines so we should see returns soon. How are things at the magazine?"

"They're going okay – it puts in some time."

There was something about the way that she said those words that struck me. I didn't want her to be just 'putting in time'. I never thought I'd hear words like that come out of her mouth.

"What about Alan? Is he happy you're still working?" I was probing about the baby situation.

"He thinks it's a good idea . . . especially now . . . after the last couple of months."

What had happened? What was she not telling me?

"Is everything okay?"

She nodded unconvincingly but said no more.

"It looks like divorce is coming to Ireland? So there's always hope for me?" I winked at her but she didn't take the bait.

There was going to be a referendum and things were moving quicker in Ireland than anywhere at the moment – maybe she would be free someday.

When Mr Owens had been laid to rest we went on to the Shieling Hotel. It was full of people and we made our way into the lounge where I got my first chance to speak properly with Stephen.

"Hey, man!" He leapt up to shake my hand. "Thanks for coming. I appreciate it."

"It's been a long time – I am sorry – I liked your dad." I meant it.

"Yeah, well, it's coming to us all. I knew that he wasn't well and that's why I moved to Dublin – I've been working for Microsoft in the States and I thought I'd get more time with him – at least I got two months."

"When did you move back?"

"In January. Things are changing pretty fast here and I'm working flat out."

"Glad to see you doing well."

"Where are you now? Frank said something about France?"

"Yes, I'm living in Bordeaux. It's good – different. I saw Linda arrive a few minutes ago."

Stephen looked around frantically. "Where?"

"Karen saw her park up her car as we came in."

"I'd like to see her." Then he smiled at me the way he used to and I was so glad that I had made the effort to come. "Wish I'd shagged her – I was mad about her."

"Well, you may be in luck – she's not married yet – mind you, she won't be single for long."

"No way!"

"Yeah – she's engaged. Working in PR so I believe and seen in all the right places."

Just then Karen and Linda walked over to where we stood at the corner of the bar and for an instant the scenario was too familiar. I was seventeen again and we were all going to the Grove.

"Hi, Stephen – Greg," Linda said mournfully and kissed Stephen on the cheek. "I'm so sorry about your dad."

"He was great, wasn't he?" Stephen said with a half smile. "It's a pity that it takes something like this to get us together – I wish Frank was here."

"Oh God – maybe not though," Linda said. "I'd feel like a whale next to Jackie Quinn."

I watched amused as they all fell into laughter. She might be Mrs Frank O'Reilly but she'd always be Jackie Quinn to us.

"You look well, Linda," Stephen remarked.

"I'm young and about to marry the man of my dreams – hey, why don't you guys come to my wedding in September – it's going to be huge and I won't know half the people there. It would be much nicer to meet under those circumstances, don't you think?"

I couldn't imagine Isabella wanting to go to an Irish wedding – too much drink and bad language and there's always a row. I nodded to be polite – I mean, for Christ's sake, we were at a funeral.

"You can get to see Karen dress as a big raspberry meringue," Linda said, poking Karen in the ribs.

"I've warned you not to do that to me!"

I watched Stephen's enthralled face as he watched the two girls. They were special – we were all special when we got together like this.

"Okay then – so will you come?" Linda wasn't taking no for an answer.

I had nothing to lose by saying yes. I had no idea where I would be in September. But the chances were I would be still in France.

I flew back to Bordeaux with my head full of notions. I was glad to be back on good terms with Stephen – I'd missed him. But Karen was an enigma and I needed to know what she was doing with her life.

Chapter 24

September 1995

Isabella was good about my decision to take an extended vacation. I could have told her about the wedding but I knew that it wouldn't really have been her thing – a crowd of Irish people in an old castle. Or maybe it would have been, but I felt better going on my own. That way there would be no questions about getting married and starting families. Why did my parents feel you had to reproduce yourself once you got to the age of thirty? And it wasn't just my parents – it was also Isabella's father and everyone of that generation.

So I decided to be a rebel and take three months off to travel around the world. I had relatives in Australia that I'd never seen and friends in America that I wanted to visit. Frank was ready and waiting for me on my last stop of the journey in New York. It would be giving the finger to middle age. What would happen when I returned I wasn't completely sure. My mother said that Isabella was a clever woman and only giving me enough rope to hang myself. They were the most profound words I'd ever heard her say and she had a bottle of Chardonnay inside her at the time.

So I set off for the wedding, having packed a shirt, tie and a suit that was probably not fashionable in Dublin but I didn't

179

care. I didn't do formal in France – since moving to the vineyard
I was always in hobo's clothes and I was happy that way. I had
wound down my food-exporting business to concentrate on
helping Isabella and it was working out well, but I did often
wonder if I was in another co-dependent relationship. This trip
was my chance to break away – I just had to be sure what it was
I wanted to do.

* * *

St Fintan's Church in Sutton was an ugly 1970s building. I was
in the last class to make our First Communion in the old tin
shack that was pulled down before the church was built. I
always preferred the shack.

It was big and crowded with guests by the time I arrived. It
reeked of roses. I spotted Frank and Jackie Quinn who were
only a couple of pews away. I wished that I had brought
Isabella now – I couldn't stand the thought of meeting Karen's
husband Alan again and felt I would cope better if Isabella were
with me.

Linda arrived looking hot – her figure was hourglass – and
walking behind her was Karen looking so beautiful I thought my
heart would stop. She was showing her bare shoulders and her
hair had grown since the funeral. This wasn't good for me – she
managed to floor me every time I saw her.

I wondered where Stephen was. He had started to date a girl
but decided not to bring her when he heard that I was coming
alone. It would be a great chance to really catch up. I'd tried to
call him a couple of times but we never did long conversations
ever.

I picked up the wedding booklet and skimmed my eyes over
the names – Linda was marrying a man who called himself Dr
Bill. I had a chuckle to myself. He reminded me of a character in
the *Muppet Show* or some programme like that.

I couldn't wait for the singing to be over so I could have a pint. I checked my watch and Stephen just arrived as the happy couple went over to sign the register. He slid in beside me in the pew.

"Well, she went through with it then?"

"'Fraid so, mate."

"Ah well – there's always divorce – or maybe she'd be up for an affair!" He winked at me.

I'd be happy with an affair with Karen, I thought to myself. A part of me wondered if the reason I had her on such a pedestal was because we never actually did the deed!

I wondered where her husband was – I scanned the pews but apart from Linda's parents and Frank I didn't know anyone.

* * *

Stephen and I decided to walk to the Sutton Castle Hotel and Frank and Jackie joined us – it wasn't that far away. I figured there would be plenty of time to talk to Karen after the photos and girly stuff was over with.

As we walked along the curve of Strand Road I realised that Jackie was really pretty sound. She was looking forward to my visit to New York in the new year. I had to admit I was too. I needed to do things now – there was an urgency to life that I hadn't felt before.

When we arrived at Sutton Castle Hotel Stephen got the drinks in and we were able to sit outside at the tables and look over the bay. There was champagne and sherry on the lawn but I'd been looking forward to the cool pint of Smithwick's that Stephen handed me.

It seemed to get more delicious each time I came home. I should take a few cans of it back with me. The French would go mad – I laughed at the thought.

"So that's another one down – only you and me left, Greg, and I'm not so sure about you!" Stephen poked me in the ribs.

And then Karen walked by – pretty in pink!

She kissed each of us on the cheek in turn and sat down beside me.

"I'm so sorry that I won't be sitting with you guys – I have to stay with the bridal group – but Alan has been put at your table so keep him company for me," she grinned.

I wondered at that moment why I had put myself through this.

* * *

The tables were set in circles and I had a perfect view of Karen at the top of the room. I realised there and then that I hated weddings and wouldn't want to go through this showy farce with anyone. I was becoming French but wouldn't want to admit it – even to myself.

The best man's speech was hilarious even though he didn't mean to be funny. He told the story of how his brother, the groom – who looked like a right pillock – a stinking rich one, mind you – was responsible for disfiguring his head with a hammer at the age of three. At least it explained why he was pig ugly. He was annoying after a while and I didn't blame the groom for hitting him over the head.

I'm not the paranoid type but Alan spoke to everyone at the table except me – he blanked me like I didn't exist. I was glad about it but I did wonder what the state of play in his house was. Karen had been different at the funeral – more nervy – and in my gut I could see beyond her husband's so-called charm – I could always sniff out a bully. By God, I swore I'd kill him if he was ever heavy with her.

Karen came down from the top table once the cake was handed out and stood at Alan's side. He pulled her down to whisper in her ear. She nodded and went away again.

"You'll have to excuse me, everyone," Alan said then, getting to his feet. "It's a right pain, I know, but I have to go now – it's been lovely meeting you all."

I wanted to punch the air. Maybe the gods were smiling on me and Karen again.

Alan made a point of shaking everyone's hand except mine as he left the room.

"What a pillock!" I said to Stephen.

"A bit of a prat but I thought he wasn't bad for a southsider – hey, are you okay?"

I nodded. I wasn't going to speak about the pillock for the rest of the evening.

Karen returned to the ballroom and walked straight over to me.

"Hey – I can spend some time with you guys – now that the formalities are over. Alan has had to go to meet a client – it's really important."

"I don't mind looking after you."

"I was hoping you'd say that – can we go outside?"

Stephen was chatting to one of the other bridesmaids and didn't notice as we slipped away.

The grounds backed onto the Hill of Howth and there were a couple of empty benches nestled in against the foliage. We sat down at a quiet bench tucked well away from the wedding party.

"It must have been a great house to live in years ago."

"Yeah – a nice setting for a wedding. Where did you have yours?"

"The Shelbourne – it was awful – I was dressed like a big meringue. We married in Trinity College. I'd wanted to do it in St Gabriel's church – my parish. But Alan wouldn't dream of asking his people to cross the Liffey."

We laughed together.

"I'm sure he was very proud of you." God knows I would have been.

"Well, seems like a bit of a blur now – four years. At least nobody is asking us about babies any more – everyone assumes that there's something wrong with me!"

"And is there something wrong?" I probed. I wanted her to confide in me – I wanted her to need me.

She nodded. "I wish I'd stayed that night – in your parents'."

Not half as much as I did!

"You said there was a reason why you didn't and that you would explain – you didn't though."

"I'm so sorry – you see, I thought I might be pregnant but it turned out that I wasn't. I was scared that if I spent the night with you and later found I was pregnant, I wouldn't ever be sure who the father was."

"That's the reason?"

"That's the main reason – I honestly thought I was pregnant."

I was shocked. I felt she had misled me with all her talk about not wanting kids and by implying she wasn't having sex with Alan.

"That was very mature of you," I said as calmly as I could. "Most people don't think and just pop out sprogs when the mood takes them."

"Well – you know me – I've always been one to think over things – probably too much . . ."

"Yes – definitely, you were always a philosopher."

"But my philosophy doesn't seem to be working – I think I've driven Alan away – I think he's having an affair."

This I couldn't believe – why would anyone who was lucky enough to have Karen as their wife mess it up by having an affair?

"You said yourself that he has a pressurised job – he was boasting at the table about his clients and cases."

"Yes, but we only live in Sandymount – there's no need for him to stay over in town as much as he does."

"And who do you think he's having the affair with?"

She shook her head. "I don't know but the phone has gone dead a couple of times when I've lifted it. He's after getting a mobile phone too."

"Lots of people have mobile phones nowadays – probably

needs it for work." I couldn't believe I was trying to convince her that her husband loved her.

"Call it woman's intuition or whatever you want, but I think that he has someone else."

I put my arm around her because it was what she needed. It was what I needed too but she had no idea how much it was wrecking my head. I realised there and then that I was still totally in love with her and I was torn between running away and staying in Dublin.

Part 4

24-10-1995

Greetings from Thailand and the
solar eclipse!

I hope that you are keeping well.
Planning to visit Dublin on my
return. Heading off to Australia
next!

You would love it here

Take care
Greg ☺

Karen Forde

21 Clontarf Close

Clontarf

Dublin 3

Chapter 25

Karen

Dublin, November 1995

The picture on the postcard was of the most beautiful beach that I had ever seen. My mother said that it had arrived on Friday. She handed it to me the moment I walked through the door and with it came her apology.

"I'm sorry, Karen, I should have told you that Greg called all those years ago – I didn't want you to be upset – you were getting very steady with Alan and, well, I knew Greg was flitting all over Europe and I didn't want you to go off with him."

"Why are you telling me this now?" I couldn't believe I was able to remain so cool with her. If she had told me at the time I would have screamed but by now I had resigned myself to my lot in life.

"Because he obviously still thinks highly of you and I know what it's like to have someone from your past that finds it difficult to let you go."

I waited for her to say more but she opened a box of John Player Blue and lit a cigarette – a signal that the conversation was over – so I let it go.

I took the postcard home and read and reread it several times and was sad that it wasn't longer. I wished so hard that I could be there with him. Life was passing me by and he was out there living it. Why was my life so filled with fear? The answer was easy. Alan. Why hadn't I the guts to do something about it? He had lashed out again. This was the fourth time and I was getting braver – or maybe I was just getting used to the threats. The thumps when they landed – on my back usually – didn't hurt as much as the fear Alan managed to instil with his threats.

So, I could be lying in a hammock with Greg in the beautiful Gulf of Thailand basking in the sunshine, instead of sitting in the office wondering why I was travelling backwards in my life instead of moving forward. I dreaded going home in the evenings. What had started out as psychological abuse turned into physical after the miscarriage earlier this year and the start of his affair.

I felt so bad after that night in Offington with Greg two years ago. I kept replaying his words over and over in my head. Did he really ask me to leave Alan and be with him? Hindsight is a wonderful thing and if I'd known that I was definitely not pregnant then I would have happily stayed the night – all he had to do was wait. But between my mother hiding his calls, his devotion to Orla and my fear of carrying Alan's child we'd been sending out mixed signals to each other for years so I didn't blame him for being confused. Then when he didn't answer my letter I got desperate.

Eventually I got pregnant but miscarried a couple of months later. I thought that being pregnant would make Alan happy but it only made him angrier when I lost the baby. Said it was my fault – no baby would want to stay in my womb – I'd make a terrible mother.

He said that the baby probably wasn't his anyway. His comments freaked me out completely and I wondered what would motivate him to say such hurtful things. Did he think I was having sex with Greg? Had he noticed my feelings for him and assumed that? Ours was always a love that was deeper than a physical relationship – it was metaphysical. But there was no way that Alan could ever understand emotions like that. Not from me or anyone. Everything was black and white in Alan's mind and if it wasn't explained scientifically then it didn't exist. What a dull and sad world it must be for my husband. I could barely call him that. So why did I stay with him? Because I couldn't see any way out.

Greg was kindness itself at the wedding but I was too proud to tell him the truth – about the abuse. I couldn't bear to tell him that I was actually pregnant and lost a baby after the fear of pregnancy holding me back from spending the night with him. I'd been in such a muddle for the last two years – since I bumped into him in the Summit back in 1992 if I was to be honest. Anyway, he had Isabella in the background – his support and confidante. I thought it unfair that he had seen my situation and knew so much about me and I knew nothing of his life in France. I sometimes tormented myself and tried to picture what she looked like. He didn't exactly paint a clear picture. But she seemed to be kind and desperately in love with him. So much in love with him that she was happy to let him go off around the world on his own for three months. She must be confident.

That is what I miss the most. My confidence. I can't even remember what it felt like. My parents would never imagine what is going on for me. My dad has tried to pry a couple of times but my mother hasn't a notion. She loves telling the neighbours about her daughter in the period house in Sandymount, married to the barrister. Alan the barrister bastard. I've been so unhappy since Greg came back into my life – I've kept imagining what might have been but I can't seem to find my way out of my situation.

Chapter 26

January 1996

It happened again and I didn't even find it strange any more. I rang Greg's mother's and he answered the phone. He said that he answered the phone because he knew that it was me. He could have been bluffing and covering up for why he hadn't called me. I had thought he would be back in France by then but something made me dial his number. I knew that the connection between us was real and that it was always there – it was a kind of telepathy.

He had promised to call me on the final leg of his grand voyage and I was relieved to hear that he would be in Dublin for five days. I needed him now more than at any point in my life. That last postcard sent from Thailand was the final straw.

Alan and I were at breaking point. Christmas was awful – I never remember one like it. At least he hadn't hit me since October. I actually thought he didn't care enough to do that any more – or maybe my threat to tell the police put a stop to it. But he still put me down with his words and his constant disappearance. My esteem was at an all-time low.

So Greg arranged to meet in the Westbury for lunch – it was his suggestion. I was surprised that he chose such a public place. He sounded buoyant and happier than I had heard him in years.

I guess I would feel that way too if I had travelled around the world.

I pulled my new low-waist jeans on and they nearly fell off my hips. I had to put a new notch in my belt too. I didn't know if it was worry or lovesickness that had brought me to this point but I had never been this skinny in my life.

My breasts had shrunk too – I was a 34C cup for the first time. I didn't feel like eating – Linda gave me a hard time over it. She was four months pregnant and the happiest I had ever seen her. I was so pleased for her – I didn't want to bring her down with my feelings so I made a huge effort to be excited about the baby. Linda knew about the miscarriage last year. I sometimes thought about what might have been – if I had the baby at least I would have someone for myself. But I was taking a terrible risk bringing it into such an unhappy home. I closed my eyes and tried to imagine what it would feel like to be pregnant with Greg's child. It would be the most wonderful feeling in the world. That would be the grand prize – the lottery on a mega scale.

I looked at my profile in the long mirror. Not even a little bit of lumpy flesh covered my stomach – only a thin layer of elastic skin. The bridesmaid dress would fall off me if I put it on now. I settled for a Donna Karan jumper with a zip-up neck and my wedged ankle boots. It was cold. I'd bought a black leather jacket that was very sixties in style in the sales and I slipped it on.

I decided to drive into town – traffic had got so bad I'd been getting the bus to work but I didn't know what Greg's plans were, so this way we could be flexible. It was a bright day and I parked in the Stephen's Green Shopping Centre.

The Westbury is far from the sort of place Greg and I used to go together. It was more an Alan place – Alan would only go to the most fashionable places in town. I hoped that I wouldn't meet him with his girlfriend here. Her name was Niamh – that much I knew from his mobile phone and I'd heard him talk about her in passing. A part of me was hugely hurt and I knew that if he actually admitted it I would be stunned but then again I knew it to be true in my gut.

Greg was sitting at a table upstairs gazing out on to Grafton Street and looking gorgeous. His hair was tossed and long around his neck and ears and I longed to go over and flick his fringe out of his eyes. He was wearing flared jeans that looked like he'd slept in them and a V-neck jumper over a stripy Aertex. He could pass for twenty-five looking like that.

He jumped up when he saw me and gave me a squeeze.

"Hey, great to see ya!"

He was tanned too but not dark brown – more a golden colour.

"Hiya – you've a great colour!"

I took my coat off and put it on the couch opposite where he was sitting.

"Wow, Karen – where have you disappeared to? You are literally fading away!"

You better believe it, I thought. "Busy life, you know," I brushed it off, "but Linda is piling it on – she looks about eight months gone instead of four."

"I didn't realise that she was pregnant – fantastic news! She seemed so happy at the wedding – I'm glad we got together for it."

"Yeah, it was a good day. And you have been jet-setting around the world since then! Thanks for the postcard by the way."

"Thailand was amazing. You'd have loved it."

I just nodded.

"They have this thing called the Full Moon party – I heard about it when I was on Koh Samui – it's held on this little island called Ko Pha Ngan every time there's a full moon. There were hundreds there the night I was and then we had the eclipse as well. I kept thinking of you and that conversation we had years ago about life on other planets. Jeez, there's a whole world out there and I think I'd like to see more of it."

"So you've got itchy feet now?" He'd never ever come back to Dublin – I was sure of it.

"I think travel helps you get a perspective on what you want," he went on. "I know now I wouldn't want to live in Australia. Don't get me wrong – I had a cool time but it's not a lifestyle that would suit me. I went to Tokyo too – now that is amazing. I'd never seen so many people in my life and I felt like a giant my whole time there."

"Where else did you go?"

"New Zealand – the west coast of the US – I took a trip down to Mexico too for a couple of days. The Mexicans will do anything to get over the border – I'd women throwing themselves at me – I'd to tell them that I wasn't American and they'd be worse off with a Paddy. Although I believe they are opening up a bit now with some new work visas."

"There was something about it in the news. So did you meet Frank and Jackie Quinn?"

"Ha – will we ever call her Jackie O'Reilly? Or even just 'Jackie'? She's started her own fashion label – Frank is making a fortune and they have an apartment in Astoria and a beach house in West Hampton. Literally living the life of Reilly!"

"Good for them." Who'd have thought that they would end up there, successful and prosperous? And Greg would be going back to a vineyard and I'd still be in the mess I was in.

"I believe Stephen is doing well too?"

"Yes," I'd seen him a couple of times, "and he's met someone."

"Yeah – I must ring him. This Windows malarkey is the next big thing from what he says."

"You only have to look around Grafton Street – there's a computer shop a couple of doors up from MacDonald's."

"And this internet thing is going to change the world according to Frank."

I wished something would change my world.

There was a pregnant pause then I said, "I don't feel like a big lunch . . . do you mind if we get some fresh air – we could pick something up on Grafton Street?"

"I've eaten so much weird stuff over the last couple of months I'd love a Big Mac," he said. "Then maybe if it's warm enough we could go for a stroll down the Burrow Beach?"

It was exactly what I wanted to do – I needed to be on the northside of the city.

We grabbed a takeaway and I drove out the coast road while he fed me chips. I was hungry for the first time in months – really hungry. And I was feeling so happy just to be in Greg's company I could shout out loud.

"How are your mum and dad?"

"That's a good one," he laughed. "My mother has gone off the booze but she's addicted to Prozac. My dad has her on it. Ella says they are a new wonder drug. She's only out of college and she knows it all. She agrees with Dad on everything now. I kinda wish she'd married that yobbo a couple of years back. Instead she's turning into a little clone like all the other Med students."

He didn't need to explain – I knew exactly what he meant after having my fair share of Med students in college.

"Funny, isn't it – the way we turn out like our parents," I said. I couldn't say I was exactly like Monica but I understood where she was coming from now.

"I guess I'm an exception to that rule."

"Yes – yes, I suppose you are."

"And there's poor Yogi who was in school with us – did you hear that he died in London a couple of months ago – heroin. So not everyone has had it easy."

I wanted to pull the car into the side of the road and scream at him. But it wasn't his fault – he had done nothing wrong – he'd tried to save me from this life that I'd made for myself and I wanted to cry. But I was too used to hiding my true feelings now and just smiled at him instead.

"Poor Yogi," I said.

We stopped the car at the 'hole in the wall' and walked out on to the beautiful strand. The light was low but there was hope in the air and the promise of spring. I needed hope – that's what I longed for.

"So what are your plans for your return to France?"

"I think I've had it too good – Isabella has been amazing and kept everything going while I've been away. I think it's time that I paid her back."

"You're probably dying to see her."

"Well . . . she came over to New York for the New Year when I was there with Frank and Jackie. My plan was not to go to New York until the end of January but the three of them had it all planned."

I felt the green-eyed monster swallow me whole. As I thought of my own Christmas spent with Alan's parents and their neighbours I wanted to burst into tears.

"Oh, thanks for the flowers by the way," I said.

"You got them okay then – that's good. It was while we were in West Hampton between Christmas and New Year's Eve. Isabella had asked me to get something for Jackie to say thanks so I rambled into a flower shop and there was this tall dark-looking chap and I thought I'd seen him before. It turned out that he was from Howth – Joe Doherty was his name. He'd been working in the plant and landscaping business for a couple of years. We chatted about the Summit and the Grove and I suppose he made me think of you. He had a dream of returning to Howth some day and setting up a place just like the one in the Hamptons. So I got a bit nostalgic and the flowers were a bit of an impulse buy!"

"They really were a lovely surprise – Mum thought that you had sent them to her. Her eyesight is gone to pot and she didn't read the card properly. I'm glad you sent them to Clontarf."

"What about you – how was your Christmas?"

"Fine – absolutely fine! Apart from . . ." I paused, not sure if I was ready to tell him exact details of my miserable life or not.

In the end I decided I had nothing to lose. "Alan went away between Christmas and New Year with his mistress."

Greg stopped where he was walking and his jaw dropped.

"You're not serious!"

I nodded. "He didn't admit it but I know he was with her."

He frowned at me in disbelief and I reached up and ran my fingers through his fringe. Dear sweet Greg, I thought, how happy I am for you but now, as you see, I am miserable.

"Karen, what's going on?"

"I'm fine."

His expression turned to one of pain. As if he felt what I was going through.

"Please tell me?"

"Let's just enjoy these couple of days – huh?"

I needed this time with him. I needed to feel like I still had a part of him and he wouldn't be here now with me if he didn't want that, would he?

The beach was deserted apart from an old man and his two collie dogs. He nodded at us as Greg slipped his arm around my shoulder and we walked in silence all the way past the Howth Lodge Apartments. There was stillness in the air that left me feeling calmer and the reassuring way that he held me close replenished my drained spirit.

* * *

That night I went to bed happy. For the first time in over a year I felt safe. I was so used to feeling scared on my own and scared when Alan was there that I didn't know which was worse. But while I was asleep I seemed to leave my body and was hovering over it as I looked down at my face for the first time. I was happy but my body was weeping. Tears stained my cheeks.

When I went back into my physical body I woke with a jerk to a buzzing noise. I looked at my alarm clock and it read 3 a.m.

I heard Alan come in and take himself to the spare room. I

199

then remembered my dream – a dream that was a recollection of something that happened fourteen years ago: that hug between Greg and me and the way he left my house when we took the break. Did he know something then that I hadn't realised? All my philosophy and life experience was worth nothing – I was at this point in my life and I still wasn't with Greg.

Chapter 27

I called in sick to work the next morning and I didn't think it was paranoia on my part but I thought they were pleased. I'd been so miserable the last couple of weeks and the magazine had become more frivolous and irrelevant over the past year – hence the huge hike in sales and delight of the publisher.

Greg agreed to get the DART out to my side of the city and I suggested we meet at Sandycove station.

"Joyce's Tower is a good spot – appropriate for us to meet on hallowed ground," he'd said.

I'd become a big fan of Joyce as my tastes matured – I hated him in college but I hated most of the authors that we had to study back then.

It was amazing the way our lives had continued to run regardless of who we had spent them with. And although we had so many different experiences with other people, we could always manage to guide the direction of our conversations as if we'd been living in some kind of parallel universe. Now, it was like each of the times that we had met up over the last few years were pointing to this moment. I wanted to believe it – I needed to.

I was determined not to let Greg return to France without

having 'the conversation'. It was hanging in the air between us when we walked on the Burrow Beach and it needed to be spoken. We both knew that it was coming.

I parked up the car and waited for the DART to pass. It was alien meeting him here – like we were both in a foreign country.

"Well, we picked a good day for this," he said as he came through the turnstile.

It was a remarkably fine day for January in Dublin and could have been twelve degrees or more. The sky was a powder blue as we started to walk along the serpentine wall that hugged the coast. Joyce's Tower beckoned and, although neither of us were quite sure what we were going to do when we reached it, we walked on nonetheless.

"I feel like I am playing truant from school." And I did.

"So do I in a funny kind of way – but I've been feeling like that since I started on my travels."

"You've done the right thing – getting travel out of your system – you will be ready to settle down with Isabella when you return."

"Have you been speaking to my mother?"

I had no idea what he meant by that but I didn't want to pry. Or maybe I was in denial and not ready to hear anything that I couldn't deal with. But he continued anyway.

"My mother says that Isabella sent me off on my travels to reel me in."

"She did turn up in New York though."

"Yeah, and I was glad that she did – we had a really nice time with Jackie and Frank."

Please don't tell me any more – I wanted to scream at him to stop.

"What is New York like?"

"Busy and a bit wild in places – certain areas are a no-go – but Astoria was good."

"You sound American the way you said that."

"Hey, give me a break – you should go over there. Frank and

Jackie love having visitors. Their pad at the beach is amazing – they really are living the American dream."

"I'm glad someone is."

"Hey, there – you don't have it too bad now – what about your nice house in Sandymount and new car? Alan's not so bad and you achieved everything that you said you would."

What had I said? What had I set out to achieve? I couldn't remember any more what my dreams were because I didn't know what I really wanted. It was what Alan had wanted that I had taken on board.

"What about his affair?" I prompted – hadn't he been listening to me?

"Are you really convinced that Alan is having an affair?"

We stopped walking and I looked up at him – did he not believe what I had said? I brushed his fringe out of his eyes the way I loved to and then we walked on.

"I've no career as such. If I don't leave the magazine they'll eventually kick me out for being too frumpy."

"Now 'frumpy' is not a word I would ever use to describe you, Karen – you've got a bit skinny but apart from that you are drop-dead gorgeous."

I slowed down and he did the same. It was a compliment of mega proportions for me, especially the way that I was feeling lately. The wall was behind us and the tide was out – we were almost at the base of the tower. We stopped walking. I ached to be held by him – couldn't he tell? Of course he could – he was a mind reader – we both were. He grabbed me and put his long strong arms around me and let me hide my face in his chest. I'm not sure how long we stood there, just holding each other, but the feeling was so powerful an earthquake could have happened at that very moment and we wouldn't have flinched. It was too perfect – I thought I could burst. I was afraid to look up at his face but I did. We didn't speak but he let his lips stray cross my face and land on mine. They were so soft – much softer than I remembered. The heat of his breath escaped and danced across my face. We didn't part our lips – it was too intense just being there like that – still. I didn't feel a need to get a room – it was enough to just be close.

I tried to calculate how many years it had been since our lips had met but I couldn't work it out. It was a sublime moment that was enough to convince me that my marriage to Alan was over.

We slowly resumed our stroll which took us along the coast to the neighbouring village of Dalkey. We stopped in Finnegan's pub for lunch and rested in the warmth and comfort of the best bits of being in Dublin.

I floated home after driving Greg to the DART that evening. Alan said nothing as I came in the door and I went straight upstairs to my bedroom. I didn't want anything to interfere with what had been for me an almost perfect day. And we had another one to look forward to tomorrow.

* * *

When I woke the next morning I could still feel Greg's lips on mine. Even though we had eaten lunch, talked and laughed for a few hours after the event, the freshness of the kiss had lingered. I hoped that I wasn't reading into it too much. But it was the first kiss we had shared since we were seventeen.

I wasn't Janis Ian 'At Seventeen' – I was Karen Forde again and I felt like a beauty queen when I was in Greg's arms. I hoped that I wasn't too late.

He said that his parents would be gone all day and night visiting his little brother who now lived permanently in Galway. Simon hadn't gone on to be a racing-car driver – he was a mathematician instead. Greg's younger siblings were the ones with the brains but from what he said Greg seemed to be at peace now with his position in the family. Maybe it just didn't matter any more.

I waited by the phone for his call until lunchtime and then became frustrated. He eventually rang at one fifteen and I was more than disappointed. We didn't have long – how could he waste a minute of possible time to be spent together?

"Hi there." His tone was a little too aloof for my liking.

"Hi ya – took your time calling – I told you I didn't have work today."

"I'm sorry. I went for a walk along the beach this morning and nearly ended up in Portmarnock – I went to Howth first and when I got back to Sutton I just kept going."

He didn't sound himself at all and I felt scared.

"Are we meeting then?"

"Yes, of course – do you mind coming over this way?"

"Not at all – I thought we had agreed – what with your folks going to Galway and all."

"Oh yes – I'd almost forgotten."

He sounded awful – what had happened since that glorious kiss in Sandycove?

"Well, what time?"

"Is about four okay? I need to get a few things to take back to France."

"Of course – I'll see you then."

* * *

Crossing over the toll bridge at three-thirty I could feel myself tremble. What if he had decided that he had made a terrible mistake by kissing me? But what was I to do? I wanted it so badly.

He opened the door to me and I wanted to fall into his arms. But he turned and walked back to the kitchen. I followed him.

The house was empty and I was relieved. We still hadn't had 'the conversation' and our time was running out. It was always easier when we were on our own in this house.

"So I'm back to France in two days – can't believe how quickly the time has gone."

It was as if we hadn't spent the entire day together yesterday – he was getting edgy and I was feeling more and more anxious.

"Can't we go into the sitting room?" I asked.

I was nostalgic for the old leather couch. We had so much history on that couch. In happier days when we would hide our courting from the others while they drank fizzy drinks in the kitchen. How intense things were between us then and how intense they still felt. I imagined Santana playing on the idle record player in the corner and wondered why they hadn't got a CD player by now.

Greg came over and stood by my side at the door between the two rooms. I longed to know his thoughts as he stared over at the old couch. "I think it's probably best if we stay in the kitchen – whaddya think?"

And instantly I felt rejected. But I was used to that feeling – it was how I lived my life. I wondered how much more I would have to take before the day was over. But still I was willing to lay my heart on the line for us – it really was our last chance.

He went over to the kettle and hit the switch so I followed him.

"Tea or coffee?"

"Or me?" I bit my lip after I said it – what sort of a fucking eejit was I?

He just grinned and reached up into the cupboard and took down three mugs in his large grip.

I gasped and he did too. It was like someone had put a pause on the moment. There were only two of us but by taking down three he had signalled another presence – a spiritual one. We both understood immediately the significance of the gesture. The third cup symbolised something we both realised without having to say it. If it had happened with anyone else in the world it would have been just an extra cup, but here and now in this context I knew this was our moment destroyed. Our fate had been sealed and there was nothing either of us could do about it.

"Who's it for then?" I asked. I had a hunch he knew the answer already. "There's another presence here – telling us something."

He seemed freaked by my outburst.

"Do you know who it is?" I had to know. Anyone watching us talking this way would think we were nutcases but this was how we were together – we were like one person and on the same wave-length which meant having unique conversations that we wouldn't have with another soul.

"I'm not sure." He started to pour tea.

"Maybe it's someone who has passed on to the other side?" I said.

"And maybe they'd like a cup of tea?" he smiled. "Okay then, we'll pour them a cup." He poured tea into the third mug. "Of course it could be someone who isn't born yet."

He was ahead of me now – all that travel and finding himself and he was no longer in the same race as me any more and I was beginning to feel it. It was like I was swimming against the tide and much as I tried I was losing the struggle.

He took the three cups over to the table and I sat down beside him but we were no longer on our own.

"So have you decided on any New Year's resolutions?" he said.

I didn't blame him for trying to change the subject.

I was desperately hiding my mood – I felt like I was beat but I had to give it one last try.

"I'm going to have fun and travel more," I said. "Might even leave dear old Ireland for a while."

Greg grinned at me without condescension. "That's one of the great things about you, Karen – the way you always bounce back – just when I think I've lost you to the dark side."

"The dark side?"

"Yeah – that's where I resided most of the time in my teens and twenties. I've always been the morose one and here I am on the downward slide again and you manage to turn around and be upbeat just like that."

He was right – I was the perfect yin to his yang and vice versa – we were like two halves of the one person. As one of us was about to fall the other was on the rise to lift us up.

I was ready to ask him now. "So what about Isabella – are you going to get married?"

He shook his head. "Nah, definitely not married. But I did feel closer to her than ever before when we met in New York – I hadn't realised how much I'd missed her until I saw her in Frank's apartment. New York is magical at Christmas and the other pair are like a couple from a Woody Allen movie most of the time so we just had to sit back and be entertained. But we are kind of different from each other – I guess being from different countries means that we have had very different experiences growing up. She wouldn't understand about the Grove – or the Trinity gigs or drinking in the Pav."

I knew what he meant but it still wasn't enough to keep us together and it wouldn't be enough to keep them apart. This was my very last chance.

"So what if I said I'd changed my mind?" I was trembling now. "That offer you made back in the sitting room the last time we were here – does it still stand?"

I could see in his eyes that the answer was no and I hated myself for putting my heart on the line in this way.

He stood up awkwardly, and defensively started to clear the third cup away – as if he didn't want it to hear.

"I meant it then but you were right," he said. "We both have other people to think about – there has been a lot of water under the bridge since and I don't want to upset other people. You have to think of Alan too."

"Alan is having an affair – I told you – we're on the brink of splitting up."

He looked at me with disbelief and it hurt.

"You said you weren't happy," he said, "but you are still together and I have to be fair to Isabella too."

No – this couldn't be – I couldn't stand to hear him speak this way. I stood up and followed him over to the sink.

"But what if I told you that I really have changed my mind completely – I will leave Alan tonight to be with you – but ultimately the decision has to be yours."

He stood with his back to the sink and propped himself against it with his palms. "Then I would have to say . . . we have to put others first."

I could feel myself well up from the very depths of my soul. I hadn't expected this – I hadn't expected the extra teacup. It was all going horribly wrong again. The gods were playing the cruellest joke.

"I know." It was all I could say – the only appropriate thing to say.

He put his arms around me and I hid my face in his chest but my tears seeped through his shirt. There was no need for more words – everything that needed to be said had been said. We had come full circle and finally met our end. I don't think I ever felt so at one with him as at that very moment. I could feel it from him too. Eventually I looked up and when our eyes met we melted into one another.

"I think I'd better go home."

His face tensed. "I don't want you to go."

"You can't have it every way – I want all of you, Greg. Now has to be the time – or never." I was hurt and couldn't conceal the sharpness in my tone.

"It's just not always up to us . . ." He let out a loud sigh. "Fuck it! Look, can you drive me around the block? I need to go for a walk on the beach."

I had no idea what time it was. Alan might or might not be home but it didn't matter – this night had been waiting to be played out for far too long and now it was over. I drove him to the Burrow Road and he was agitated and angry as he jumped out of the car, banging the dash with his clenched fist, and I knew then that he was concealing the truth from me.

I drove home in a flood of tears that made it difficult to see the road ahead.

As I crossed the Liffey to the other side I decided there and then that I needed closure with Alan, now that I had finally got it with Greg. The lights were on but I knew Alan wasn't home – his car wasn't there. I would tackle that situation tomorrow – I had been through enough for one day. I went upstairs and the house smelt different – cold and musty. I walked into my huge bedroom and threw myself onto the bed where I hid my head in my pillow and sobbed my soul to sleep.

* * *

I decided to have it out with Alan in Finnegan's pub. It felt like the right place to do it. Maybe I wanted to torture myself because I had shared a happy time in Finnegan's with Greg not so long ago.

Alan was very surprised because it had been months since we had met this way during the week for lunch.

I ordered a smoked salmon sandwich and Alan went for a hot pot.

"So why did you want to meet?"

He was such a typical barrister – always sussing the other person out. I wouldn't miss his interrogations.

"I've come here to ask you a simple question and I want an honest answer, Alan."

He seemed amused and plumped up his shoulders as if ready for any response.

"Are you having an affair with a woman called Niamh?"

He had just taken a sip from his pint of Guinness and almost spat it out across the table.

"Do me a favour – I'm a big girl and I'm ready for it – the truth."

He recovered from his surprise and grinned at me smugly like a Cheshire cat. "I'm impressed with your observation – I thought I'd hidden her pretty well."

I was trembling by now – hearing the truth and having a hunch were two very different things. I was surprised by my reaction and I was shaken.

"I'm ready, Alan – I want out of this sham of a marriage."

"We haven't been happy for a long time, have we?"

"No," I had to agree – we hadn't been happy since the day I saw Greg again – it was while I was with him that I realised I would never be happy with Alan.

"So what do we do?"

"I'm not sure."

"We could always try and give it another go."

"And you'd break it off with Niamh? Do you love her?"

"I suppose I do."

"Well, then, be happy."

He nodded at me – more fondly than he had in years.

Chapter 28

Three months later

The last three months had been frustrating and traumatic. I don't know what I had expected but I thought that once we had decided our marriage was over it would all be done and dusted nice and neatly and quickly, but that's not the way things happen with a solicitor and most definitely not with a barrister. At the rate he was going I'd be lucky to get out of the marriage with my shirt – even the car was looking dodgy. Until one of Alan's colleagues, who had an axe to grind with him for a stunt he pulled in a very high-profile case, offered me legal advice and put me in touch with a new solicitor. It looked as if she knew the right buzz words and demands that I needed to make in order to ensure that I got some compensation from my shambles of a marriage. I was so pleased that I went along like a puppy on a lead because I had lost everything as far as I was concerned – I had lost Greg who was the only person in the world that mattered.

Then I got an urgent call from my mother a couple of weeks later to call around to her after work – I was surprised. What could be so urgent?

I decided to play the CD *Foreigner 4* in my car – I sometimes liked to revert back to old Grove classics in the car. There was a certain solace to it. My own private guilty pleasure.

My mother met me at the door as if she had been anxiously waiting for me and when I saw her I thought instantly that something had happened to Dad.

"What's wrong, Mum – is everyone okay? Dad?"

"Your father is fine – he's in the front room watching the TV." Then she drew me inside the door and took my shoulders in her hands. "Karen, love, you have been through an awful lot these last couple of months and no one knows that more than me . . . but . . ."

"Mum – what's wrong?"

"You have a visitor."

My mind boggled – who could be visiting me here?

My mother saw the confusion in my face and took me by the hand.

"I've brought him into the kitchen. Karen, it's Greg. And, Karen, I'm sorry – I feel this is all my fault – if I had told you that he was trying to contact you when you were dating Alan you might be with him now."

I put my hand up to my mouth. "What's wrong – why has he come to see me?"

"He has some news."

What was he doing back in the country so soon and what news could he only tell me to my face?

"I've been so naïve, love – I feel terrible. Greg sent a wedding invitation to this house for you and I opened it when I saw his name on the back of the envelope. I was thinking that you've been through enough this last couple of months without getting news like this. When he said that he was coming home this week I asked him to come and see you – he was very sorry to hear about yourself and Alan."

"Greg is getting married?" I could hear what my mother was saying but none of it was being absorbed. He had only just told me that he would never marry Isabella . . . unless! The scenario was getting worse.

"Karen, pet, he already is married. I'll leave him to explain."

I was in a trance – like I was driving a vehicle in a head-on collision – everything was happening in slow motion.

"I'll keep your brothers out of the kitchen so you can have some peace – all right, love?"

My mind was abuzz and I felt like I was walking on the moon taking those few short steps from the hall to the kitchen. And there he was sitting at the table drinking a cup of tea. He didn't get up and I was afraid to get too close to him so was pleased with the distance. I pulled back a chair and sat opposite him.

"Your mother made a pot of tea – will I pour you some?"

"I don't think I could drink it." The shock on my face must have been as tangible as the concern that was etched across his.

I looked down at his hands and that was when I noticed the shiny band of gold on the ring finger of his left hand. He sensed my stare and started to play with the ring, twisting it around like a child who had been forced to wear an uncomfortable collar and tie.

I wasn't going to mince my words here – there was no point. Our history was too recent.

"Congratulations. So we finally know who the third cup of tea was for."

"Yeah – eh, what do you mean?"

"Isabella must be pregnant – congratulations."

He was spooked by my comment and I wondered how we had so quickly lost the bond between us that I thought would never be broken.

"Eh, yes, but how did you know? We've come back to tell my parents the news – nobody knows it yet." And all the time he twiddled the band around and around.

"You said that you wouldn't marry Isabella. But when you lifted the third cup from the cupboard that night you must have had a hunch that she was pregnant. Now three months later you've got married quickly and there can only be one reason."

He laughed nervously and I knew that the years spent living

with a solicitor had served some purpose. I could always be a private eye if I wanted a change of career.

"I'm sorry, Karen – I knew there was a chance that Isabella could be pregnant after we met in New York and she was. You were in the same situation yourself when you wouldn't leave Alan that time that I asked you."

"We've been on a see-saw, haven't we?"

He nodded. "Please, I feel so uncomfortable in your house – can we go around to the castle or something?"

"Sure." The walls were paper-thin in my mother's and we were always comfortable in the castle.

I drove the car as quickly as I could because I hated being with him and not being able to look at his face.

"I thought you were exaggerating when you said things were bad with you and Alan."

"But this isn't about me and Alan – it's about you and Isabella and, no matter how things were with Alan and me, you and Isabella were always going to do this." I felt very proud of myself for having the strength to say the words without crumbling. If anything Greg was the one mumbling and fumbling and caught in a mess.

I wished he'd stop playing with his ring. He must have sensed that because before we got out of the car he took the ring off and I saw him slip it into his pocket.

"Put that back on – I won't be responsible for you losing it in my company," I demanded.

"I'm sorry – it's very difficult to wear it with you present."

It was the most powerful I had felt in years. So, I still unnerved him – after all that had been said and after all that we'd been through – it was still there.

He reluctantly put the ring back on.

"Karen, I don't know what to say – our timing has been terrible."

"Eh, you can say that again!" There was no kinder way to put it. In fact, it couldn't be made up.

Once we found a quiet intimate corner of the castle, which was easy to do at this hour of the day, I was ready to ask. "So what happened after you got back to France in January?"

"Isabella told me that she had conceived in New York – as I said, we'd known there was a chance."

I just looked at him – what could I say?

"Then we had to decide if we would have a wedding or a quiet affair. She was keen for us to go to a registry office and do it quickly so we went to Paris for the weekend and did it on the spot. Her family are Catholic so we're having a blessing next month in Bordeaux. I sent you an invitation but your mother got her hands on it first and called me to explain that your marriage had broken up and that it might be upsetting for you to hear about my wedding while going through the mill."

I nodded. What else could I do? But I was baffled. How could he expect me to go to witness him and Isabella being bound together for life? And, even if he didn't actually expect me to go, my mother was right – even at the best of times it would have been a huge shock for me to receive such a missive in the post. Had he become so out of touch with my feelings?

"Yes, our timing has indeed been fairly pathetic," I said. "So while I was issuing an ultimatum to Alan you were running off to Paris to get married. Bad timing of epic proportions, Greg!" I wasn't even angry – it was too bizarre to be anything but sad. "So I guess this is the way it's meant to be." I didn't quite believe it though.

"I can't believe it." He fiddled some more with his ring and I had to ask him to stop.

"I've had more women chat me up in the two weeks since I've been wearing this thing than in the four years before it – I had no idea that wedding rings on men were a babe-magnet."

"You'd better believe it – there are women who only go for guys who are already committed. They seem to have some sort of twisted thinking that if he can commit to one woman he might commit to them. Alan's girlfriend is a typical example of it. She's over the moon with our marriage developments – even has the colour charts out for how she's going to change the décor in our house."

"You won't let her kick you out of your home, will you?"

"I don't give a damn what they do with the house – I just want enough to be able to move back to the northside and get a little house for myself in Clontarf somewhere."

"Oh Karen, I'll be glad when you're back in Clontarf – that really is for the best."

I didn't want to see him so smug – things weren't all right in my world now. He might have difficulty getting used to a band of gold but I had lost a lot here and there was still the news of his first child that I wasn't relishing.

"I'm not sure how I'm going to feel when your baby arrives – I won't pretend that it doesn't affect me."

He nodded. "It's a big change."

It was indeed. We had been going around in circles for years, but had I finally truly lost him? "We couldn't have been more out of sync for the last twenty years if we had tried."

"I agree – it's not easy for me, Karen. My whole world has changed dramatically now."

"And so has mine."

"Will there ever be a time for us?"

I looked at his hands and the band of gold. I didn't have the answer. But our time certainly wasn't now.

Chapter 29

September 1996

Emer invited me to live with her in Boston when I told her that I needed to get out of the country and it seemed like a plan. Emer was a mate from school days, not close, but we'd kept in touch. She was so generous with her offer of support and help to get settled in 'Beantown' that we quickly became firm friends. She lived in a lovely old part of the north end of Boston; it was another world and it was easy for me to forget about all that had transpired over the past few months. I had even managed to put the birth of Greg's child out of my head.

My poor mother was heartbroken – she had gone from having her daughter settled in Sandymount and married to a barrister to being a separated emigrant's mother. I knew she felt guilty too for keeping Greg away when I was dating Alan all those years ago. She did what she thought was best at the time, but I suspected she would never again play Cupid.

It may have been a tragedy for my mother but I felt emancipated. I'd had to get away from Dublin. I understood everything that Greg had been saying to me now. Dublin was so parochial, so out of touch with the rest of the world, and America was the place to be. My mother had bumped into Mrs O'Sullivan a couple of days before I left for Boston and she told me that Greg and Isabella had a little girl and they had called her Gina. It made me even more glad to be in America – safe enough to be away from anyone or anything that might mention Greg or Alan or any part of the life that I had carved for myself in my twenties. I felt bad leaving Linda when she was in the throes of motherhood but she had made lots of new friends who were young mothers too and my place was not with them.

I was much better off with Emer who was in a good scene in Boston, and it was such a buzzy place, coming from Sandymount. Our apartment was on Prince Street not far from the landmark Paul Revere house. We were right on the Freedom Trail and it was so cool to be able to hang out the window and watch the tourists *ooh* and *ahh* at our old building. We were also in little Italy which meant that we never went hungry. We had so many choices with takeaways and cheap restaurants we never ate at home. I was plumping up nicely after all the time I had spent like a stick insect married to Alan – especially towards the end.

Most nights we'd go down to Faneuil Hall and Quincy Market and hang out with the guys. Emer even got me a job working with the *Boston Globe* – she was a tax accountant and knew and helped out so many business people that they were super-generous to her friend – lucky for me.

It had all happened relatively quickly – my decision to move and the separation. I suppose Alan had his reasons to look for the best financial deal – Niamh was pregnant and he was beside himself with joy. I was grateful in one way because it made the final stages of separation so final. But then there were my feelings which I hadn't considered to be so mixed – I was so consumed with how I felt about Greg that I hadn't bargained for the feelings of hurt and betrayal that I felt at the hands of Alan. Why wasn't I just deliriously happy to be out of such a miserable marriage? For a few months I found myself thinking about Alan just as much as I had been thinking about Greg. It wasn't that I wanted him back – I was certain of that. But I was sad for the loss of what might have been. I was sad for our baby that was never born. When I had married Alan I had genuinely hoped that it would work – nobody goes up the aisle thinking anything else surely? Maybe they do but I can only speak for how I felt. I was happy to be marrying Alan back then and now after just turning thirty I was feeling sad and empty. I was a thirty-year-old woman very much alone, on the other side of the Atlantic from my family and all that I had been familiar with for my entire life to this point. That made it hard – but maybe hard was how it was meant to be.

Emer put me in counselling a week after I arrived. It hadn't occurred to my family to do that. I guess they are old school and counselling is really more of an American thing to do. Emer had been getting counselling for two years and swore by it – she always went for a manicure straight after and sometimes got her highlights done just before.

Boston was crazy – the Americans were crazy – but I loved it.

My counsellor – or should I say therapist – was called Martha and she had rooms not too far from Prince Street where we lived. She was fascinated by Greg and our story and said that we must have been soul mates in a past life. She wasn't a fruit cake – even though at the beginning I did think she was. She was incredibly intuitive and for the first time since I was a teenager and dating Greg I was feeling really much happier in my own skin.

* * *

Boston is a university town – Harvard isn't the only university there – and it's a great place to be a student. I wished I was one again and I suppose in a way living there made me feel like one.

Emer took me up to see the campus shortly after my arrival and I was very impressed. The whole of Boston is beautiful, and rich with historic buildings – and it's too European for an Irish person to feel completely homesick. I guess that's why so many of the Irish traditionally emigrate here. And Harvard bears an uncanny resemblance to Trinity – I know the colours of the bricks are red and Trinity is grey, but the layout in a quadrangle and the green areas where the students sit are so like Trinity.

I found I could be any age I wanted to be in Boston. For fun I'd been twenty-five a couple of times when guys chatted me up and they believed me – good for my ego. But of course I hadn't met anyone that I would consider dating – I was still too raw inside. Some days I cried for Greg; some days for Alan. Martha said it was natural and that I had been co-dependent for too long. She loved that word – *co-dependent*; I hated it.

But, she said, dating again was something that would probably help me. Emer heartily agreed – I had to tell her to lay off when she actually set me up on a blind date but didn't tell me anything about it until I walked into the bar. She said I needed to get 'back in the saddle' again. So I told her gently that I wasn't and would never be a cowboy and I'd find Mister Right in my own good time.

Emer had been brilliant and she knew the Greg story too – I didn't know how she listened to me those first two weeks when I moved over. No wonder she sent me to therapy.

Anyway, work was excellent. I had two jobs. It wasn't unusual in Boston – all the Irish had at least two and some had three. I decided to give retail a go and got a weekend job in Victoria's Secret, which was a lingerie shop unlike anything I'd ever seen in Dublin. Incredible size selection too.

For my weektime job, I was at the bottom rung of the ladder in the *Boston Globe*, but my boss Larry was really cool and he loved my accent. He kept saying that he'd give me more responsibility soon. I was happy simply to be occupied and distracted in a new city like Boston.

My poor father rang constantly to tell me about houses that were coming up for sale. He warned me that they were going up in price all the time and if I didn't buy something in Clontarf quickly with the money that I got from the house in Sandymount, he would spend it. I'd left the money in a joint account so he could invest it if he wanted to – he was afraid it might burn a hole in his pocket. So I told him to look for a place for me to return to. Of course, I didn't see myself returning anytime soon – I'd made the break and I needed to stick to it. He had been to see a house on Mount Prospect Avenue and he was insisting that I see it when I came home at Christmas if it was still available – I hadn't the heart to tell him that I wouldn't be home for Christmas – it would be too unsettling.

I was loving the lack of responsibility and Martha thought I just needed to be free and easy for a while after all that I had been through. I used to think that Americans were freaks, the way they talk things through, but now I could see a side of myself that was completely denied while I was married to Alan and I was looking forward to finding it again. Emer wasn't going back to Dublin for Christmas either so we were all set to have fun here.

Chapter 30

December 1996

It was almost three weeks to Christmas and I had already broken the news to my parents that I wasn't coming back. When the phone rang, I was on my own – Emer was at the gym.

"Hello, Karen? Is that you?"

"Dad – hiya, yes, how's everyone at home?" My heart always jumps when he rings in case there is something wrong with Mum or the boys. I was never like this before – distance is difficult at times.

"Did you get the photographs that I sent?"

"No, Dad – and I think the Christmas post is going to slow things down. What's up?"

"I went to see a fantastic little house off Stiles Road today – it needs a lot of work but has been rented for two years and you could buy it without a mortgage."

Mortgages, houses, rent – I was not in the zone for this conversation but I didn't want to upset my dad. He was so desperate to get me home – I wished he would just let me be.

"I don't want to be giving you any hassle, Dad, and I won't be home for a while."

"I know that but wouldn't it be nice to know that you had a place waiting for you when you get back?"

I could hear the pleading in his tone and I felt so bad for him. Maybe he was right but my head and heart were a million miles away from Clontarf. He prattled on about the house in the hope of getting me excited about it.

"Dad, go ahead and buy if you think it a good idea – I really don't want to think about it." My sigh was so loud I'm sure he felt it on the line across the Atlantic.

The question of a house didn't matter to me and if it kept him occupied for a while then so be it. I could rent it out, and sell it if I needed to later on. I'd never known Dad to be so determined about anything. It was totally out of character for a man who was usually so laid back and not driven. My mother said it was his way of coping with me living abroad. Niall had moved out too so my mother was getting desperate.

Emer came in from the gym a few minutes later, elated, and I announced my news.

"I think I'm about to become a home owner again."

She shook out her long black hair and threw her bag down on the table.

"What? I go to the gym and you go make a major decision like that! You mean you're really letting your dad go ahead and buy you something? What about this co-dependence Martha and I talked about."

"Oh, Emer, I feel so bad for my dad – he's just missing me and he wants me to buy a place in Dublin in the hope that I will come home."

"Give me a hug!" she said and I half-heartedly hugged her. Emer always thought a hug was the answer to everything, but I had just agreed to something that I did not want to do.

"You will find your own voice, Karen – it will just take some time." She plonked herself down on the futon, which doubled as our guest bed and TV couch. "Anyway, come on and spill the details."

"He has a plan to buy this house on Stiles Road and he says it's suitable for rent."

"I'm sure he knows what he's doing . . ." Her tone, however, wasn't convincing.

"I'm trying so hard to find myself here and I'm really reaching deep inside, but it's more difficult than I ever imagined."

"That's growing up, babe – and, hey, I'm sure the house won't drop in value so you will still have your money for when you do need it – you might want to buy a nice condo over here eventually?"

And when she said that it struck me that I definitely could never imagine myself buying a condo or anything else in America. I was only here a couple of months but this was my version of reliving my youth and finding myself in a way that I hadn't by marrying Alan when I was really much too young. This was my round-the-world trip that I should have taken with Greg. I intended to enjoy every moment that I spent with Emer while I lived this side of the Atlantic.

"Okay then," I said. "How about celebrating my potential new house purchase? Fancy hitting Clarke's?"

Emer jumped up and grabbed her bag. "Give me ten minutes – and you'd better get yourself a cuter look – it's Thursday night and I can feel a rough weekend coming on." She winked at me and I felt blessed to have such a positive loving person around me.

* * *

"Finally – dressing as if you want to pick up a guy!" Emer grinned at me as I came out of the bathroom.

"You don't think the top is a bit tight?"

She was brushing her hair and nodding vehemently. "Absolutely way too tight – that's why it is exactly right!" She lapsed into Phil Collins' 'In the Air Tonight'.

I joined her in song and soon we were laughing our way down Prince Street and North Street where the flyover was being constructed. I still got the shivers when I reached Quincy Market and all the beautiful shops and restaurants come into view. America was alive in a way that I could never imagine Dublin ever to be – so many different ethnic cultures and such choice.

It was nine o'clock when we got to Clarke's – a bit early for the evening punters but the bar was still crowded with the people who came there straight after work. We ordered our usual pitcher of beer and took a place at the square bar – it had the same layout as the *Cheers* pub on TV and I was so chuffed to be living in this buzzy city.

Emer loved chatting people up and an Irish accent was a passport to instant adoration from the American guys. I ordered some kebabs while she spoke to a tall blond guy with an English accent.

I was pensively enjoying my own thoughts of the happiness my father would get from buying the house when a tall guy with shaggy brown hair pushed in at the bar beside me. He smelt good and although he didn't notice me at all, which was odd at such close proximity, I felt a thrill.

He ordered three pints of Guinness and I felt like I was in the Summit or somewhere as he spoke. I turned to look at him and he seemed vaguely familiar, but I couldn't place him.

Then he looked at me and smiled. "I didn't think they'd be this busy on a Thursday."

"This place is always hopping," I said.

He tilted his head with a vague glimmer of recognition. "Ah, so you're a Dub like myself. Where are you staying?"

"I'm in the North End – with all the Italians – that's my flatmate over there – Emer." I pointed to her.

"I'm Tim," he said, holding out his hand, and there was something so charming about him I could only smile. "And you are?"

"I'm Karen – Karen Forde."

He frowned slightly. "You wouldn't have a brother called Niall, would you?"

This was so typical of Boston – it was like London in the

eighties – you couldn't walk down the road without meeting someone's brother or sister or boyfriend.

"I do actually – he went to St Paul's."

"Like myself – but he was a good bit younger than me. In fact, I think you and me might have met before."

I had no recollection of meeting Tim despite his familiar Celtic looks because I'm sure I would have tried to get to know him better. Mind you, my head was more often than not filled with Greg and dreaming of him so I could have missed out on lots of opportunities with nice fellas. Since hearing of the birth of Greg's child I had tried to be ruthless with my emotions and blank him from my memory.

"Well, I'm Niall Forde's sister all right. Maybe you used to go to the Grove?"

"I don't know anyone on the northside that didn't." He grinned and had a wonderful smile. "Yeah, I was a Grove-head – I heard they're thinking of shutting it down."

"That would be a catastrophe," I said and meant it.

"In fact, come to think of it, I'm sure I danced with you one night but you were very distracted and dumped me very quickly."

I was shocked – how could somebody remember me after all this time?

"Oh, I'm sorry – I really have no recollection."

"It was New Year's Eve too – mind you, I don't blame you – I was spotty in those days."

I tried hard to remember but my head was always full of Greg in the Grove.

"Well, it is nice meeting you again," I said, trying to glaze over the past.

"It is indeed," he said, taking three pints skilfully in his grip. "And I do hope I get to bump into you again sometime, Miss Forde."

With that he walked over to his friends at a table by the door and left me feeling a little unsettled. What else had I missed while living my life with blinkers? That was how I'd felt since I'd moved to Boston – like I was a horse who had blindly been galloping along but not seeing my full surroundings.

Emer turned around and smiled as her blond too disappeared into the night. "Did I miss anything – who was the bloke you were chatting to?"

"Someone that apparently I met at the Grove many years ago."

"He was tasty – what's his name?"

"Tim."

"What's his surname?"

I shrugged. "I didn't ask."

"Karen – don't let a hunk slip away without at least getting his full name and place of work!"

"We didn't get that far – he seemed to know my brother though."

"I find blokes are like horses – you can lead them to water but then you have to take over and be firm and show them that they are bloody thirsty."

I laughed and we clinked our glasses together.

"Here's to home ownership and picking up hunks in bars!" she declared and I drank to that.

I turned around but Tim was nowhere to be seen. It didn't matter because he was only a messenger from my past to show me that there is hope and new life out there – I just had to believe.

Chapter 31

My dad phoned me so many times I was worried that my parents wouldn't be able to afford the bill once Christmas came around. He had rung to tell me every step of the property transaction and was more excited about this house that he was buying than anything I'd ever heard him talk about before in his life. I did catch Niall on the phone one evening and asked him about Tim – he told me that the only Tim he knew in school was Tim Doyle. There was no point quizzing him any further as his head was in the clouds most of the time.

But I was pleased for my dad and the fun he was getting out of planning for the house. He even had tenants lined up to live in it after all the paperwork was signed in the New Year. I went through all the photos and details that he had sent by DHL and I was sure he had almost had a heart attack paying for them.

But it did take the sting out of our separation and he was very jolly when he rang on Christmas Eve.

"Where will you be spending Christmas Day?" he asked.

"We'll probably go to Clarke's."

"Who are they?"

"It's a pub, Dad – the pubs open on Christmas Day over here. There's a big gang of Irish meeting and it should be fun."

"Well, as long as you'll be all right – I'd hate to think of you on your own."

"Emer will be with me – we have a short holiday, only two days, and then it's back to work."

My mother took over the receiver. "And what about New Year's Eve – will you do anything special?"

"We've planned a dinner in a restaurant on the Charles River with a few friends – we'll be able to see the fireworks as they blast over the city."

"I'm sure it'll be marvellous. And is it cold?"

"Absolutely freezing, Mum, and there's talk of snow next week."

"Oh dear God, just be careful now and don't slip, sure you won't?"

You would think I was six sometimes but I assured her that I had snow boots ready for the weather – they were still not convinced.

As I hung up I was sad that I wasn't home but also glad to be in a different environment to the year before – was it really only 365 days since I'd had dinner with Alan and his parents? It felt like it was years ago and I realised that I had changed so much more in the last year than at any other time in my life.

I did think of Greg and wonder about his first Christmas with his own family. His baby would be three months old and I'm sure the apple of her father's eye. How I would love to be with him, sharing all those emotions and first stages of parenthood!

I wasn't surprised that I hadn't heard from him again after we parted that day – there really was nothing more to say. But I wondered at how our great love story had come to such an abrupt end. I couldn't imagine us meeting ever again on our own and experiencing life the way that I only ever could in his company.

* * *

Christmas morning arrived with a flurry of snowflakes and I was going to experience my first white Christmas at thirty years of age! I didn't realise how much I would miss my family until after our quiet lunch of lasagne and red wine in our little flat.

"Hey there – don't be getting all maudlin on me now," Emer said as she came into our little kitchen. "You haven't had anything like a Boston Christmas Night, I assure you."

"Oh, I'm fine – I was just talking to my dad there and he was all chat about the house and trying not to say too much about Christmas."

"Your first one away is hard but it does get easier and sure you can always go home next year."

I realised that Emer wasn't like me – she had no intention of going home for a very long time.

"We have to get through this one first." I tried to smile.

"It's only a day, Karen – but we'll have fun tonight."

I nodded.

"So, are you ready for Bernie's?" she asked.

I was confused. I thought that we were going to Clarke's. "Bernie's?"

"Yeah, we're going to have a few drinks there first and then meet the crowd in Clarke's later – okay?"

I didn't mind. I would be led by Emer wherever she wanted to take me this Christmas. It had to be better than the last one.

* * *

There were ten of us in convoy from Bernie's flat to Clarke's as the evening crept on. All Irish of course and in a way it felt like the Christmas Eves that I used to spend in Dublin with Linda when we met the old college crowd. The Americans did Christmas really well – I had never seen decorations like the ones in Boston. And everything lit up or sang or danced or said *ho-ho-ho!*

Bernie was from Galway and great fun – with red hair and a

233

raucous laugh that vibrated through walls. I bet her neighbours were glad when all the Irish decided it was time to go to Clarke's.

But there was no way Bernie would be heard above the noise in Clarke's – the place was heaving like Bruxelles in Dublin on any Christmas Eve.

I was feeling giddy after three Irish coffees and two mince pies with cream. Then I spotted him at the bar. Tim was surrounded by a big gang and telling a joke to an enthralled audience. He looked even better than I had remembered and I suddenly felt unsteady and searched frantically for Emer.

"Are you okay, Karen?" she said when she saw me.

I smiled. "Look over at the bar – that's him – the guy from a couple of weeks ago."

She glanced in his direction. "Sure is – and if you don't go for him I will!" She winked at me naughtily.

Maybe it was the Irish coffees or maybe it was the fact that I wanted this Christmas to be memorable but I walked straight over and tapped him on the shoulder. It was so untypical of me to do something like that and I felt brave. He stopped his lecture mid-flight and turned and smiled at me. I noticed then that he must have been drinking for the best part of the day because he almost keeled over as he turned.

The tall guy at his right-hand side steadied him, propped him up against his shoulder and held out his hand to me.

"Thomas Horan, lovely to meet you – do you know my mate Tim here?"

I shook hands and then Tim pushed me aside and made a dash for the toilets. I could tell that he was about to puke and I'm not sure if he made it. This was going to be a disastrous day – the very sight of me made the only guy that I liked in Boston sick.

Emer saw what had happened and pulled me over to the group that we had walked with from Bernie's house.

"Karen, have you met Gill – he's American but he's all right, aren't you, Gill?"

I wanted to just get out of Clarke's and go home to the flat and cry. I could tell after ten seconds that Gill was not all right and we had less than nothing to talk about. I sneaked out the side door and walked through the slushy streets back to Prince Street. I'd told Emer I was leaving of course and she wasn't happy about it at all, but I insisted.

When I got back to the flat I put on my fluffy slippers and dressing gown and watched TV. Just because it was Christmas didn't mean that it had to be a great day. But I was tortured by thoughts of Greg, Alan and my family and I fell asleep in the chair.

Emer woke me the next morning as she came into the flat. I had slept through the TV noise – oblivious to my own sad display on Christmas Day.

"Karen – you missed a great night. Look outside. I was so worried about you getting stuck in the snow."

I was confused in my half-awake state. "Stuck in the snow? It was only slush when I got back."

"Take a look out the window."

A snow plough was driving up the street and everything was covered in a blanket of white.

"Wow, is that why you're only getting back now?"

"Not really. You missed a great party! I was in Thomas and Tim's apartment – they had a céilí. I really wish you had stayed."

I sat up in the chair. "Tim – the cute guy?"

"Yeah, and his friend Thomas – most of the pub went back – they live in Beacon Hill – amazing pad. And I asked them to join us for New Year."

A part of me was annoyed that I had missed such a great party but another part of me was intrigued and thrilled at the prospect of what might be – I wasn't doing myself or Greg any good by moping like this for Christmas. My body was in shock after spending years in conformity with Alan. But those days were all over now. It was time that I pulled myself together and got on with the rest of my life.

* * *

I had hidden a really gorgeous black sequined cocktail dress in Filene's Basement – it was Donna Karan and had been reduced from three hundred dollars to one fifty and now after three weeks it was down to seventy-five. I couldn't believe that nobody else had picked up on it. Emer had shown me when I moved over how to shop in Filene's. Each garment had the date of its arrival on the tag and the longer a garment stayed on the rails the more it dropped in price. The trick was to hide it in a place where no one would snap it up just before the due day for a price drop. The percentage drops were placed on boards and each day showed the dates related to drops.

I was determined to look beautiful on New Year's Eve and my resolution was to try and stop thinking about Greg and what he was doing, and accept that the way I had lived with Alan was miserable and there was now a whole host of options opening up to me.

I took my shower first and saved showing Emer my new purchase until after she came out of the bathroom.

"I much prefer New Year's to Christmas!" Emer almost sang the words as she applied her make-up.

"It will be very different to last year, that's for sure." I bit my tongue as I said the words – I'd be getting a telling-off any minute now.

"This is one of the nicest restaurants in Boston and we are really lucky to get the table."

Emer had been out the night before with Thomas and was covering up a hicky on her neck. In Dublin I'd have thought a hicky was juvenile but every day here challenged what I used to believe. I was living like a college student since moving to Boston.

I walked into the bathroom and Emer caught my reflection in the mirror and swung around.

"Oh wow! What a fab dress! Where did you get it?"

"It's the one I was holding in Filene's over Christmas – it wasn't found – what do you think?"

"It's amazing – I've never seen you look so good. And what fantastic pins you have, Karen – how come you never show them off?"

Alan had teased me about my legs and called me 'stick insect' on a couple of occasions but I saved the melodrama and didn't mention that. "I never felt comfortable in dresses but I'm going to give it a go – New Year's resolution and all that."

"Karen, I'm thrilled." She shook her head in delight – in a *Pygmalion* type of way. "I think you may well be on the road to recovery in that dress. I can't wait to see Tim's reaction."

She didn't have to wait long.

We were late getting to the restaurant and the rest of the party had arrived. I pulled the dress down a bit but realised that it was futile – if I bent over at all everyone would see my Victoria's Secret knickers.

He was sitting at the other end of the table but I had noticed him catching my eye a couple of times. Emer was hitting it off big-time with Thomas and I was pleased for her. I wasn't sure how I was going to get to speak to Tim though and it was already forty-five minutes to the New Year.

Then Angela, one of the girls, suggested that we all swap places and talk to someone new before the dessert arrived.

I didn't mind giving up my view of the river because my newly allocated spot was beside Tim and I was pleased at the chivalrous way that he had orchestrated the move. I was feeling a flutter in my stomach for another man that wasn't Greg and it felt good. I was thinking of Greg all too often still. I hadn't yet got the knack of switching him off like Martha wanted me to do, using her relaxation and control methods. But for tonight – wearing my lovely new bargain-basement Donna Karan frock I was thinking of someone else and was about to sit beside him.

"At last," Tim said as I sat down.

I'm sure that I blushed. "Nice to see you again."

"I believe I was a disgrace on Christmas Day." His tone was apologetic. "I always lose it in that pub – that's why I don't go to Clarke's as much as I used to in the early days."

"Don't worry. I wasn't really in great form – my first Christmas in another country and well . . ." I didn't want to get into my past – I was here with a clean slate and determined to see 1997 in on a positive note.

"I checked with some people back in Dublin and I *was* in school with your brother."

"Yes – I did ask Niall."

"Did you now?" He leaned over and refilled my glass with white wine. "I'm trying to get the others to buy champagne but they're too mean."

"I wouldn't complain, Mr Moneybags!"

"I'm not Mr Moneybags yet but believe me I'm working on it."

For an awful moment I thought of Alan and then of the money conversations I'd had with Greg and I hoped that this wasn't an omen.

Tim must have read my mind because he said. "But I don't care too much for money – 'cos 'money can't buy me love'."

It was like music to my ears – someone who appreciated the meaning of music and used a song to say how he felt. Even Greg didn't do that.

"Oh, do you like the Beatles?" I had struck a chord, I could tell.

"Love them – and I don't give a hoot about the Oasis begrudgers – Noel is a genius and it's about time someone went back to the Beatles for inspiration."

I knew that this was a man that I would be able to talk to for a long time.

We almost missed the twelve o'clock countdown. We were busily charting the top ten for three decades. But as the fireworks broke out and people chanted Auld Lang Syne we kissed – a soft and slow kiss that marked the start of something that was completely new for both of us.

"I only had to wait fourteen years," he whispered in my ear after he pulled his lips away. How could he have remembered me all this time? Had I got it wrong with Greg – was this man my destiny? Maybe Greg had come into my life to help me break up with Alan and maybe Alan had married me to keep me from marrying anyone else so that I would be available for Tim? I needed to make sense of all that had happened because there were nights when the whole timing of my life did my head in even more than the concept of what there was if there was no universe.

Tim and I went back to his place that night and made love. I can call it that because it was something really special. He seemed to know me better than any other lover I had ever had. Part of me wanted to take it easy and slow but another part was urgent to have him. I was thirty and I didn't want to waste time dating someone that I wasn't compatible with sexually.

Emer was disgusted to lose me so quickly. Within three weeks I moved in with Tim and we made love at least twice a day for those first six months. Was it any wonder that I soon fell pregnant?

Chapter 32

September 2004

I didn't feel up to walking all the way to St Anne's Park with the baby. Stiles Road was that little bit far. I would have put Oscar on his trike and pushed him but my hands were so much fuller since little Nathan had arrived. Besides, he was in the horrors teething – unlike Karl and Oscar who had dribbled through the cutting of their first teeth without much pain. Now at seven and four they were over many of the important stages. I thought having kids later in life would make me a more understanding parent but when I looked at Linda and the ease with which she popped out five offspring it baffled me. Linda turned into the perfect earth mother and each one of her children was as beautiful and talented as the next. I cherished her friendship more than ever since becoming a mother. There was nothing that I was experiencing that she didn't have an answer for and she always made me feel better about myself.

Even with Tim's long working hours I managed to maintain my part-time job and had an au pair to help me out. But she always took Sundays off. She was a Spanish girl and deeply religious. I felt sorry for her at times when she went off to Mass on her own. Things had changed so much in Dublin – there was a time when the churches would have been full on a Sunday. But since the economy had been booming people were too busy playing golf or shopping on a Sunday.

I cursed the Celtic Tiger because Tim was working harder than ever before. Sure, he was making more money and he wanted to get a bigger house for us but prices were jumping by the tens of thousands by the week. I was more concerned that we enjoy the kids, and free time was more important to me than moving to a massive rebuild on Seafield Road or Castle Avenue. Some of the women at the school drove me insane with their one-upmanship and showiness. I didn't know where it would all end.

Sometimes I thought Tim and I were on totally different tracks – Tim was ambitious when I met him but not in a material way. At least we still had the music. We went to concerts together and I loved it when the oldies came and played in the Point or the RDS.

I was so fortunate to have Tim – I sometimes thought it funny the way things work out.

With my three boys buckled into the car I drove down Sybil Hill and the trees looked more colourful than usual for autumn.

* * *

"Quiet in the back!" I yelled at my eldest.

Reflected in the rear-view mirror, behind my son's cheeky grin, was the figure of a tall man with sandy hair. His face was firmly etched in my memory. I'd had seen him over the years but this had been the longest gap ever. I started to shake. Almost crashing into a parked car at the side of the road, I pulled over, rolled down the window and called out.

"Greg!"

He turned his head suddenly and walked straight over to my car, ushering two little girls in front of him. My heart pounded as he leaned in through the open window.

"My God, Karen, it's so good to see you." His blue eyes, wide with shock, had turned to amazement.

"What are the chances?" I smiled. I wished now that I had

242

thrown a bottle of dark-brown colour in my hair that morning to hide the silver threads at my temples and roots. I was almost forty years of age but had got away without hair colour for longer than many of my friends.

He grinned, then looked down at the two little girls who were staring in at the boys.

"This little lady is Gina," he indicated the child on his right, "and this is Lisa."

They looked just like their dad and I didn't need to ask any more.

"Hello, girls! My boys are Karl, Oscar and Nathan. I can't believe this. We don't normally come to the park this late in the day and we haven't been on a Sunday in six weeks," I said – trying to be normal.

"Well, I never come to the park. In fact, I haven't been back in the country for two years."

My heart pounded so loudly I hoped that he couldn't hear it. I did some quick mental arithmetic. Eight years – it had been eight years since we had clapped eyes on each other and it felt as if not a day had passed since I'd left him in my mother's house after hearing the news that had changed our worlds forever. But bumping into him at this stage of my life felt sublime.

"It's not just a coincidence, is it?" I said.

"You and I both know there's no such thing."

Without prompting, he opened the car door and took the baby out of his seat.

Everything speeded up around me now. I took the buggy out of the boot and Greg placed the baby into it, expertly strapping him in, and started to push while I walked along at his side. Lisa grabbed Oscar's hand and started skipping towards the park entrance, while Karl and Gina lagged a little behind – more aware of the opposite sex than the younger ones but still anxious to get to the swings and all that the playground had to offer.

"I've just finished reading a book by Deepak Chopra about coincidences," I said.

"I don't need to read it, do I, Karen?"

I threw my head back and laughed. I knew what he meant.

He had aged well since we had last seen each other and the eight years didn't show in his face.

Our eyes were smiling as if it was twenty years before and we were taking our usual Sunday afternoon stroll in this very park.

"So quickly, tell me all your news – you and three boys and everything. You look so happy."

"Well, I wouldn't say any relationship's perfect but I'm married to Tim and we get by very well. After Alan and I split up I went to Boston for a year and met Tim who was doing a Master's in Harvard . . ."

He stopped me in my tracks and pointed to his maroon-coloured sweatshirt. It was ragged and faded but the logo and letters were clearly legible: *Harvard University*.

"But it's just a coincidence," he grinned.

I gave him that knowing smile – the one that I saved for him.

"We came home then. I couldn't marry Tim straight away but we had Karl shortly after our arrival and then Oscar four years ago and little Nat six months ago. I'm currently on the brink of becoming a desperate housewife!"

He laughed. "I knew you'd be okay. I could feel it. I've thought about you a lot over the past few years – especially on the14th of August."

I was touched that he remembered my birthday.

"Where do you live now?" he asked. "Clontarf?"

I nodded. "Stiles Road. Are you doing any photography?"

He shook his head. "I've been working too hard. The last eight years feel like eight months. We had to sell the vineyard and anyway we wanted to spend more time with the kids. They were growing up before our eyes. We invested the money in property and now we're living in Spain. I suppose you could say I'm at a crossroads."

By now the children had reached the swings and climbing frames and were doing acrobatics in turn. For a moment our eyes met but a loud thud broke our stare.

"*Papa! Papa!* Karl's fallen off the pole!" cried Lisa.

My heart sank.

We hurried over to where Karl had fallen on the gravel but he was already on his feet and there was only a scratch on his leg. I held him tightly and kissed his grazed knee. He ran off, embarrassed by my fussing, and joined Gina on the climbing frame.

"Kids!" I rolled my eyes.

"Will you have any more?" he asked.

"No way! I can barely cope with three and I've an au pair."

He knelt down and took the baby's hand. "They are beautiful at this age, aren't they?"

I nodded. "What about you – will you have any more?"

"No, Isabella wouldn't be able." He hesitated and I longed to know what he was hiding. "We're blessed to have the two girls."

"Absolutely, two healthy children are as much as anyone can ask for." Then I added, attempting to be kind about the woman who had cheated me out of sharing my life with my first love, "Is Isabella with you?"

"No, but she'll be over on Saturday. My brother's getting married. It's been five years since my family have met up. We're living all over the world! Hey, let's try and meet up this week."

"Yes," I replied, scared and excited at the prospect of seeing him again.

We stood in the autumn sunlight, soaking up the moment. Greg's hands rested on the handle of Nathan's buggy and we looked on as the other children played.

My muscles turned to jelly. So this is how it would have felt if I had married Greg. This is how it would have been if we'd had a family together. Just like all the families who took their children to St Anne's Park on a Sunday – just like I usually did with my husband. It was strange that Tim happened to be away today but not so strange now that I was here in this present company. I felt an ache in the pit of my stomach. The gods had given me and Greg this time, albeit just a few minutes, to feel like a family, and I knew that he felt it too.

"We obviously weren't meant to be together," he said sadly. "Or these little ones would never have been born."

We turned and stared at each other and for an instant all the other people in the park disappeared and we were locked in our own private moment. I couldn't feel my body, I was outside it now and so was he. I felt as if our spirits embraced way above the ground, touching the top of the beautiful autumnal trees and came back to earth together, hovering before landing with a thud. I closed my eyes for what felt like an hour and when I opened them he had his phone in his hand.

"Please, Karen, will you give me your number? I'd really like to see you again before I go back."

I looked over at my boys and back at the man I'd loved before anyone else. I could do the right thing for them or the right thing for myself. The number rolled off my tongue.

* * *

I was shaking when I got back to the house after the walk. Poor Karl, who is the most sensitive of my boys, knew that there was something wrong with me from the moment I pulled over after seeing Greg.

Greg O'Sullivan. I had just walked through St Anne's on a glorious colourful day with Greg O'Sullivan and his children and my children.

Raquel was humming in the kitchen and I never felt so relieved to hear her.

"Karen, are you all right?" she asked as I pushed my way into the kitchen with the baby.

"Could you please put some Dettol on Karl's knee and then take the boys for me. I know it's your day off but I'm not feeling too great. I just need a short rest."

"Of course." She took Nathan from me and I poured myself a glass of water and went up to our bedroom.

I threw myself on the bed and felt the pain in the pit of my stomach radiate through my body until it peaked in my throat and I let out a primal scream.

Poor Raquel came running up the stairs and peeked her head in the door.

"Karen, are you all right?"

"Yes, thank you, Raquel – sorry – just a stomach ache." How could I explain to her or anybody how I felt?

When she shut the door tight on leaving I put my head into my pillow and sobbed louder and harder than I had ever done in my life. All the grief I had hidden after my break-up from Alan – all those years spent watching Greg with Orla as they walked through the gates of Trinity College – all those emotions burst out and I wasn't sure if they would ever stop. My head and ears and nose filled up with tears that seemed to have been hidden in the very depths of me. I thought that I was going to burst. I was an empty vessel – depleted beyond anything I had felt before. My pregnancies – my heartfelt emotions – the death of Tim's father – all were nothing compared to this pain. Why was I feeling this now? How could a short stroll through the park inflict such deep and dark emotions? I wasn't happy or sad – I was brought back to my young raw self and I couldn't see my world through the cloud of tears that flooded my eyes.

I didn't even have the energy to speak to Linda about it. There was no way that she would understand. Her children were everything to her – there was nothing else. She even called her husband 'Daddy' and he loved it. I was sixteen again and suddenly I felt very old.

Part 5

Cambrils
12-10-2004

Hi Karen

It was great seeing you.
I don't have your address so I'm
writing to your mother's. I wanted
to say how great it was to see you
in Dublin.

Miss you, Greg ☺

p.s. I know you like postcards –
hope you like the picture on this one

Karen Forde

21 Clontarf Close

Clontarf

Dublin 3

Chapter 33

Greg

October 2004

It felt silly sending her a postcard but it was what I had always done. It felt right to send it to her mother's because I felt thrown back to another time and place after meeting her this time and wasn't sure where we fitted into each other's lives any more. I trusted that Monica would see that she got it – after meddling in our lives all those years ago when Karen was dating Alan, she'd promised me that she would never do that again. She had risen to the occasion after our last dramatic meeting when I had just married Isabella.

I wanted to give Karen something tangible from me. Texting is too impersonal and you can't express emotions with an SMS. Sometimes texts are difficult to interpret and I don't know whether the sender is joking or angry. I've had difficulty responding to her last two texts. I don't want to be deceitful to Isabella but she knows me so well I wonder if she suspects that something is wrong with me. I shouldn't be a fumbling idiot at this stage of my life. I'm almost forty for Christ's sake, with two children and a life as far removed from Dublin as it could ever be. But Dublin is all that I can think about at the moment. The timing couldn't be worse. Isabella and I have to struggle to do even the smallest things together and she is always good-humoured despite the agony she must feel inside her crippled body. Why the fuck did it happen to us? We were happy and she had worked so hard to get the vineyard working productively. I suppose we wouldn't have the money to start our new life in Spain if she hadn't sold the vineyard. After her father died and she was diagnosed with Parkinson's our entire world changed. We had to make some serious life decisions.

I can't help wondering what my life would be like if Karen and I had got together that time in my parents' house. I know that I made the right choice because I had my daughters and I wouldn't change that part of my life. But what if I had given Karen and me that bit more time before I launched off on that round-the-world trip? I was selfish and pigheaded back then.

Now it's so difficult to even make love. Isabella often loses control of her movements with the trembling and I long to hold her like I did back in New York all those years ago when we made Gina.

Fuck! I say this to myself a lot. I'm angry with God even though I know he doesn't exist and I'm angrier with myself. Isabella doesn't deserve to have a husband thinking of another woman this way. And the thoughts I've been having are X-rated.

We should have got *it* out of our systems years ago but instead she's always going to be on that bloody pedestal.

I thought I was going to have a heart attack when I saw her that day in St Anne's with her three small boys. I got the shock of my life. The strange thing is I knew that I was going to see her. The minute we got into my father's car to drive to St Anne's I felt she would be there. When she told me that she had lived in Boston it was like I already knew. I had picked the old sweat-top out from a pile of dad's clothes that he used when doing the garden. My gut told me that it was what I was meant to wear that day.

But I had to stop hypothesising and putting explanations to the reason things have turned out the way they have. I had to forget what might have been.

I went back to my parents' house that day and tried my best

to be all chat with the girls but Gina noticed that something was wrong with me.

"Daddy, who was that woman?" she asked.

"She was somebody that I used to know when I was a few years older than you are now." I don't know what sort of an answer that was supposed to be but I could barely put a sentence together after the bizarre experience that I had just had in the park. My whole body had been lifted into a crazy void like I was in a living computer game. It's difficult to describe but it was like time had stood still and I was neither in the past, present or future but somewhere that all three existed at once. I know it sounds like the wacky sort of thing Karen would come up with but, then, I was with her. For eight years I had locked a part of me away into a box somewhere that I never allowed myself to go. I had found a part of me that hadn't existed before too – the feelings that I had for my girls was beyond any caring emotion that I thought I was capable of feeling.

So, two days after our family reunion and my brother's wedding, I couldn't wait any longer – I had to see her. I rang her while she was at a service station filling her car with petrol. It made me laugh to think of how much technology had changed our lives. Everyone is available so immediately nowadays. Sometimes I long for the past and the simple way we communicated when we were kids. But it was helpful for now because Thursday was the only opportunity that I had to meet her as Isabella was taking a trip into town with my mother and the girls.

Karen sounded flustered when she heard my voice. I wondered if she had doubted whether I would call or not.

"Thursday is okay for me," she said. "I can come out your way if you like?"

"I don't mind – whatever suits you best?"

We decided on Howth pier – the East Pier.

* * *

253

I parked my car and waited by the large red gate that stopped traffic from going down to the lighthouse. She appeared out of nowhere like a vision in denim jeans; I couldn't wait to see her rear – some things never changed. I was nervous – and felt in a funny kind of way like the previous eight years had never happened. I could see in her face that childbirth and the years hadn't taken that sparkle away from her eyes.

"Hiya," she smiled.

I melted. I was seventeen again – I was fumbling and goofy and this was one of our first dates. I didn't kiss her – I hated to think how I'd react if my lips touched any part of her skin. That teenage lust was running through my veins and it felt great.

"You got such fine weather for the wedding. It must have been lovely."

Ah yes, we were back in Ireland where everyone talks about the weather at the beginning of a conversation. I went along with it.

"Ha – it went well considering my father behaved disgracefully. You'd love Simon's bride – she's a feminist and always putting it up to Dad."

"It must be difficult for men of that age to see the changes in this country."

I wondered how she felt about them. "And it most certainly has changed a lot even since the last time I was here – everything has speeded up and got more expensive."

"If you mention house prices I will scream – it is just ridiculous. People call property the new porn – you won't be able to have an evening out without someone telling you how much their house is now worth."

I laughed. Karen hadn't changed – unlike so many others whose heads had been inflated by the property boom. Stephen had agreed to see me but lives in a mansion in Killiney now and, although it's huge, I wonder sometimes how his head gets in the door. I'm not jealous – it's just Ireland has changed at such a pace that I wonder if it is capable of catching up on itself.

"So all this property porn isn't for you?"

She shook her head crossly and looked sexy. "We needed to change – the church needed to stop having the influence and hold that it had – but there is a whole new set of values now and I wonder how long we can sustain the bullshit."

"Karen, you are sounding like a revolutionary," I teased. "It's great to hear you back to yourself."

"I did lose myself for a while, didn't I?"

I nodded. "I was worried about you when you were married to Alan – I hope you don't mind me saying it but it was like he kept you down."

"That is possibly the understatement of the year. After a year of therapy in Boston I am now finally able to accept what I lived with and move on from that chapter in my life."

"Therapy – that sounds heavy. Do you want to talk about it?"

"I suppose I should come clean and fill you in – Alan was a bully – physically and mentally abusive. I was in a mess when I saw you again that time in the Summit and I realised that I had lost myself. I guess that's why I made some bad decisions."

My heart ached for her and I wanted to hold her.

"Karen, that's really bad – when did it start?"

"A while after you went back to France – that time we spoke in your parents'. You see, when you didn't answer my letter I did something foolish – I became pregnant. I wanted my marriage to work. I'd lost you."

"What happened to the baby?"

"I miscarried but then Alan flipped and the abuse became physical. He had been having that affair all along."

"That bastard – and where is he now?" If he'd been in front of me I'd probably thump him. And to think she had been pregnant – why hadn't she told me this before?

"Riding high on the ass of the Celtic Tiger and screwing all his clients no doubt with extortionate fees. Last I heard he'd split from Niamh and has an even younger model."

"You must have felt vindicated when he did that."

"No, I felt bad for her – she has a child on her own now and no money can compensate for having to stay associated with that bastard for the rest of her life." She gave a little laugh. "No, I was the lucky one that got away and I have you to thank for that."

"Me?" I was surprised.

"Yeah, you helped me to see that I wasn't being true to myself – you gently pushed me back into my own skin whether you realised it or not."

"Hey, I was a fumbling mess back then – remember? Running off around the world without responsibility. I guess we have helped each other get to where we are now."

I knew what she was getting at but wondered if there wasn't a bigger plan that we didn't know about lurking in both our destinies. I'd become philosophical about a lot of things since Isabella's diagnosis.

"I still haven't found my voice though. I'm back writing in a newspaper but it's all so boastful and affluent – we are more American than the Americans and more European than the Europeans. Yet you won't find an Irish person to serve you in a shop, bar or restaurant."

Now that she mentioned it I had noticed that the shops and bars employed mostly Eastern Europeans. Even half the posters at the bloody airport were in Polish.

"So you don't altogether like this new Ireland?" I asked.

"It's good to see everyone doing so well but I can't help thinking that we are all going around with these plastic smiles saying how fantastic everything is, all having a great time, but . . . something is missing."

I understood what she was saying. It was glaringly obvious to me but I was coming from another country – she was the first person who was still living in Ireland who was articulating what I felt about the changes in my old home.

Treading the harbour walk on this sunny autumnal day I felt like we were in a vacuum, away from the world that the rest of the walkers inhabited. The seagulls cried over our heads and the gentle lap of the tide could be heard over the clanging halliards of the yachts in the marina. This was the old Karen that I had loved amongst the heather and gorse on the other side of the hill but she spoke with a new and mature voice and I still loved her.

"You've become very wise, Karen."

"And pedantic and probably boring . . . now tell me about you. How is life in Spain?"

"Hot. Sunny and much more laid-back than here. We had a difficult couple of years after selling the vineyard and relocating to Spain – we live in a town south of Barcelona called Cambrils."

"Why did you sell it?"

I dreaded telling her about my life. I was surprised that she hadn't heard from Stephen but then, on the other hand, he was so up himself it had obviously not been a priority for him to tell her.

"I'm surprised Stephen didn't tell you – have you spoken to him lately?"

"I bumped into him three years ago in town and we said that we would meet up but of course we never did – people are so busy chasing their tails in this country I really wonder what the hell they are doing half the time – making work for themselves."

Wow, she was feisty but it was good to hear – it was great to see her in such good shape. It was a credit to how well she must be getting on with her husband.

"The reason I'm asking is because I told Stephen four years ago about our problem – you see, Isabella has Parkinson's."

Karen's face dropped. We stood on the pier just looking at each other and I could tell that she couldn't find the words.

"It's okay – she's doing well – she can walk and talk and do everything but the stress of the vineyard was too much for us and we needed to find a new venture – something that was more my thing so I could take the strain off her. We wanted to go to a sunnier climate before the girls became too settled – they now speak Spanish better than French."

"Oh, Greg – that must be so hard for you both."

"We're happy – we have our lovely girls and we have holiday apartments that we rent and they are doing well – we will be all right."

I wondered what was going through her head. Usually I could tell but not this time. She seemed to be thinking deeply but her thoughts were not for sharing with me.

We reached the end of the pier and came to the rail that surrounded the unmanned lighthouse. Without speaking we stood at the spot where we had walked as teenagers. It was where I had once carved our initials into the metal railings. GOS ❤3 KF. It was barely visible over the years of erosion and all the layers of fresh paint that had been applied. But it could still be made out.

We took a stroll up to the village. There was building going on everywhere. Dublin city had more cranes now than London had in the eighties.

We sat in a smart little café in the centre of the village called The Country Kitchen and ordered coffee.

"At least the coffee has improved since last time I was home," I commented.

"I suppose so. There are good things about living here but sometimes I wish we had stayed in Boston a bit longer."

"How long were you there?"

"Only a year – I got pregnant and of course couldn't get divorced because Alan and I weren't the statutory four years living apart. So, Tim and I moved back to a house that my dad insisted I bought with the money left over from my marriage and we've been there ever since. I got a column in the *Evening Herald* and for the last five years have been commenting on parenthood and children. Ironic, when I'm far from an expert on mothering. I have to consult Linda to check what to write about each week!"

"Now Linda being an expert on mothering is one thing I could never have predicted."

"Could we have guessed how we all would turn out? Have you heard from Frank and Jackie at all?"

I felt bad – we hadn't contacted them in at least four years. We hadn't bothered with Christmas cards since Isabella's diagnosis. Somehow they seemed irrelevant in our scheme of things.

"No, I haven't – have you?"

"Frank was home a while ago and we met for a coffee – he has got so thin and is super fit – he is running marathons all around the world. Jackie of course is busy being fabulous and designing dresses for the Grammys."

"I should have known. I'd love to go back to New York – maybe someday."

"Greg, you are sounding like an aul' fella! For Christ's sake, you are only forty!"

"Yeah, but there is something about being that age that is hard to accept."

"Believe me, it's worse for a woman – I sag in places I didn't know you could sag."

And then she smiled that beautiful smile at me and we hardly noticed the waitress putting our coffees on the table.

"So are you happy? You look happy." I knew I was prying but I wanted to know her again.

"I am – Tim is a good man and he's great with the boys – he's really into doing things with them and he's been great with babies – he gets up in the night with Nat now that he's teething. But other than that he's not into domestic duties and that's why we got Raquel to stay with us."

"Is she your au pair?"

"Yeah – actually she's Spanish."

I had to laugh. "Another coincidence?"

"She's been speaking to the older two in Spanish and they are picking it up. She speaks only Spanish to little Nat so he will probably have the accent."

"It's a great gift to have another language – I struggled with French and now I've had to start off from scratch with Spanish."

"I'm truly sorry to hear about Isabella. I have to say I'm still in shock – I didn't think you could get Parkinson's unless you were ancient, like the pope."

"It usually doesn't kick in until you're over fifty but, yes, you can get initial symptoms in your twenties. It's unfortunate for Isabella that she has it so young. She is on medication but there are side effects."

"And what is the prognosis at this stage?"

"Well, she can't get better but there is new technology being found all the time and we are hopeful that she can maintain her current degree of health for as long as possible."

I was grateful for her concern but really wanted this time to be for us – I had to live with the Parkinson's and I wanted to be selfish and indulge in the moment. "So what about you? Tell me more about your life . . . it's so great to see you."

She beamed at me with a knowing look that lifted my spirit. "Well, I think I've filled in the blanks – life is steady and good and I am where I'm meant to be."

"That's a good way to put it – I must be there too."

She nodded – licking the frothy milk from her top lip. "But somehow I feel like I've been living all this time with you in my life – I can't explain it."

"I know – I've thought about you so much and not just on your birthday – I have to admit I've tried to forget you at times because it is difficult to think about what I am missing."

She blushed at my remark. I was touching a chord in her.

"While we were walking through St Anne's Park I felt like we were in a different universe," she said. "Like both our lives had been different and we had got married and the kids were ours."

I felt that too. For some reason it made me feel sad in my soul.

"It was a good feeling, wasn't it?"

"Is that all that we are getting for this life?" she prodded and I felt awkward answering.

"Who knows what the future holds for either of us," I said, "but, one thing for sure, we might have thought that we had commitments and obstructions eight years ago but we certainly have them now."

She sighed into her cup – she was almost finished and I hadn't started my coffee.

"I wish I had the gift of time travel and then I could go back and give my sixteen-year-old self a good slap," she declared.

"Hey – I was the one that needed the slap – my foolish pride just couldn't cope with the thought of you kissing another guy. It was Pete just being a bloke and not your fault – I shouldn't have taken it out on you."

"I didn't help things going around kissing fellas every time I went out." Karen gave me that sad look that floored me.

"That didn't make it easy for me but I was the one needing my ego massaged and Orla knew just how to do that. I shouldn't have let her control me."

"We can't beat ourselves up about our past – look at what we have – our lovely kids."

"So you probably wouldn't change a thing – would you?"

"Oh – I might have been better off missing out on the whole Alan experience but it's part of who I am and I feel that I'm a stronger person for it. But I wouldn't change my family, no." Then she smiled and said, "I do wish I'd had more time with you."

"We had golden moments over the years, Karen – maybe that is all that we were meant to have – if we were caught up in the day-to-day hassle of living together I wouldn't have you on that pedestal and you would see me for the difficult and annoying bastard that I am."

There it was – my melancholy coming out – and true to form she smiled cheerily at me.

"Greg O'Sullivan, you are most annoying sometimes – and I do understand what you're saying." She looked almost pixie-like as she sipped the last drop from her cup of coffee.

"Will you have another?"

"Why not? We aren't going anywhere."

"We can have some food if you're hungry?"

"No, thanks, another coffee will be fine."

I'm not sure how long we spent philosophising in that little café but I was on a plateau that I hadn't ever experienced before. Maturity mixed with teenage infatuation is a head-wrecking cocktail.

"Will I be able to see you again before you return to Spain?"

"I'm not sure – I don't know from one day to the next how Isabella is going to be – she gets depressed with the medication. I'm feeling guilty for having such a good time with you."

She put her hand across the table and rested it on top of mine, sending shivers up my arm.

"I am and have always been here for you."

I nodded – I knew. "I had a feeling that you would be okay over the past few years – we are so connected that I'm sure I would have felt it if there was something wrong. It wasn't easy because I was heading into a marriage that I was unsure about and I hankered for you for longer than I want to admit."

She blushed. "I found it difficult to listen to people sympathise about my marriage break-up when I was missing you – not Alan. But it's good that we're both okay and we have our beautiful children, which is our priority now."

"And for the rest of our lives more than likely. I wonder is there ever going to be a time when we stop worrying about our kids?"

"I'm not sure – my dad still worries about me – although not so much since I married Tim – he loves him."

"That's good – you're lucky that you get on so well with your parents."

"And how are you with your dad now?"

"Still much the same but he doesn't *get* to me any more. As I think I told you last time, my mother has been off the booze but on tranquilisers for years, so I really hope that her health doesn't give at some stage."

"How short life is!" she said.

I wholeheartedly agreed.

Chapter 34

November 2004

I was fixing a light switch in one of our properties when my phone rang. I knew instantly without looking at the number that it was her. I'd been thinking about her all morning; I'd been doing quite a bit of that.

"Greg, it's Karen – is this a bad time?"

"Karen – no, not at all – just doing a bit of maintenance. Good to hear from you."

"Thanks for the postcard."

"Ha, you're welcome – it's a picture of our apartments – Cambrils is a beautiful town."

"Yes, it looks very pretty – I looked it up on a map. You're quite near Barcelona."

"Yes, about an hour's drive."

"What's the temperature?"

"Today it's about 23 degrees. Warmer than usual for this time of year."

"Oh, I'm so jealous – it's freezing in Dublin – probably about 8 degrees."

"Yeah, but it can get up to the high thirties in July."

"Don't rub it in," she laughed. "I was thinking of taking the older boys and Tim to see a Barcelona game after Christmas but don't know how to go about it and I was wondering if you would?"

"I'm the worst person in the world to ask about football – you know me, it was never my sport. I used to pretend to support Manchester United when talking to your dad. But leave it with me and I'll see what I can do. Do you have an email?"

"Yes, I'll text it to you – that would be cool. But I'm sure you've guessed that's only my excuse to ring you."

"You don't need an excuse, Karen – I'm always at the end of the phone if you ever want to speak to me."

Here I was offering my friendship and I couldn't honestly say that I was capable of staying true to my word. I was confused and generally in bad form since seeing Karen again. Instead of it helping me with Isabella, I was feeling resentful and I was angry with myself for having these feelings.

"Greg . . ."

Yes, I know, no need to say it – in fact, it would be easier if you don't, I thought. I pleaded with all my heart for her to hang up and leave me with my guilt.

"Thanks, Greg. It's just good to hear your voice."

"For me too. I will email – I have to go here – there are workmen coming in to paint the apartment."

"Bye."

And when she was gone I went over to the chair in the corner of the room and sat on it and put my head in my hands. An awful pain pounded in my head and I hated myself for it. Why were these stupid juvenile emotions swallowing me up?

* * *

I went through the market on the way home to pick up some vegetables and bread for dinner. There had been a lot of development along the strip but Cambrils still managed to maintain its strong Catalan heritage. I'd have loved to bring Karen over here and visit Reus and the mountains – she'd be fascinated with the stories of the Spanish Civil War. My mind had really opened up since living in Spain – it was completely different to France. Or maybe I felt more at home here because it wasn't Isabella's home. Her mother died when she was a teenager and she had no brothers or sisters so she was happy to move to a new place after her father died – a fresh start where she wasn't known as the beautiful athletic woman that is no longer there. I sometimes wished I was the one who had got the disease because it was so difficult to help her to see the bright side. It was when I was at my most melancholy that Karen always knew to cheer me up – Isabella was different. Even though she was only forty she acted much older than her years. But she was always that way – a bundle of sensibility. I was the rebellious one, selfishly searching for myself, while she was already a wise woman.

I drove an old Merc that we brought down from Bordeaux. It did the job and the girls were able to walk to school which was really helpful for Isabella. She had been advised against driving at all now. So she shuffled her way to meet the girls some days when I didn't collect them. We were fortunate that we had money and had invested in the properties which would give us the income that we needed to go on and educate the girls.

There was no room for ambition or drive in my life and when I should have been at the peak of my career I felt like I was a failure.

I did meet up with Stephen on my last day in Dublin and that was a mistake – I didn't think we would be seeing each other again for a long time. I never thought money would change him. He was married to the most annoying woman I had ever met in my life. She was very beautiful but when she spoke I was disappointed by how cruel and thoughtless she was. And as for the way they treat the people that mind their kids and keep their house for them! Well, I was disgusted that I was friends with those silly people. I wondered what his father would think of his showy son – how easily Stephen had forgotten where he came from and the values that used to make him sound.

But I had to be careful that I wasn't jealous of him – I was definitely not jealous of his trophy wife, but I wouldn't have minded a slice of his fortune and position. I did get a smug sense of satisfaction from the thought that he probably didn't get a ride from the witch more than once a year. She looked like the type that would make her husband beg.

Then I thought of my lovely Isabella and what a great sex life we used to have.

She was sitting on the couch reading a book when I got home – we were living in a medium-sized villa close to the beach – and as always I was glad to see her. I felt guilty for speaking to Karen earlier and feeling the way I did when I listened to her voice.

"*Bonjour, amour!*"

She always calls me '*amour*'.

"I got some veg for dinner."

"*Ah, merci.*"

"Where are the girls?"

"Today they are swimming in school."

Wednesday – yes, how did I forget?

"Do I need to collect them?"

"No, Rosario will bring them home."

I put the vegetables on the kitchen table and sat down beside her on the couch.

"I had a call from a friend in Dublin today who is wondering about tickets for Barcelona football club. Who would know about getting them?"

"Carlos – Rosario's husband – he is football crazy."

"Of course – I'll ask her when she drops the kids off."

"And how is Dublin?"

"Rainy and miserable, I'm sure."

"Yes, but you have been sad since our last visit, *amour*."

I wanted to put my arm around my wife and hold her to me but I was confused and trembling inside.

"Do you wish you could live there?" she asked.

266

I had no great love for my hometown but Isabella was right – I was disconnected from her since my return. I hated the feelings I was having and the constant thoughts of Karen.

I felt like I was cheating on her and my girls.

"Nah – we are happy in Spain – the cost of living is too high over there. I'm glad we moved here."

And as I spoke her hands shook more than usual and I leaned forward and hugged her as tightly as her body would allow. I wanted to cry and I didn't know why.

Chapter 35

March 2005

Karen began to email me after we spoke in November. I deleted her mails after I'd read them a couple of times – it wasn't that there was anything in them that would hurt Isabella but I didn't want her to find them. There were times when I expressed my feelings to Karen in a way that I couldn't to my wife. It was my fortieth birthday last week and she texted me while I was out in a restaurant with Isabella and the girls. I was certain that Isabella sensed my reaction after reading it. Why did life have to be so hard?

And now Karen was coming to Barcelona next Friday with her husband and two of her sons and she wanted to meet me and I was scared. You would think I was having an affair – there is no fool like an old fool.

But I would think up an excuse to be in Barcelona on Saturday and meet her. The match was starting at five o'clock so we would meet at about four while her husband and sons were in Camp Nou. Was I being deceitful? The fact that I was asking myself this meant that I must be. It would have been different if Isabella wasn't suffering with Parkinson's. In truth, I felt like a bollox. But I had to see Karen – we only got a snippet of each other's lives and, since we had been in contact for the last six months with phone calls and emails, I was realising how much I missed her.

* * *

The traffic along the motorway into Barcelona was always frantic but especially when there was a match in Camp Nou so I took a right to miss the Avinguda Diagonal and made my way down towards the port to La Rambla. She was staying in a hotel at Plaça Catalunya so I asked her to walk down La Rambla and meet me in a well-known tourist café called Café de l'Opera. It was a quirky little place and I felt I'd like to take photos in there some day. I'd started to think about photography again since moving to Spain – there was such stunning architecture there, especially in Barcelona. I was not a huge Gaudí fan but you have to give the guy respect. He produced an incredible amount of work and it was ground-breaking when you realise that he inspired the art-nouveau style. There were parts of Park Guell that were so mind-blowing I could stay and snap away for hours.

I would have loved to take Karen there but she was clear that we only had three hours – maybe less. There was so much that I wanted to do with Karen but I'd have needed a lifetime and we didn't have that so I would be content with these three hours.

I could literally feel my heart pound in my chest as I approached the little café. It was kind of touristy on the outside but I knew that she would love the décor. The walls were lined with green-painted panels and all the details and lighting around the bar were authentic art nouveau. It was packed but I figured we would get a table at this time because the locals ate late and the tourists would be looking for more than tapas at this time.

I took a free table in the window – perfect timing. Unlike the way the rest of our lives had been up to now. I checked my phone for messages but there were none – I wondered again what we did without these bloody things. The anticipation was just as bad as when I was a kid waiting for a birthday or Christmas. Ridiculous. But then through the window I saw her silhouette at the door and I couldn't describe the feelings I had for this woman.

She spotted me instantly and came over to the table. I got up of course and we hugged awkwardly before sitting down at our little round table.

"So you found it okay?"

"Yes, sure it's impossible to miss. I love it – what a great suggestion!"

"It's really a tourist haunt but the atmosphere's great – it's very old – was open all through the civil war."

She laughed out loud.

"What's so funny?"

"You quoting the Spanish Civil War – dear lord, when you think of all that schooling we had – how much of it was wasted!"

"There's no better teacher than travel."

"I'll agree with you there – but you've had my share too. Maybe someday I will get to travel but probably not until the kids are a lot older."

And then we looked at each other and that was one of the moments that I held tight, deep inside me to charge my soul for all the time that we would spend apart.

"What happened to time?" I asked.

She shook her head. "I don't know where it's gone – it's running out – that's for sure."

"Does everyone feel this old at forty?"

She shrugged and I wanted to grab her there and then.

The waiter took our order of *chocolate* and *churros*.

"You have to try this before you go home," I said. "I think you'll like it."

"I had no idea there was so much to see in Barcelona – we took a bus tour this morning and the city is huge."

"How do your boys like it?"

271

"They were so excited to be on a bus – terrible reflection on modern Ireland when kids don't get to go on public transport."

"We never minded the bus."

Then she gave that knowing grin and we were off again to 1982.

"When you think of it – we hadn't even the DART in those days."

The waiter put two cups on the table and a plate of *churros*, which were delicious local doughnuts.

I nodded at Karen. "Go ahead."

"What do I do?" she asked.

"Dip your doughnut in the chocolate and slurp it up."

She looked so funny doing it. I laughed and joined her.

It all felt so natural and good. I wanted this to be my Groundhog Day and live it over and over with Karen but as each second passed I realised we couldn't go on staying in touch. Well, at least I couldn't.

"Can we go and see more of the Rambla – would you believe this is my first time walking down it?" Karen sounded giddy like a little girl and I realised I would do anything for her.

"Sure," I said. "I'll get the bill."

I took out a fifty-euro note and waved it at the waiter – not sure why I felt the need to be flash or ostentatious – I just did. He had the change in his wallet and I handed him a generous tip.

"Ready?" I asked and when she stood up beside me I could feel my heart pound again.

The sun was lower in the sky now, which meant La Rambla would start to come to life soon. Already, a troupe of tango dancers had started their routine. They were dancing to the music from a beat box but dressed in full costume. The passion in their movements struck a chord for Karen – her eyes were bulging with excitement and I wanted to hug her.

"Wow, look at how they move! I wish I could do that. There are so many street artists on La Rambla they nearly outnumber the pedestrians."

"Straight from Argentina, I bet – this is a really cosmopolitan city."

"Oh Argentina! There's so much of the world that I haven't seen . . . and I'll probably never get very far now."

"Do you ever wonder about life? What might have been if you had travelled more or done other things?"

"Don't go there, Greg. Not today. I'm having a lovely time. You've no idea how much I've been looking forward to these few hours."

"And you think I haven't? Jesus, Karen – since I saw you in Dublin it's been impossible to think of much else."

She stopped walking and turned to me and looked up into my eyes.

"For me too. I'm feeling so bad and yet it's so good just being around you again. Knowing that I can ring you means so much." She paused, looking troubled. "I'm not sure how I'm going to be when I get back to the hotel and Tim and the boys are there waiting to hear about how I got on without them."

"Did you tell them that you were meeting me?"

She shook her head and I wasn't surprised – I hadn't told Isabella the truth either.

"And what if I hurt Tim? It's better just to hurt myself."

"When does this stop, Karen?" I didn't want to ruin our time but there wasn't going to be a good time to have this conversation. It didn't look like we were going to be getting a room to pass our time together. God knows I'd thought about it – I'd imagined it all the night before. Making love to her for three solid hours – but already one had passed.

"I don't know," she said and we started to walk again.

This time we strolled off La Rambla and into the Plaça Reial where there were some nice restaurants and bars. There was also a small hotel in the corner and I wondered if there were rooms available.

I was shaking inside as I spoke.

"Do you fancy stopping here for a drink? Or something?"

273

She stopped again. "Or something?"

"Karen, I know this is probably a big mistake and I hadn't planned on it but we only have a couple of hours left . . ."

"Are you saying what I think you're saying?"

My legs felt like jelly but I had to go for it.

She looked at her watch. "It's six o'clock."

"Two hours – that's all we have and I know where I'd like to spend them."

I was getting braver now and she responded by taking my hand. She reached up to my ear with her lips.

"Yes, now."

We didn't talk as I steered us towards the hotel on the corner – it was a little three-star but I didn't think we would notice our surroundings.

* * *

Karen

I was going to do this. I was going to be with Greg at last. I'd been trembling since we left the little café because I knew then that I wanted this but I still couldn't believe that we were actually going to do it. I wondered had he planned this all along? I had always hoped that this day would come but never in a million years would I have thought that it would be here in a square in Barcelona. I thought it was a good choice. The palm trees were enormous and buildings so beautiful. It was somewhere I would always be able to picture in my mind's eye when I needed to.

The foyer of the little three-star hotel was pretty bleak and I was sure the rooms wouldn't be luxurious but I didn't care. It was a match day and we would be lucky if there was a room available.

I stood back as Greg went up to reception and spoke in accented Spanish to the girl at the desk. I became painfully aware of the infidelity that I was about to commit and hoped that the girl didn't realise this.

I was so excited I could hardly stand. He returned with a big key hanging off a huge keyring.

"Don't want to change your mind?" he asked.

Not a chance! I just shook my head and we waited for the little lift to arrive. We were on the second floor and it was dark on the way to our room. I hadn't thought it would happen like this – all the times when we could have consummated our love and it was to be now in this strange place.

He rattled at the door and it opened to a bright room with shutters open over the hustle and bustle of the square. There was a large bed and a small dresser and nothing else in the room.

I switched on the light while he closed the shutters.

I was going to burst at any moment. And then he looked down at me as I was still wondering could I do this. He stroked the side of my face and planted a gentle peck on my lips.

Oh no – I hoped desperately that he wasn't having second thoughts.

He put on the small lamp above the headrest and knocked off the main light, giving me the space to ask him what I needed to.

"Do you feel bad – for Isabella?"

"Tim and Isabella have us the rest of the time. I'm forty – if not now, when?"

Then he gently took my face in his hands and looked deep inside me. Our connection was total – he had a part of me that no one else would ever have.

He was right – we had our opportunities in the past and missed them. I was trembling at his touch and felt like crying I was so overcome.

Then he put his lips on mine – more firmly this time and our mouths opened as we French-kissed like we used to in the Grove. It was more intense at this moment and we were more nervous than in those days when we didn't have responsibilities and spouses.

It felt familiar and yet new – he tasted the same – he smelt the same and yet this was so different.

He peeled my jacket off my shoulders and it dropped to the floor. Then his hands rambled along my shirt, nervously opening the buttons. I helped him along as he removed it to reveal the black lace bra that I had specially picked for the occasion. I couldn't wait, and opened it at the clasp as he undid the buttons on his own shirt.

I could smell him so strongly now – I was transported back to 1982 and his bedroom.

Then he picked me up and carefully lifted me onto the bed. It was a subtle gesture but meant so much – like our own mini matrimonial ceremony.

He curled his naked torso into my back and started kissing the nape of my neck. This was new. His hands caressed the line of my body as he ran his hand along my thigh, slipping under my skirt.

"Take it off," I begged him and he did – my underwear too. I was naked now and twisted myself around to face him. He was pushing his trousers down to reveal his naked body. It was unrecognisable in the same way as mine was, so different to the nubile toned figures we had in our teens – but it didn't matter.

Everything was slow and in complete synchronicity – even our breaths.

It didn't feel like any lovemaking that I had done before. This was unity. The build-up of years of love and soon it would be complete.

I was so full of desire for him to touch me between my legs I was afraid that I would burst.

He put his head between my breasts and started to kiss his way to my right nipple. My saggy breasts became a portal to more emotion than I could take.

I grabbed his hand and put it between my legs. His fingers were no longer familiar with my stretched and newly moulded entrance after the wear and tear of childbirth.

Our eyes were open and locked on each other all the time as he moved on top of me. I opened my legs to guide him in but he knew the way. He was going home.

I was lost now – couldn't think – no thoughts just feelings – incredible feelings that had been bottled up for decades. I was in the here and now and this was as real as I could be. I was whole as we moved together, coiled as one being. I felt and smelt colours as he erupted inside me and I was the happiest I had ever been. The most intense I had ever been. Even giving birth wasn't like this.

Satisfied, he cradled my head in his strong arm and we lay side by side in silence for a minute but it felt like an hour.

Then he turned his head and looked at me with love.

"I love you," I said because it felt like the only thing that could be said.

"I love you," he responded. "We will always have this."

Oh no – don't say this is it! Please don't say that we can't do this again!

"Greg, I don't think I can go on without you."

"You have to. We both have to." And the sorrowful way the words dribbled from his lips made me cry and we held each other tightly and stopped breathing.

I knew this would be the outcome before I came to Barcelona but I didn't want it to be the end.

"So can't we stay in touch?"

"It's too difficult for me, Karen – I know that I seem in good form when we speak but that is because I'm speaking to you. When you hang up I'm left with an emptiness that I can't hack and it isn't fair on my family."

I would have been lying if I said it was different for me. It hadn't been good for my relationship with my family either and I wasn't dealing with the same obstacles as Greg was.

"So after today, that's it?"

"I'm sorry – it's been wonderful having you in my life again but I can't do it to Isabella – she knows me too well. She could

277

never meet you or she would know how I feel about you and I don't want to hurt her. I know I'm selfish coming here but I had to have you, Karen – I couldn't give up so much without being with you this one time."

"That's how it felt for me – I was you while we made love."

"Maybe if there is reincarnation we will be together – I'll be holding out for it in the next life – but I'm glad we made love in this one."

"Sometimes I feel like I lived before and have spent all my other lives with you. If this is how it is without you then in our next life I want to go back to the way it was."

"I'll do my best – but we have now. We have one more hour and I need to love you again before we say goodbye."

I let him take me in his arms and his head buried itself in my breasts for one more time.

* * *

Greg

When I left her and returned along the motorway to Cambrils I felt like shit. I don't know how I was expecting to feel. I loved my wife, I loved my family and I was content with my life in Spain. But what had just happened was going to stay with me for the rest of my life. I would carry the guilt and never ever tell Isabella. What purpose would it serve to hurt her with the truth?

I would stay at her side for the rest of her life. Who knows, I might die before her – nobody knows how long they have.

But making love to Karen was amazing – I knew it would be. There was something about her every move that grabbed me and I was hers. God, I wished I could turn back time! But if I could, where would I go? How far back? I'd probably go back to O'Neill's pub and grab her hand that night when I got back from London. I wouldn't let that bastard take her away to dinner.

I'd save her from those years of torture with him and then I'd marry her and we would have . . . but it was only going to annoy me more if I daydreamed.

She seemed to realise that we couldn't be friends – it must have been too much pressure for her too. Somehow, though, I thought she handled her emotions better than I did – women are like that. I was all or nothing – I had to box off my feelings to cope and while we were still in touch with each other I couldn't do that. At least I had the memories of our two hours in that little hotel – they would keep me going when it got tough with Isabella's illness – as I knew it definitely would.

Chapter 36

Karen

April 2005

When I returned from Barcelona I was thrown immediately into the day-to-day manic activities that I called my life. But it was different. Everything was different because I had shared myself with my soul mate and I couldn't get it out of my head. That was what he called me as we left each other at the top of La Rambla.

I made it into the hotel only twenty minutes before Tim and the boys. I flicked on the TV and Barbra Streisand and Robert Redford were on it in the old movie *The Way We Were*. I understood that movie now. The song rang around my head as I showered and I cried as the infidelity and love were washed from my body. A part of me wanted to keep his scent on my skin – another part was sad that I had broken my vows to my husband who I loved and didn't deserve this. It would never happen again – and that thought made me cry even harder. At least I was able to blame my tears on the movie when the boys and their father returned.

They said that they had found a MacDonald's and that was just the place to cheer me up. I agreed and went with them out into the night and did everything I could for the rest of the weekend to show them how much I loved them all.

Back in Dublin I decided that I needed a new challenge and

something to inspire and stop me from thinking about Greg all the time. It was easier for him – he wasn't being reminded of me everywhere he went. He was in a faraway land and I was here with the park and the pier and all the places that were ours.

I wanted to do something for my boys that would make them laugh or give them pleasure. I contemplated decorating their bedrooms – but I was no interior designer. I could do a cooking course – my dinners were often bland and unimaginative but my boys liked their food simple and Tim wasn't fussy either. But I could bake and do something nice and it might make them interested in their mum's creations and in turn more imaginative with their eating.

My mind wandered and I started to dream of all the good things that I wished for the boys. I longed for them to have a happy life and wished that they would find love and keep it. I had been lucky to find it twice. Tim was a wonderful husband and the best father that anyone could ever be. I loved him deeply and it caused confusion in my head every time I thought about Greg. Tim and I were always very much individuals. We were one big happy family unit but Tim allowed me to be my own person and vice versa.

It pained me to think of my time in Barcelona – when I was with Greg there was just the two of us in the world and that was not good for conducting a normal healthy life. So I decided to try to finish the story of Greg and me. There had to be a reason why our universes were so intertwined – I just couldn't figure it all out.

The next ten years or so would be difficult for him and there was every chance that Isabella could live to be a very old age but with an unhealthy body that would limit her in her relationship, and Greg's life would be affected by her condition. I had to be understanding for his sake. He couldn't care for her and have me on the side. It would eventually lead to a mess that our consciences wouldn't allow.

So my first concern was to put a distraction in place that

would keep me focused – stop the memories and thoughts and dreams of what might have been. And try not to question why I didn't feel guilty.

* * *

"I just wish you had told me how it was between you in those days – I didn't really understand," Linda said.

"It's too late to rake up old feelings but I always realised that we had something special – I just didn't realise how special it was."

"Did you feel tempted to do anything?"

It was like she was reading my mind. I still couldn't admit to her what I had done.

"I had to think of Tim and I would be distraught if he had an affair with someone – in fact, I don't know how I'd be consoled," I said, evading a direct answer.

"I understand."

I nodded in agreement. Linda had become the most incredibly wise rock of sense, which was quite a surprise when she was the wild one of the pair of us in our youth.

"So how do I get over this?"

"I'm not sure that you ever will."

I feared that she was right. "I've taken up baking."

"That's good – anything to get your mind off him, I guess. But he must be under incredible stress and pressure if his wife has Parkinson's."

I closed my eyes and tried not to think about how awful it must be for her. I hoped and prayed that he was in a happy place with his lovely wife, despite her illness. It was simply not to be for us – the end of our story had been written and we had to carry on.

* * *

Bedtime was a job in itself but I liked to do it with Tim and save Raquel's help for the mornings. She went to the gym after dinner most nights.

Tim put Karl to bed with a story – he had grown so much he even brushed his teeth and washed his hands without prompting, which was remarkable for a seven-year-old.

After Nat had his last bottle of the evening I went into my bedroom with the booklet of night classes that was dropped through the letterbox a few days earlier and I started to search for courses or things that I could do and I found a local cake-baking course.

And then Karl crept into the room.

"Mum, can I have a huggy?" He tried so hard to be the big man with his brothers around but really he was my little baby – my first little baby.

I put the booklet on my bedside locker out of the way and he hopped up and on to the bed. I squeezed him tightly and he smelt of soap and I was filled with everything delicious that a mother can feel for her child.

"I love you more than Pod," he said, looking up at me with his father's brown eyes.

He couldn't sleep without his little teddy Pod. "I love you more than peaches," I said.

He laughed. "I love you more than the sky!"

"Good one!" I kissed him for that. "I love you more than daisies."

"I love you more than this house."

I could tell that he wanted a bigger response. "I love you more than chocolate."

"Cool – that's a lot because you really love chocolate."

I was pleased that he was happy.

"Mummy," he said and paused. "Tell me about a day that you spent before I was born when you were really happy – your best day ever."

I kissed him on the forehead and pulled him to me. The days

started to flood back in my memory – the walks on Dollymount beach – the old pond – Hyde Park – Howth Head . . . and they were all days that I had spent with Greg. It was the most thought-provoking question that I had ever been asked and it took a seven-year-old to make me see myself. All my happiest days were ones that I had spent with him and I wished I could make it stop. Because I loved my husband and I loved my family and I shouldn't be having these emotions at this stage in my life.

* * *

I baked hard – I baked every day. When the boys and Tim wouldn't eat what I baked I gave it away. I resorted to baking cakes for the children in my boys' classes and since they were becoming popular some mothers asked me to bake for special events. I was doing christenings and birthdays – within a few months I got to the stage where I found it difficult to find time to write my articles. I was bored with them and the paper was happy to let me go. All I wanted to write about was my baking.

Linda was pleased that I had found something new and she encouraged me – she knew how deeply I was affected by just seeing Greg again. Besides, she loved my cupcakes – even Dr Bill liked them. I had found something to distract me and it was productive and people liked me and my cakes. It didn't make me feel like I felt when I was with Greg but there was nothing in the world that made me feel that way except being with him so I just continued on baking. And the weeks and months passed and Greg didn't make contact but I kept baking.

Chapter 37

Greg

July 2010

Dad's death had been the making of Mum. She was a different woman. I didn't think she would stay in the big house in Sutton on her own, but she seemed content and had carved a busy life for herself with the other widows in the neighbourhood who went to the bridge club twice a week. I didn't often go back to Dublin because she was happy to jump on a flight to Malaga and visit us. I would rather not be in Dublin because when I was there I felt the urge to contact Karen.

But I was more mellow about my feelings for her – it was such a relief to finally make love to her that day in Barcelona. It was something that had to happen and now it was over I could get on with my life and accept my situation. The girls were getting that much bigger and I was like a single parent in many ways so it was tough . . . Isabella had remained stable on the drugs but her quality of life was so poor at times.

But I still had the memory of that afternoon in Barcelona.

Moving to Malaga had been good for Isabella and our family. My dad came out and stayed with us before he died but he thought my new business was another foolish pipe dream. I had accepted that I would never please him and at this stage in my life I didn't care. It was sad that he had to die without us resolving our differences but, as Isabella would say: *C'est la vie.*

I had to go to Dublin to help Mum sign for the probate and get all the paperwork out of the way. I hired a car for the journey from the airport – Mum wasn't so good on the motorways any more and usually only pottered around locally in the car.

And then I heard *her* on the radio. My heart stopped.

"Today we are very privileged to have Karen Forde with us in the studio – thank you for coming into see us today – I'm sure you have a hectic schedule."

"It's lovely to be here, Mary – thank you for having me."

"And I see that you have brought some of your cupcakes into the studio – there will be a row over who gets these, you know!"

They talked on and on but I couldn't concentrate on what they were saying. I heard words but they didn't make any sense – it was her voice, the tone, that struck me and I was wrapped in a time warp in the past.

"So where to from here? Your success has been immense and you have a TV series starting tonight, is that right?"

"Yes, Bake the Cake *starts tonight on RTÉ 2 at seven-thirty."*

"And your cupcakes are for sale in three franchised shops with two more opening up this year?"

"That's right, Mary – it has been hectic. Our first store in Cork will open in September and then our Galway shop will open in October."

"Well, it's great to hear a story like yours in these recessionary times. And thanks so much for the cupcakes."

I turned the radio off. My head was aching. She was a TV cook! How had that happened? I wondered why my mother hadn't told me about her success. My siblings were all living abroad so they might not have heard. I wished I'd stayed in touch with Stephen – I hadn't spoken to Frank in many years. We swapped Christmas cards but that was the limit of our correspondence. In truth it was probably my fault. I had been hiding Isabella away from people for the last six years – trying to protect her. Or maybe I'd just been trying to protect myself.

When I pulled into the drive of my mother's house in Offington I was stressed out. Karen still did this to my head. Or, rather, I was letting her into my head again. In truth, she had always been with me – since I let her into my heart over twenty years ago. *Karen Forde, I wish I didn't love you.*

My mother came out to meet me.

"Greg, darling – how was your flight?"

"Good, thanks, Mum – you're looking well."

She shoved my arm away playfully like a little girl and grinned from ear to ear. It was a relief to see her this way. I had found that living abroad, away from an elderly parent, meant that I was always waiting for that dreaded call that something has happened and it was difficult.

"Stop it now – oh, and you'll never guess who was just on the radio?"

"I heard her."

"Isn't that amazing – she's on the radio all the time and her recipes are in every newspaper and magazine that you open. Cupcakes she bakes and other stuff – they were fairy cakes in my day. I suppose if you give something a fancy name and dress it up that's how it becomes the latest thing."

I wondered how Karen went from the philosophical girl who worried about the world to a cupcake-maker. Maybe she felt that this was what the world needed at the moment. I couldn't figure it out and I'd be too scared to delve deeper into her life to find out more.

"So how are you, Mother?"

"I'm going to the Active Retirement later in the parish hall so I was hoping that you wouldn't mind? I'll be back to have dinner with you – I thought you would like a lie-down."

"Of course I don't mind. Let's go out to dinner when you get back."

What the hell was I going to do with my time? I didn't want to see anyone. I'd go into town – that was probably the best. I'd promised the girls that I would get them each a present.

289

* * *

I decided to take the DART – it had become impossible to park in Dublin and I hated driving around it even more than Malaga. Karen popped into my head again and I thought of her voice on the radio. Where did she say her shop was? Somewhere on Grafton Street?

The landscape hadn't changed much along the DART line until I got to Clontarf Road station. Then the development at East Wall became visible. The changes got more apparent as the train reached Butt Bridge. The buildings to my left weren't there ten years ago – apart from the Custom House of course – and I saw a new bridge that looked like a harp. I felt like a tourist. The cranes had left the skyline, leaving behind space for the sky and I felt nostalgic for the Dandelion market and the Diceman and nights spent in the Neptune Bar.

On my right was the Ha'penny Bridge and it made me think of that video of 'Old Town' by Phil Lynott that was shot there. That was the Dublin I remembered – girls with big hair and boys without tattoos. The loss of innocence and the passing of my parents' generation made me see Dublin without blinkers. I hankered for it – I hated it and I loved it all at the same time. I'd never move back here because I wouldn't want to be reminded of her constantly. So why was I really going into town when a walk on the Burrow Beach would probably have done me more good? I was on a mission to see her shop and I knew it.

Trinity was the same but clean – the air was less polluted and there was an order about my city that wasn't there when I left in the eighties. The lines and markings on the road were a new addition. Bike lanes, bus lanes, like in any modern European capital. I passed the Molly Malone statue – feeling anxious with each step – what was the name of the shop? I walked up and down and past Bewley's and the Westbury but couldn't see it anywhere. And then there she was, in two-dimensional full colour. Smiling and wearing a pinafore with pink roses printed on it. But all I could see was her smile. The poster had been photo-shopped but it was unmistakably Karen, on the inside of the window next to the display of cakes and buns. Her hair was shorter and she was wearing pearls. And I hoped that she hadn't turned into Martha Stewart. I didn't know what I expected to gain by coming here – it had been a bit of an information overload for one day. So I went into Brown Thomas and asked the girls at the counter what a thirteen and a fourteen-year-old girl would like from the cosmetics counter. They gift-wrapped some perfume and a set of make-up stuff and that was my job done.

I was tempted to take a peek in at the cake shop on my way back down the street but there was no point – she probably wouldn't be there. So instead I walked straight past Trinity and tried to forget the past.

* * *

The next morning I woke up sad and empty. I hadn't realised how much I had blocked thoughts of Karen out of my head for the last five years. The time had flashed by and years felt like months. I was forty-six.

I woke with a hard-on like I always do when I'm in Karen mode – like now. I was all right until I heard her voice – or maybe until I saw her picture. It made me a bit sad to see her packaged up in a pinny – not like the Karen I knew. I was not jealous of her success. Christ, I was pleased for her – as long as she was happy.

I took out my Blackberry and flicked through it – I didn't have her number any more – I had to delete it. But I had her email still and hoped that she hadn't changed it. What was I hoping to achieve by this? But before I realised it I'd typed up a message.

Hi Karen

It's me here – I heard your voice on the radio yesterday and wanted to tell you how great you sounded. You're a big star in Dublin now – I saw your shop too and it looked the business!

Take care

Greg X

I hit send and off it went. It was too late to stop it and I wondered what I'd done. Opened a can of worms more than likely?

She was so sad when I said goodbye to her that day in Barcelona. I couldn't stand to see her cry – but I was crying too. Like a fucking baby.

I hadn't cried since. I wondered if I ever would again. Even at my father's funeral I didn't feel the same terrible sense of loss. I got the horrible wake-up call and sense of mortality that strikes everyone when they lose a parent but I didn't feel empty – that was how I felt when Karen and I left each other that day and that's how I had probably felt since. I'd had good times – I was not being ungrateful for my beautiful wife and family but there was always something missing.

I checked my phone again, half hoping for a reply, but that was foolish. She was probably too busy with her TV show – I was glad I was out with my mother last night and couldn't watch it.

As I pulled myself out of bed I saw a text from Gina on my phone – she was a good kid. She was a better version of myself and I was so proud of her. Lisa was more like her mother. She had that subtle and stylish Frenchness about her. I truly was blessed to have my girls.

My mother knocked on the door. "Greg, are you ready? Ella has just been on the phone and she's waiting for us at the hotel."

Ella was coming with me and mum to the solicitors and she

had become so like Dad we didn't really get on any more. Of all the people! She was the *rebel*. And yet she was now the most conservative in our family. She was in the process of moving back from the States where she had been for the last seven years. Her husband was American and a bit odd – a computer whiz. I thought he must be half machine to be able to tolerate her. It was a shame they wouldn't stay with Mum while they were in Dublin – the house was big enough. But Todd needed to have access to a swimming pool at all times and that was why they were staying at the hotel. They were looking for a house close by for when they move. Ella had done remarkably well in her career and she had a little girl when she hit forty. Now, she wanted her educated in Ireland – hence the big move. She was upset that the girls' schools don't have nuns in them any longer. It never ceases to amaze me the way things work out and the way people change. Ella of all people, I thought, would be the most liberal.

I looked at my watch. It was already a quarter to eleven. I had to stay focused on the job at hand. My mother was my concern now.

We sat into the car and I turned on the radio. The advert was a jingle for cupcakes.

Chapter 38

Karen

August 2010

It had hit me like a slap on the face and I'd been pondering over the bloody email for four weeks now but I still didn't know how to reply. I could just send a couple of lines saying lovely to hear from you and hope the family are well. That was probably the best thing to do. But there wasn't a right way to answer.

My life had changed quite dramatically since we met in Barcelona. I was fortunate to be in the position that I was in now. I never expected that I would turn into a cook – with my own TV show! I knew it seemed crazy but I did put the change down to that trip to Barcelona. I really didn't think that I would be doing any of this if I had kept in touch with Greg.

I realised that my new career had taken me away from the boys a lot of the time but Tim was so supportive and proud of me and we had Amelia to keep house and to help. I never could have imagined how my life would turn out. The new house was wonderful – I was glad we waited until that year to move – house prices had really gone crazy and now we have our perfect home.

I was so lucky with my life. So I should have been able to answer Greg. But when I thought of him I felt disturbed and I shouldn't have – what happened in Barcelona was inevitable – it had to happen. I wanted it probably even more than he did. It had been such an overwhelming experience and I thought I could handle it but I couldn't. To block him out was the only way I could carry on with my life – and I had to admit to myself how much I missed him.

But if I answered this email it would not be the end of our story. I would be opening up old wounds and, worse than that, I would be opening up my heart. I could only think of him with a passion that transported me to another time and place.

So I went up to the attic and found the box that I had discreetly packed away in a corner of the purpose-built wardrobes. I was living in my dream home – everything had a place and the safest place for this box was in the farthest out-of-reach spot in the house. But as I opened the small green wooden box where I had stored my most precious mementos I started to shake. There they were – the postcards that he had sent me over the years. And never a letter – I would have loved a letter. But I had the photographs too. I ran my finger over the copy that he had given me from our time at the Baily lighthouse. I hardly recognised myself. I wished that I could reach out and tell my young self everything that I knew. We looked so good together – we always did – and if we were to stand beside each other now I am sure that we would still.

But everything had turned out all right – hadn't it? I did wonder how he was – I hoped that his wife wasn't suffering. His little daughters were so beautiful. I remembered when I saw them that day in the park and I wondered how they looked now.

Karl was growing out of his skin. Somehow that thought made me concerned. I still thought of my son as a child and not capable of the deep emotions and attachments that I had felt back when I was a teenager myself. When I was with Greg we seemed so old – we really thought that we knew it all. Already Karl was breaking out from his childish ways and asserting his own opinions and preferences, and I should probably pay more attention to his needs.

There were times when it was difficult to juggle all the balls in the air. The cookbooks and show were one thing but the day-to-day demands of being a mother to three young boys was quite another. My days were full and I was a lucky woman to have so much fulfilment in my life.

But when it came to Greg I was stumped. I really didn't know where I was or who I was or even what year it was.

Did I want to go back to that place? I was in such a different space in my head now. A part of me was angry that he hadn't kept in touch but I'd got over that. I had to be empathetic and think about all that he was going through or would have to go through with Isabella.

In the end I decided not to reply. There was nothing to be gained by it. We could continue our lives and our paths would never need to cross ever again. It would probably be for the best.

Part 6

Hi Mum

Here is the postcard as promised.
I am having a brill time.
There's a nice girl in the school.
The weather is hot but the school
is cool and there's air-con
in the house where I am staying.

Say hi to Dad and Oscar and Nat.

Love
Karl ☺

Benalmádena
25-06-2012

-Karen Forde

-6 Seafield Lane

-Clontarf

-Dublin 3

Chapter 39

Karl

Benalmádena, Spain, June 2012

I put the postcard in the yellow postbox – at first I thought it was a bin because I was looking for a green letter box. I'd been to Spain before with Mum and Dad when we went to Barcelona. That was amazing – I don't remember it very well because I was only seven but I'll never forget the noise in Nou Camp when the players ran out on to the pitch. We didn't have Nat with us either because he was too little. I don't really remember much else.

Oh and I remember Mum crying – she was crying really bad when we got back from the game. She was probably scared on her own. She isn't like that any more.

My mum could be such a pain sometimes and she's always going off to places around the country by herself. Dad doesn't seem to mind. I think he secretly likes it when she has to go off and do her demonstrations. Amelia cooks better food as well when Mum's away – she does amazing pizzas that she makes herself. Everyone in school thinks I must have the best dinners but Mum isn't really a cook – she even says it herself.

I can't stand cupcakes – they are for girls. Dad always says that it is *her thing* and she needs to have a girlie thing to do. True, our house is always full of sports stuff and that isn't her thing. But Mum doesn't have to do as much as other mums because we have Amelia. Sometimes I wish she didn't work but then it is cool when she gets free tickets to things like movies and concerts and she knows famous people so that is okay.

Shane and David are on this trip with me and I thought I'd be sharing with them but instead I got stuck with Alex. He's such a weirdo! But at least our house is near the other guys. All of our houses are on the same street and near the beach a bit outside Benalmádena. The town is crazy busy at night but we have to stay close to the school. Sometimes they organise things for us to do and that's cool.

There's this girl who helps out at the school – her dad owns it and she has brilliant English. When she speaks you'd think she was from Dublin. She doesn't look like she's from Dublin though. She isn't tall, has blonde hair and blue eyes and looks kind of Swedish. She smiled at me one day when we came out of class. She's about my age – maybe a bit older – but she's not like the girls in school in Dublin. She doesn't wear make-up like the girls in our school and her hair isn't dyed either. She has this amazing smile. I wish I knew what to do – I told my mum about her in the postcard and now I wished I hadn't. She could be so embarrassing sometimes . . . like asking me to send her a postcard. That was so random! I had no clue what to do – I'd never sent one in my life. But I asked Maria, she's the woman we are staying with, and when it was done I didn't have to think about home until Mum texted me later. She always did at about nine o'clock. But nobody goes to bed early in Spain. They have siestas in the afternoon and then everyone goes out at night and we are all allowed to stay up until midnight.

There's going to be a disco on for everyone in the school. I won't dance at it but it will be good fun with the lads, slagging all the girls. I hope that cute blonde will be there . . .

Chapter 40

Karl had a few disposable razors in his toilet bag that his father had packed for him. He flushed with pride when he spotted them.

They hadn't had much of a chat about sex before or anything like that but his father had told him that he was underage to have sex and he would be committing a crime if caught with a girl who was under sixteen.

Karl had joked that he'd only go for older girls and Tim had laughed. He then showed him what a condom was and said that there would be no need for it – however, he was better off knowing what it was used for and when to use it. It was embarrassing for both of them and they were relieved when the conversation was over.

This was the first time that Karl had left his family behind to go to a foreign country so it was a big adventure and he appreciated his dad for being cool. He'd been at the Gaeltacht the year before and that was where he'd met a few girls but no one that he wanted to meet for a second night. In his head girls were too clingy and they had weird ideas about dating and stuff. That was why he liked to stick to hanging out with the lads in school.

Tonight Karl wanted to look his best. He lifted the razor and ran it across his top lip. His hair wasn't as dark as his parents' but removing the strands made a difference. He had got used to doing it. He put some sweet-smelling tonic on his skin that his dad had given him. He was a man of the world.

After eating dinner he walked with Alex to a house down the road. Shane and David were coming out of it and the four continued walking for about half a mile until they came to the building where they attended classes each day. It was really hot and the boys all wore shorts and T-shirts.

"So what did you have for dinner tonight?" Karl asked.

"That weird bloody ham and bread with this olive dip and potatoes – I think I'll have to get a bag of chips from one of the stalls later," Shane replied. "What did you have?"

"We had pizza tonight – makes a change from paella."

"We wouldn't mind that, sure we wouldn't, Shane?" David said. "I think she's trying to poison us!"

Karl was pleased that he got the house with better food. "I wonder will there be others here from all the classes?"

"You like that blonde but she's too hot for you!" Shane said with a wink.

Karl hated it when he was caught out. He hadn't said anything to Shane or David about her. Maybe they liked her too – the thought worried him.

Suddenly his phone beeped. He read the text message quickly.

Hope you are having a lovely time. It's pouring rain here. Be careful.

Mum xx

"Who's that?" David asked.

"Just my mum."

They walked through the pretty squares and bustling streets filled with holidaymakers and locals. It was almost dark but there was a buzz on every corner with music and lights, promising that pleasure was the order of the night.

Some girls in miniskirts passed by – they could have been

eighteen but looked any age. They were like lifesize Barbie dolls and the boys all looked back at them as they walked in the opposite direction.

Karl felt nervous as they approached the school. It was set in a street close to the promenade and the lads already had it planned that if there was no action at the disco they would get some beers and drink them on the beach.

David nudged Karl. "She's here."

Karl realised at that moment that he wasn't the only one who liked the blonde girl.

David often did this. Karl had kept his mouth shut but David still sussed that he liked her. It was the same when he tried out for the basketball team – David had no interest in basketball until he heard Karl was trying out to get a place. David had a Samsung Galaxy and he wasn't happy with it when Karl got an iPhone for his birthday.

"I like the English girl Susan or what's her name?" Shane was always was a little forgetful when it came to names.

"Suzanne," David prompted. "You can have her – not my type."

Karl wouldn't be surprised if David tried to meet her too.

The common room was transformed from earlier. Paper lanterns hung from the ceiling and the long doors were open into the patio when there were torches burning and a barbeque in the corner.

"Hey, I didn't know we were getting food!" David said, his demeanour changing to one of excitement. "I'm starved."

Half the classes from the Irish and UK schools were there already and the teachers were serving Coca-Cola and Sprite from tables that were propped up along the walls.

Karl turned to Alex who had hardly spoken since they had joined up with the other pair.

"I'm not hungry, are you?"

Alex nodded and went over the barbeque with the others.

Karl was left standing alone and he scanned the room to see

where the blonde girl was but he couldn't see her.

The school was buzzing one hour later. Groups of students filtered out into the hall and some were hiding out in classrooms. There were plenty dancing and Karl was getting restless because there was still no sign of the pretty blonde girl. Had she left?

Then he spotted her. She was cornered by David over near the barbeque. He felt anger inside but didn't know what to do. Shane had scored – he was meeting an English girl outside the school – and Alex stood silently at Karl's side.

Karl wanted to just go home. He couldn't stand watching the girl meeting David. But his eyes were transfixed on the couple and David was getting closer and closer to her. Eventually the Irish boy lurched towards her and Karl felt a compulsion to do something. He marched over to the barbeque. But as he approached he saw that she wasn't having any of David's attentions and had ducked out of his way. She looked around and saw Karl coming towards her.

"Hi," she said and quickly walked away.

David frowned when Karl appeared. "What did you do that for? I was in there."

"Didn't look like that to me."

"I would have been – I had her eating out of the palm of my hand."

Karl wanted to punch him. Maybe Alex wasn't so bad – better to be with a nerd than someone who claims to be your friend and then does things like this.

"There's no action here – we should go to the beach," David said.

"You go – I'm going home," Karl said and walked back through the crowd.

He had never felt this way before about a girl. He'd met plenty at the rugby club disco so he guessed that girls liked him. But this girl was so cute he found himself thinking about her while he was meant to be learning his verbs in class. She was fluent in English as well as Spanish and so clever. At least he guessed that she was – he had never technically spoken to her but when she came into the classes with notes and messages he did catch her eye and she always smiled at him.

He walked along the corridor and passed a classroom where the lights were on and there she was – piling some books up on to a shelf for the class in the morning. He stopped still, just looking, and flinched when she stopped what she was doing and saw him staring at her.

"Sorry!" he said and then felt foolish for apologising.

"Hello," she smiled. "You're with the Irish school, aren't you?"

He nodded, in shock that she had actually spoken to him. He was frozen to the spot and couldn't think of anything to say.

"Do you like it here?" she asked.

"Oh yes, yes," he nodded enthusiastically. "I like it."

"Warmer than Dublin anyway."

"Anywhere's warmer than Dublin." He was feeling braver now. "You've got a bit of an Irish accent."

"I learned my English from my dad."

"He's Irish then?"

"From Dublin."

"He owns the college, doesn't he?"

"Yeah – he used to teach here but it has expanded so much he is busy with the managing end of things. He always spoke to me in English so I never had to learn it."

Karl edged his way inside the door of the classroom.

"That's so cool – I'd love to have a second language that I had naturally from when I was a baby. I had a Spanish au pair when I was little and she tried to teach me. Her name was Raquel."

"I've heard you talk – *muy bueno*!"

Karl blushed. "But I could never speak Spanish the way you do."

"Actually French is my mother tongue so I have a French accent in Spanish!"

"Oh, so you're not half Spanish?"

She shook her head but didn't elaborate. "Are you going home already? It's only getting started now?"

"It's good – it's just that my friend wanted to go to the beach and I've lost my other friend – I think he's gone off with an English girl."

"If you wait for me I'll walk back with you – where are you staying?"

"Calle Acebo."

"I live near there – I'll be glad of the company – wait till I get my bag, will you?"

Karl's insides were flipping. This was so cool. He'd wait all right.

David came walking along the corridor. Karl's heart sank.

"I thought you were going home?" David said.

"I am."

"What are you standing there for then?"

"I'm walking with someone."

"I'll come too then – this party is lame," David said, pulling his shoulders back.

Karl didn't know what to say. He looked at his watch. He didn't want David to mess things up.

"I thought you were going to the beach?"

"Changed my mind."

They stood for five minutes then David convinced Karl that they might as well go on. Karl hadn't admitted who he was waiting for and didn't want to either.

* * *

As they walked out the door Gina saw them disappear. She had taken a call from her father and was too upset to walk home. He would be along to collect her soon, because her mother had taken a turn and was in hospital.

Gina didn't have long to wait. She ran to her father when she saw him and he hugged her tightly – gently kissing the top of her head.

"Where is Lisa?"

"I'm going to pick her up now."

"Is Mum really bad?"

Her father couldn't lie. "She collapsed but the doctors are doing all they can for her – she will be fine."

Gina jumped into the car. They drove silently home and collected her sister Lisa before making the difficult trek to the hospital in Malaga.

* * *

"Are you sure you don't want a beer – we can get one in MacDonald's?" David asked.

Karl shrugged. "Why not?"

The beautiful blonde girl must have dumped him, he thought. She seemed so interested and lovely to him though. Girls! He couldn't figure them out – just as well he didn't have any sisters to wreck his head.

"Did you see Shane before we left?"

"Still eating the face off that Brit girl last time I saw him. I'll text him and tell him to tell Alex where we are."

Karl ordered a bottle of San Miguel. He felt old – they never asked him for ID in the MacDonald's because he was so tall. He'd easily pass for eighteen even in the pubs at home. But he hadn't tried it yet. It was so cool to be able to buy beer in MacDonald's.

"Do you want anything to eat?"

"Might as well have a burger while I'm at it."

"I'm getting a Big Mac meal – the woman in our house is trying to starve us with that Spanish muck."

David had been so arrogant since they'd come to Spain – he had changed totally from the person he was back home in Dublin. Karl felt like he had changed too. He found it an incredible experience to be away from his parents – it was no wonder that so many different emotions were erupting.

Chapter 41

Karen

June 2012

I was having a Greg moment – they happened much less regularly these days but sometimes when I worked late at night like this he would just creep into my head. I just acknowledged that he was somewhere doing whatever he did with his family and I was happy to be here in my lovely home with mine. My life had become so full and busy I seldom got moments to think of anything except the next job to be done.

Karl had grown up before my eyes. He was taller than me and had been since he turned twelve. I loved the gangliness of his body when I held him. I was so lucky to have my affectionate boys – they all hugged me – surprisingly, Oscar was the one who was least tactile but he clung to Tim for attention.

I supposed it was natural to feel this bond with your eldest child. Karl was getting more independent each day and it worried me sometimes. I wished that I could bottle him now – bottle all of them and keep my family exactly the way they were.

He arrived home one day a couple of months ago with a note from his Spanish teacher informing us of an exchange that had been organised by the school. He went to the local co-ed school which was good for him – I wanted him to be around girls as he didn't have sisters. I would send all the boys there. He'd been going away on scouting trips since he was nine but leaving the country worried me. But it was all part of the process of letting him go as he had become a teenager.

The note read that it would be of huge benefit to my child if he took part in the exchange and he would be living with a Spanish family along with another student from his class.

Karl, of course, was aching to go away. He was at that stage where he wanted to assert his independence and I suspected that he liked one of the girls in his class. It was a pity that there was no Grove any more. It was a rite of passage for so many teenagers in my day. Teenagers had changed so much with all this new technology and Facebook and Twitter. I could barely keep up with it. My agent insisted that I tweet but I hated doing it. That's why I'd employed Lucy to work for me three mornings a week. I had a lovely Seomra office built at the end of the garden where she happily went through all my paperwork and sorted me out.

But I had to pinch myself and remember that Karl was fifteen now. Just a little bit younger than I was when I was going out with Greg. I shuddered when I thought of him having the depth of emotions that I had back then. But kids were growing up even younger these days and the chances were that he would be doing just as much as I did. I hoped not. Maybe I would have been better off if I was one of the geeky girls who didn't kiss a boy until I was in college. Did it matter? So what if I had drunk underage – done things that would have made the nuns ship me off to a Magdalene Laundry? And there were Magdalene Laundries and all sorts of sinister things going on in eighties Dublin while I was in love with Greg. There still were horrors out there and it was customary now to wrap our kids up in cotton wool and protect them from the harshness of reality.

I thought of my cupcakes and wondered if I had sold out. It was a million miles from where I thought I would be at this stage of my life. I didn't think I'd be this successful but I did think I'd be doing something that was more worthwhile – like commentating on the state of the nation – heaven knows it was in a state! Now the only thing that anyone wanted to read from me was a recipe with a pretty picture and me wearing a silly apron. Maybe it was comfort we needed at this stage in our lives. Anyway, I knew that what mattered to me was my family and keeping us all well and happy. There might not be excitement and passion in my life but there was love and I was blessed with that.

I typed the last few details of my itinerary for the next week into the email for Lucy and pressed send. I looked at my watch. It was after twelve. I had worked a solid four hours at the computer and it had felt like twenty minutes.

I had heard Tim putting Nat to bed – it wasn't easy to convince him that it was night-time on these bright evenings but the incessant rain did make it seem more like autumn than the height of summer. At least Karl would be having a good time in the south of Spain. I could do with a break myself.

Tim popped his head around the door.

"Coming to bed?"

I nodded. "I'll be up in a few minutes."

Tim was so understanding – such a good husband. I wished that he had something more for himself but he seemed content to focus on his children and liked his odd game of golf and watching the rugby on TV. Since my career had taken off he had put the brakes on his ambitions and work had slackened considerably in his office. He didn't have the same passion or drive for his career. I could see it in so many of our friends' husbands. Even Linda's husband was feeling the effects in the medical world – his practice was flying during the Celtic Tiger years but now sometimes the middle-class clientele didn't have money to go to the doctor. I decided to text her and have a much-needed catch-up – it had been three months at least since we had seen each other.

* * *

313

Karen and Linda met next day in Bay restaurant on the Clontarf Road, close to where the little wooden bridge used to bring them down to the statue of the Virgin Mary.

Linda was already there when Karen arrived.

"The nearer the church – the further from God!" Linda said, getting up to give her friend a kiss.

"I'm glad we picked here – home from home in a kind of way. Sorry I'm late – I'd a call as I was coming out the door – deliveries to Superquinn went astray."

Linda smiled. "Who would have thought that you would be the big businesswoman? I don't know how you do it!"

"I don't have five kids!" Karen said, slipping into the seat and taking a menu from the waitress who had just popped over. "What are you having, Linda?"

"Goat's cheese salad."

"Make that two, please, and some sparkling water," Karen said with a smile and turned her attention to Linda. "How are your folks?"

"Mum needs a hip replacement and Dad had a couple of stents put in last week but, apart from that, they are fine."

"Ah, God help them!" Karen said, touching the top of the wooden table – the superstitious reaction was something that Monica would have automatically done.

"How's Monica and your dad?"

"Grand, thank God – I always worry about Mum and she's still puffing away on the cigarettes but she's keeping well – says that her ciggies keep the germs away."

Linda laughed. "It's funny when you look at their generation – how clinical and robot-like we have all become – don't you think?"

"Do you know, I've been so caught up in my own world and business I don't really think any more – thank God things have quietened down for Tim or I wouldn't be able to get through the day."

"I saw you on the telly on Tuesday – you looked great."

"Ha – just as well there are no cameras on me now!"

314

"I know – the state of ya!"

For Karen it was heaven just relaxing with her best friend and being the person she was when she was a kid – they always fell into this childish mode when they were together and, apart from Greg, Linda was the only person she felt this way with.

"I'm really glad that you rang – when I got the text to meet I thought that you were psychic."

The change in Linda's expression warned Karen that a revelation was about to be made. "What's up – everything okay with the kids?"

Linda sighed heavily. "I think Bill is having an affair."

Karen froze. It brought back horrible memories that churned around her stomach.

"Hold on – you don't know for sure?"

Linda shook her head. "I just know. You've been there – I didn't understand when you were explaining it to me about Alan but I do now."

Karen felt Linda's pain and reached out to put her hand comfortingly on top of her friend's. "I'm so sorry to hear this – but you must speak to him about it – you can't be sure."

"It's his secretary – so bloody obvious. Sure why wouldn't he? He sees more of her than me."

"I don't know what to say – I believe you but still hope that you are wrong."

"I never thought I'd end up like this – I don't even have my own bank account – everything is joint or in his name. I didn't keep my running-away money like my mother warned me to."

"But, Linda, you can't say that you will run away – what about the kids? You have too much to lose. You both have."

"I don't know what to do!"

"When was the last time that you had a break?"

"On my own?" Linda sat back and tried to think.

"Or a girlie weekend?"

"I haven't had one since I went to London with my mother three years ago."

"Then it's long overdue. I think if you were just not there then Dr Bill would have to sit up and take note."

"And where do you suggest I go – and with who? Money isn't flush at the moment either."

"Don't worry about money – I was only thinking last night about how much I'd love to go for a break somewhere that I wasn't demonstrating how to make cupcakes."

Linda sat up – her eyes widened and Karen knew that she had made the perfect suggestion.

"It's been so long since we went away on our own together," Linda said. "I would love it so much."

"That's settled – tell you what, how do you fancy popping down to Marbella? I miss Karl terribly and it would be great to have a little check-up on him."

"Where is he exactly?"

"Benalmádena – it's up the coast from Marbella."

"He won't thank you for landing on his doorstep."

"I'll keep it as a surprise until the day before. We could go this weekend. What do you say?"

Linda was beaming – it looked as if the decision was out of her hands.

"You know, maybe when Dr Bill sees you all relaxed and beautiful after your weekend with me he'll start to take care of you again?"

Linda hoped so. Karen was amazing – the best friend in the world.

* * *

The news of Karen's impending trip was announced to Tim as she put his plate of lasagne down in front of him at dinner that evening.

"And what about your TV show and the new cookbook?" he asked.

"I've finished filming – I told you. The new book is being edited."

"It would be nice for us to get away for a couple of days on our own together."

"I promise when I get back we will go to Monart – like we did for our anniversary."

Tim smiled. He had enjoyed that weekend. They wore bathrobes all the time and made love twice a day – it had been a long time since they had both had the energy for that.

Karen wrapped her arms lovingly around her husband's neck.

"Thanks for being so understanding and I promise I will make it up to you in Monart," she said with a dirty look.

Tim slipped his arms around her waist. "You had better – and you can start by making up to me tonight!"

"You've got a deal," she said.

Their lips met briefly before Amelia stomped into the kitchen with Nat and his dirty tennis whites.

"Oh, I am sorry!" Amelia apologised.

Karen and Tim pulled apart and Karen straightened down her top. "No, that's fine – we were just about to dish out dinner – weren't we, Tim?"

Karen counted her blessings – she was married to a wonderful man and her life was good.

Chapter 42

Karen

June 2012

The taxi was ordered for nine o'clock because I had to swing by Malahide and collect Linda en route to the airport.

"How was Bill when you were leaving?" I asked, as my friend plopped down with relief on the back seat of the car.

"He was okay – but not that happy with me going away and leaving him with the kids. I guess I should take time off more often! I probably shoulder too much of the burden all right. To think I lived a champagne lifestyle once!"

"Linda, you were crazy in college – I was the one that was pulled along on your coat-tails."

"And now I'm the one tagging on to yours!"

"We've always been there for each other – and always will be."

Linda's red hair was now a dusty blonde – I'd insisted she treated herself to highlights and a manicure and pedicure before she came on the trip. It was important that she felt good in herself – I had been concentrating so much on my own work and family I hadn't noticed the steady decline in my friend.

I didn't trust Dr Bill completely but still found it hard to believe that he was having an affair – he was always so crazy about Linda. However, since becoming an earth mother of sorts she had changed. It was time to bring my friend back to her true self.

* * *

The hotel was exactly as I expected it to be. A large high-rise with a man at the door ready to take our bags. The rooms had a view looking out over the Straits of Gibraltar and I felt giddy at the prospect of three days with my best friend.

"It's like being sixteen again, isn't it? Only we can go out and drink without sneaking around!"

"I can't believe that I'm here – no kids to collect or drop off or dinners to make. Thanks so much for making this happen."

"No – thank you – I need this break just as much."

"Did you let Karl know that you were here?"

"I rang him two days ago and he was less than impressed. Said that he was too busy in school and I wasn't to call in to see him there – he'd meet me tomorrow."

"Ah, the poor lad – he must have had a terrible fright – nothing worse than your mother appearing on the scene just as you are trying to assert your independence!"

"I'll just meet him the once tomorrow. I'm really more concerned about you and me having a fabulous time."

After we checked in I booked a massage for us both. Then my phone rang. It was a business call. I tried to keep it brief, explaining I was in Spain for a break.

"Who was that?" Linda asked when I hung up.

"Cheryl from Weddingsonline – they're giving me an entire page on their site."

"Wow, you really are a high flyer!"

"Hey, no slagging, please! Tell you what, I'll turn my phone off once I hear from Karl, okay?"

"I don't mind really – anyway, where are we going for dinner?"

I'd already decided that dinner was going to be in a nice

restaurant in Naranja Square. I remembered Raquel telling me about that place all those years ago and was excited at the prospect of being there – I could use it for inspiration for some cake recipes – cooking with oranges! My head was spinning – I realised then that I worked every minute of every day – my head never stopped. I would see to that when I returned. For now my mission was with Linda.

Chapter 43

The doctor came out to the corridor with a nurse at his side.

Gina wished her dad would come out of her mother's room because she couldn't bear to look at her body any longer. She lay so still, so grey and cold. The life had suddenly been zapped out of her – like in a vampire movie. She didn't need to be told that her mother was dead.

Gina held her sister's grip tightly, sobbing back the tears. But Lisa couldn't cry. She was too shocked to cry. It was too cruel – to die of a blood clot – it didn't make sense. She didn't know much about medicine or treatments but why should that kill her?

The girls had always been careful to ensure that their mother was catered for – they had spent most of their time helping her to do chores and get around well.

Being the eldest, Gina felt a renewed sense of responsibility – she had to take care of her father and her little sister. Lisa might be only a year younger but she was not as sensible as her and Gina would need to mind her now.

* * *

I hung around school for a few minutes every day that week but there was no sign of her anywhere. How could she have disappeared like that? And if it was her dad's school why wasn't she working here like she was the week we arrived?

I was kind of looking forward to seeing my mother. I wondered why she came down with Aunty Linda – she wasn't my real aunty – my mother had no sisters but Linda was my godmother and my mum's best friend. She was always really generous at my birthday – which was nice of her because she had loads of kids of her own. I was really annoyed at first when I heard they were coming 'cos I thought Mum was checking up on me. But that was when I was into Gina. I'd have loved to ask my teacher where she was. Maybe I would.

* * *

I had a MacDonald's with Alex and some of the other Irish kids from the school. It was hot today – well over thirty degrees.

"Have you seen that blonde girl this week – you know Gina – who helps out?" I asked around the table.

"She's hot!" one of the lads said. "No – not this week."

"I heard her mother was sick – she's in hospital and you know the tall man with the grey hair, well, he's her dad." Tracey Smith was a gossip and she found out everyone's business but in this instance it helped me – I now knew why I hadn't seen Gina. I hope that her mum will be okay – whatever it is that's wrong with her.

After school I hung around for a little while and spoke to my tutor, Gabrielle. She's young and really nice. And she wears skirts that are a distraction when she writes on the board!

"Is everything all right, Karl?" She smiled at me and I felt myself blush.

"I was just wondering if Gina was okay – I haven't seen her in school and someone said that her mother was sick."

"How nice of you to ask – you are a kind boy, Karl. Yes, it is very sad – her mother died yesterday. The staff are very upset for our boss – it is his wife."

I felt devastated at this news. The poor girl – how awful! I couldn't imagine how it must feel to lose your mother and I felt very glad that I would see mine soon.

I ran most of the way back to the villa in the blistering heat. I don't know why I'm so upset – I don't know this woman and I hardly know her daughter. I didn't go down to the beach with the gang as I'd planned. Instead, I laid on my bed and thought and thought and kept thinking about nothing at all.

* * *

In the Spa area, Linda was searching for Karen who was already lying on a cushioned lounger.

"That was the best massage I have ever had in my life – you really know how to look after yourself, Karen."

"I've had to learn and I've found balancing all the balls in the air has made me good at some things and time management is one of them – you have to look after yourself or you won't be able to look after anyone else!"

"And there was I thinking I was the wise one – what happened to me?"

Karen sat up on the lounger and made sure that her friend was comfortable. She handed Linda a glass of water.

"I hope you don't mind me saying this but I noticed lately that you have been consumed by the kids and looking after them. That may be why you have been distant with Bill. Isn't that possible?"

"It's true I'm very focused on them. They were so easy when they were smaller – I could control them – but I'm at my wits' end with teenagers. Not all teens are saintly like your little Karl."

"Karl's no saint but he's a good lad – I don't know where I got him from – I have Tim to thank for giving him the grounding that he has. I know that there have been times over the years when I was all over the place – like when I saw Greg back in 2005."

"Yes, and I wasn't much support – I was swamped with five tiny kids so was on a totally different vibration to you."

"And I wasn't much help to *you*."

Linda was startled. "You have always been a wonderful friend – you are solid, Karen – that's why I've always had difficulty understanding your obsession with Greg. I suppose I'm envious of that depth of love that you felt so young."

Karen sighed. She realised, if she wanted to help her friend, the time had come to tell her the truth – the whole truth. "Linda, I think life isn't black and white and an affair isn't necessarily the end of a marriage."

"Well, I know you're not speaking from personal experience!"

Karen hesitated and then plunged in. "I am."

"What? What do you mean?" Linda's eyes were about to pop out of her head.

Karen couldn't get herself to say the words.

"Are you going to make me fish or are you going to spill the beans?" Linda was being her old stroppy self.

"It's time to spill the beans, I guess . . ."

And Karen told an astonished Linda exactly what had happened in Barcelona.

"So you see," she concluded, "even if Bill did have an affair – which I don't believe he did – he would still love you more. I'm a married woman and Tim deserves a lot better – I would hate him to ever find out but I want you to see that even if Bill did slip up once or twice it doesn't mean that he doesn't love you. I adore Tim – he is the best husband and father – I doubt I would be as happy with anyone else."

"Even Greg?"

"I came to the conclusion some years back that if I was married to Greg I would be so obsessed by him I wouldn't be able to do anything with my life – we would be the most neglectful parents because we would be too caught up with each other."

Linda wasn't convinced by her friend's answer. "I wonder – is that just the way you cope with being apart?"

Karen shrugged. Maybe Linda was right – either way she had no choice – if she had stayed around waiting for Greg to become available she would have missed out on having a beautiful family and all the happy years with Tim.

"I guess I've learned to be philosophical about it all – I had no choice. I'm lucky the way my life has turned out."

"And you still haven't contacted him since he sent you that email a couple of years ago? When he was in Dublin and heard you on the radio?"

"No. I sometimes wonder whether I should have replied."

"Well, I think you did the right thing – if you'd replied you'd have arranged to see him and you always got upset after seeing Greg."

Karen shrugged. "I'm just doing my best to survive like everyone else."

"Do you ever wonder how the lads are? I'd love to know how Frank and Stephen are doing."

"I've seen Jackie Quinn Designs in lots of glossy magazines – *Vogue, Marie-Claire, Coco* . . ."

"Well, I had a glamorous life for a short while in my twenties, didn't I?" Linda said unconvincingly.

"You saw through the smokescreen and concentrated on what truly matters in life – your kids."

"You're just trying to make me feel better. And, as you just said, I probably focused too much on the kids and neglected Bill. Do you know, we haven't been away on our own since 2006!"

"Therein lies your problem – he must be feeling ignored." Karen stood up. "Let's work on getting gorgeous and showing our fellas what a benefit it is to send their wives off on a spa treat like this and maybe we can make a habit of it?"

Linda joined her. "Okay – where to, now?"

"The swimming pool – gotta get a bit of a tan – don't think we will be seeing much sunshine when we get back to Dublin."

* * *

Karen stepped out of the pool and dried herself off with her towel. Her phone bleeped with a text:

Mum I can get bus to Marbella and c u tonight 4 dinner. Wot ur hotel Kx

Karen's heart jumped a little. She hadn't expected him to want to see her at all and was giving him time to get used to the idea. She looked over at Linda and hoped that she wouldn't mind their first night being interrupted in this way. Already Linda looked like a new woman – the few hours away from routine were doing her good.

"Who's the text from?" Linda asked, looking up from her book.

"It's from Karl – he wants to see me for dinner tonight."

"Great! We'll all go to Naranja Square," Linda said immediately.

"But I thought we were having a quiet night? I could put him off . . . though, God, I hope there's nothing wrong with him."

"Isn't it wonderful that he wants to see you? Tell him to come along."

"Are you sure? I wanted you to have a nice time away from the kids and seeing Karl might ruin that."

"He's my godson – tell him to meet us."

"I'll tell him to get a taxi to our hotel then – are you sure?"

"Positive – poor lad must be missing you."

Karen dialled his number.

"Hello?"

"Karl, darling – it's Mum – I'm so pleased that you want to see me and Aunty Linda – we're going to Naranja Square for dinner, okay?"

"Sure – will I get the bus?"

"No, no, get a taxi to our hotel – it's called the Hotel Fuerte Miramar – can you write that down?"

"Will you just text it to me?"

"Okay – how long will it take to get to Marbella?"

"I don't know – it's really far – I was there one day with the school – we got the bus."

"Will it take an hour?"

"Not as long as that."

"Okay, then get a taxi – it's four o'clock now so maybe if you get here for seven . . . is that all right?"

"Yeah – I'll see you then." He hung up.

He had sounded so sad and distant. Karen held the phone to her chest and wondered what was up with him.

Chapter 44

As the sun dipped beneath the horizon Greg sat listening to the crickets and watching the heat rise from the stones beneath his feet. He was numb. His daughters were being consoled by their Aunty Tara and their cousins. He was expecting his mother to arrive any minute with his brother Simon. It wasn't exactly the sort of impromptu family reunion that he could look forward to. Time had no meaning at the moment and he wished that he could slip away to a retreat somewhere and escape the next day. It was too cruel the way that she died – a blood clot in her leg. The entire week had been so random and suddenly she was unconscious and then she was in a coma and then she was dead. It wasn't the Parkinson's that had killed her after all – or not directly. But life had been hard for all of them for the last two years – they had been a blur for Greg.

His daughters were so wonderful with their mother – such caring young girls – he was blessed to have them. They were far more mature than their sixteen and fourteen years. He thought of how selfish he had been fighting with his father and criticising his mother. His daughters were so much more accepting.

It was just the three of them now – he wasn't alone. He would make sure that they got the best education possible and become the finest that they could be. He would make Isabella proud of his parenting as she watched from heaven. Who was he kidding – he didn't believe in heaven – Isabella was stardust floating around in space and he would never see her again. For his daughters' sake he said that he believed she was in heaven now and they would do the whole Catholic funeral in the morning. But it would be a hardship as he trudged through the next few weeks and months and years – there was still a lot of pain that he would have to endure, but for now he had to concentrate on the future and his daughters.

* * *

Karl went out to the corner of the street where the taxis lined up. Maria wanted him to get a taxi from the house but he was confident that he knew what he was doing. He was fifteen after all.

He hadn't gone far when he saw her – walking along the street with a woman. He got such a shock he didn't know where to look. What was he going to say to her? Her mother had died.

She spotted him and waved over.

Karl's heart pounded. She was so pretty. The woman who was with her didn't look like her at all but she did look Irish. He decided that he had better go over to the other side of the street. He wanted to say something. The woman lagged behind as Gina walked towards him.

"Hiya – I'm Karl from the school – we spoke the other night."

"Hello, Karl – yes, I remember your name – I'm sorry that I didn't walk home with you – you see, my dad called to say that my mother was ill."

Karl kicked the ground awkwardly, his hands in the pockets of his shorts.

"I'm sorry to hear about your mother – I found out in the school today."

"Thank you – the funeral is tomorrow." Gina looked so sad and so beautiful.

Karl was overcome by the moment. "I wasn't sure if I would see you again – I'm going home next week."

"I don't know what I'll do after the funeral – I may not see you – maybe you'll come back next year?"

"I would like that – or I could Facebook you if that was okay?"

"Yes – my Facebook is full of messages – I haven't looked at it yet. You know, when something terrible happens and everyone leaves a comment – I've done it myself but it does feel weird when the messages are for you and it's not your birthday or something nice."

Karl couldn't imagine it. He understood what she meant though.

"I hope it goes okay – the funeral."

Gina looked at him and he melted. He wanted to put his arms around her and protect her and tell her that it would all be okay. But how was he to know? He was only fifteen and he didn't feel very big any more. He was just so happy that he was going to see his mother.

* * *

The marble-lined foyer of the Hotel Fuerte Miramar was an impressive oasis of calm. This did not, however, ease Karen's concerns as she padded up and down waiting for her son to arrive. What if he had got into a cab with a dodgy taxi driver? She should have gone to Benalmádena herself – they could have left dinner in the square until the next night. How was Karl going to get back? He could stay on the couch – yes, that would be the best idea and she could send him back in the morning. She had to remember to ring Maria and tell her that he wouldn't be back.

Then a taxi pulled up and a tall figure got out of the car. He had grown in the two weeks while he was away, she was convinced. Karen rushed over and hugged him tightly.

"Oh, Karl – it's so good to see you, pet!"

Karl leaned down and kissed his mother on the cheek. "I'm glad that you are here – it's like you knew that I was going to be sad today."

"Here – pay the man," Karen said, thrusting a fifty-euro note into his hand.

Karl paid, then Karen slipped her hand through the crook of his arm and they walked together into the hotel.

"How are Dad and the others?"

"They are all fine – I think Oscar is missing you terribly – although he's getting on better with Nat than he usually does. I think they will both be ecstatic to see you."

Karl grinned. He was pleased to be missed. The trip had gone really well until the other night. He had hoped since the first day that he would get to know Gina better and now there was no hope.

"So have there been any girlfriends?" Karen pried and Karl winced.

"Mu-u-um!"

"Okay, sorry, I realise that I'm an embarrassment – I wanted to check before we go up to your Aunty Linda – I'm sure that she will want to know."

"She won't! She's much cooler than you!"

Karen didn't care how she acted – she was so happy to see her son.

* * *

It was almost nine o'clock when Jean O'Sullivan and Simon arrived. Greg greeted them in the hallway and what was left of the O'Sullivan clan sat around the veranda in the balmy night air. Ella had apologised – she had a major surgery case that needed to be performed the next day and couldn't make it. Greg didn't mind – they had grown apart with time and he had enough support and distractions around him. In fact, he would rather be left on his own with his daughters to put Isabella to rest in peace but that was not going to happen.

"Would you like something to eat?" Greg asked his mother and brother.

"We had our dinner earlier and then we had something on the plane," Simon said.

"Grand, so."

"When will the funeral be – the morning?"

"Yes – after eleven Mass. Then to the crematorium in Malaga."

"What will you do with the ashes?" Simon asked.

"Simon!" Jean O'Sullivan berated her youngest son.

"It's okay, Mum," Greg said. "We'll be taking her home with us. The girls will want her to stay in the house with us."

* * *

Plaza de las Naranjes was accredited with being one of the quaintest squares in all of Andalusia and Karen and Linda were very anxious to get there.

"I never thought that it would take me this long to get to Marbella – even the cast of TOWIE made it before me!" Linda said.

Karen laughed. "Hey, I'm sure we can't be compared to the TOWIE cast."

"No – domestic goddess and domestic mess – that pretty much sums us up!"

Karen hated to hear her warm, bright, intelligent friend speak about herself this way.

Karl was lagging behind and Karen hoped that he was okay – he seemed very distracted since getting out of the taxi. Karen had rung Maria and said that she would put Karl on the bus in the morning and he would go straight to class. The young lad was happy to be with her and she was overjoyed by this closeness that they shared. He was a rock of sense – so unlike Oscar – and, as for Nathan, she had grave concerns that he would be a juvenile delinquent. It was her own fault – the younger pair hadn't received the same attention as Karl and it did show.

"This looks nice – what do you think?" Linda asked as they came to a restaurant tucked into the corner of the square. The restaurants were separated by different-coloured parasols and some had white linen tablecloths.

"Lovely – let's hope it's not too busy to take us."

A waiter rushed out and pulled back the chairs and the three sat in the clement heat as the hustle and bustle of the locals and tourists mingled around the fountain and the sculpted hedgerows.

Linda got up to use the bathroom and Karen seized the opportunity to squeeze more information from her son. His quietness had her concerned.

"Is the house nice where you're staying?"

"It's fine."

"And Maria? She sounds lovely on the phone."

"Yeah, and she cooks nice food."

"So you're having a lovely time?"

He nodded. "I'm just a bit sad because there's this girl in the school and her mother died the other day. I'm glad that you decided to come here now."

Karen's heart melted. Her poor boy – he was only a kid. Just because he was six foot tall she shouldn't forget that. Of course he would be worried about her dying. She had felt the same as a teenager and was so blessed that, despite the years of puffing tobacco, Monica was still in the best of health.

"Give me a hug," Karen said and she breathed in his smell. The cologne Tim had given him reminded her of her husband and she felt blessed for the men in her life.

Chapter 45

Karen was wandering down a narrow lane behind Naranja Square. There was a man following her and she was searching for Karl who was nowhere to be seen. She had lost her son – Linda was nowhere to be seen either. A deathly silence hung in the air.

The shadow of the man following her grew bigger and longer. No matter how fast she tried to walk he was gaining pace all the time.

She broke into a jog and the man did the same. She had no idea where she was running to – the streets were turning into Dublin and she was on Talbot Street now. Dirty old Dublin streets crowded with men in reefer jackets and women with headscarves.

Karen was frightened because the man was still following her and his silhouette stood out against the crowds that he was pushing out of his way.

"Karen!" he called. "Please stop!"

Karen turned and recognised the figure at last – she wondered what she had been so frightened of.

Karen opened her eyes and let out a sigh of relief. It was only a bad dream.

* * *

Greg sat up in the bed in a state of panic, remembering only snippets of his nightmare. The sweat was streaming from his body. Dawn had broken and already the heat of the day rose from the balcony outside. He remembered what day it was and put his head into the palms of his hands.

So soon – he had to bury his wife too soon. And why was he dreaming of Karen now? He hadn't thought of her in months. He felt guilty for thinking of her.

He looked around the room and spoke inside his head. "If you're here, Isabella, you probably know what I did. I'm sorry." But he felt nothing – Isabella's spirit had left this planet and wherever and whatever she now was it didn't matter. Life was all a game and their lives a drop in the ocean. If only he could have seen it that way when he was a kid – he might not have got caught up with things that didn't matter. But he had lessons to learn and now he hoped that he had learned them. Maybe his entire life was a big lesson. And what had he learned?

He knew that his girls were the most precious part of his life and all that really mattered. He had always known that – but Karen was important to him too and she had been a part of his life for so long. It was no surprise that he should think of her now on this, the most difficult day of his life.

* * *

Karen roused herself to go to the bathroom. Linda was fast asleep in the bed next to hers and Karl was still asleep on the couch in the suite. She looked at her watch. It was only seven o'clock. She wondered why she was dreaming about Greg now – probably because she was in Spain. She had lived that afternoon in Barcelona over and over in her head at times – whenever she felt cross with Tim or low in herself. It always did the trick and helped her feel that she had lived. She looked at herself in the mirror. There were too many lines – she was on the wrong side of forty – not long until she would be half a century. If she wanted to be depressed about it, the best of her health and looks were over. All that time – had she spent it well – had she managed it to the best of her ability?

She had certainly lived a full life and with the joy of her sons there were plenty more years of wonderful experiences to be shared with her family and friends. So why was she feeling so maudlin today of all days – while the sun was shining and she was with her best friend? She wasn't going to be able to make sense of any of it so it was probably best just to get on with it. Getting her son up for his day at school was a priority.

* * *

The cavalcade drove along the motorway to the crematorium in Malaga. To his left Greg looked out at the haze of heat rising in front of the Sierra Nevada mountains. The serrated contour of the peaks created a perfect contrast to that cerulean blue sky. What a beautiful place he lived in!

His mother was sobbing quietly to herself in the back of the car and holding on to Lisa's hand.

"Will we get to take home her ashes today?" Lisa asked.

"I don't know." And he didn't – his father had been laid to rest in St Fintan's Cemetery in Dublin so he didn't know what happened after a cremation in Spain.

He brushed his palm along the back of his daughter's hand – over and over – trying to soothe his own soul as much as hers.

As he looked out to the mountains again his mind wandered back to the dream – why was he chasing Karen in that way and why was she so much in his head this morning? Of all mornings!

* * *

Karen watched Karl wave from the bus as it drove off down the road to Benalmádena. She was satisfied that he had been filled with enough motherly love to help him through the next week. She would be happy when he was home for good.

It was a short walk back through the labyrinth of narrow streets to their hotel on the beach. Linda was already propped up on a lounger under the shade of a parasol, with a book in her hand, enjoying a Diet Coke.

"Is he okay?"

"He's fine now – last night at dinner he told me why he was upset – a girl on the course lost her mother this week and it shook him up a bit."

"He's a lovely sensitive lad, Karen – you've done a great job with him."

"And your kids are a credit to you, Linda."

"Enough of the mutual admiration – get yourself a drink."

"I will and I might even get something to eat."

They lazed by the pool for two hours until the heat became too much and they decided to take a siesta. As they gathered up their towels and bits and pieces Karen felt the urge to tell Linda about her disturbed sleep.

"You know, I had a bit of a nightmare last night."

"Ooh, I hate them – what happened?"

"It was weird – I was in Naranja Square and there was someone following me and then I was in Dublin and the man was still following me – it was terrifying – and then it turned out to be Greg!"

"That was probably after talking about him yesterday."

"Yeah, but it was so real. I can't explain it."

"Maybe he's thinking about you?"

"We used to be that way but not for years – I thought I'd got him out of my system in Barcelona and I've been so busy I wasn't dwelling on him too often."

Linda frowned. "Are you sure you're okay?"

"I have this ache in my stomach as if something awful is

about to happen – everything has been going so well in my life – I'm out of sync or something."

"Maybe Greg is the one out of sync and you're feeling it?"

"Linda," Karen sighed, "do you think it might be some sort of sign?"

"I always told you that I was psychic – I think we all are – only some of us choose to use it. Maybe he feels that you are in Spain."

"Yeah, but we are hundreds of miles from Cambrils where he lives."

"It's natural when you are away like this to have dreams and strange feelings."

Karen nodded. "You're probably right. I suppose I should just forget about it."

"Concentrate on enjoying yourself."

* * *

Greg returned to Benalmádena with his family – a few friends had gone with them to the crematorium but he wanted to go back home now and he would meet everybody later at dinner at the square in Mijas. It was Isabella's favourite place and he wanted to honour her memory by taking her friends up to the restaurant where they had been so happy together. His life would change radically – he was a single parent and all the decisions regarding the girls were his. He felt so deeply for them – girls especially needed their mother. How would he fulfil the roles of both parents adequately for the next ten or twenty years or however long they needed him to support them in their education and personal life?

It all felt too daunting and he excused himself to go up to his room where he threw his head back in the air and let out a roar that was loud enough for his family to hear downstairs. He then lay on the bed and closed his eyes and cried.

* * *

"What do you want to do tonight?" Linda asked as she stepped out from the shower in a fluffy white robe.

"I wouldn't mind going back to Orange Square – what do you think? Or we could get a taxi up to Mijas – it's meant to be stunning."

"That sounds great – let's try Mijas. Did Karl ring you today?"

"He texted to let me know that he had got to school safely."

"That's the main thing. Sure he'll be back before you know it."

Karen started to put on her make-up. "I'd love a bottle of Cava now while we get ready – what do you think?"

"Dear lord, now you are talking! Will I ring room service?" Linda asked.

"Yes, let's do it. And will I get them to book a taxi to take us to Mijas while we are at it?"

"That sounds like a plan."

* * *

Greg gathered his family around and started to organise lifts for everybody.

"Are you sure that you feel up to this?" Jean asked her son.

"It's what Isabella would want – she loved this place – do you remember we brought you up to Mijas last year?"

"Yes, yes, of course I do – it is nice." Jean looked at her son and put her hand on his shoulder. "Will you be all right?"

"I have to be – for the girls."

Jean shook her head. "Life's difficult – I wish there was something I could do, son."

"I want the girls to remember their mother – they need to spend some time in France – remember where they came from too."

"And I'd like them to spend some time with me – maybe next summer they will come stay with me and give you a break?"

Greg nodded. "They would like that – I'm sure."

Tara walked over and gave her brother a hug for no reason other than to tell him how much she loved him. Then Greg and the girls got into his Jeep with his mother, and the others followed behind in their hire cars.

It wasn't far to Mijas but everything was happening in slow motion today. It was a day that Greg wouldn't forget in a hurry.

* * *

The taxi drove up along the steep and narrow streets that wound their way through whitewashed villages. It stopped at the Bull Ring in the centre of the town where the scene was picture-perfect under a velvet sky and a host of restaurants awaited discovery.

"The view is spectacular here. Look at the lights!" Linda gasped as she looked behind at the coast where they had come from.

"I'm so glad we made the effort to come up – this is my producer's favourite place in the world. He has a villa down the road and is always raving about this restaurant . . . what's the name of it? I can't think . . ."

"It's a world away from my busy life – thank you for taking this time with me, Karen. I needed someone to shake me up a bit."

"Have you spoken to Bill today?"

"Yes, and he said that he missed me!"

"There you go – I bet he isn't having an affair at all."

"I really hope not – I've been feeling so insecure in myself. I think it's part of growing into middle age and feeling that life might be passing me by."

"Look at what you have – look at those beautiful people that you have made."

Linda smiled. "Always the philosopher, Karen – how lucky I am to have you."

343

"Now stop the maudlin stuff – we are getting a nice table and another bottle of Cava quickly – looks like the car journey has wasted the effects of the bottle that we had at the hotel."

They found a table in a nearby restaurant called El Olivar and took in the view of those around finding their place among the olive trees and under the stars.

* * *

The funeral party had to park a brief walk away from the Plaza del Toros. They meandered through the winding streets to the restaurant named after the white blackbird. Greg called Isabella his white blackbird on occasions – it was private joke. One he wouldn't be able to share with anyone ever again.

"What's the name of that place Isabella loved, Greg?" Jean asked.

"El Mirlo Blanco."

"Ah yes, I remember us all going there – I think it's a good idea now."

They were a party of eighteen in total after Isabella's friends and Xavier, the school manager and a couple of others from the school arrived.

Xavier was tall with hair as black as coal and a strong Andalucian accent.

"How is everything in the school?" Greg asked his colleague as he sat down.

"It is all very good. You have nothing to worry about."

But Greg felt like he had the weight of the world on his shoulders at the moment. He was overwhelmed.

A waitress dashed around handing out menus and the group gelled well considering the circumstances. They dipped bread into the pesto and olive oil and spoke about the lovely Isabella and how much she was going to be missed.

* * *

"I think that was the nicest meal I have had in ages!" Linda said, pushing her empty plate away.

"It was yum, wasn't it?" Karen nodded. "I kinda wish we were staying three nights now."

"We have all of tomorrow by the pool – what time is our flight?"

"Not until ten o'clock."

"That's great. I have to hand it to you, Karen – you really picked out everything perfectly. I feel like I'm ready to take on the world now when I get back."

"Well, as long as you're ready to take on Bill, that's the most important thing."

Linda shook her head. "I don't know if I have the nerve to ask him straight out if he is having an affair or not."

"Think twice before you do – because you have to be able for the answer. I mean, you don't really have any evidence."

Linda moved around uncomfortably on her seat. "I suppose it's a gut feeling that I have really."

"And could that gut feeling be telling you something else maybe? Perhaps you are feeling neglected and being sharp with him and in turn you are both falling into a spiral of bad behaviour?"

Linda didn't answer – she paused and scrunched up her face. "I don't know any more. I find it difficult to manage everything – I'm out of routine or order – it's crept up on me slowly since the kids became teenagers."

"It is a difficult time, and I know that I have help, but you could have help too."

"I guess so – I was always so proud that I did everything myself."

"Well, it's time to put pride aside and concentrate on your marriage. That's what I had to do and it worked."

"When did you?"

"When I came back from Barcelona – I had to decide what I wanted and who I wanted to be with and thanked my lucky stars that I had Tim. He may not be perfect, but I certainly am not either. We have to make the most of life – especially when all that we have is now."

Linda took a gulp from her glass of Cava. "You are on a roll tonight, Karen – if you could bottle what you just said to me you could sell it and make millions – I bet you'd even get a slot on Oprah."

Karen decided then to shut up – she had said enough. "So what do you want for dessert?"

"Another drink. Then we'll hit the road."

* * *

While the rest of the party sipped on coffees and wine, Greg got up to pay the bill.

He felt the hairs on his chin as the waitress took his card and put it in the machine to process his payment. He hadn't shaved in weeks and had grown a beard without noticing it very much. It was just easier to do so.

From the corner of his eye he spotted a woman walk by who looked like Karen. He wasn't surprised, after the dream he'd had the night before – it was the sort of thing that happened when he started to think about her. This was not the night to think about Karen – this was the night to give thanks for Isabella and all that she had given him. But there was one condition that he could do without – his melancholy was back and he had no clue how to combat it this time. Only his girls mattered – he had to concentrate on his girls. They gave him a reason for living. Because right now his world had ended and he needed one.

* * *

A pleasant incline on the road helped Linda and Karen walk down to the taxi rank.

"Look at that guy over there," Linda pointed. "Isn't he the

image of Greg with a bit of a beard?"

Karen craned her neck – it was difficult to see in the dark of the street and the lamplight surrounding the restaurant.

"Nah – he's too skinny from the side – Greg had plenty of muscle on him last time I saw him in Barcelona. He was never thin."

"Yes, but it's funny to see someone that looks like him after that dream."

Linda was correct – that is exactly the way that Karen used to see the world. A wonderful mishmash of coincidences and spiritual happenings – it was this belief that had helped her to achieve so much with her cupcake business. But she didn't want to think about Greg – she had swept all emotions under the carpet since the last time she had seen him because she wasn't in the place to deal with how she would feel if she ever saw him again. Having a nightmare about him was a warning of sorts and it would be much better if she didn't feed those thoughts.

"Come on, let's get back to the hotel. I want to ring Tim before it gets too late."

They grabbed a taxi near the Bull Ring and held a post mortem on their delicious dinner as the car weaved its way down the winding hill.

Chapter 46

It was the last day before he was due to return to Dublin. Karl had given up hope of seeing Gina again and was ready to go home. He missed the lads from school and there had been a couple of parties that looked like great *craic* on Facebook. He scanned through the tablet that his mum had given him for his birthday and typed Gina's name into the search bar. There were loads of Gina O'Sullivans but thankfully the one he was looking for had a photo of herself as an avatar. He clicked on it and sent a friend request. The last party of the week was on tonight and he wasn't sure if he wanted to go or not. David was spending every second with a girl called Alison and Shane was stapled to the hip with Suzanne. It would have been okay if he hadn't seen Gina – there were plenty of cute girls that had shown their interest in him but he hankered for Gina and the news of her mother's death had affected him in a weird way.

Suddenly he got an email: **Friend request accepted.** Gina was on line.

He decided to be brave and clicked his chat line on.

Hi there how r u feeling?

He had it sent before realising how lame he sounded – her

mother had just died – how did he expect her to feel?

I'm fine. R u still here?

Karl was shaking as he typed.

Yes but I'm back 2 dub 2moro.

Immediately her answer came back.

Pity I won't c u to say bye

She could say that again, he thought.

Do you have an iPad?

Yes

We can facetime if u like?

Wot ur email?

Karl texted his address and waited with bated breath; suddenly his tablet rang.

"Hi!"

The pixels moved at a steady pace but blurred the line of her perfect face and long blonde hair. He was ecstatic to see her image – distance didn't matter.

"Hi, thanks for accepting my request."

"I told you to find me on Facebook."

"Will you be in the school later?"

"No – I'm here with my dad – my granny has gone back to Dublin today – we had family staying for the last few days."

"Where does she live?"

"In Dublin in a place called Sutton – do you know it?"

"Yeah, it's not that far from where I live – Clontarf."

"Oh, I've been there. My dad used to take us to St Anne's Park when we were little and staying with my granny."

"My parents always took us there too."

"Tell you what – I could meet you in MacDonald's in a few minutes if you like – I don't think my dad would mind if I took a walk."

Karl's heart pounded. Of course he would like it. He would love it.

"Great – how long?"

"Twenty minutes?"

* * *

Karl was shaking as he ran down the stairs to Maria.

"But your dinner is ready in half an hour," she protested.

"Can you keep it for me, please – I really want to go to MacDonald's and meet someone."

Maria shrugged. He would be gone soon and another teenager that she would have to lay down rules and regulations for would take his place. "Okay."

Karl checked his hair in the mirror – it was a bit flat with the heat so he brushed it to the side in a sweeping style. He ran down the street – checking his pockets for money. He had managed his allowance well and was all set for the highlight of his time in Spain.

Gina was already there when he arrived – standing in the queue, looking up at the menu board.

"Hiya," he said nervously – she was a lot smaller than he remembered. Maybe he had grown.

"Hi – what do you want?"

"I'm not really hungry – what are you having?"

"A strawberry shake."

"I'll have one too then."

Gina looked behind her. "Maybe we can take them onto the beach – what do you think?"

"Yeah, that would be good."

He couldn't find words now that he was actually here and with her – but she must like him or she wouldn't have suggested that they meet up.

The promenade was full of tourists and revellers and they slipped onto the sand where most of the bathers were packing up for the evening.

"I'll miss your sunny weather – my mum says that it's been raining every day in Dublin since I've been here."

"I like Irish weather – you don't get too hot in summer and

you can go out at any time that you want."

"You would hate our winters though – especially when it's windy and wet – it's colder than anywhere."

She nodded. "I understand what you mean. But the Irish always talk about the weather – my papa doesn't too much now but when his family come to stay with us they always talk about it."

They strolled down to the water's edge and brushed their toes against the incoming foam where they walked.

"It's funny because you sound Irish – some of the girls at home have American accents from watching too much TV – you sound more Irish than them."

"I think I don't sound like I am from anywhere– the Spanish always ask where I am from because of my French accent and I lived in Catalonia for a few years."

"I was in Barcelona once – my dad brought me to a match in Nou Camp."

"I've never been to one – my papa doesn't like football."

Karl loved hearing more about her life and her world and where she came from – he loved the sound of her voice and the way she spoke. He wished that he had more time with her – this was the best time that he'd had since he arrived.

Every few steps they walked closer and then walked away from each other once their skin brushed off each other. Hormones were flying in all directions and Karl wanted to grab her and kiss her. Time was running out for them but he wanted it so bad.

* * *

Gina left him at the corner of Calle Acebo and walked slowly home. She suddenly remembered that her mother wouldn't be there and wanted to cry but swallowed hard and choked back the tears. She would feel like this for some time – the doctor had warned her in the hospital. She was a lovely lady and she had explained to Gina that over the next few months she would need time to express her feelings and come to terms with the loss of her mother.

Karl was a nice guy – she could have stayed and talked with him all night but her father would be worrying about her and she needed to be with him now. The visitors were all gone and it was their first night in the house just the three of them alone, knowing that her mother would never come back.

Gina felt a wave of emotion sweep over her again as she approached the gate of her house. She slipped in through the side gate and went around the back to enter through the back door.

Her father was sitting on a chair outside on the patio, reading the paper.

"I was getting worried about you – where were you?"

"I went for a walk with one of the students. Karl Doyle."

"I can't say I know him."

"He's only with us for three weeks – going home tomorrow."

"You are kind to the students, Gina – I wouldn't be surprised if you end up being a teacher."

"I wouldn't mind, Papa."

"Well, this will be yours one day to do with as you please."

Gina hated to hear her father so sad – it was like he had given up.

"Papa, you are so young!"

She went over to him and wrapped her arms around his neck and he put his head on her shoulder. He needed to feel loved – he was the lost child and his children were his saviours.

Chapter 47

Karen

July 2012

There was a distance between Tim and me when I returned from Spain and I couldn't understand it. Like I had done something wrong but he wouldn't talk to me about it. The time on my own with Linda had helped me to appreciate how much I loved my home and my family and I had made a decision on the flight home that I would spend more time with them and cherish them all.

Tim's behaviour was unusual and scary – I was so confident that I knew what was best for Linda but had I failed to see what was going on with my own marriage?

Maybe I was taking him for granted – but Tim was so easily pleased I didn't think I needed to do anything else.

Then I got an email that shook me – it was brief but it said a lot.

Hi Karen, I found your address from your website – aren't you doing great – so delighted for you. I just thought you would like to know that Greg's wife died. Two weeks ago – none of us knew – I'm still in shock TBH – she was a good woman. Must catch up one of these days but I'm seldom home since my mum passed away last year.

Jackie says hi and she loved your new recipe book – got a copy of it in Barnes and Noble.

All the best

Frank

I read it and re-read it and then I rang Linda.

"Oh my God, that's just awful – did he say how she died?"

"No – he didn't – I thought that you could live to be really old with Parkinson's."

"Exactly – doesn't that guy from *Back to the Future* have it?"

"Yeah, Michael J Fox. I'm stunned – poor Greg – and his little girls."

"What age are they now?"

"The eldest is not much older than Karl," I said and shook my head sadly. I was lost for words.

"Are you going to write to him?"

"I don't know – what would I say?"

"I'm sure he'd like to hear from you."

"I'm not sure I could handle it though."

"If you want I can meet you and we can chat about it?"

"Thanks, but I think I'll just go for a walk. Figure out what I will do then."

But my head was in a muddle and there were recipes to discuss with the girl who was writing my new book. I did the only thing I could cope with doing – I baked.

* * *

Tim was late home again last night and I've decided to have it out with him tonight. Since our return from Marbella Dr Bill has lavished his attentions on Linda – she was way off the mark and he laughed when she admitted she'd thought he was having an affair. I felt vindicated and punched the air when she said that she was going to look into getting a part-time job for herself and a bit more help with the house and kids. It is easy for a woman to lose herself in her family and I could see this is what had happened to Linda.

As for me, I had to ask myself what I was doing with my relationships. I had been so consumed with my business and being super-efficient and organised that I wasn't getting the full picture.

Oscar let it slip that Tim didn't come home one of the nights when I was away. Amelia was very defensive when I asked her about it – admitting that she had promised Tim not to say anything about it. It made me so suspicious that I was imagining all kinds of scenarios.

Then when I was driving back from the supermarket the most awful mood hit me. I randomly switched the radio over to Classic Hits and 'The Look of Love' came over the airwaves. I don't know what hit me but I felt a wave of emotion that I hadn't experienced in years. I was driving along the coast road and had to pull in. I felt like I was sixteen again and couldn't think of the person I had become. My mind blurred and all I could see and feel was tremendous emotion for Greg. I would have given anything to see him at that moment. My heart swelled and tears erupted from my eyes. I'd been holding back this tsunami for too long. No matter how busy I was or how successful I had become, I was just like Orson Wells crying for Rosebud in the movie *Citizen Kane*. The simplicity of life when I loved Greg and he loved me was something that I yearned for – but it was an impossibility. I tried to be philosophical about my emotions but it was useless. That song had come on the radio at the very moment that I needed to accept what I had lost all those years ago. Would my life have been better if Greg and I had stayed together? Would we be divorced by now? I'd never know.

But that love that I felt was very real and very pure and I realised in that moment that the power of first love had stayed with me through all my relationships. It was irreplaceable and unique. No matter how much I wanted to have those feelings again I would never have them with another human being – not even my husband.

Hiding behind cupcakes and nurturing my family were good excuses to safeguard against ever being open to that kind of deep emotion again. How could I safeguard my sons against the ravages of first love? The answer was that I couldn't – it would find them and take them over and they would never be the same again.

I felt sad for my husband and sad for myself but I had to sort our relationship out.

I texted Tim in work to say that I needed to speak to him that evening and he texted back: **Fine.**

Nothing else, just that. He'd never been like this before and I was feeling scared.

* * *

I looked at my watch and it was nearly six o'clock as Tim drove up the driveway.

I had baked a cottage pie and made sure the green vegetables were crisp and perfect. All sorts of thoughts were rushing through my head and I felt so foolish. We knew that Bill wasn't having an affair but what if my own husband was? I thought after sussing Alan and Niamh out all those years ago that I was now the expert, but the truth was I hadn't a clue. I was so efficient in the way I ran my life I had everyone and everything neatly boxed off and in their place while I strode through my humungous workload at speed. What if I had been missing the plot all along? After listening to the song on the radio earlier I had to admit that I had been fooling myself so it was not impossible that my husband had been fooling me too.

Tim smiled at me as he came in the door of the kitchen and I felt thrown. He flung his coat on the chair and ran over to me with all the excitement that the boys showed whenever they won a football match or got a day off homework in school.

With arms outstretched he grabbed me.

"Karen, I've just had the best news in the world!"

He was scaring me now – what could be so big in his life that I didn't know about? Had I lost the plot completely?

"Well, tell me!"

"I have been doing something for several months now but I didn't want to tell you in case it came to nothing."

"Tell me quick!" I was bursting to know and somehow I didn't think he was having an affair any more.

"You know how I love to sing?" his eyes danced wildly in his head, like a child after winning the egg and spoon race on sport's day.

"Yes."

"Well, I've been going in to the Academy of Music for lessons after work some days."

"Singing lessons? Why?" I couldn't have been more surprised.

"Because I want to have a passion – you have your cupcake business and it isn't easy for me to be in your shadow all the time. I decided this year that I was going to do something that I really enjoyed and it has been the most incredible experience."

"What are you singing?"

"Opera."

You could have knocked me over with a feather – it was the very last thing I expected him to come out with.

"And what about that night you didn't come home while I was away in Spain?"

"There was a show down in Cork and I had the chance to go with some professionals, including my tutor. As it turned out I was given the chance to audition with Lyric Opera and I have been given a part in the chorus of *Aida* which is going to be in the Gaiety in November."

I was truly delighted for him but speechless also. Had I made him feel inferior with my drive and determination to succeed with my pet project? I was proud of him for pursuing his passion but secretly a little hurt that he hadn't told me until now.

"That's wonderful news – I'm delighted for you. Why didn't you tell me before this?"

"Because I didn't want to fail and make a fool of myself. I know I'll never be a professional singer but this is as good as it gets and I have to say with all the negativity around over the last few years and all this austerity I want to punch the air and say I did it!"

I held him to me and I felt his passion like a great heat surrounding him. He was happy and alive and I never wanted him to let me go. We didn't have first love but what we had was good.

* * *

Going to the opera was something that Tim and I did infrequently – it was however something that I only ever did with him. Our love of music had bonded us when we met first and naturally our tastes had matured over the years but I'd never heard him sing opera. I was shocked to think that he had put so much time and effort into his goal without sharing it with me or anyone. It made me realise how little I knew my husband. We were so busy going through the daily routines and jobs of being a family and I was so intent on pursuing my passion that I had failed to even consider that my husband had a passion that he was harbouring and nurturing behind my back. It was much better than having an affair he had said and that frightened me a little because the intonation in his voice suggested that that was the alternative. I didn't want to know if he had seduced someone or if someone had tried to seduce him – I was pleased that he had his 'thing'. Everybody needed to have their own thing and, when so much has been invested in family and work, sometimes it is easy to forget your passions.

A part of me was hugely proud of him – I knew that he loved to sing and he had a nice tenor voice but I never thought that he would be able to sing in an opera. However, with numerous lessons and coaching sessions he had turned into an opera singer and I was going to see him in his first production – the ambitious *Aida*. There's nothing like starting at the top and that was where Tim wanted to go. He had left it all too late but the achievement of appearing in this would be one thing crossed off his bucket list.

Linda agreed to come to the opening night with me and Amelia stayed at home with the boys. I did think that Karl would like to come in to see it as he is old enough to appreciate music but he had to study for his Christmas exams. I didn't know if his diligence was being used as an excuse but it didn't matter. Tim, however, was disappointed that I was the only member of the family who would be in the audience.

* * *

The curtains drew back and I spotted my Tim straight away. The set was breath-taking and I was transported on a wave of emotions – Radames was torn between his love of Aida and the princess who was his chosen wife. Music had always been so important for me – I spent my youth recording the music from each year as a method of remembering my life. I was older now and, although we had been to see bands like Take That recently, we were at a different stage in our lives and the emotions of opera fitted where we were now as individuals and a couple. I was filled with such pride for my man.

"You're not going to cry, are you?" Linda whispered in my ear.

"I just might – sorry!"

"And we thought our fellas were having affairs – instead yours is wearing a white towel in front of hundreds of people and my fella – well, he's just Bill but he's mine."

"We're blessed, aren't we?"

An elderly lady shushed us and poked me in the back.

Linda nearly got the giggles but I looked away and had to

concentrate very hard on something sad to stop me from bursting into the giggles too. Suddenly I remembered Greg and the giggles stopped. It was difficult to think of him and not feel sad. I said a silent prayer to him and hoped that he was all right. Somehow I thought that I would feel it if he wasn't. To contact him now wouldn't be right – this wasn't the right time. Maybe there would never be a right time but for now I needed to just be.

Chapter 48

July 2013

The plane descended slowly over Howth Head and Gina knew that she was approaching her destination. She could pick out her granny's house from the Google earth map that she had studied with her father before leaving Spain. As a little girl he would point down to it and she could never make the house out but she could now. This was her first time travelling on her own on a plane and it was exciting.

Lisa was meant to come too but she didn't get on so well with her grandmother and anyway it was probably better for her father that he wasn't left on his own. He would get upset sometimes and storm off to his bedroom, leaving the girls wondering what they could do – then at other times he would gather them close to him and the three would have a cry together.

So much had changed in a year. Gina felt like she was older than her years because her father had got her special driving lessons even though she wasn't old enough to drive on the road in Spain – he wanted her to have independence and be ready for college. She had discussed it with him in detail and liked the idea of attending Trinity College.

Gina loved everything Irish and this was the best chance to

study and learn more about her father's heritage. Lisa on the other hand was more interested in France and all things French.

It was the same with boys – the only boys that Gina liked in the college were the Irish ones. She could spot them before they opened their mouths. Unlike the Spaniards who worked in the college, she didn't get confused between the English and Irish accent. She was even able to recognise the difference between the rural Irish and the Dublin accent.

It was an adventure for Gina to visit in this way and a chance for her to really get a feel for how it would be if she were to come to Dublin to study next year and live with her grandmother.

Then there was Karl – he sent her messages on Facebook every few weeks and they had Facetimed about once a month. He didn't seem to have a girlfriend. There was a time around Christmas for five weeks that they didn't chat much and she had her suspicions that he was with someone – it was after his friend posted about a party they were at. But it didn't really matter because they had a special kind of friendship that she hoped would turn into something else once they met up – which would be very soon now.

* * *

Nerves had a grip of Karl as he walked along Offington Park. He wasn't familiar with this estate – the houses were all very nice. A couple were nearly as nice as his own home on Seafield Lane.

He counted the numbers as he walked – almost there and Gina had mentioned that he should look out for her granny's car. It was an old blue Alpha Romeo. He spotted the car in front of the house and turned in. He was tempted to walk on the grass instead of walking that bit further along the drive – but he didn't.

The doorbell was hard to find and by the time he did Gina was already at the porch. She looked amazing and her hair had grown so long it was way down to her elbows.

They looked at each other for a moment, neither going to make the first move, but the tension and anticipation had been building for a year for them both. Now that the moment was here they were afraid to speak.

"Come inside – my granny wants to meet you."

Karl followed her into the kitchen where an old lady sat drinking tea from a china cup – she seemed very dignified yet distant.

"Hello – you must be Karl."

"Yes, Mrs O'Sullivan."

Gina had him primed – she had warned that her granny was old-fashioned about certain things and she liked to be addressed properly by young people.

"Where do you live, Karl?"

"I live in Clontarf – in Seafield Lane."

"Lovely to meet you – would you like a drink of 7Up or something?"

"No, thanks, I'm fine." He wanted to disappear out the door with Gina – the sun was shining and his father had suggested they should go to the Burrow Beach.

"What have you two got planned for today?" Jean asked.

Gina blushed and looked at Karl.

"We could just go for a walk if you like?" he said. "It's a nice day for the beach."

"A little cold but I can wear my jacket."

"We'd call this the height of summer – wouldn't we, Karl?" Jean chuckled.

Karl nodded his head. He wanted to get in Granny's good books.

"Be off now, the two of you – I'm playing bridge in the community centre in a couple of hours and I want to get something for dinner." She watched the two young teenagers walk down her drive and felt a familiarity about the situation – it reminded her of Greg and Karen many years before and she wished she could turn back the hands of time and recover those years that she lost looking at the world through the bottom of a wineglass.

It took less than ten minutes to walk from Offington to the sea and Karl was ecstatic to finally be alone with Gina.

She walked very closely to him and he thought a couple of times about slipping his arm around her shoulders but he hadn't got the nerve yet. She was a little bit older than him after all and he only hoped that she didn't have a boyfriend back in Spain. A lot of time had passed since last summer and their chats were sometimes weeks apart.

"When were you last on this beach?" he asked.

"It was a long time ago – my dad prefers to take us to Howth whenever he is with us. He loves the place on the hill where you see the lighthouse and the bay."

"Yeah, I know where you mean."

Karl had met a couple of girls around Christmas time but none that he wanted to date. None of them made him feel the way he did when he thought of Gina. He hoped that she felt the same too.

"When do you finish school?" she asked.

"I have to do my Leaving Cert in two years and then I go to college."

"I'll be finishing school next year – and I would like to study in Trinity College. My papa said that it's the best place in Dublin to get a degree."

"My mother went there. My father went to UCD."

"Oh, my papa did too but he didn't finish his degree. I think that is why he's so worried about my education. He has no need to worry because I don't mind studying. Which college will you go to?"

Karl shrugged. "I like maths – I also like physics and astronomy – I'm a bit of geek when it comes to space, so I guess I'll go wherever I can do those."

"I've seen images that you share on Facebook and sometimes

I look them up so I have learned about *Star Trek* and *Star Wars!*"

Karl laughed – he was chuffed that she showed an interest in things that he liked.

"And what about you – what will you study if you do go to Trinity?"

"I would like to do English and possibly Spanish or French."

"Languages aren't really my thing – although I did tell you about an au pair we had one time who was Spanish and my mother says I was good at speaking with her. That was a very long time ago though. Other au pairs we had after that were more interested in improving their English."

"I remember you telling me that – Raquel, wasn't it?"

"Yeah, that was her name."

Karl was in awe of her memory and interest in him. He had hoped that he wasn't imagining it when he thought that she liked him – his confidence was growing as they took each step. He wondered when would be the best time to make his move. It was the first day but she would only be here for three weeks and already he decided that he wanted to spend most of those with her.

* * *

The kitchen was full of his brothers and parents but Karl didn't feel like talking to them. In order to avoid the quizzing that his mother would give, he slipped up the stairs and went straight to his room. He opened his phone and found the picture that he had taken of the two of them on the beach. Ireland's Eye was placed perfectly in the background and he had a clear picture of Gina. She was the most beautiful girl in the world. He would give anything to kiss her. Tomorrow – she had agreed to see him tomorrow and he would have to kiss her then.

* * *

Gina stood waiting for Karl at Howth DART station. She was ten minutes early but the walk from Offington had been much shorter than she expected. It didn't look like it would rain so she was wearing a T-shirt with a light cardigan and skinny jeans. Her hair was swept up in a ponytail for a change.

She looked at her phone to see how much longer she had to wait. Her credit was running out quickly because her granny's connection to the internet was so slow she preferred to ring her father and it cost a fortune. She had time to put on another layer of the lip gloss she had bought at the airport when leaving Malaga.

Suddenly the train let out a beep to signal its arrival at the station and she started to feel her heart pound in her chest. It was amazing seeing him the day before but they were both nervous. Today was different. She was ready.

Karl was the first passenger to walk down the steps and she wanted to run to him but held her nerve very coolly. She propped herself up against the railings around the Bloody Stream Pub.

"Hiya – good day at last!" he said.

"Ha – yes, and we talk about the weather again!" She gave a little laugh and he blushed.

"I'm just going to pop into the shop here to get some chewing gum," he said. "Do you want anything?"

"No, thanks, I'm fine."

Karl bought a packet of extra-strong gum and then the walk started.

Without prompting they moved together along the promenade in the direction of the East Pier. It was a busy day in Howth. The harbour was thronged with tourists perusing the restaurants that lined the West Pier, their time in Dublin incomplete before seeing this historic beauty spot. The locals went about their daily business up and down the town and around the eclectic mix of shops and cafés.

Overhead the seagulls followed Gina and Karl on their route

past Beshoffs chipper – they scavenged in their pathway on the remains of the white chipper boxes scattered beside the aluminium bins. They passed the children's playground next and they both recalled visiting it when they were younger.

"I used to love the playground in St Anne's Park," Gina said.

"Me too – my parents used to take us most Sundays when we were little."

"My dad always took us there too when we visited my granny." Gina paused for a moment. She recalled the park so clearly and wondered if they had ever been there at the same time. "The yachts are so pretty! I would love to sail over to Ireland's Eye."

"Did you ever get the motor boat? It goes every half hour or so."

"No – but I'd love to."

"We can do that another day if you like?"

Gina nodded. "I'd like that."

Karl was aching to put his arm around her. But this wasn't the right moment. At the start of the East Pier a Romanian gypsy was playing an out-of-tune saxophone poorly and the two giggled – but Karl gave him fifty cents anyway.

"I'm glad that noise is out of earshot!" Karl said once they had reached 'the elbow' – the gradual bend in the pier – where the direction of the gentle westerly breeze met them head on.

A gang of youths wearing swimming trunks were taking turns to push each other over the side of the pier into the freezing cold water. Their girlfriends stood close to the wall, shivering in bikinis and taunting the boys to pick them up and throw them into the water.

"I wouldn't go in there – it's freezing!" Karl said.

"I'll miss swimming in the sea if I do come to study in Dublin next year."

"There are some locals who swim in the sea all year round – even in January – even if it's snowing."

"That's crazy!"

"I think so too. But we are members of Westwood Gym in Clontarf. It has a big pool. If you like you can come there one day with me?"

"I'd like that."

Karl was bursting with delight – he was making plans and she was responding exactly the way he had hoped. As they passed the boat sheds and Howth Boat Club a cool breeze danced around them.

"I love this lighthouse." Gina's eyes glistened in the sunshine as they started the short climb up to the extended pier with the unmanned lighthouse waiting at the end.

They both realised that they were almost there – it was time.

Black railings surrounded the ugly pillar-like lighthouse that served its purpose well – directing the yachts and fishing boats towards the harbour mouth.

Gina stopped and leaned back against the railings, looking out at the coastline of Baldoyle and Portmarnock in the distance.

"Do you ever read graffiti?" Karl asked, pointing down at some vague cuttings that had been painted over after years of decay and disintegration.

"I love looking at trees with initials carved in them – but we don't have lovely trees in Andalusia like you have in St Anne's Park. It's difficult to see these letters . . ." She leaned closer and gasped as she spotted something that she recognised. "Look – it's GOS ❤3 KF. I'm GOS – Gina O'Sullivan – I wonder who KF is?"

Karl shrugged. "It's just a coincidence. KF – I'm K but Doyle is my surname – will that do?"

Gina blushed and put her hand up to her hair to sweep her fringe out of her eyes.

Karl knew this was the moment – despite it being a beautiful day they were miraculously the only two people on the slice of pier jutting out to sea. All he had to do was make that first move.

She moved about on the soles of her feet restless, anxious and ready.

There was no need for words. The tension between them could be cut with a knife. It would be easier after it was done.

Karl leaned forward slowly, only closing his eyes the second that his lips touched hers. She gave a little moan of pleasure as he put his hands gently on her waist. Her hands slipped naturally onto his shoulders and they melted into each other with a natural rhythm that they had both been waiting for since the first time they had spoken at the dance in the school in Benalmádena.

Karl reluctantly moved away first.

"I've wanted to do that for ages."

"Me too – it was worth the wait. This isn't going to be easy, you know – we live in different countries."

Karl knew what she was saying but he didn't care – he knew that she was the perfect girl for him. "It's going to be as easy or as difficult as we make it – we have three weeks now and I wanted to say it to you yesterday but I hope that we can see each other every day."

"I hope that too. When my mother died I was so sad and I know this sounds crazy but I was happy that I had met you – I knew the first time I saw you that one day I would kiss you."

"I did too. Come on, let's go – I'll show you the seals!" he said, slipping his arm easily around her shoulders. He was young and in love and the happiest he had ever felt in his life.

* * *

There was no escaping the inquisition later on that evening when Karl entered the kitchen. His mother was filling the kettle with water for her final cup of the tea for the evening.

"Where were you all day?" she asked.

"I told you I was with a friend."

"And would this be the friend you were with yesterday by any chance? And would this friend be female?"

Karl rolled his eyes. "Mum, you can be such an idiot sometimes."

"I'm sorry, love, I just like to hear your news. You seemed so happy last night. And this girl lives where?"

"She lives in Spain."

Whenever Spain was mentioned Karen always thought about Greg – maybe only for a split second but he did register with her.

"Where in Spain – how do you know her?"

"She lives near Malaga – I met her at the Spanish college last year. Her dad owns the school."

"Is she here with her family?"

"No – she's on her own."

"Oh? So where is she staying?"

"She's staying with her granny in Offington for three weeks."

"Offington is nice. Not in the park by any chance?"

"Yes, Offington Park. Her granny is Mrs O'Sullivan. She's pretty cool."

Karen went white in the face and had to sit down.

"Mum, are you all right?"

"What's her name? This friend?"

"Gina. Gina –"

"O'Sullivan," Karen finished. It couldn't be – it was too much of a coincidence. Karen felt a shiver up her spine and tingling in her head running all around the hair follicles. Her son and Greg's daughter? It was too much to take in. O'Sullivan was a common enough name – anybody could have moved into the area. But her psychic self knew better.

"Is she the girl whose mother died while we were in Spain?"

"Yeah – how did you guess?"

"I-I-I think I may know her father. Do you know if his name is Greg O'Sullivan?"

"Yeah, that's him."

"But I thought he lived near Barcelona?"

"They moved a few years ago – she told me they used to live there – how do you know him, Mum?"

Karen wasn't sure what to say – the truth seemed like the only option.

372

"I dated her father when I was your age."

"No way!" Karl felt sick at the thought of his mother with anyone apart from his father. He knew that his mother had been married before but he had managed to box that part of her history off as a non-event. But dating Greg from the school was creepy. And it was too close for comfort. It didn't change how he felt about Gina – he loved her. He hadn't said the words or thought it before but after today's kiss he knew that he did.

Chapter 49

Karen

After I had digested my conversation with Karl I sat down at the laptop and did something that I should have done years ago. I still had his email address. I had drafted several emails but none of them seemed like the right thing to say and it was never the right time to send them. Today I seemed to know exactly what to say.

I drafted the letter and pressed send without rereading – I knew that it was right.

Dear Greg
Thank you for your email with your congratulations which I should have answered a long time ago – I really appreciated it. I have been consumed by my business and family for so long now and the years and my life seem to be flashing by.

I was so sad to hear about Isabella – I'm sure you have been through the most awful time. I feel selfish now for not writing sooner. I was worried about my own reactions if I saw you again. I won't pretend that I haven't thought about you – you know how fondly I think of all the times that we shared. You were and always will be an important person in my life. But I wasn't ready to see you and I'm sure I wouldn't have been of much help.

I only discovered this evening that you moved to Malaga. I have been very bad at keeping in touch with the old crowd. My career and family have taken up so much of my time I don't get to socialise the way I would have before the cupcake business took off. It may seem like a glamorous lifestyle choice but it is a huge amount of effort and hard work and probably something I would never have done if it were not for you. When I returned from Barcelona I needed a distraction to stop me from thinking too much about you and what had happened. I suppose if you put so much energy into something it will reap rewards and my little hobby has grown into a business that is rewarding and fulfilling.

I'll never forget our time together and really didn't think that I would ever see you again after Barcelona. I had to shut all thoughts of you from my mind and get on with living my life in Dublin. Sitting writing this now I am shaking and right back on Howth Hill looking out at the Baily Lighthouse.

You might wonder the reason why I am writing to you now of all times. It is simple. My son Karl told me this evening that he spent the day with Gina O'Sullivan from Spain, so I wondered if she was related to you. Then he told me that her granny lived in Offington and I knew.

It's incredible to think I was in Malaga last year when Karl was in your college and I never knew. I suppose our lives are inextricably linked and will always be. I don't know if you are coming to Dublin while your daughter is here but I would like to see you if you do visit. I can honestly say that I am finally ready to be friends if that is okay with you. It looks like we may have no option. The path of young love doesn't always run smoothly as we well know but I think it's best to clean out the skeletons in the closet.

So what do you say, Greg – do you think the time is right – and we can finally do friends?

Sending you best wishes from Dublin

Karen

* * *

I went upstairs to the attic to look for them and I was able to read the postcards without crying or having any of the old emotions that used to take over whenever I was in contact with Greg. Maybe I had reached a plateau at last and our children were helping us along in this quest to be our best and who we were meant to be.

* * *

The reply came back two hours later. I hadn't expected to hear from him so soon.

Dear Karen

I don't know what to say. I'm in shock after getting your email. I have to admit that thousands of students pass through the doors of my school each year and I can't put a face to your son. I wish I had known as I would have had a special interest in him. However if he was here last summer then I admit that I probably was too caught up with Isabella and the trauma and upset at her death. She was such a brave woman and it was cruel the way she was taken so suddenly from us. I've tried to make peace with myself over what happened. She developed a clot in her leg and that is what killed her in the end. I think the body has a funny way of working and she detested the thought of becoming an invalid so much – she even discussed euthanasia with me and she did die while still able to walk and had movement to do everything she needed for herself. So I have to be philosophical about it. Naturally I would love to have her still here with me and the girls. I am inadequate as father and mother. But I tried to do something that she would have wanted me to do after she died – I started to take photographs again. I believe Isabella was trying to direct me from the other side of the grave because one day my old camera that I had in Paris miraculously appeared at the bottom of the wardrobe. I took it to a camera shop and while there bought a new digital one that I've enjoyed using ever since. Gina pestered me to take my photos to a local gallery and that was where I met Vanessa who owns the gallery. Vanessa has been a wonderful addition to our lives. She is a widow too with no children and we are good companions for each other and it is important for the girls to have a woman around the house for them.

Although like me I'm sure you find it difficult to let the kids go, Gina already has her head set on going to Trinity when she finishes school. It is funny the way life goes around in circles. I suppose I shouldn't be surprised that she has fallen into a relationship with your son. It is kind of the way our lives have always been, isn't it, Karen? It's like we have been the one person and, although this little friendship that our children have may not make it past the summer, it is nice to think of them experiencing what we had. Although if I catch your son in the shower with my daughter I may have to hang him!

It's so good to hear from you. I will be over to see my mother briefly before the autumn and I hope we can catch up for a coffee and a chat.

Take care, I've missed you,

Love Greg X

I read and reread the email so many times. It was my first proper letter from him. For all those years I had only ever received brief postcards and now I had a true heartfelt letter that was full of so much emotion I wanted to cry with joy. The circle of life was all we had and all that we were assured of. We were at a new stage in our relationship and I was excited. I did love him and I always would but I loved Tim and my children and my work and I loved life. Maybe Greg and I had perfect timing – we needed to miss each other with such perfection to get to where we were meant to be now. Otherwise we wouldn't have had our beautiful children and we wouldn't be doing what we love. Life is an adventure to be lived and love is something that you learn along the way if you are fortunate. I was so lucky to have been loved by Greg. I was so blessed to have my wonderful husband Tim and beautiful boys. Maybe I had it all and didn't realise it all along.

Epilogue

Karl

Dublin, 14th August 2025

I was shaking when I left Gina's side. I didn't want to be away from our beautiful little girl who was only twenty minutes old. But our parents would be anxious so I slipped out to the corridor to phone my mother with the good news.

"Mum?"

"Karl – any news yet?"

"Yes! We've a girl!"

I could hear the overwhelming joy as she let out a little squeal – having no daughters of her own I knew that she secretly had been hoping for this.

"Oh Karl – I can't begin to tell you how happy I am! Is everything okay – how's poor Gina?"

"She's good – doing better than me – I had no idea that it would be so gruesome – I thought I was going to throw up at one stage."

"Well, it's probably for the best that you can appreciate what your poor wife had to go through."

"I do – women are amazing. Thanks for having me."

My mum laughed down the phone – I knew she'd like that.

"Has Greg arrived?" I asked.

"Your father picked him and Vanessa up at the airport a

couple of hours ago – their timing couldn't be more perfect."

"Are they in our house?"

"Yes, and your dad gave them the keys of Gina's car – the poor girl won't be driving for a while."

"Happy birthday, Mum – sorry, I nearly forgot!"

"Darling, you have given me the best birthday present that I could ever hope for."

"Well, here's another one – as it is your day *and* a big birthday . . ."

"Less of the big – I've decided I'm going to lose ten years – I'm telling everyone I'm fifty!"

"Well, this may make it easier – we're going to call her Karen."

"Oh Karl – oh darling, I really didn't expect that – I thought you would want to call her Isabella."

"Hey – we will need more names for her sister when we get over this."

"I don't know what to say. Thank you so much, darling. Are you quite sure?"

"Positive – she has your birthday. It was an easy decision to make. Gina suggested it."

"When can we come in and see them?"

"Visiting times are really strict – this evening, and only two visitors allowed at a time. I'm staying here with them for the day. Gina's wide awake and feeding Baby Karen already."

"My darling, I'm over the moon – oh, your father is coming in the door now – I'm going to tell him. Congratulations and love to Gina!"

I had to ring Greg now and I felt a lump in my throat – the emotion of becoming a father was so big I never realised what a huge day this was for our parents. How great for them to see the next generation – a new life that would perpetuate the loving homes that we had been given – this precious life was a testament to them and their love. I felt like the universe was revolving in perfect motion – my whole life was full of meaning.

Everything that had happened to me in the past was leading to this moment. And I thought of my mum and the postcards she had shown me when I told her that Gina was pregnant. I understood why her eyes watered as she spoke. Our family was complete – we were all connected and part of the one whole.

After calling Greg with our news I went back in to the delivery suite to Gina and took my baby in my arms while her beautiful mother drank tea and ate toast. I stared down at her perfect little fingers and sharp nails – her face was angelic. This child was my destiny – my whole family's destiny.

I was home.

THE END

Also published by Poolbeg

Two Days in Biarritz

Michelle Jackson

They're chalk and cheese but always the best
of friends ... until Biarritz!

Meet best friends Kate and Annabel, all set to celebrate
a big birthday in style. And where better to do it than the chic resort
of Biarritz – packed with yummy food, heady wine and surfers?

Kate is an artist and lives in France, while Annabel's only ambition is
to hang on to her Yummy Mummy status back in Dublin. But
Annabel has been keeping a shocking secret from Kate for years.
Then in Biarritz, in a haze of alcohol, she at last lets it slip.

Kate is devastated and runs back home to the Pyrénées.
Then her mother's illness forces her to return to Dublin ...
to Shane, a pilot, the one-time love of her life ...
and to Annabel.

Meanwhile Annabel's perfect suburban life is rocked and she throws
herself into setting up a small business. Her husband Colin is
appalled at the new Annabel ... new friend Gary, however,
approves ...

Can the women's friendship survive deception, betrayal and anger?

Can they survive Biarritz?

ISBN 9781842233290

Also published by Poolbeg

Three Nights in New York

Michelle Jackson

3 girls, 3 guys, and 3 unforgettable nights
in trendy downtown New York!

Eve doesn't believe in knights in shining armour. As director of
Just for Coffee dating agency she reckons you need the correct
profile and bank balance to find love. Fate, however,
does not agree!

This is single mum Nicky's first time in New York and she has
come to shop! But she gets more than she bargains for!
For Rachel it's time out from her stressful marriage and a chance
to visit her hunky brother Conor. A holiday fling is the last thing
she needs. Until she meets sexy Alex who uncovers the dark secret
she lives with in her cosy secure life back in Dublin.

From the High Line to SoHo and the Boathouse to Chelsea
– the magic of New York transforms their lives forever!

ISBN 9781842234150

Also published by Poolbeg

One Kiss
in Havana

Michelle Jackson

Emma, Louise and Sophie are sisters. Talented, artistic and creative, they have a lot in common – especially when it comes to men.

When Emma receives two tickets to Cuba in the post from her late husband she is more than surprised. She decides to take her sister Sophie along in his place – not realising that he had always intended Sophie to go.

Louise hankers for her lost love Jack Duggan. She trudges through her suburban life with husband Donal while her sisters soak up the Caribbean sunshine. But a chance encounter with the love from her past means that she will have plenty to deal with in Dublin while her sisters are away.

Meanwhile, in Cuba, Emma meets Che Guevara lookalike Felipe and Sophie meets Greg, a Canadian art dealer. Against the backdrop of Salsa music, rum cocktails and balmy tropical nights, the girls have no idea what *One Kiss in Havana* will lead to . . .

ISBN 9781842234846

Also published by Poolbeg

4 a.m. in Las Vegas

Michelle Jackson

It's Halloween in Las Vegas and things are crazier than normal for Connie the wedding planner. Vicky and Frank are in town for their nuptials but she soon realises that he has more on his mind than wedding bells. Vicky's teenage daughter Tina is less than impressed until she meets Connie's moody and enigmatic son Kyle. Frank's brother John is trying to hold everyone together but then something happens that turns the wedding party on their heads at 4 a.m. in Las Vegas!

Life and love seem to have slipped through Suzanne's fingers but then, new to Facebook, she stumbles upon more than she expected when she receives a friend request from old flame Ronan in Boston. He's on his way to Las Vegas for a work convention and Suzanne's friend Eddie convinces her that she should go too.
What has she got to lose?

When they all meet in Binion's Casino the cards have already been dealt – but will there be a winner?

ISBN 9781842235089

Also published by Poolbeg

5 Peppermint Grove

Michelle Jackson

Emigration, emigration, emigration . . . Ruth Travers is leaving Ireland like so many unhappy members of the Irish Diaspora who have gone before her. But Ruth is travelling business class on a Boeing 777 and will be landing in sunny Perth, Western Australia, to take up an exciting new job.

Leaving behind her married boyfriend of ten years, Ruth hopes to make a fresh start. Her mother Angela, who lived in Perth in the seventies, is distraught when she hears that Ruth is Australia bound. It is only when Ruth discovers a sealed airmail envelope, with *5 Peppermint Grove, Perth*, scrawled across it in her mother's handwriting, that she wonders what else Angela may be hiding.

Her best friend Julia Perrin gently orchestrated the move to Perth for her friend's own good. She is a successful businesswoman with her own travel company and so busy fixing everybody else's life she sees no need to do so with her own . . . until she visits Ruth in Perth!

Sunshine, sandy beaches and barbeques abound but there may be more than Angela's secret waiting for them in Peppermint Grove . . .

ISBN 9781842235515